LAKE OSWEGO JR. HIGH SCHOOL
2500 SW COUNTRY CLUB RD
LAKE OSWEGO, OR 97034
503-534-2335

prized

CARAGH M. O'BRIEN

prized

THE SECOND BOOK IN THE
BIRTHMARKED TRILOGY

ROARING BROOK PRESS
New York

The author is donating a portion of the proceeds of this novel to the Global Greengrants Fund, a non-profit, international, grass-roots organization that provides small, pivotal grants to people dealing with environmental destruction. Interested readers may find more information at www.greengrants.org.

Text copyright © 2011 by Caragh M. O'Brien

Published by Roaring Brook Press

Roaring Brook Press is a division of

Holtzbrinck Publishing Holdings Limited Partnership

175 Fifth Avenue, New York, New York 10010

macteenbooks.com

Library of Congress Cataloging-in-Publication Data

O'Brien, Caragh M.

Prized / Caragh M. O'Brien.—1st ed.

p. cm.—(The Birthmarked trilogy bk. 2)

Summary: Sixteen-year-old midwife Gaia Stone is in the wasteland with nothing but her baby sister, a handful of supplies, and a rumor to guide her when she is captured by the people of Sylum, a dystopian society where she must follow a strict social code or never see her sister again.

ISBN 978-1-59643-570-4

[1. Midwives—Fiction. 2. Sisters—Fiction. 3. Survival—Fiction. 4. Genetic engineering—Fiction. 5. Parents—Fiction. 6. Science fiction.] I. Title.

PZ7.O12673Pri 2011

[Fic]—dc22

2010048505

Roaring Brook Press books are available for special promotions and premiums. For details contact: Director of Special Markets, Holtzbrinck Publishers.

First edition 2011

Printed in the United States of America

1 3 5 7 9 10 8 6 4 2

For Nancy Mercado

contents

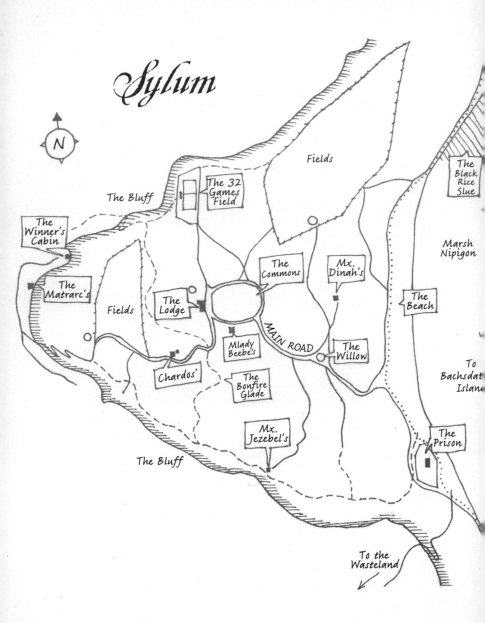

CHAPTER 1

the wasteland

SHE GRABBED THE HILT of her knife and scrambled backward into the darkness, holding the baby close in her other arm. Beyond the fire, the wasteland was still, as if the wind and even the stones had frozen in the night to listen, and then she heard it again, a faint chink, like a footfall in pebbles. Someone or something was out there, watching her.

Gaia turned the knife in her palm, resettling her grip, and peered toward where the far edge of the firelight touched the boulders and the gnarled, wind-stunted trees of the gulch. Without dropping her gaze, she felt by hand that the baby was secure in the sling across her chest, her warm, light weight hardly more than a loaf of bread. She'd left the baby bottle on a ledge of rock, out by the fire, and she hoped whoever was watching her wouldn't take that bottle, whatever else they might do.

The chinking noise came again, drawing her gaze to the far side of the fire. Then a head, an enormous, animal head, big as a cow's but long of face, appeared at the edge of the firelight, looking directly at her. A *horse?* she thought, astounded to see

1

an animal she'd believed was extinct. She checked its back for a rider, but there was none.

Inadvertently, she lowered her knife. In that instant, a powerful hand closed around her wrist and another touched around her throat.

"Drop it."

The voice came softly from behind her right ear. Sweat broke out along her arms and neck, but still she clasped the knife. His grip did not move, did not lessen or increase at all, conveying his confidence that he simply had to wait until she obeyed. So completely, so imperceptibly had he crept up around her that she stood no chance of fighting back. Below her jaw, she could feel her own pulse beating against the firm, pernicious pressure of his thumb.

"Don't hurt me," she said, but even as she spoke, she realized he could have killed her already if that had been his intention. Rapidly, she imagined trying to twist free of him with a kick, but the baby might get hurt. She couldn't risk it.

"Just drop it," came the voice again. "We'll talk."

With a sense of despair, she dropped her knife.

"Do you have any other weapons on you?"

She shook her head.

"No sudden moves," he said, and his hands released her.

She sagged slightly, feeling the adrenaline still coursing through her. He picked up her knife and took a step toward the glow of the fire. A broad-shouldered, bearded man, he wore clothes and a hat of the same worn, dusty color as the wasteland.

"Step forward where I can see you properly," he said, and held out a hand to invite her forward. "Where's the rest of your group?"

"We're it," she said.

Gaia stepped into the firelight, and now that the burst of fear

2

that had given her strength was receding, she doubted she could stand for long. The campsite, she knew, must reveal how she'd been reduced to the last, pathetic shreds of survival. He picked up the baby bottle. She watched his gaze settle on the sling that crossed her chest and the protective hand she kept there. He jogged up the brim of his hat with his thumb in obvious surprise.

"You have a baby?"

Gaia braced a hand against the tree trunk. "You don't have any baby formula with you, do you?"

"I don't usually carry that. What's in this?" He gave the bottle a little shake, and the translucent liquid caught the golden firelight.

"Rabbit broth. She won't take it anymore. She's too weak."

"A girl, even. Let me see her."

She curved back the edge of the sling for him to see, and as she had done a thousand times since she'd left the Enclave, she checked her sleeping sister to see if she was still breathing. Firelight flickered over the little, pinched face, bathing it in brief color before sending it back to black and white. A delicate vein arched along Maya's right temple, and a breath lifted her little chest.

The man touched a finger to the baby's eyelid, lifted it a moment, then let it go.

He gave a sharp whistle, and the horse came nearer. "Here we go, then, Mlady," he said. Decisively, the outrider lifted Gaia from the ground and up to the saddle. She grabbed the pommel to balance herself and Maya, and swung a leg over. He passed her the bottle and her cloak, then collected her meager things into her pack and slung it over his own shoulder.

"Where are we going?" Gaia asked.

"To Sylum as directly as we can. I hope it's not too late."

3

Shifting, she tried to arrange some of the fabric of her dress between herself and the saddle. She could feel the dark, cool air touching her legs above the tops of her boots. When the outrider swung up behind her on the horse, she instinctively leaned forward, trying not to crowd against him. His arms encircled her as he reached for the reins, and then he kicked the horse into motion.

"Hey, Spider."

The horse's movements seemed jerky to Gaia at first, but when her hips relaxed into the horse's stride, the ride became smoother. Behind them, the gibbous moon was low on the western horizon, casting a light strong enough to create shadows in their path, and Gaia peered to her right, toward the south, to where the Enclave and all she'd left behind had long ago dropped beneath the dark horizon.

For the first time in days, Gaia realized she might live, and hope was almost painful as it reawakened inside her. Inexplicably, she thought of Leon, and a lightless, lonely feeling surrounded her, as real as the outrider's unfamiliar, protective arms. She'd lost him. Whether he lived or died she would never know, and in a way, the uncertainty rivaled the unhappiness of knowing definitively that her parents were dead.

Her sister could well be next. Gaia reached her hand into the sling, easing her fingers between layers of fabric so that she could feel the baby's warm head in the palm of her hand. She made sure the cloak couldn't smother the little face, and then she let her eyes close. She nodded gently with the rhythm of the horse.

"Maya is dying," she said, finally admitting it to herself.

The man didn't reply at first, and she thought he must not care. But then there was a careful shifting behind her.

"She may die," he confirmed quietly. "Is she suffering now?"

4

Not anymore, she thought. Maya's crying, before, had been hard to bear. This was a much quieter, more final form of heartbreak. "No," Gaia said.

She slumped forward, dimly aware that he was helping, with singular tenderness, to support her and the baby both. Why a stranger's kindness should amplify her sadness she didn't know, but it did. Her legs were chilled, but the rest of her was fast becoming warmer. Lulled by despair and the soporific, distance-eating gait, she gave in to whatever relief oblivion could bring, and slept.

It seemed like years passed before Gaia became dimly aware of a change around them. She ached everywhere, and she was still riding, but she was leaning back against the man whose arms were supporting her and the baby securely. The baby's body was warm. Gaia took a deep breath and opened her eyes to search Maya's face. The baby's skin was translucent, almost blue in its pallor, but she still breathed. When sunlight flickered over the little face, Gaia looked up in wonder to see that they were in a forest.

Tiny dust motes floated in shafts of sunlight that dropped through the canopy of leaves and pine needles, and the air had a lush, humid luminosity that changed breathing fundamentally, filling her lungs with something warm and rich each time she inhaled.

"What is it, in the air?" she asked.

"It's just the forest," he said. "You might be smelling the marsh. We don't have much farther to go."

Even when it had rained in Wharfton, the air itself had remained sere between each raindrop, aching to suck away any moisture, but here, when she lifted her hand, she could feel a trace of new elasticity between her fingers.

"You talk in your sleep," the outrider said. "Is Leon your husband?"

The thought of Leon as her husband was too ludicrous and sad to bear, no matter what she might say in her dreams. "No," she said. "I'm not married."

She glanced down, checking to see if the necklace Leon had returned to her was still around her neck. She tugged the chain so her locket watch rested on top of the neckline of her dress and loosened her cloak. As she straightened, the man let her go, using only his right hand to hold the reins. His fingers, she saw, were clean, with stubby fingernails.

"Where are you from?" he asked.

"South of here. From Wharfton, on the other side of the wasteland."

"So that still exists?" he asked. "How long have you been traveling?"

She thought back over a daze of time in the wasteland. "The formula for Maya lasted ten days. I lost track after that. I found an oasis and caught a rabbit. That was, I'm not sure, maybe two days ago." There'd been a corpse at the oasis, a body with no visible wounds, like a harbinger of her own pending starvation. Yet she'd made it this far.

"You're safe now," he said. "Or almost."

The path rose one last time, turned, and the earth dropped away on their right. Stretching far toward the eastern horizon was a great, blue-green flatness that reflected bits of sky between hillocks of green.

She had to squint to see it clearly, and even then she could hardly believe what she was seeing. "Is it a lake?"

"It's the marsh. Marsh Nipigon."

"I've never seen anything so beautiful," she said.

Lifting a hand to shade her eyes, she stared, marveling. Gaia had spent much of her childhood trying to imagine Unlake Superior full of water, but she'd never guessed it would be like having a second, broken sky down below the horizon. The marsh expanded across much of the visible world: part serpentine paths of water, part patches of green, with three islands receding into the distance. Even from this height, she could breathe in the cool freshness of it, laced with the loamy tang of mud.

"How can there be so much water?" she asked. "Why hasn't it all evaporated?"

"Most of the water *is* gone. This is all that's left of an old lake from the cool age, and the water gets lower every year."

She pointed to a swatch of dark green that rippled in a slow-motion wave as the wind moved across it. "What's that area there?"

"There? That's the black rice slue," he said.

The path took a long, left-handed turn along the bluff, and as they rode, Gaia could see where the landscape dipped down to form a sprawling V-shaped valley. At the wide end, the forest descended to meet the marsh. A patchwork of woods, farmland, and backyard gardens seemed to be stitched together by dirt roads and pinned in place by three water towers. Where the path curved down to meet the sandy beach, a dozen groups of men were working around canoes and skiffs.

"Havandish!" the outrider called. "Hurry ahead and tell the Matrarc I've brought in a girl with a starving baby. She needs a wet nurse."

"We'll meet you at the lodge," a man answered, swinging onto another horse and bolting ahead. People turned to stare.

"Who's the Matrarc?" Gaia asked.

"Mlady Olivia. She runs Sylum for us," he said.

He steered his horse rapidly up the shore and through the village, and for the first time, the horse stumbled. Gaia clutched at the pommel, but the horse regained its footing.

"Almost there, Spider," the outrider said. "Good boy."

Caked with sweat, double-burdened, the horse flicked back an ear and pushed onward. The road turned to abut a level, open oval of lawn, edged with oaks and ringed farther out by sturdy log cabins. Simply dressed people paused in their work to follow their progress.

Ahead, a sun-scorched strip of dirt separated the commons from a big lodge of hewn, dovetailed logs, and in this area stood a row of four wooden frames, like disconnected parts of a fence. Puzzled by the jumbled sight, Gaia stared at a hunched form in the last frame until understanding came to her: they were stocks, and the dark form was a slumped prisoner, passed out or dead under the noonday sun.

"Why is that man in the stocks?" she asked.

"Attempted rape."

"Is the girl okay?" Gaia asked. *What sort of place have I come to?*

"Yes," he said, and dismounted from behind her. Rugged and lean, bearded and strong, the outrider ran a hand down his horse's neck and turned to look up at Gaia. *He isn't old*, she thought, surprised by her first clear look at him. She'd seen the outrider only by the light of the fire, and she was curious now to see how this man, to whom she owed her life, matched his voice and clean hands.

He tilted his face slightly, regarding her closely, and she waited for a question about the scar that disfigured the left side of her face. It never came. Instead, he took off his hat to rake a hand through hair that was dark with sweat. Decisive, percep-tive eyes dominated his even features with inviting candor.

8

Beneath his beard, the corners of his mouth turned down briefly with a trace of regret.

He donned his hat again. "I hope your baby makes it, Mlass," he said. "For your own sake."

Startled, she instinctively held her sister closer, but before she could ask what he meant, a light tapping noise came from behind her. She turned. A wide, deep veranda spanned the width of the big lodge, and a white-haired woman with a red cane was coming through the screen door. She stood straight, and her pale blue dress draped over her pregnant form with regal simplicity. A bit of gold and glass hung from a necklace, gleaming against her dark skin.

Six months, Gaia estimated. The Matrarc was six months pregnant.

Half a dozen women were coming out of the lodge behind the Matrarc, openly curious, and more people were gathering in the commons.

The Matrarc held out a slender hand in a gesture of expectation. "Chardo Peter? You brought in a girl and a baby?"

Gaia noticed a subtle disconnection between the Matrarc's gesture and the direction of her gaze, and put it together with the significance of the cane: she was blind.

"Yes, Mlady," he said. "The baby's a girl and nearly dead from starvation."

"Bring them here to me," said the Matrarc. "I suppose the girl is weak. Carry her if you must."

Chardo propped his hat on the pommel and reached up to help Gaia. She shifted her sling to make sure Maya was secure. As her feet touched the dirt, her knees buckled, and he caught her before her legs gave out entirely. "Forgive me, Mlass," he said. He scooped her up in his arms and delivered her to the top of the steps. Gaia steadied herself against a log pillar and glanced furtively around. She didn't know why she was uneasy, but something felt wrong.

"Please," Gaia said. "We need a doctor."

The tip of the Matrarc's red cane nudged Gaia's boot, but then she set the cane aside and extended her hands. "I want to see the baby." There was a melodious, deep quality in her voice that took the edge off her direct command, and yet she clearly expected to be obeyed.

Gaia gently extricated Maya from the sling and lifted her into those expectant hands. Unbelievably scrawny and fragile, the baby was hardly more than a listless bundle of blankets. The Matrarc cradled Maya in one arm and ran quick fingers over her face and arms, settling at the baby's throat.

Up close, Gaia saw the Matrarc's complexion was a deep tan, with darker freckles splayed across her nose and cheeks. Her wrinkles were few. Despite prematurely white hair, which was arranged in a soft, heavy bun, the Matrarc was in her mid-thirties, Gaia guessed, and obviously competent with a baby. The clear, translucent brown of her sightless eyes was lit by an alert, trenchant expression, and then she frowned with concern.

"You see?" Gaia said.

"It's not good," the Matrarc said. "When was she born?"

"About two weeks ago. She was premature."

"Where's Mlady Eva?" the Matrarc said.

A woman was hurrying across the commons carrying a baby of her own. "I'm here!" she called. Her apron had streaks of red, and her dark hair was coming loose from its ponytail. "I was just putting up my preserves, but Havandish told me this couldn't wait. Why do you need my baby?"

"You'll need him to get your milk flowing," the Matrarc

said. "A baby has just arrived who's too weak even to suck. Do the best you can for her. Mlady Roxanne, take them in. Quickly, please."

The Matrarc passed Gaia's sister to a tall, angular woman who gave Gaia a swift look through her glasses, then took the baby into the lodge. Mlady Eva was untucking her blouse as she hurried after them.

"Wait for me," Gaia said.

"No, stay," the Matrarc said. "We need to get acquainted. What's your name, child?"

Gaia peered anxiously through the screen door, but already the others were out of sight. She tried to follow, but her legs were still too wobbly. "Where are they going? I need to be with my sister."

"She's not your own child, then?" the Matrarc asked.

"No. Of course not." Gaia glanced at Chardo to find him regarding her with faint surprise, as if he had been operating under the same misassumption as the Matrarc. "I would never have been feeding her rabbit broth if I could have nursed her myself," she said to him.

"I didn't know what to think," he said.

"Obviously, you've been through an ordeal," the Matrarc cut in, lifting a hand. "Let me see your face."

Gaia backed against the railing to avoid the Matrarc's touch. "No," she said.

"Ah!" said the Matrarc in surprise, dropping her hand.

"Mlass, you need to cooperate with her," Chardo said.

Cooperating, Gaia had learned, could be dangerous. "I need to be with my sister," she argued. "Take me to her and then I'll cooperate."

The Matrarc drummed her fingers on top of her cane. "You

have that backward, I'm afraid. How old are you? Where have you come from?"

"I'm Gaia Stone," she said. "I'm sixteen. I left Wharfton two weeks ago. Now let me in there. We're wasting time."

A puzzled crease came to the Matrarc's forehead. "Why do I know this name?" she asked. "Who are your parents?"

"They were Bonnie and Jasper Stone." A thought hit Gaia. "Do you know my grandmother, Danni Orion? Is she here?"

The Matrarc touched her own necklace, and took a long moment before she replied. "Danni Orion was the Matrarc before me. I'm sorry to tell you she's been dead these ten years now."

As the Matrarc released her necklace, Gaia saw the pendant clearly for the first time. It was a gilt-edged monocle, and the familiarity of it stunned her. Years ago, in one of her earliest memories, she'd seen the same monocle in the sunlight as her grandmother twisted it to dazzle her.

"You have my grandmother's monocle," Gaia said in wonder. Gone was the chance to ever know her grandmother, replaced by a concrete truth: this was the place she'd been seeking for weeks in the wasteland, her grandmother's home, the Dead Forest that Gaia's mother and Old Meg had urged her to find. She gazed out at the big, shady trees and lush greens of the commons, proof that nothing here was dead except the possibility she would ever be reunited with Danni O.

"Gaia Stone," the Matrarc said slowly, testing the name. "Your grandmother told me about your family. A brother was taken away from you, I think. I remember now. They burned your face, didn't they?"

Everything inside Gaia slowed down, and she let her gaze drift up to the woman's sightless eyes. It was beyond strange to come all this way and meet someone who knew, without seeing

12

or touching her, that her face was scarred. She untucked the hair behind her left ear to let it slide forward.

"Two brothers," Gaia said, correcting her, as if it still mattered. "The Enclave took both of my brothers. One I've never met. The other left for the wasteland shortly before I did."

"Why weren't you taken into the Enclave? I don't understand."

"The burn scar kept me out of consideration for advancing or I might have been taken, too."

"Where are your parents now?" the Matrarc asked.

"Dead, back in the Enclave. My father was murdered. My mother died giving birth to my sister."

"I'm sorry," the Matrarc said.

Gaia stared bleakly toward the screen door. "Please," she said. "Let me go to my sister. I need to be sure she's okay."

"You can't do anything more for her, and there's something we need to settle," the Matrarc said. She made a gesture. "Bring her a chair."

Chardo fetched one from farther along the porch, and Gaia eased down upon it gripping the edge of the wooden seat.

"Tell me something," the Matrarc said. "Why did you go into the wasteland with a baby? Why would you risk her life?"

"I didn't have a choice," Gaia said.

"Maybe you didn't for yourself," the Matrarc said. "But why couldn't you leave the baby behind? Surely someone in Wharfton would have cared for her."

Gaia's eyebrows lifted in surprise. She had promised her mother to protect Maya, and for Gaia, that had meant staying together as a family. "I couldn't leave her."

"Even knowing it was likely she would die?"

Gaia shook her head. "You don't understand. I had to take care of her. I didn't know it would take us so long to cross the wasteland." Then she remembered that her friend Emily had offered to care for Maya, and she'd refused. Had that been a mistake?

"Or what you would find on the other side, I expect," the Matrarc asked. "It was a terrible risk. A desperate, suicidal risk, in fact. Were you persecuted in your home? Were you a criminal or a rebel of some kind? Did you leave to escape the law?"

Gaia looked uneasily at Chardo and the others.

"I resisted the government in the Enclave," she admitted. "But I didn't cause any rebellion. I did what I thought was right. That's all."

"'That's all'?" the Matrarc echoed, and then laughed. She pensively circled her cane tip against the floor while her eyes grew serious again. "You have a decision to make, Mlass Gaia. Staying in Sylum is like coming through a one-way gate. You can enter, but anyone who tries to leave Sylum dies. We don't understand fully why this happens, but we find their bodies."

Gaia's eyes grew wide. "I saw a corpse," she said. "At the oasis two days ago. He was only recently dead. I was afraid it meant the water was poisonous."

"A middle-aged man with a full beard and glasses?" the Matrarc asked.

"Dressed in gray," Gaia said. It had both frightened her and given her hope that she was nearing civilization.

"There's your crim, Chardo," the Matrarc said. She turned to Gaia. "He escaped from prison here four days ago. It happens to anyone who leaves. We've had nomads pass through, but if they stay with us even two days, the same thing happens."

Gaia had never heard of anything like it. "What could cause that? Is there a disease here?"

"We think it's something in the environment," the Matrarc explained. "There's an acclimation period while your body

14

adjusts to being here, but after that, there's no harm to those of us who stay. Beyond the obvious."

Frowning, Gaia gazed at the gathered crowd, trying to see what was so obvious. Aside from the man in the stocks and the Matrarc's own blindness, the people looked healthy and fit. There were tall people and short, a few chubby ones, and none very skinny. Old men and young lounged nearby, with a fairly even distribution of skin tones, from pure black to birch white. There were plenty of children, and attire suggested a mix of affluent and poor.

"What do you mean?" Gaia asked.

Laughter came from the women on the porch. Gaia turned to Chardo, puzzled.

"We don't have many women here," Chardo said. "Only one in ten babies is a girl."

Gaia looked around again in amazement, seeing how few women there were, mostly congregated on the veranda around the Matrarc. Out in the commons, nearly every face was masculine, and many had beards. Even the children were nearly all boys. How had she not noticed?

"It's more than that," the Matrarc added. "The last girl was born here two years ago. And since then, only boys."

"How can that be?" Gaia asked.

The Matrarc shrugged. "You don't have to understand it to realize you need to make your choice. Leave today, or stay forever."

"But that's no choice at all. Where would I go? How would I survive?"

"There was a small community west of here a few years ago," the Matrarc said. "And there are nomads who cycle through from the north. You could take your chances in either direction, or you could head back to your own home in the south."

Gaia couldn't possibly go back, not in her weak condition. She could hardly stand. "I can't go," she said. "Besides, I'd never leave my sister behind."

"I thought you'd say so," the Matrarc agreed. "Here's the other side of your decision. If you stay, you must agree to follow the rules of our community. You might find them strict at first, but I assure you, they're fair."

"I can put up with anything as long as I'm with my sister," Gaia said.

A faint breeze moved along the porch, and a tendril of white hair shifted across the Matrarc's face. She smoothed it back, blinking. "Tell me," the Matrarc said in her soft, lyrical voice. "What would have happened to the baby if Chardo Peter hadn't found you?"

Gaia swallowed back the thickness in her throat. "She was dying," she admitted.

The Matrarc nodded. She drummed her slender fingers around the top of her cane again. "She still might die. If we didn't have a mother here to nurse her, she'd have no chance at all. Correct?"

Gaia nodded.

"Is that a yes?" the Matrarc pressed.

Gaia didn't like where this was going. The Matrarc's gentle manners belied a quiet, unyielding brutality.

"Mlass Gaia?" the Matrarc said, waiting. "Say it."

"Yes," Gaia said. "My sister would be dead."

The Matrarc eased back slightly. "Then from now on, we will consider your sister to be a gift to Sylum. A small and precious gift. What's more, in light of your gift, and depending on your compliance during your probation, we may pardon your crime."

"My crime?"

"You knowingly, deliberately put your sister in deadly harm."

"You're implying I tried to kill her," Gaia said, rising stiffly in alarm. "I didn't! I've done everything I could to keep her alive."

"You admitted yourself she would be dead without our intervention," the Matrarc said. "You have forfeited any claim to the child. *Your* sister, the one *you* cared for, is dead. The only baby that's alive is the one Chardo saved, and right now, she needs stable care and a new mother."

Gaia had a terrifying glimpse of what it must have been like for the mothers when she herself had taken their babies to be advanced to the Enclave. "Oh, please. Let me see her," Gaia begged. "She could be dying right now. I need to hold her."

The Matrarc turned slightly, tapping her cane once on the wooden planks. "I'm sorry for your loss, of course. It's terrible to lose a child."

She was speaking as if Maya were already dead.

"You can't do this!" Gaia said. "You don't know what we've been through. I've lost *everyone* I care for." Gaia impulsively grabbed the Matrarc's cane, jerking it in protest. "You can't steal my sister!"

The Matrarc released her cane and lifted her hands, stepping back. "Take her."

Gaia was grabbed from behind and instantly dragged down the stairs. The cane fell rattling to the floorboards. Gaia's arms were wrenched behind her while half a dozen men sprang between her and the Matrarc.

"She's my family!" Gaia shouted, struggling to break free. "I can't lose her!"

The Matrarc smoothed the tendril of her hair back again, and then held out her right hand, palm up, in a silent request. One of the men put the handle of her cane in her hand, and Gaia watched the Matrarc grip it with steely fingers.

17

"I want her all the way down," the Matrarc said.

Gaia was pushed down so fast that her knees hit the ground hard, and she had to catch herself with her hands in the dirt. It was humiliating. Her chin was millimeters from the dusty ground. She was so weak that it didn't take much for a guard's heavy hand to keep her there, physically, while inside she screamed in defiance.

"She's down," said Chardo, and she realized he was the one holding her there. She struggled once more, unbelieving. He'd been so gentle with her before, but now he had the force of a stone block.

"You'll listen to me, Mlass Gaia," the Matrarc said, and her voice had dropped to a honey-smooth alto. "There is only one leader here. One. And I speak for everyone. You will learn to obey our rules, or you will be sent back to the wasteland to die."

"What would my grandmother think of the way you're treating me?" Gaia demanded.

"Mlady Danni would be the first to support me," the Matrarc said. "She taught me everything I know. Chardo," she called.

"Yes, Mlady," he said.

"Where's Munsch?"

"I left him back at our camp. There wasn't time to circle back to him."

"Return to him as soon as you can get a fresh horse. And keep an eye out for her brother or anyone else. I'll send out extra patrols. I don't for a minute believe she's the only one out there. Something must have happened down south."

"Yes, Mlady," he said.

"Gaia Stone, are you ready to cooperate?" the Matrarc asked.

Gaia ground her teeth. She would get her sister back, whatever it took. Groveling included. "Yes, Mlady," she said, parroting Chardo's words.

"Bring her up, then," the Matrarc said.

At the first indication his grip was loosening, Gaia jerked free and staggered to her feet. She flashed a scathing gaze at Chardo. "You rescued me for this?"

The outrider met her gaze without flinching, as if he wasn't sorry at all. "It was the right thing to do."

The right thing. He'd known all along that the Matrarc would take her sister.

Sylum was as bad as the Enclave. But the women were running it.

CHAPTER 2

libbies

GAIA TURNED ON HER PILLOW, hearing the soft pattering of rain on leaves just outside her open window, and then she heard a faint cry in the night. She sat up slowly, listening, anxious that it might be Maya. A thin line of light glowed under the door.

Since her encounter with the Matrarc that afternoon, the villagers hadn't treated her poorly, but they'd kept her in the lodge, and Maya had clearly been moved elsewhere. They had run Gaia a bath while she ate a bowl of soup, and they'd provided a white cotton shirt and a beige skirt of soft homespun to replace her torn, dirty blue dress. As she swung her feet to the floor, she could feel the floorboards through the wool of new socks. Her boots were nowhere to be found.

She listened intently until a second cry came floating through the rain, a wild, eerie, spiraling birdcall, as if the marsh itself had found a voice. Gaia shivered, then second-guessed if the earlier cry had truly belonged to a baby. She had to find out.

Her sore muscles tightened as she first stood, and a faint groan hummed in her throat. Trying her door, she found it locked.

She turned to push the window sash up higher and inspected the slats that crossed the opening in a grid, imprisoning her. Mist stirred against her face as she squinted, trying to see. The spaces were barely wider than the span of her hand, but as she tested the solidity of each slat, she found the two on the right side were loose at the nails, just waiting for a good shove. They gave with a crack.

By twisting and squeezing through the tiny opening, she was free, and she dropped down into the soggy garden. Her socks were instantly soaked. She had no idea where to look first, or even how large the village was, but that didn't deter her. She began with the cabins around the commons that had lit windows, peering inside, and progressed slowly downhill. For an hour, she succeeded only in getting drenched, and finally, shivering, she ducked under the shelter of a willow tree. A trace of unfamiliar tobacco smoke laced into the clean smell of the rain, and then a man on horseback slowly passed the willow.

She didn't want to get caught, nor did she want to give up. She listened as the horse's splashing footfalls diminished into the distance. A flash of sheet lightning exposed the marsh in a vast, black-and-white landscape, desolate and alive. Hoping for more lightning, she peered into the darkness, and then, as the thunder rumbled away, Gaia heard another cry, only it wasn't a baby or a birdcall this time. It was the moaning cry of a woman in labor.

For an instant she froze, her inner strings reverberating with the familiar sound, and then she was hurrying down a lane toward the echo of the cry. She didn't stop until she arrived on the narrow porch of a peak-roofed, one-story cabin, where the cry came again. As it faded away, she knocked loudly on the frame of the screen door.

"Will?" called a woman's voice from inside.

"It's Gaia Stone," she called. She blinked back the raindrops on her lashes and waited.

Nobody came. Gaia peered through the screen into the high-ceilinged room, noticing that shelves of books ran waist-high all the way around the walls. More volumes were piled high on the mantel over the fireplace. A lamp with a rose-colored shade was burning on a table. She stripped off her muddy socks and tried to shake off some of the rain that dripped from her arms and hair. When still no one came, she pulled softly at the screen door and stepped inside, hearing the rush of the rain on the steep roof above.

"Hello?" she called again.

She tiptoed down a short hallway to a curtained doorway. She fingered the curtain aside to find a tableau of contrasts: a slender, red-haired woman in tidy brown trousers and a white, delicately pleated blouse stood beside a bed where a distraught, disheveled, pregnant girl was clenched in the pain of childbirth.

The woman's gaze traveled from Gaia's soaked clothes to her muddy feet. Her lips curved. "Sure you have the right party?"

Gaia laughed, rolling back her wet sleeves. "What's her name? How long has she been in labor?"

"This is Mx. Josephine. She started just after lunch. I'm Mx. Dinah. Welcome."

Josephine's face was dusky and flushed, her eyes half wild with fear. In a sweat-soaked, gray nightgown, she curled to her side in a thrashing motion.

"Oh, no!" Josephine said. She wiped a strand of black hair out of her mouth in a panicky gesture. "Here comes another one. Mx. Dinah, help me!" She grabbed for Dinah's hand and held her breath, gritting her teeth for one long, torturous suspension of time.

Not good, Gaia thought, hoping the mother's frenzy didn't presage an underlying complication. She had to be ready before the next one.

She took a quick survey of the room to see what she had to work with, noting the lit fireplace and a pile of clean linens. Two oil lamps gave good light, and the bed jutted into the middle of the room so it would be easy to get to both sides. As she washed her hands in the corner basin, she knew she would need more water and a knife. If only she had her old midwifery satchel.

The next moment Josephine expelled her breath rapidly, panting, and her eyes, glazed, rolled back in her head. Dinah looked back over her shoulder, her expression grim. "I don't suppose you've had any experience with this."

"Actually, I have." Gaia leaned near to the mother. "Here, now, Josephine. Let's see if you can sit up a bit more before the next one, okay? And try your knees here." She took the girl's hand and moved a couple of pillows along her back. "Is this your first baby? How old are you?"

"It's my first," Josephine said. "I'm seventeen. It just hurts so bad. Is it supposed to hurt this bad?"

Gaia smiled. "It's normal to hurt some, but you'll be all right. I'm Gaia and I want you to listen to me. When the next contraction comes, I want you to look in my eyes, okay? Don't close your eyes. And see if you can keep breathing. I'll help you. All right? Can you do that?"

The girl pushed the black curls out of her face and nodded, already a little calmer. "Okay. You look younger than me. What's wrong with your face?"

Gaia smiled. "It's just a scar. I'm sixteen. How much time has there been between contractions? Ten minutes? Five?"

Josephine looked at Dinah, as if she didn't know.

23

"Closer to three or four, I'd guess," Dinah said.

"I'm going to need some hot water and a knife," Gaia said, taking her locket watch from around her neck. She dried it on the corner of a blanket before she flipped the catch and set it on the bedside table. "And Josephine's probably thirsty. Do you have any motherwort? Any black cohosh?"

"I have some chamomile. I'll get it, and the water. You can't believe how happy I am that you're here," Dinah said.

"It's coming again!" Josephine said urgently.

Gaia ran a sure hand down the girl's back and gave her the other to hold. "You're going to be okay. You're doing a fine job. Just breathe easily here, ready? Breathe in, now." She took a deep breath herself, inviting the anxious mother to follow. "Josephine, look at me." She could feel Josephine's focus on her own lips. "That's right," Gaia said, smiling slightly. "A good deep breath now." She showed her again.

Gaia could feel Josephine's eyes fixed on hers in pain but not panic, and when the contraction stopped, she relaxed backward, exhausted.

Gaia glanced up at Dinah, who had paused in the doorway to watch.

"Why didn't you just say you were a midwife?" Dinah asked.

"I wasn't sure I still was," Gaia answered, and laughed somewhere between surprise and despair.

The last birth she'd handled had gone completely, desperately, fatally wrong. Part of her had never wanted to deliver another baby after her mother's death, but now, with Josephine needing her, she knew her mother would expect her to take up her duties again. She looked down at her hands as she wiped them again on a clean white cloth.

"Where's your usual midwife or doctor?" Gaia asked.

"Our last doctor died a few years ago and our midwife died

in childbirth two summers ago," Dinah said. "The best we have now is Chardo Will, who's pretty good with animals. I sent a boy for him an hour ago, but he hasn't come."

"The outrider who brought me in?" Gaia asked, confused.

"That was Chardo Peter. Will is Peter's brother." Dinah went to gather what supplies she could.

Gaia met the gaze of the tired girl on the bed. "Do you mind if I examine you?"

"Okay." Josephine's voice was small. She pointed toward a little table. "Could you hand me my bear first?"

Gaia saw a ratty brown thing with one button eye. "Sure," she said, and passed it over before she gently lifted the mother's gown. "You might feel some pressure."

She examined Josephine with steady, perceptive hands. The mother was fully dilated, and the baby's head was hard in the cervix's opening. Everything was in line naturally for an uncomplicated delivery, and Gaia was relieved.

"It's not too much longer now," Gaia said. "You did the hard work before I came."

Within an hour, it was true, and the mother lay back, spent, while Gaia passed the infant to Dinah.

"You've done so well, Josephine," Gaia said. "Truly. She's a beautiful baby girl."

"A girl?" Josephine asked. "Really?"

Dinah tucked a clean blanket around the newborn and set her gently in Josephine's arms. "A girl. I can't believe it," Dinah said. "The first one in two years. The Matrarc will be ecstatic."

Gaia cleaned up gently between Josephine's legs, making sure the afterbirth was complete. More memories of her mother came back to her as she massaged Josephine's abdomen, helping the uterus to contract. There was nothing dangerous about the blood flow, or Josephine's coloring, and the baby was full term

25

and healthy, yet Gaia felt an urgency to make sure everything went just right. She kept her head down, working silently, until finally she tucked a wadded towel tightly between Josephine's legs and settled her sideways where she'd be comfortable for a few hours.

As she stepped back, a touch of dizziness hit her, and she braced a hand against the wall.

"You all right?" Dinah asked.

Gaia touched a hand to her eyebrow. "I'm fine. A little dizzy maybe."

"Here, take a seat while I finish tidying up here," Dinah said, pulling up a chair beside the fireplace and guiding Gaia to it. Dinah laughed. "Your clothes are clammy still. Let me get you some dry things."

"I'm okay," Gaia said.

"Something for your feet at least. Your toes are blue. Why are you barefoot?"

"I couldn't find my boots. I left my socks on your porch."

Dinah threw on a couple of logs and gave the fire a poke, then rummaged up some dry socks and a pair of worn, over-sized loafers. Gaia inched her shod feet toward the warmth, and then she reached for her locket watch, the only gift she had left from her parents, and tilted it toward the firelight. She ran her thumb over the engraved words: *Life first.*

Now that her parents were both dead and her sister taken from her, Gaia took little comfort in the credo. Putting life first hadn't worked for her parents. If anything, her parents had found things worth dying for. Or being killed for. She closed the lid with a little snap.

Gaia looked over to see Josephine's tired eyes gleaming from her pillow. Her damp black hair curled vividly around her bright eyes, and there was a winsome loveliness to her smile as she traced the little face of her daughter.

"I don't know how I can ever repay you for tonight," Josephine murmured. "Either of you."

Dinah gave the girl a quick kiss on her forehead. "It was no trouble at all."

Gaia felt the same way.

Now was the time Gaia would normally have a cup of tea with the mother and birthmark the infant's ankle with the Orion tattoo, but she had no needle, no ink, and no mother of her own to keep the tradition alive for. The onslaught of sadness hit her then, fast and hard. She missed her mother so intensely she could barely take in air. "Excuse me," she said, rising. "Where's the washroom?"

"There's an outhouse out the back door," Dinah said. "Just go down the hall there. Here, take the lantern." She lit the little candle and dropped the pane of glass back in place.

Gaia held herself together until she stepped out the back door, but as the rain curtained around her off the overhang, she sank down on the back stoop of the little cabin. She set the lantern beside her, but tilted it so badly the flame went out. She curled her legs up in her arms, resting her forehead against her knees. She had just assisted a birth again. Babies were still coming into the world while, in some far off city, her mother was dead. Thunder crashed around her. Gaia didn't even get to bury her. Or her father.

She squeezed hard around her knees, gulping in big, impossible, ragged gasps of air. Blind grief wracked through her, and she wished, she just wished she could have her mother back. She didn't care at all about getting burned for her scar. She just wished she could take all of the last months back, erase them all, and be back in her old home with the comforting rattle of her father's treadle sewing machine and her mother kissing her good night.

But she would never see either of them again.

She moaned over a little ache in her throat. *I hope they at least buried Mom beside Dad.*

The door behind her bumped into her back as it was pushed partly open, letting out a crack of light.

"Mlass Gaia? Are you all right?" Dinah asked.

Gaia sniffed in hard and wiped her nose on her wet sleeve.

"What are you doing out here?" Dinah said.

"I'm sorry. Is Josephine okay?"

"She's fine. But what about you?"

Gaia dragged herself to her feet. She couldn't meet Dinah's gaze. She could feel it coming again, and she was ashamed to cry in front of anyone else. Then she did, anyway.

"You poor kid," Dinah said. "Come on in here. Let's see if we can't warm you up."

"It's just so unfair," Gaia sobbed.

Dinah hugged her hard, and then picked up the lantern and guided her back inside again. She held the curtain aside for her and nudged her toward the fire.

"Is she okay?" Josephine said.

Gaia dropped off the big loafers and pulled her feet up on the chair. She had to stop crying. Just had to. She hid her face and felt a big soft towel settling around her shoulders. A shudder rippled through her, and then a hiccup. She clutched at the edge of the towel until finally the worst of it passed.

When she peeked out again, a bowl of soup was waiting for her. She reached wearily for it and slowly spooned bits of chicken and black rice from the hot broth. To her left, Dinah was softly talking with Josephine, and the baby snuggled in to nurse for the first time. When Dinah came to take the bowl out of her fingers, Gaia stirred enough to thank her.

"You hardly ate anything," Dinah said. "Better? A little?"

Gaia nodded.

"You've come far, haven't you?" Josephine said.

Gaia closed her eyes to slits, making the fire blur. "From another world," she murmured.

Dinah sat on the end of Josephine's bed, and as she leaned forward, resting her slender forearms on the knees of her trousers, her braid slipped over her shoulder. Her wide gray eyes caught the firelight as she spoke.

"I wish I could do more for you," Dinah said. "But I'm afraid you might be in even more trouble for coming here."

"How so?"

Dinah picked a bit of lint off her trousers. "I'm guessing you didn't exactly have permission to come down. We're libbies, outcasts from the cuzines. The mlasses of the lodge don't normally mingle with us. Since this was a medical situation, I'm hoping the Matrarc will overlook it."

Gaia frowned. "What's a libby?"

"You're my new hero," Josephine said, then spoke to Dinah in a hushed squeal. "She's never heard of a libby!"

Dinah regarded Gaia curiously. "Where you're from, what do they call the women who don't marry?"

"I don't know. 'Single'?" Gaia said.

Josephine laughed again. "I love that. 'Single.' I want to be single."

Dinah's expression remained somber. "Okay. You need to understand something," she said to Gaia. "It's very important here for women to marry and have children. Ten children is the goal. Even after they have ten, most mladies keep on having children. They consider it a duty and an honor."

29

Ten children. "That sounds just insane," Gaia said.

"Not if you think of it this way. We have roughly two thousand people here in Sylum," Dinah said. "Nine out of ten are men, and that proportion is getting worse each generation. The men, of course, can't have children. That means, for our population just to stay the same, each of our two hundred women needs to bear ten children."

"And if they don't?"

"We'll die off. We've *been* dying off for generations," Dinah said, but there was something in her voice that Gaia didn't understand, as if Dinah was reconciled to this extinction.

"What does that have to do with you and Josephine?" Gaia said.

Dinah dovetailed her fingers before her. "Mx. Josephine and I have broken the rules. We're not getting married. We've opted out."

"*You* opted out," Josephine corrected her. "Some of us got kicked out."

"If it mattered to *some* of us to stay in the cuzines, *some* of us shouldn't have been sleeping around with men in the pool," Dinah said.

Josephine pouted, reminding Gaia of a cornered, petulant kitten. "Xave is not any 'man in the pool'," she said.

"No. He's the biggest, handsomest, meanest one of them all," Dinah said dryly. "Good choice."

"I take it you're not going to marry him," Gaia said, still watching Josephine.

Dinah laughed. "It's too late for that now. Besides, he won't have anything to do with her."

"He might feel differently once he meets his daughter," Josephine said stubbornly. "We had a *girl*." She pushed her black curls back and tucked them behind her ear.

Dinah clunked her hand against her forehead. "Walker Xavier is not coming back to you now, not after all he went through insisting he was innocent. He's not going to forget hours in the stocks and a month with the crims."

"You don't know Xave," Josephine said.

"I don't have to know him!" Dinah said. "He's ignored you utterly for what, seven months now? You think that's an accident?"

Josephine's face closed. "I really don't need this right now."

Dinah smoothed the blanket around the girl's feet, and as she did so, Dinah's expression softened. "I don't mean to pick on you. It's him I'm mad at when I think of the hardships ahead of you."

Gaia glanced up. "What do you mean?"

Dinah flicked her gaze to Gaia's. "We're practically men, with no rights and no vote. Second-class citizens at best. Mx. Josephine will keep her daughter as long as she nurses her, up to a year, and then she'll give her over to one of the regular families with a mother in the cuzines. It won't be fun."

"But why?" Gaia asked.

"Libby mothers are unfit to be parents," Dinah said mockingly. "We don't demonstrate the proper family values."

"Just because you don't want to marry?" Gaia asked, surprised.

"It's the whole thing," Dinah said. She retucked her blouse where it was a little loose at the back. "Remember what I said about the ten children? The cuzines are devoted to sustaining the population, and they need every girl to take up her duties of motherhood. The costs are very high for a girl who doesn't. After all, we libbies are accelerating the extinction. That's hardly patriotic."

Gaia looked again at Josephine's little baby and thought of

her own sister. No wonder the Matrarc had been so implacable about taking Maya away, considering that she was accustomed to reassigning libby babies to new parents.

"You don't seem to have any illusions about it," Gaia said.

Dinah laughed. "I've never been one to delude myself."

"Do you have any children yourself?" Gaia asked.

"I have Mikey," Dinah said. "He's seven now."

"And who's raising him?" Gaia asked.

Dinah picked up a blanket from the end of the bed and re-folded it carefully. "My brother and his wife. They're one of the Munsch families, down by the marsh. They dote on him, and he's happy there now. I visit him often. He calls me his Aunt Dinah."

Gaia didn't understand how she could be so calm about it. Either Dinah had an incredibly thick skin, or her nonchalance was a façade. "Why didn't you just marry the father of your child?"

Dinah smiled with amusement. "I wasn't going to shackle my life to a man's just to keep my child and then be bound to have nine more children by him. Besides, I was already a libby by then."

"But you must have loved him, at least for a time," Gaia pressed.

"I don't love anyone," Dinah said. "I'd rather have my books."

"Don't believe her," Josephine said. "She was chosen as the prize in the thirty-two games five times before she became a libby, and she's had plenty of expool boyfriends since then. She has to beat them away."

"Enough of that," Dinah said, smiling. "That's none of your business, or Mlass Gaia's. We're not supposed to be corrupting her."

Gaia was impressed, and curious. "What are the thirty-two games?"

"They're a competition where the men try to win a chance to live with a woman in the winner's cabin for a month. It's ridiculous," Dinah said.

"It's fun," Josephine argued, smiling. "You'll see."

"Maybe I should be a libby," Gaia said.

"Don't you start thinking like that," Dinah said. "This isn't the life for you. I can tell already."

"Why not?"

"You're smart. You'll want to do things with your life, and for that, you have to be in the cuzines," Dinah said. "You have to stay on the Matrarc's good side."

Gaia had her doubts about how likely that was. "She thinks I'm a criminal for endangering my sister."

"I know. I'm not sure what she'll do to you if the baby dies," Dinah said. "Sorry. I didn't mean for that to sound so blunt. I'm just trying to think ahead. For lesser crimes, a woman's confined to the lodge, but we've never had a woman convicted of murder before." She straightened slightly. "I guess she could exile you, and then the gateway sickness would kill you. Did you say you saw a corpse at the oasis?"

"The Matrarc said he escaped from prison."

"It's what will happen to you if you get dropped out there. She's exiled traitors before, men and women, but I don't know what she'd do in your case. You're a pretty valuable person."

"Because I'm a girl?" Gaia asked.

Dinah smiled. "Don't underestimate how much that matters, and you're a midwife, too. To be fair, I should add that the Matrarc is unfailingly decent to her loyal followers, and that's pretty much everyone except the crims and a handful of libbies."

33

Gaia could hear the admiration in Dinah's voice. "You respect her?"

"Of course I do," Dinah said, laughing. "I'd be a fool not to."

"No, I mean you really do, don't you? You sound like you admire her, as a person," Gaia said.

Dinah gave her an odd look. Then she turned to a dresser and began opening drawers. "The Matrarc's a curious person. She's strong and smart, of course, but it's more than that," she said, her voice thoughtful. "I can't explain."

Gaia was surprised. Puzzled, she glanced over at Josephine.

"It's true," Josephine said sadly. "When the Matrarc trusts you, you want to tell her things. You can feel how she cares about you, so then if you disappoint her, you feel awful."

Dinah turned from the dresser with a shawl and held it out to Gaia. "Here. Take this. You really should go. You can bring it back with the shoes another day. If the shoes fit, I'd say you should keep them, but they're obviously boats on you."

"Thanks," Gaia said. She stood stiffly. A bit of light was coming in the window now, and the rain was barely a drizzle. She didn't want to leave. "What will you name your daughter, Mx. Josephine?"

The new mother smiled. "I'm naming her after me. Fitch Josephine, Junie. I'll call her 'Junie.'"

Dinah touched a hand to her heart, and then to the baby's head in a gentle, motherly gesture. "You do that," she said.

The cabin was quiet, with only the sound of the fire crackling and the soft drum of rain on the roof. As Gaia took a last look at the fire, the warmth penetrated the scar on her left check, almost like pressure. For a moment, she was able to imagine an invisible kiss from her own lost mother, a gift of quiet approval, and Gaia held on to it.

CHAPTER 3

a deal

THE SLATS had been hammered back on.

Even though she could see that they were secure, she tried the wood anyway, fruitlessly hoping. It wouldn't give. She looked to her left along the log wall, toward where there was light in the windows of a kitchen. Gaia's pulse elevated as she quietly crept nearer, climbing the two steps to the door. She tried the knob, but it was locked.

She peeked in the window screen and saw the back of a man's head and shoulders. She knocked softly.

"Back so soon?" came a terse voice.

"Please. Let me in," she said quietly.

There was a thumping noise, then a click, and the door opened to reveal a thickset, gray-haired man with a peg leg. He kept his swarthy arm on the door, barring her way, and lowered his bushy white eyebrows into a stern line.

"Hi." She tried a little smile. "I'm Gaia. The new girl. Sneaking back in."

The man gave her a once-over, and she could just imagine the picture she made, half wet, carrying her dirty socks, standing awkwardly in the too-large, muddy loafers.

He backed up with a grunt. "You're wanted in the atrium."

The kitchen smelled of warm oatmeal, and on a rocker near the hearth, a black cat lifted its chin to inspect her, revealing a long patch of white on its chest. Herbs hung from the rafters, and a row of three copper-bottomed tubs hung over the windows. Gaia closed the door and slipped out of her muddy shoes.

"Is there news about my sister? Who wants me?" she asked.

"Who else? The Matrarc. Don't leave those there," he said. "There's a boot tray behind the door."

"Is she mad?"

He stepped over to his stove, the peg making a hollow noise on the floor as he strode. "She doesn't get mad. She makes decisions," he said, and smacked a pan onto the stove.

For all Gaia knew, this man was this grumpy always, but she didn't have a good feeling about it. She set the shoes and dirty socks in the tray beside a tall, solitary left-footed boot. She spotted a row of pegs behind the door and hung Dinah's shawl there.

"What do you think the Matrarc will do?" Gaia asked, turning again to the cook. "She won't send me back out to the wasteland, will she? Just for sneaking out?"

"Depends."

"On what?"

"On what you did while you were out," he said.

A laugh escaped her, and the man glanced up, frowning.

"You weren't with a boy, were you?" he asked.

"No," she said. "Nothing so romantic. Should I take time to change?"

"I wouldn't. She's been here half an hour already. Here. Bring her this." He poured steaming tea from a ceramic pot into a teacup and set it on a little tray.

"May I have some, too?" Gaia asked.

He looked at her briefly, morosely, but then he took another cup off the shelf, added it to the tray, and poured again.

"You don't have any honey, do you?" she asked.

He reached for a brown honey pot and dropped a dollop into her tea, spinning off the last strand of gold on the edge of the cup.

"Thank you," she said.

He added a spoon to the tray and waved her off. "Take it. Go."

"I don't even know your name," she said, picking up the tray. "Or your cat's."

His bushy eyebrows lifted, then lowered again. "I'm Norris. The cat there is Una. Now run along. I've got work to do."

From the kitchen, she turned left down the hallway until she came to a large, open room. The ceiling rose three stories to a clerestory of windows, just lightening with rosy, fresh-washed dawn. Tiers of balconies bordered three of the walls, creating an atrium with the fourth wall, which was dominated by a great stone fireplace. Before this, in a high-backed chair, the Matrarc sat with her cane and a ball of white yarn, knitting. Her red skirt glowed in the firelight, and her feet looked tidy in black, beaded moccasins. She stretched out a length of yarn and lifted her face.

"I thought I heard voices. Is that you, Mlass Gaia?" she asked.

"Yes. How's my sister doing?"

"She's better. I came from there to tell you so. Imagine my surprise when I found you gone. Have you brought tea?"

"Yes. From Norris."

"Set it here, please." She lightly tapped the round little table on her left, and then gestured to the chair opposite hers. "Take a seat."

Gaia glanced down at the cushion. "I'm afraid I'm too wet still."

"Is that so? Let me feel your skirt."

Gaia set down the tray and stepped nearer, holding up a bit of the cloth until it touched against the Matrarc's fingers. The older woman fingered it thoughtfully before she dropped it. "Why don't you pull up one of the other chairs then, or sit on the hearth?" the Matrarc said.

Gaia glanced over to where a dozen straight-backed wooden chairs were drawn up around a table. Beyond were other group-ings of tables and chairs, some in cozy combinations by the windows where sunlight would touch soon, others arranged more like a dining hall or a school. With a glance at the oval braided rug at her feet, she dropped to the hearth, bringing her cup of tea and the spoon with her, and huddled her back to-ward the warmth.

"Is Maya really better?" Gaia asked.

"She started nursing. I wouldn't say she's out of the woods yet, but she can be roused and her pulse is strong."

She had turned a corner, then. Gaia was so relieved. For a moment she didn't care about anything else, or anything that could happen to her. As long as her sister lived, that was all that mattered.

"Save us both some time and tell me where you've been," the Matrarc said, her voice as melodious as ever.

Gaia glanced down into her teacup and realized the Matrarc would know soon anyway. Babies weren't exactly top secret news. "I went to Mx. Dinah's. I heard a girl there in labor, so I went in and delivered the baby."

"Mx. Josephine's?" the Matrarc asked. "She was due about now."

"Yes. She had a girl. A healthy one, and Mx. Josephine is fine, too."

"Wonderful news," the Matrarc said, looking pleased. "You seem so young to be a doctor."

"I'm a midwife," Gaia said. She considered adding that she had experience assisting doctors in the Enclave, but decided against it. "I assisted my mother for five years, and I started delivering babies on my own this past summer."

"This makes a difference," the Matrarc said. "A very big difference. We need you here more than you know. In the two years since the last midwife died, we've had half a dozen babies die in childbirth, and three mothers as well. Why didn't you tell me at first?"

Gaia gave her tea a slow swirl with the spoon, disturbing the honey at the bottom. "I wasn't sure I could do it anymore," she answered.

A slow clicking came from the Matrarc's lap as she knit a few stitches. "There's much about you that I don't understand," she said. "But the grief in you I sense clearly. For your parents, I assume. I think you've come to us for a reason, and maybe you need us as much as we need you. What brought you north? Why didn't you go in some other direction?"

Gaia lifted the steamy cup to her lips and took a sip. "My mother told me to come here. I've wondered about it. My grandmother left when I was only a baby, years ago, but only a month ago my mother told me to come find my grandmother here, as if she thought my grandmother was still alive. Could they have corresponded somehow?"

"It's remotely possible, but not likely. I know Mlady Danni tried to send messages to the Enclave with nomads who passed through, but that was, as you say, a decade ago. I don't know that she ever received any letter back but I doubt it. Such news would have been enormously exciting to all of us and she never said anything."

"It could have taken the nomads a long time to deliver a message or letter to my parents," Gaia mused. "My grandmother didn't leave any papers behind when she died, did she?"

The Matrarc looked thoughtful. "Come to think of it, she had a sketchbook. I'll see if I can have my husband Dominic find it." She tilted her face slightly and pressed her knitting needle idly against her chin. "I think we need to work out a deal."

"You'll give me my sister back?"

She shook her head. "Please face the truth, Mlass Gaia. You're sixteen. You're still weak from crossing the wasteland. You're in no condition to watch over an infant who needs constant care and nursing. I have a mother here who will love her and care for her as her own."

"You just don't think I'm fit to raise a baby."

The Matrarc smiled. "You've been talking to Mx. Dinah. You'll be perfectly fit to raise your own baby in a loving home someday. I'm certain of that."

"Unlike Mx. Josephine," Gaia said, with an edge.

The Matrarc took a sip of her tea. "You liked them, didn't you? Mx. Dinah and Mx. Josephine are wonderful women. They've just made different choices, and trust me when I say they made them with their eyes wide open. But I don't care to go into the matter of the libbies at the moment. We have things to work out between us."

"Like when I can see my sister? Where is she?"

"You broke out of the lodge to try to find her, obviously," the Matrarc said.

Gaia drank another swallow of her tea. "I'll do it again, as soon as I can. You might as well just let me see her."

The Matrarc's eyebrows arched slightly. "You sound so much like your grandmother sometimes. Come here. Kneel before me." She set down her teacup and held out her hands. "I want to touch your face, child. Don't resist me this time."

Gaia's gut instinct was to back away as fast as possible, but the Matrarc merely waited. Gaia eyed the woman's slender fingers, her pensive face, the rich red color of her skirt draping around her pregnant shape, and gradually her wariness yielded to the Matrarc's wordless patience. She set her cup lightly on the hearth with a faint clink, then she shifted nearer so that she could gently lean her face up against the Matrarc's waiting fingers.

She closed her eyes as a trembling coolness rippled through her. Ten impossibly light fingertips touched along her face, instantly sensitizing every millimeter of her skin. Her eyebrows were traced in simultaneous curves, and then her cheeks. She could feel her scar respond as the Matrarc's touch returned across the mottled skin of her left cheek a second time, examining, smoothing, and then the touch glided tenderly down her nose, and lips, and chin. The touch came to pause at her jawline, holding her, memorizing her. Gaia could hardly breathe.

Gaia opened her eyes to see a question in the Matrarc's expression. No matter how many times people had stared, no stranger had ever touched her this way before, and the intimacy unglued Gaia. The Matrarc's inspection went deep into her marrow, a cross between suffocation and a kiss.

The Matrarc's own face was a study of concentration, and her clear, sightless eyes flickered with prisms of firelight.

Confused, Gaia knew it was time to shift away, but somehow she couldn't. Nor could she speak. The Matrarc's hands slid lightly over her hair and down to her shoulders, meeting the chain of her necklace.

41

"What's this?" the Matrarc asked. As she lifted the locket, the ticking became audible.

As if released from a spell, Gaia could breathe again. She leaned back slightly. "My locket watch. My parents gave it to me."

The Matrarc lowered it carefully. A belated shiver lifted along Gaia's skin, and she crouched back to her old place beside the fire, hugging her arms around her. *What did you do to me?* she wondered.

"I didn't realize things were so complicated," the Matrarc said finally.

Gaia felt the heat of a blush start up her neck. "Don't pretend to know me just because you've felt my scar."

The Matrarc laughed gently. "You think that's all I saw?"

"I don't know what you mean."

"You need so badly, Mlass Gaia. Every part of you is reaching for someone to care for you." The Matrarc's eyebrows arched, and she turned her lips in a contemplative expression. "The men will be drawn to you. They'll want to protect you. You're young and full of promise, of course, but it's the longing inside you that will intrigue them."

Gaia hardly knew what to think. She didn't want be the vulnerable girl the Matrarc was describing.

"How do I manage this?" the Matrarc added softly.

"You don't have to manage this at all. I'll take care of myself."

The Matrarc laughed. "Such independence. You haven't said anything about leaving a boyfriend behind. Did you?"

A dim silence came back from her heart where the lonely place was. Explaining Leon would not be possible. It was so much easier when she didn't think of him at all.

"Never mind," the Matrarc said, even more kindly. "As you

42

say, you can take care of yourself. The fact is, you're here now. I'd like you to look after our pregnant women. There are at least six I can think of off hand, and I'm sure there are more. Could you do that?"

This, at least, was something Gaia understood.

"Yes, but I don't have any supplies," Gaia said. "Did your last midwife leave a garden?"

The Matrarc nodded. "She lived near the shore, a bit out of the way. Her place is all overgrown now. I had most of her herbs transplanted to the kitchen garden when she died, but I don't know how well Norris has done with them."

Gaia was curious to see what was there. "If I do this, if I take care of the pregnant women for you, can I have my sister back?"

The Matrarc's hands stilled on her yarn, and she tilted her face as if she were listening. Gaia heard noises above in the building, the sounds of people waking and moving in their bedrooms. There was a distant sound of water in the kitchen as well.

"I'll be honest with you," the Matrarc said. "The answer is no. I'll never let you raise your sister, but I'll let you see her."

"When?"

"When I can trust that you aren't trying to undermine my authority here. You can't go sneaking out of the lodge anymore. You can't go down to the libbies to socialize. I want you attending school with the other mlasses and learning our ways."

Gaia could do that. "School?"

"Mlady Roxanne can teach you in the mornings with the others. Are you literate?"

"I can read," Gaia said. "I'm a little slow, though. She won't make me read out loud, will she?"

The Matrarc laughed with open humor for the first time. "No, she won't. You'll like Mlady Roxanne. Everybody does."

43

Gaia smiled slowly, letting her gaze drift out to the tables and chairs again, seeing bookshelves in the corner. She'd never had the chance to go to school before. She'd always been jealous of the Enclave kids, but now maybe she'd get to read good books, too, and study about all the things that had always left her curious and hungry.

"I need one other thing," Gaia said.

The Matrarc was smiling easily. "What is that?"

"I need to know that if my sister's dying, I can go to her and hold her one last time. Promise me that, and I'll agree to the rest."

The Matrarc's smile faded, and her eyebrows narrowed in genuine sympathy. "I'd be an ogre to refuse you," she said. "I promise."

"Will I be attending to your pregnancy, too?" Gaia asked.

"That would be reassuring, actually. This is my eighth pregnancy," the Matrarc said. "It feels different, but I don't know why. I had some spotting earlier, and then it stopped."

"When are you due?"

The Matrarc smoothed a hand contemplatively over her belly. "In twelve weeks. I'm praying for another girl. My oldest, Taja, is my one daughter so far. Imagine, having a girl first."

"How old are you?" Gaia asked.

"Thirty-three."

The sound of a door opening carried from above.

"I tell you what," the Matrarc said. "Get yourself cleaned up and eat and rest. Until you're stronger, I'll tell the pregnant mladies to come talk to you here at the lodge. I'll ask Mlady Maudie to set up a room upstairs where you can see them with some privacy."

"And the libbies? They'll come here, too?" Gaia asked.

The Matrarc hesitated. "It would be better if you met them at Mx. Dinah's."

Gaia was about to object, then decided she would wait to fight that battle.

The Matrarc was standing, reaching for her red cane. "This has been most promising," she said. "A much better start. You haven't been feeling dizzy or sick yet?"

"Only a little."

The Matrarc put her knitting in a small bag. "Soon, you'll be sick. There'll be no mistaking it. This is your last chance if you want to leave Sylum," she said. "You could still go."

Gaia felt a shiver of foreboding, but she stood, bringing her teacup with her, and reached for the tray. "No," she said. "I'm staying."

"Then there's one other thing you should know," the Matrarc said. "It's important. I don't think any of the men would take advantage of your ignorance, but they might. Men can't touch you here. They normally shouldn't even speak to you unless you speak to them first."

The Matrarc had to be joking.

"Why not?" Gaia asked.

"It's to ensure you some space because otherwise you could be overwhelmed with men competing for your attention. It's the same for all the mlasses. And you should respect the men, too. They're inclined to do anything you ask because they'll want you to like them, but it's rude to boss them around."

Gaia let out a laugh.

"I'm quite serious," the Matrarc said. "Especially about the touching."

"The outrider Chardo already touched me," Gaia pointed out.

"Contact for emergencies and direct orders is condoned, obviously. Any tender touch, any kiss, is strictly illegal until you choose the man you want to marry."

Gaia laughed again. "That won't happen in any hurry."

"Respect our customs," the Matrarc said. "They may seem strange to you, but they work for us."

"Don't worry," Gaia said. There was no danger of her touching or kissing any man in Sylum. That was the last thing on her mind.

She slept. When she woke in her back bedroom with the slats crossing the window, it was afternoon and someone had put her white boots just inside her door. Her pack was on the chair, and the blue cloak Emily had given her back in Wharfton hung from a peg. They'd given her back everything she could still use, and kept her sister.

How long, she wondered, would it take to prove to the Matrarc that she deserved to see Maya?

She spent much of the afternoon seeing half a dozen pregnant mladies. When the first asked if there was any way to know if she was carrying a girl, Gaia smiled, amused. "You must know I love my sons," the mlady said. "But a girl would be so wonderful." By the time she'd been asked the same question for the fourth time, Gaia could feel the anxiety that drove the women to ask. When the last woman, not yet pregnant, asked if there was a way to be certain she could conceive a girl, Gaia felt helpless.

Drained, weary, she made her way back to the kitchen and was grateful when Norris pointed her toward the rocking chair. The day had grown warm, and even with the windows open, the air was uncomfortably still.

"You're a midwife, huh?" he said. "You look too young."

"So I've heard."

"My niece Erianthe is expecting."

"I'll probably see her tomorrow. There were six moms today."

All the talk of babies had made her miss Maya even more. She'd spent a whole day without her now, and it just felt wrong.

Norris passed her a bowl of soup and hot slice of black bread, right from the oven. She hardly ate half of it before she felt full. She gazed absently around the kitchen, noting the pipe that brought in water, and the tray of black loaves. They reminded her of Mace, and the night in the bakery when she'd talked to Leon. He'd been so klutzy with the little toy eggbeater. When she closed her eyes, she could actually see the pieces of the broken toy he had been holding, but not his hands. That's what she wanted to see. And his voice. She missed that, too.

She wanted to believe Leon was still alive: that after he'd been knocked senseless, the guards had brought him to the Bastion with nothing more than a bad headache. He could be playing chess with his sister right now, all safe and reconciled with his family. He could be in the solarium, surrounded by ferns and flowers.

Who was she kidding? If she was going to let herself dream the impossible, why not imagine that Leon was coming across the wasteland to find her?

"You should finish that," Norris said.

She opened her eyes and looked down at her bowl, still half full. "I think my stomach shrank."

"I'd say that's likely. But you need food. You won't have your energy again until you eat enough."

Gaia nibbled a few more bites of the bread. She did feel weak still, and she knew she looked haggard. A glance in the bathroom mirror earlier had confirmed that for her.

"Have you heard anything about my sister?" Gaia asked.

47

"No."

His peg made a sturdy noise as he moved around the kitchen, putting away a grater, onions, spices, and other odds and ends. Though there was nothing rhythmic about his steps, the peg noise made a kind of music in the kitchen, a comforting sound that didn't match his abrupt speech and persistently glowering expression. She could feel her guard coming down a little. His cat, Una, watched the end of Norris's peg with studious attention.

He passed Gaia an apple. "Try that."

She palmed the apple, one with golden specks in the red, and a slightly rough skin. It was almost too pretty to eat.

"Thank you, Mabrother." She caught her mistake. "I mean, Norris," she added quickly. "Is that your first name or your last?"

The man lifted a bushy eyebrow. His forehead gleamed with sweat, and he ran his forearm across it. "'Norris' is my mamname. My given name is Emmett. Norris Emmett."

"Your mamname? Is 'Norris' your mother's family name?"

"That's what I said."

It worked backward, she realized. Not only were the names reversed, first to last, but children carried on their mothers' family names, not their fathers'. "Back home, women take their husbands' names when they marry, and then their children have the father's last name," she said. "Like for me, Gaia Stone. 'Stone' was my father's last name."

Norris appeared to consider a moment. "That doesn't make sense. You only know for certain a child is his mother's. Of course a family bears the mother's name."

Gaia could see his logic, but it seemed peculiar. "So, technically, I'd be Orion Gaia here." She laughed. "That's not me." She stood and walked to the sink to clean out her bowl. A faucet provided a stream of cool water. "Is this potable?"

"You have to boil it before you drink," he said. "But you can wash with it. Rinse the soap off with the hot water. The drain will take it out for the garden." He nodded toward the stove where a black kettle was steaming on a back burner.

"We didn't have running water back home," she said. "They did in the Enclave, but we didn't outside the wall. Where's the water from? A well?"

"The marsh. We have an aqueduct system, and there's a water tower out back. I have a few minutes now, and I could show it to you, and the garden. Want to come? It'll be cooler out there."

He passed her a spare straw hat on the way out. The garden was large, and a couple of boys were working at one end of it, harvesting beans. Norris introduced them as Sawyer and Lowe, and they tipped their hats in greeting. Norris took her through the garden slowly, pointing out each vegetable and herb, but as they progressed, Gaia was increasingly disappointed. There were less than half of the herbs she had routinely used back home, and the prospect of filling out what she would need all by herself was daunting.

She tossed her apple core onto the compost pile.

"You're not happy," Norris said bluntly.

"No. It's all right. It's a start."

"You can transplant anything you want," Norris said. "There's no shortage of help. Just tell us what to do."

She glanced again at the boys, who had paused to look up at her again. "Is this the most extensive collection of herbs in the village?" she asked.

He seemed to consider. "Everyone has a garden. The Chardos, come to think of it, might have more variety with their herbs," he said. "You could try there."

She asked directions, and though Norris offered to send

Sawyer along to guide her, Gaia was eager for a chance to walk alone and think.

"Don't be gone too long," Norris said. "The acclimation sickness can come on suddenly and you don't want to be alone when it hits."

She hadn't gone five minutes before she heard footsteps coming fast behind her, and when she turned, a dark-haired girl was running toward her. She was surprisingly fast considering she ran with a hand on her hat, and her yellow skirt flapped out behind her. Gaia stopped to wait, listening to the cicadas starting up their slow buzz in the trees overhead.

"Hey," said the girl, out of breath. "I wanted to talk to you. I was hoping I'd catch you alone. I'm Mlass Peony."

"Nice to meet you. I'm Gaia."

"I know. You'll never believe how happy I am to know you're a midwife."

Gaia looked at her more closely, noting Peony's curvy figure and the bright eyes under the pale brim of her hat. Brown, lustrous hair fell loosely to her shoulders, and she wore a necklace of fine blue and purple beads. She was the picture of sturdy, farm-girl healthiness, with her cheeks rosy from running, yet she wasn't smiling.

"What can I do for you?" Gaia asked.

Peony hesitated, her eyes darting to be sure they were alone. "I'd like to know if you can help me miscarry."

peony's request

GAIA FELT THE BRIGHTNESS seep out of the afternoon. She had known this day would come. Her mother had tried to prepare her for it, but being prepared in the hypothetical wasn't the same as facing a girl on a road asking for her help. Until this moment, she'd always only used her skills and knowledge to help mothers have healthy babies.

Peony was watching her closely. Gaia gave a weak smile before turning up the road again.

"Can you help me? Do you know how?" Peony asked.

"I know how," Gaia said slowly. "I haven't done it before."

"You don't want to," Peony guessed.

She didn't want to. Not at all. "I need to think."

"What are you thinking? Tell me."

Gaia shook her head, unsure where to even start. "It isn't simple. Back in Wharfton, where I come from, it was my job to advance babies into the Enclave. I took them when they were just born and handed them over to the authorities, and their parents would never see them again."

Peony looked horrified. "How could you do that?"

"I didn't really have a choice, and I didn't much think about it. The mothers let me. We all accepted the system because it was supposed to be good for the babies. They were going to families that loved them and could take care of them better than we ever could outside the wall. Advancing a baby was an honor. That's what I'd been taught to believe, at least, but then I began to see."

She thought back to her first solo delivery. The mother had been poor and alone, and she'd named her baby Priscilla, believing she'd get to keep her. Gaia also remembered how she'd girded herself up to be strong enough to take the baby, how she'd even been proud of what she did. There were some things Gaia wished she could forget.

Peony was waiting, her eyes troubled. "How does this relate to me?"

Gaia glanced down and saw a dried drop of apple juice on the back of her thumb. She sucked it away, pressing her thumb hard against her teeth. "Here's the thing," she said. "That shouldn't have been my job. The only one who should have been making a decision about that baby was her own mother. Keep it, give it away—that should have been *her* choice to make."

"I agree with you," Peony said.

Gaia frowned down at the road between her feet. "I think the person who has to live most closely with the consequences of a decision should be the one to make it."

Peony took a step nearer. "Does this mean you'll help me?"

Gaia slowly looked up to see the agony and hope in Peony's eyes. "Are you absolutely certain it's what you want?" Gaia asked. "Have you talked it over with the father and with your parents?"

"I can't tell my parents." Peony turned to look up and down the road again, and then rubbed the heels of her hands against eyes underscored with dark circles. Now that her blush from running had gone, she was visibly pale and restive. "I've talked to the father. He's a lot of things right now, but supportive is not one of them."

"Will you be in trouble if anyone finds out?" Gaia asked.

Peony laughed. "Whoo-boy! But here's the thing. I'll be in much, much worse trouble if I have the baby, won't I? Like Mx. Josephine. I can't do it. I just can't."

Gaia looked up at the sound of wheels. A horse-drawn wagon was approaching down the road, and Peony smiled. When her face wasn't troubled, she was an unusually pretty girl, with wide cheekbones, a generous mouth, and large, expressive eyes. She even gave a cheery wave as the wagon passed. Immediately afterward, she was all tense anxiety again.

"Please say you'll help me," Peony pleaded. "Please, I'll do anything for you."

"I think we're going to need to talk," Gaia said. "Not here."

Peony nodded eagerly. "There's a path just ahead in the woods. We should be okay there."

Gaia turned doubtfully toward the green woods on the side of the road. "I can't go far," she said, reluctant to admit her weakness. "I'm not my usual self. Where does this lead?"

"It runs back to the bluff and meets another path there, but there's a little glade before then, with a bench. Not far, I promise. We have bonfires there."

A few paces farther, the sylvan path veered to the left, then branched again and dipped into a small, open area between old, arching trees. Three big, rough-hewn logs for sitting had been pulled up around a ring of blackened stones. Gaia took the end of a log and sat.

It was only as Peony sank to the log opposite her that Gaia

saw the undisguised misery that consumed the girl. A small, choking noise came from her, and then she slumped forward and covered her face with her hands.

Gaia didn't know what to do. She moved around to sit beside Peony and put a hand on her shoulder. She didn't know this girl at all, and she felt like she was way out of her league. "Are you sure we shouldn't talk to your mother?"

"I can't tell anybody else. You must think I'm terrible," Peony's voice was hardly more than a whisper, and then she sobbed once.

"I don't think you're terrible," Gaia said gently.

The girl pressed her skirt against her eyes. "Just tell me you'll help me," Peony said. "You have to. There's nobody else who can. If you don't, I don't know what I'll do. I almost killed myself a couple of nights ago, but then I chickened out."

"You can't kill yourself," Gaia said.

The girl gave a hysterical laugh, looking up again. "No?" Her face crumpled in anguish. "I've been so terrified. And then I heard this morning you were a midwife. I couldn't believe it! It was a sign. Please, please tell me you'll help me."

As Gaia met Peony's distraught gaze, she suddenly realized it didn't matter that she didn't know this girl. She wasn't being asked to help a friend. She was being asked, as a responsible midwife, to practice her skills, and it humbled her.

"If I can, I will," Gaia said. "It's okay. Try to calm down a little. How far along are you?"

Peony bit her lips together before she answered more calmly. "I missed my period two weeks ago. I know you're thinking it might be a fluke, but I've been regular for the last four years, like clockwork, and I just know."

"You aren't too far along, then," Gaia said. "I'll have to examine you later to be sure, but we'll assume you're right. Do you want to talk a little? Is there any chance you'd change your mind? I know it's a lot to adjust to, even in the best circumstances." She closed her fingers around her locket.

Peony took a deep breath and seemed to settle a little. "It's like this. If I have this baby, I'll be cast out of the cuzines just like Mx. Josephine was, but she at least has a sister. My whole family's depending on me," she said. "I'm the only daughter. I'm the one who's supposed to inherit after my mother someday and take care of my brothers, but I won't be able to once I'm cast out."

"I don't fully understand," Gaia said. "Is your mother old or sick?"

"No, but I'm the one carrying on the family line. The farm and everything, that's all tied up in me to inherit, mother to daughter, when my mother eventually dies. I wouldn't just disgrace my family if I was cast out of the cuzines. My family would end up impoverished because of me. Don't tell me I'm thinking too far ahead. That's how it is."

"You'll hate me for asking this," Gaia said, "but why didn't you think of that before?"

"When I was with him, you mean?" Peony sniffed, wiping at her eyes again. "Have you ever loved somebody? A boy?"

Startled, Gaia thought of Leon. "Not that way."

"Not at all?"

Gaia glanced down to where the tips of her boots poked out from the hem of her skirt and frowned. "I left someone behind that I cared for," she admitted. "We only knew each other a few weeks, now that I think of it."

"So you never slept with him?"

Gaia laughed. "No."

"But you kissed him at least, right?"

"Does this matter?" Gaia asked, hugging her arms around herself and leaning over her knees.

55

"Just tell me."

"Yes. We kissed."

Peony sat back a little, looking more hopeful. "So it was se-rious. What was he like?"

Gaia wondered why Peony cared about this, but she could see it was making her less anxious when Gaia talked a little about herself. She thought back for the first sign that he'd cared for her. "Leon gave me an orange once, before I even really knew what he was like. He sent it through prison walls to me when I needed hope more than anything. I didn't find out until later that it was from him."

Peony nodded, smiling slightly. "You would fall for one of the nice ones," she said. "I can tell."

Nice, Gaia thought. Intense, generous, troubled, smart: those were all Leon. But nice?

"He wasn't exactly nice in the normal way," Gaia said. "We never had any normal time together."

"What were you doing in prison?"

Gaia rocked her heels in the dirt. "I was only hoping to res-cue my parents, but then I saw a pregnant woman being hanged so I had to save her baby. I got caught, of course, and I ended up arrested. I was kept in prison for weeks, without a trial." She didn't want to go into it further.

Peony's eyes were wide. "You're really tough, aren't you?"

Gaia shook her head. "I don't think so. Listen, I'd rather that people here don't know about my jail time."

"We have mutual secrets, then," Peony said. "Despite what I've just told you, it's hard to trust anybody with this."

"You can trust me," Gaia said. "Confidentiality is part of my work."

"How old are you?" Peony asked.

"Sixteen."

"I'm seventeen," Peony said. "You seem a lot older."

"It's my scar that does that," Gaia said.

"No, it's something else. You're different," Peony said thoughfully.

Gaia had always been different. She felt a rumbling in her gut and frowned. "I think I'd better head back. Are you sure you've thought this over?"

Peony came to her feet. "All I've ever dreamed of is being a mother. If I have this baby, they'll take it away from me and I'll never be able to have a family of my own. But if I miscarry, I can marry and have a dozen kids and love every single one of them."

"Can't you marry the father?"

"He won't do it. He says it isn't his." Her voice rose to a squeak, and then she brought it back down. "If I tell on him, he'll be punished, but I'll be ruined, too. It's all a mess."

"Would anyone else marry you?"

Peony laughed. "I thought of that. I thought of just picking someone, but he'd know, eventually. And what kind of life would that be, married to someone I lied to right from the start? He'd hate me."

"What if you tell the truth?" Gaia said. She stood, brushing off the back of her skirt. "I mean, this may seem brutal, but if girls are in such short supply, probably some man would want you even if you're pregnant with another man's child."

"In that case, I'd enter into a loveless marriage with a man who's doing me a favor in exchange for a meal ticket," Peony said. "I can't do it."

They were nearly back to the road again, and Gaia paused, setting a hand on Peony's arm.

"Listen," Gaia said. "There's one more thing you haven't even mentioned. There's a life starting inside you. It isn't much yet, hardly bigger than a grain of sand. But you need to think of that, too. You'll always, always know you lost that life through your own choice. Can you carry that?"

Peony went very still and her gaze went lost and lonely. She closed her eyes. "It's going to eat me up," she said in hardly more than a whisper.

"Then don't do it," Gaia said.

"I have to! Don't say that!" Peony's face contorted with misery and then Gaia reached to pull her into a hug. The choice was not simple for Gaia either, nor free of grief, but she had to support this girl in whatever she decided. Never again would she be party to the crime of taking choices away from mothers.

"You'll still help me, right?" Peony asked anxiously.

"Yes. If it's really what you want."

"It is." Peony stepped back and wiped her eyes once more. "How do I look?"

"Like you've been crying," Gaia said.

Peony's smile was rueful. "I'm supposed to have dinner with my family tonight. I'll just take the long way back." She walked backward into the forest again. "You know your way?"

Gaia nodded. "I'm on my way to the Chardos' to see their garden. Norris thinks they might have some of the herbs I need. I'm looking for some tansy and blue cohosh especially."

"I'd help but I don't know a thing about herbs. It's not far," Peony said, pointing up the road. She told her to watch for a barn on the right with some new construction. "I'll see you around the lodge, okay? I live on the second floor there, in the corner room nearest the chimney. Will you come find me privately?"

"Give me a few days to prepare what I need," Gaia said. "And think it over. You can still change your mind."

"I won't."

58

Gaia waited to watch the other girl start back into the woods, and then, feeling much wearier than she'd been before, she continued up the road.

As she reached the Chardos', she heard hammering coming from the direction of the barn, where a scaffolding of pale, new lumber indicated an addition in progress. Beyond, a couple of horses grazed in the pasture, and she recognized Chardo Peter's horse, Spider.

To the south of the house, on the sunny side, a fenced garden offered inviting colors, and more flowers ran along the wood rail fence by the road. Gaia spotted tansy before she even started up the drive, and her heart lifted. Perhaps she could take some on her way back to the lodge to start a tincture for Peony. The rhythmic bangs of the hammer grew louder as she reached the barn door, and as she paused there, a man inside propped a nail on a box of wood and hammered it home with one sure stroke. In brown trousers and a gray tank top, with bits of sawdust salting his brown hair, he worked in focused concentration, lining up the next nail.

She didn't want to startle him, but she didn't want to spy, either. "Hello," she said. "I'm sorry to interrupt."

The man turned his head, then straightened and took another nail from between his lips.

"Mlass Gaia," he said, his voice lifting in surprise, and then his gaze shot to a workbench along the wall. He set down his hammer, walked over, and twitched a blanket over a form on the bench.

"We haven't met yet," he said. "I'm Peter's brother, Will. He's gone, you know. Back out to the perimeter." He reached for a gray short-sleeved shirt and, despite the heat, slipped it on, doing the buttons.

"I know," she said.

She tried to see how he resembled the outrider who had rescued her. Will's face was more square than long, and he was clean-shaven, with a distinct jaw line. Something pleasing in his voice was like Peter's.

"He felt bad about your sister," Will said. "He was afraid you wouldn't understand. Have you seen her?"

"I haven't been allowed to," Gaia said. "Do you know where she is?"

He shook his head. "No. Is there something I can do for you?"

"Norris told me to come see your garden," she said. "We need some herbs for my midwifery, and I thought I could take a look. I already saw you have tansy and ginseng out by the road."

"Peter planted them. He brings back plants he finds sometimes. I'll show you around," he said.

"I don't want to interrupt, though," she said, glancing at the shape he'd covered. "I can see you're busy."

"It can wait."

She couldn't take her eyes from the blanket, for the distinctive shape of a profile was becoming clear through the material. Then she looked back at the box he'd been hammering. It was not a bit of wood for the addition as she'd assumed, but a coffin.

She backed up a step. "I'm terribly sorry. I had no idea."

His smile grew strained. "It's really all right. My client has an endless supply of patience. No one told you I was a morteur?"

"No." She was still adjusting. He took care of bodies. She'd never thought of a young man as a morteur, but here he was. Now that she knew what to expect, she could smell in the barn, very faintly, the first hint of decay.

"Let me show you the garden," he said.

Instead, she took a step farther in. She'd never seen her father buried, or her mother, and now she couldn't resist her own attraction to the death in the barn.

She was intrigued by how inexplicably familiar it felt. "I'm sorry," she said. "Who died?"

"Jones Benny. He was a retired fisherman. He never had kids, but he and his nephews were very close. I always liked him. We're having the service tomorrow up on the bluff, at dawn, because that was Benny's favorite time of the day."

How she wished something like that had been done for her parents.

"That's beautiful," Gaia said.

Will nodded, watching her attentively. "You've lost someone recently, haven't you?" he said.

She nodded mutely. Who, she wondered, had taken care of her parents? Were they dressed nicely? Did someone comb her mother's hair?

"Was there a burial?" he asked. "Were you there for it?"

She shook her head. She kept looking at the blanket that covered the corpse, as if it might move, as if it were a mistake. She touched a hand to her forehead and squeezed her eyes shut for a moment.

"Please. Won't you sit down?" he asked, gesturing to a bench by the wall.

"It's been a big day," she said tightly. "I'm afraid if I sit, I'll never get up again."

"Give me just a minute to hitch up the wagon, and I'll take you back to the lodge."

She didn't want to go back. Not just yet. "I'm really fine."

"If you'll permit me, you're not fine. When's the last time you had a regular night's sleep?"

She tilted her face with a twist of her lips. "Good point."

His smile was slow and genuine. "You know," he began, "you don't need a gravesite to honor the person you lost."

"It was my parents," she said.

"Your parents, then," he said quietly. "Do you have anything from them?"

"My locket." She realized she already reached for it often when she thought of her mother or father. It comforted her. She rubbed it slowly along its chain, back and forth. "It was a gift for my midwifery. I think it would be nice to have something different, though. Final. Something to honor them, like you said."

"Suppose you pick a time that's special to you," Will said. "You can keep that moment sacred for them. I have rain to remember my mother, whenever it first starts."

She regarded him thoughtfully. "When did you lose her?"

"When I was seven. There was a fever in the village. My two youngest brothers died then, too."

"I'm sorry," she said.

Will smiled. "I don't expect I'll ever get over it, actually, but I don't even try to anymore. It's just been part of me for so long. What about you? Is there something like rain for your parents?"

She already knew what it would be, and a calmness settled around her heart. "Orion," she said. "The constellation. Whenever I see it, I think of my father anyway. He taught me about the stars."

"It won't be out in the summer," he reminded her. "But it's the looking for it that will count, even if you can't find it."

She glanced up at him. "You're good at this," she said.

"You were ready," he said simply. "That's all."

She inhaled slowly and let out a long breath. Her eyes turned once more to the corpse under the blanket, and she slid off her hat, striding idly toward the workbench. "How'd Benny die?"

"It was sudden," Will said. "They said he clutched at his chest before he went. I'm guessing his heart gave out. If you please, don't go any closer."

"Why not?"

He stepped in front of the body. "I'd just rather you didn't. Let me show you the garden."

"Are you doing an autopsy?" she asked.

Will lifted a hand to his jaw and rubbed his chin. Then he laughed. "What are the chances?" he asked the ceiling.

"What?" she asked. "I mean, it's not surprising. You must do them all the time."

He shook his head. "I've never done one before. I could hardly get myself to cut into him. I had to stop because I thought I'd be sick. And now the one person who might know something about bodies shows up in my barn."

"News travels fast here, doesn't it?" Gaia asked.

"News about a new midwife? Yes. I'd say so."

She went to hang her hat on a peg by the door. "Just so you know, being a midwife does not make me an expert in autopsies, but I was born curious. Want help?"

in the morteur's barn

S HE GLANCED BACK to see his eyebrows raised in gentle surprise. He put his fists on his hips and cleared his throat.

"You're serious?" he asked.

"Sure. I find it hard to believe you haven't done this before."

"There's no point, normally," Will said. "It can't change the fact that someone's dead. It's my job to clean up the corpse the best I can, dress him, and make the coffin. I try to do it as respectfully as I can."

"Then what's different this time?" she asked.

"Benny was an expool," Will said. "It always bothered him that he couldn't be a father. He begged me before he died to try to see if I could find out anything that would help anyone else. I tried to tell him I wouldn't know what to look for, but he made me promise. He said it was time I learned."

"Are many men here infertile?"

"The expools are," he said, nodding. "Every boy is tested around his fourteenth birthday. If his sperm aren't viable, he's out of the pool of eligible men who can marry."

"You're kidding," she said. "Is it very many men?"

"It's a lot. Maybe four or five hundred out of the eighteen hundred men here."

"I had no idea," she said. "That's horrible! What do they do?"

"What can they do? They just go on like everybody else," Will said. "Some try to get in with the libbies when they can. They really aren't much different from the men in the pool who never marry. There aren't enough women in any case."

Josephine had said something about Dinah having expool boyfriends, she recalled. She looked curiously at Will, wondering if he was an expool. She glanced at his hand to see his wedding finger was bare.

She absolutely was not going to ask him if his sperm were viable.

He smiled. "It's okay to ask. Yes, I'm in the pool."

She closed her eyes, feeling her cheeks burn with color. "I wasn't going to."

"We'll just forget about it then," he said, laughing. "On with the autopsy."

Grateful, she looked again at the form under the blanket, to where she could make out the ridge of his nose to the points of his toes. "I really don't have much experience with dead people," she said. "Just two up close. Once I had to cut into a dead pregnant woman to save a baby. I didn't have much time, obviously, and certainly no chance to look around inside, but I've thought about it since."

"I can see why," he said. "Who was the other dead person you knew up close?"

"My mother."

He took a long look at her. Then he walked behind her, reached for the great barn door, and rolled it closed, blocking

out the sunlight. She was thankful he didn't ask for any details.

"Will anyone come in?" she asked.

"No. My family's down with Bennie's people. Unlike you,
most people avoid this place when I have a cadaver."

"Does Benny's family know what you're doing?" Gaia asked.

"No."

He handed her a carpentry apron, which she looped over her
head and tied around her narrow waist. A rectangle of sunlight
fell through an open window of the loft above, and Will pushed
the workbench with its burden into the light. When she touched
the cloth by the cadaver's head, Will put out a hand.

"I'm keeping his face covered," he said.

She nodded.

When he slid the blanket up, it was a lot of dead body, with
only a modest undergarment covering his loins. A long, blood-
less incision had been cut from collarbone to below the navel.
The skin, devoid of the normal hue of blood in the capillaries
near the surface, looked tough and gray. Benny had been a thin
man, and his hipbones showed through his skin. She looked at
the way the man's ribs held up his skin over his chest.

"It was the idea of cutting away the ribs that made me
stop," Will said. "I couldn't think of any other way to get to
his heart."

"Maybe we could look at other things first," she said, "and
come back." There had been an anatomy chart in Q cell, and she
remembered talking it over with some of the imprisoned doctors,
but it had been a tidy drawing labeled with bright red and blue
colors. There were no labels here. She gently tugged the cold,
supple skin to the sides, and Will helped without needing to be
asked. Everything inside was the color of skinless potatoes and
turnips, glistening and streaked with black and green.

66

She had nothing to compare it to, no way of knowing what was healthy and normal, or what might be diseased. *I'm way out of my league*, she thought for the second time that day.

"That must be the lower intestine," Will said, pointing to the most obvious thing.

"You've done some studying?"

"A little."

He passed her a wooden slat, and gently she nudged the white, soft, bulbous hoses aside, slowly following the lower intestine upward to find the smaller intestine and the stomach. She found what she thought might be the liver, and then the gall bladder. It surprised her how much of the anatomy chart came back to her, maybe because the connections all made sense.

"Do you have another slat?" she asked. "Here. Hold this aside."

She nudged some of the larger intestines to the side, looking for a kidney deeper in. It was a darker, smooth color, and she carefully followed a ureter to the man's bladder. Just below the bladder, she found a dense, slippery lump.

"Hey," she said.

"What is it?"

She was so surprised, she put a finger in to gently push the bladder aside to see it more clearly: a uterus. The man had a uterus. It even had little fallopian tubes attached, and little round glands that might be ovaries.

She leaned in so closely to peer at the uterus that a strand of her hair fell in the cadaver. "Woops," she said.

"What did you find?" Will asked.

She straightened, her eyes wide, and blinked in amazement. She brought up her apron to wipe her hair and tucked it back. Then she lifted the man's undergarments to confirm he was truly a man, externally. He was.

"I don't know what to think," she said. Confused, she went back in, nudging around with her slat and one careful fingertip.

"Are you ever going to tell me?" Will asked. "Because I have no idea what's going on."

"He has a uterus," she said. "I think it's connected to his urinary tract. Look here. It doesn't make any sense at all."

Will was silent a moment. "This may come as a surprise, but I have no idea what a uterus looks like."

"It looks like that," she said impatiently, giving it a nudge.

When she looked up at him, his mouth was turning in mirth. "And now I know. Thank you very much," he said.

She straightened. "I thought you knew something about animals giving birth. Mx. Dinah told me that."

"From the outside," he said, smiling more.

She laughed, relaxing a little. She liked Will, she realized. "This is a bizarre thing to do together."

"No, really?"

She glanced back at the cadaver. "Do you think the other expools could be like Bennie? With uteruses?"

"I have no idea."

"It sure would be nice to know," she mused.

"That's definitely connected to why he couldn't have children, isn't it?" Will asked.

"Absolutely."

"How do you think it happened to him?"

She didn't know, but an inchoate idea was coming to her. It must have happened early in his development. He could have even been a girl first. Possibly, just possibly, some hormone was affecting the pregnant mothers of Sylum, changing their girl babies so they developed into boys before they were born. She wished Leon were there. With his knowledge of genetics and the infertility that plagued the Enclave, he would have a plausible theory. She would have to remember what she could on her own and see if the library had anything.

"Do you know if there are even numbers of male and female animals in the village, like horses and sheep?" she asked.

"As far as I know. If you don't mind, I think I've had enough."

She glanced up and saw Will frowning slightly, troubled.

"I'm sorry," she said.

"It's just, I was sure I wouldn't find anything, but in a way this is worse," he said. "It's so hopeless, really. There's no cure for this kind of infertility, is there?"

"No."

She tucked her hair behind her ear again and began pulling the man's abdomen back together. A churning turned over in her belly, enough for her to notice, and then it passed. "Do you have any thread? I can do this," she offered. "My dad was a tailor."

Will passed her a spool of white thread and a large needle, and she sewed the sides of skin together in a neat seam. He used a wet cloth to carefully clean smudges of dark blood around the incision. After he covered the body again, Will braced his hands on the workbench and bowed his head. In the quiet barn, he lifted his right hand and touched it to his heart for a long moment. When he looked up again at Gaia, his brown eyes were searching, pensive, and transparent with grief.

"This was a mistake," he said finally. "We can't ever tell anybody what we've done here. You know that, don't you?"

She was tempted to argue. They'd discovered something huge, something that might be relevant to many of the men in Sylum, and yet what, practically, did the information do for them? It was only a tease, an explanation with no cure. Will was right.

"I know," she said softly. "Poor Benny."

"I'm not sure you see," he said. "People trust me here. If they knew I did this, they'd think twice about having me take care of the ones they love. They'd worry I did it to others who are already buried. Any comfort I could give would never be the same. Why didn't I realize this before?"

"Is there another morteur in Sylum?" she asked.

"I'm it," he said.

Just as I'm the only midwife, she thought. "We're like the life and death team," she said, and wrapped the loose end of the thread back around the spool.

When she glanced up again, Will was watching her oddly. A cautious, curious smile gradually warmed his features, and she realized that Will could be very handsome if he wanted to be. Or rather, he already was handsome, whether he wanted to be or not. There was a small mole at the base of his throat she hadn't noticed before. Her gaze drifted to his square shoulders, his modestly buttoned shirt, his strong hands braced on the workbench, and she went still inside.

Standing across from him over a cadaver had become a private, binding thing, and the longer neither of them moved, the stronger it became. If she looked up to meet his gaze, they would both know it was true.

It made her miss Leon.

In the loft above, some invisible mouse skittered in the hay.

She took a short step backward and held up her hands. "I should clean up."

"Let me get you some fresh water."

Her stomach rolled unpleasantly, and she stepped back to the bench beside the wall. By the time Will returned, she was leaning over and hoping she wouldn't throw up.

"I think I'm getting sick," she said.

He set the water down before her and bent to look at her

face. "It's probably the acclimation sickness. It can come on fast."

"Is it nausea? Headache?"

"Yes. It can get intense."

"Will Maya get it, too?" Gaia asked, alarmed. "She can't afford to lose any more weight."

Will hesitated. "I don't know what to tell you."

She closed her eyes and leaned forward again. "Is there any treatment?"

"You're asking the wrong person."

"Who do I ask, then?" Gaia said. Her stomach clenched in a slow roll, and her mouth salivated ominously. *Oh, no,* she thought, gritting her teeth. She lurched through the door, headed for the grass at the side of the drive, and retched up her breakfast.

"Great," she muttered. Sweat broke out across her forehead and the back of her neck. She spat, trying to clear a drooly line of saliva, and then spat again. Waiting to see if any more would come, she braced herself on a wooden fence rail. The sunlight on the drive multiplied itself before her eyes. Her stomach cramped, then eased, then rolled again.

"Here," Will said, and passed her a damp cloth.

She touched it to her forehead and her lips, waiting. Before long, another wave rose in her and she leaned over, expectant for an awful, hovering moment before she threw up again. The shakes started next.

"Can I do anything for you?" he asked.

"If I had any idea what this is, it would help," she said. "Ginger or peppermint tea, maybe, for the nausea. With honey and salt, if you have them. I don't want to get dehydrated. Will I get a fever?"

"I think maybe you'll have hallucinations," he said.

71

She glanced up. He was serious. She gave a piteous laugh. "Take me back to the lodge," she said. "At least there I can be sick in private."

In moments, he had a horse hitched up to a flatbed wagon, and he helped her crawl onto the seat. The wagon seemed to find every rut in the road, and each bump pounded directly into her head, creating a new kind of headache with spiky bursts of color and pain. Lights and sounds tilted around her, and a tiny speck of dirt on her skirt magnified into a giant bull's eye.

"We're here," he said quietly when they finally reached the lodge. "Wait there and I'll come around for you."

"Please make it stop," she whispered.

"Take a message up to the Matrarc," Will said to someone. "Mlass Gaia has the acclimation sickness. Where's Norris?"

She felt a tender hand on her arm and tried to focus. Will was looking up at her, his brown eyes warm with concern. His face swam, and for an instant he was Leon. She felt joy rising through her, but before she could speak, he shifted back into Will again. Despair overtook her. And then the wagon shifted, and the ground.

Black things were coming to chew at her feet.

"Get them away!" Gaia said, curling up into a ball.

She kicked at the black things, but they only grabbed on with their spiky, shrieking teeth. She tried to fling herself away. Strong arms held her tight, and she crawled up onto the raft, pulling in her toes. *Hold your breath*, she thought. *That will make it stop. Hurry.* She sucked in a huge breath while the inky dry wave, coming closer and reaching taller to blot out all the stars, crashed over her.

concoction

THE SOUND OF A BELL tolling came from somewhere nearby: three rich, resonant bongs. Without moving, Gaia tested her eyes to see if any dizziness or pain came when she dared to look around the bedroom, but the morning sunlight stayed where it belonged, touching along the wall and the golden wood of the floor, with the slats adding a grid pattern of shadow. She lifted a hand to inspect her fingers in the light, and slowly flexed them in and out of a fist. The brown from her days in the wasteland was fading to more of her natural tan color.

"Are you back with us?" a woman asked.

Gaia tried to speak, but her voice had dried away to nothing.

The woman stood from a rocker and poured a glass of water from a pitcher. Gaia pushed up slowly enough to take it, and sipped.

"How's Maya?" Gaia asked.

"She's okay. Hers didn't start until the next day. She had the shakes for a few hours and cried some, but she nursed almost continuously and she's gaining strength. It didn't last as long for her. She's moved from Mlady Eva's to her permanent home now. How do you feel?"

73

Gaia thought about it. "Alive."

The woman smiled, revealing a gap in her teeth that gave her a quirky charm. She was a tall woman in her late thirties, with glasses and a dark, thick braid that fell over her shoulder. "You don't remember me," she said. "I'm Mlady Roxanne, the teacher."

Gaia searched her face more closely. "You're the one who took Maya, with Mlady Eva."

"You don't remember anything else?" Mlady Roxanne laughed. She sat again and reached for her sewing basket. "I should have known. You've been delusional on and off for four days. We weren't sure you'd make it."

Gaia was barely convinced she had. It felt as if some drug had completely derailed her mind and her nervous system, everything that made her work right. She never wanted to feel that way again.

"Do you know what causes this sickness?" she asked.

"I think it's an adjustment to the environment here, something in the food or the water," Mlady Roxanne said. "Maybe even the air. Beyond that I don't know, but you're through it now. It won't come back."

"Unless I try to leave, right?"

"Right. And then the reverse of it will kill you."

It didn't make any sense to Gaia. She pushed a hand through her hair. *I need a bath.*

"Mlass Gaia," Mlady Roxanne said gently, hitching the rocker a bit nearer. "You talked a lot when you were hallucinating. You've been through some horrible things, haven't you?"

"What did I say?"

"Something about your father being shot and your mother bleeding to death. That wasn't real, was it?"

Gaia fixed her gaze on the pegs that held her clothes on the

74

wall. "I don't want to think about the past. None of that will help me here." She rolled and felt something restricting her arm. "What's this?" she asked. Gray, wrinkled cotton was wrapped around her wrist, and as she pulled it loose, she saw it was a shirt.

"It's Chardo Will's," Mlady Roxanne said. "You wouldn't let it go."

He had to leave it behind? she thought.

Mlady Roxanne laughed. "He was very concerned about you. He's come by every day to see if you were better. Some-times twice a day."

Gaia felt a flash of alarm. She hoped she hadn't said any-thing about the autopsy. Or about Peony. *The miscarriage.* She still had to help Peony with her miscarriage, and she didn't even have the right herbs yet. "I need to get up," she said.

She pushed herself fully upright and swung her legs over the side of the bed, but all of her strength was gone. The knobs of her ankles stuck out, making her feet look narrow, and even the dots of her birthmark tattoo seemed more delicate than usual.

"You're going to need time to recover," Mlady Roxanne said. "Why do I get the feeling you won't be patient with yourself?"

"Because I won't. I feel better when I'm doing things," Gaia said. "I need to be out in the garden, harvesting what I need for medicines. I need to go find the other plants I need. That'll help me gain strength better than anything else." It frustrated her to think of all the work she'd missed already, lying in bed for four days. The world could have changed in that time.

Mlady Roxanne set her sewing into her basket and rose to her feet. "In that case," she said, "I'll start heating the bathwater and tell Norris to get something for you to eat."

* * *

75

As Mlady Roxanne predicted, it took Gaia days to regain her strength, but as soon as she could, she began harvesting catnip, myrtle, primrose, nutmeg, ginger, and the other herbs she could from the garden. She saw Peony around the lodge, but only once to talk to alone, and then their conversation was brief. Peony had not changed her mind. If anything, she had grown more desperate during the time Gaia had been sick, fearing Gaia would change her mind.

"Soon," Gaia reassured her. "I just need the right herbs."

Norris let her take over one side of the pantry where there was a wide counter and racks for storage, and he found her a collection of pans she could devote exclusively to boiling and distilling tinctures and salves. Gaia sent a boy up to the Chardos for some tansy, ginseng, and blue cohosh, and Will came that afternoon to transplant some into the garden at the lodge for her.

"Thanks for the shirt," she said, giving it back to him, clean and folded. "I didn't mean to steal it from you."

"That's all right." He ran a hand across the fabric, and smiled before he set it aside and reached for his shovel again.

The bell tolled, three resonant bongs, and Will paused where he was to touch his hand to his heart. Gaia looked across the garden to see young Sawyer and Lowe doing the same thing. A bee floated through the air, catching light in its wings, and as it got lost in the shadows under the water tower, the boys stirred again.

She lifted her gaze to Will's, waiting for an explanation.

"It's the matina," he said. "It reminds us to be grateful."

She remembered hearing the bell when she woke up from her illness, and at other times. "How often does it come?"

"Usually every day, but not always. It comes at different

76

times. You never know when, and part of you is always waiting for it."

"That's all?"

He laughed. "That's all."

So simple, she thought. Yet she felt a subtle change around her, as if a peaceful spell had passed over the village. It was so different from what she'd once imagined it would be.

"Have you ever heard of people calling this place the Dead Forest?" Gaia asked.

"Some of the nomads do," Will said. "We prefer 'Sylum,' even if it is deadly."

"You think it is?"

He gave her an odd look. "You saw, in the barn. What do you think will happen when we run out of girls completely?"

She looked across the garden again, at the beauty and profusion of vegetables even now, as summer was waning. "I don't understand this place," she admitted.

Will dug his shovel and turned over a bladeful of dirt. "You will."

Later that night, after Norris left the lodge, Gaia made a concoction for Peony, stirring it slowly over the stove. Una meowed once from under the table and Gaia glanced over.

"I know," Gaia said. "I'm not happy about it, either."

She poured a tall dose of the concoction in a cup and put the pan in the pantry to cool. Then she dipped a bread roll in honey and set that in another dish. She had a supply of bulky, absorbent cotton fabric and a basin for washing. She ran water into a pitcher. Then she washed her hands once more, banked the fire on the hearth, picked up her tray of supplies, blew out the lamp, and moved quietly through the lodge. The atrium

77

was still, with wan moonlight drifting down from the clere-story as Gaia passed the dark fireplace and started up the stairs. She paused when one creaked, listening, and then proceeded softly to the second floor.

She had to pass around the three sides of the balcony to reach Peony's corner bedroom, and then she balanced the tray along one arm in order to knock softly.

"Peony?" she whispered.

The door opened and Peony let her in. Gaia waited with her back to the door, blinded by the darkness, until Peony struck a match and lit a candle on the desk. Her room was cozy, with a watercolor of the marsh on one wall and curtains of a sheer, soft rose color. A quilt with primarily white patches and a dainty, lavender design was smoothed across the bed, and a potted spider plant grew by the open window. The soft night breeze brought the sound of crickets through the screen.

"I was afraid you would never come," Peony said. She was dressed still, though her feet were bare. "Is that it?"

Gaia set the tray on the desk and tried to banish her ner-vousness. "I need to examine you first."

"I'm sure I'm pregnant."

"I don't want to give this to you if I don't have to. It will make you really sick."

Peony climbed onto the bed. "I have something for you. I heard Mlady Roxanne talking about your sister, and I know where she is."

"You do?"

Peony nodded. "She's out on the first island, with Adele Bachsdatter and her husband."

"Why with them?" Gaia asked, both excited and curious.

"I think because Mlady Adele had a stillbirth just before you came," Peony said. "They're good people, Mlass Gaia, and

78

I know Mlady Adele was crazy with grief. It's possible the Matrarc thought your sister would help her."

Gaia tried to think if Mlady Adele would be able to nurse Maya, and guessed she could. "How do I get out to the island?" Gaia asked.

"Don't go. You aren't even supposed to know where she is. I just told you because I thought you deserved to know."

There was no way she could stay away now that she knew, but that wasn't Peony's problem. The candle flickered in the breeze from the window, and Gaia smiled. "Thank you."

"It's the least I can do." Peony hugged her knees to her chest for a moment. "Can we please get this over with?"

There was nothing for it, then, but to get on with the miscarriage. Gaia washed her hands and gestured for Peony to lie back. A gentle, competent internal examination showed her Peony's cervix had changed from the normal bump with the near firmness of beeswax to a more yielding softness. The other signs of color change were there, too, convincing Gaia that Peony was, indeed, pregnant. Carefully, she settled Peony's skirt down again.

"You can sit up," she said quietly, and Peony shifted up on the bed, crossing her legs.

"I'm right, aren't I?" Peony asked.

Gaia nodded and poured more water to wash her hands again.

"So what do I do, just drink this?" Peony said, pointing to the concoction.

Gaia searched her face, seeing the anxiety and hopefulness there.

"Is there really no chance the father will marry you?" Gaia asked. "You're sure?"

"Xave?" Peony asked. "No chance. I don't even want him anymore."

Gaia couldn't believe she'd heard correctly. "You can't mean Mx. Josephine's Xave."

Peony gave a bitter smile. "Small world, isn't it? Hundreds of men to choose from, and we both get suckered in by the same snake."

"I don't understand," Gaia said. "Why don't you turn him in?"

"I have a secret to keep, don't I?" Peony said. "If I tell on him, everyone knows. And I'm an idiot. I should have known what he was like after what he did to Mx. Josephine, but I believed in him. Now do you see?"

"So you're absolutely, positively sure?" Gaia asked.

"I am," Peony said. "I swear, I was ready to do something drastic if you changed your mind. I didn't dare ask anybody, but there are old stories. I knew it could go wrong, but that wouldn't be any worse than if I set out to kill myself anyway, would it?"

"That is absolutely not an option," Gaia said.

"But you're here. I'm going to be okay."

In a quiet, steady voice, Gaia explained what Peony could expect. The bleeding would be heavy and persistent, but it shouldn't be a gushing flow. Peony would have cramps, sweating, diarrhea, and nausea, but not a fever. The embryo would be shed with everything else, so tiny that Peony would not know exactly when it happened.

"You need to know one more thing," Gaia said. "There's a chance, a small chance, you could die. If you start bleeding too much or you get an infection, it will be nearly impossible for me to save you."

"I trust you," Peony said.

"It isn't trust," Gaia corrected her. "It's a true risk. I haven't done this before. My mother always handled miscarriages. I

80

think I'm right about the herbs and the amounts, but I could be wrong."

"You don't understand," Peony said. "I'd take any chance. I can't have this baby."

Gaia threaded her fingers together and searched her own heart one last time.

"You would never do this, would you?" Peony said.

Gaia glanced up and felt misery move through her like slow, dark molasses. "No," she said honestly. "I wouldn't. To me, keeping my baby alive would be worth anything that happened to me, even if I had to give up my baby later. At least, that's what I believe now, but I've never been in your position. Listen, Peony. It's because I feel so strongly about it myself that I respect how completely this has to be your own decision. You're the only one, the *only* one, who can make the right choices for your family."

"My family," Peony whispered.

Gaia stood. "I'd stay with you, but then everyone would know."

Peony nodded. She turned bleakly toward the cup on the tray.

"The honey bread's for after," Gaia said. "The taste is foul."

"How soon will it start?" Peony asked.

"Soon."

"And when will it be over?"

"By morning."

There was nothing more Gaia could do. She took a step toward the door, and suddenly Peony reached out to grab her hand with cold fingers.

"Stay with me one more minute, just while I drink it," Peony begged.

Gaia squeezed her hand back. "Okay."

She watched while Peony took the cup and brought it to her lips. A last moment Peony held it there, rigid with fear and determination, and then she tilted the cup to drink. She didn't stop until it was all down. The honey bread went untouched. When Peony climbed onto her bed and hid her face in her pillow, Gaia quietly let herself out.

CHAPTER 7

chainmates

GAIA COULD NOT SLEEP. Two hours later, she snuck back up to Peony's room to check on her, and later, hearing noises in the bathroom, she checked on her there as well. By dawn, she was anxious to check on her again, but people were stirring in the lodge, and she was afraid it would be noticed and remembered if she went up to the second floor.

She waited anxiously for breakfast, and when the mlasses came down to eat, Peony was the last to appear, wan but managing to act enough like normal to avoid calling attention to herself. That was it, then. She'd made it through the night. Images that had been hovering at the back of Gaia's imagination of the girl's bed awash with blood were finally put to rest, and she sagged in her chair.

"Are you all right?" Mlady Roxanne asked, looking over.

Gaia picked at a button on her sweater. It wasn't chilly, but she was cold. "Yes. Still just a little tired, I guess."

"You've been working too hard. I warned you," Mlady Roxanne said.

"I'm okay. I think I'll take a walk." She couldn't abide the idea of being cooped up inside.

"I thought you would start lessons with the other mlasses this morning," Mlady Roxanne said.

"Just one more day," Gaia said. "I'll start tomorrow, I promise."

Mlady Roxanne touched Gaia's shoulder gently and smiled. "All right. But take it easy today. Give the garden and herbs a rest."

Gaia was more than willing to agree.

She took a furtive glance down the table to where Peony was eating her oatmeal, and then ducked her head over her own bowl. She would go down to the shore, she decided. Maybe someone there would take her out to the island, or at the least she could look out to where Maya was. She needed something to ground her again.

It was the first time she'd walked downhill since she'd arrived, and soon she found a row of dark, solid cabins where a cooper, a blacksmith, a weaver, a cobbler, and a potter were all busy with their trades. Trees had been felled to make way for gardens and pastures, but most of the cabins and roads were in shade, and the people, she saw, were not as scrupulously careful to wear hats and long sleeves as they had been back home. They looked more comfortable, more carefree than the people in hardscrabble, sun-baked Wharfton, and she took her hat off, too. She liked the feel of lightness around her hair and neck.

Several lesser roads converged at an arching willow, and she recognized the place from the night Josephine had her baby. The marsh was visible farther below, and the main road curved down to the right toward the shore. A pretty, narrow path headed in roughly the same direction, and Gaia took that instead, winding past a dozen small, tidy, welcoming cabins, where children played in the yards and pumped on swings that hung from the trees.

A voice was singing, and a man was pinning laundry on a line. The matina bell sounded, and everyone paused wherever they were, even the children, touching their hands to their hearts. Their contentment was almost palpable, and Gaia waited politely, motionless herself until they resumed their activities. Even though the homes and lush terrain were vastly different from those in Wharfton, the neighborhood reminded her of home. Her parents, she knew, would have liked it here.

The path dipped, leaving the cabins behind, and the rich, mottled greens of the woods enveloped her. She ran her fingers through a bed of tall, delicate ferns and peered ahead to where the blue and green of the marsh beckoned between the tree trunks. Newly careworn about Peony, Gaia felt how easy it would be to slide into loneliness for her parents and her sister and Leon, but she focused on the gentle, powerful beauty of the forest, and she breathed deeply, filling the tiny, empty pockets of her lungs with the fragrant smell of pines and shade. *It's possible, just possible*, she thought, *that I could grow to love it here.*

A moment later, the path took a last turn and opened onto a ledge that overlooked the prison. To the left, farther below, fishermen were working and canoes were pulled up on the long, curving beach. Beyond, in the marsh, a wind rippled through the fluid expanse of the black rice slue, bending back each individual stem in a fleeting wave. The first island rose out of the flatness like a very small, green-topped hat. Hope lifted within her.

"Maya," she said. "I'm coming."

A clanking noise drew her gaze to the prison. Just below her, in a dirt yard surrounded by a tall, spiked fence, gray-clad men waited in line for bowls of steaming food. A hint of smoke from the fire below the big cook pot drifted to where she stood, and she sneezed. There were seventy or eighty crims, many chained by their ankles in pairs. Two men worked the ladles, and she was near enough to hear voices as they passed bowls and spoke a word or two to each man. Black-sashed guards armed with short cudgels and swords occupied a station near the gate, and other guards stood by the entrance to the barracks.

The path to the beach sloped nearer to the prison fence. Uncomfortable, feeling oddly exposed, she put on her hat again, crossed her arms and tried to pass at a normal, unhurried pace that wouldn't draw attention.

"Malachai! You want to finish the pot?" called one of the cooks.

A few laughs rose from the prison yard, and then several shouts of Malachai's name. On the far side of the yard, a black-bearded giant of a man stood beside a row of seated crims, and he turned to say something that Gaia couldn't hear. More men laughed this time, and when the tall man, Malachai, shifted his weight, she saw he was chained to a smaller man who sat on the bench. The implication was obvious: Malachai couldn't get seconds because his chainmate wouldn't move. Or couldn't. Malachai crossed his massive arms and leaned his shoulders back against the fence.

Malachai's chainmate was leaning forward, his elbows on his knees, his forehead on one fist, his other hand holding a bowl. He straightened and sat back, passing his bowl to Malachai, and then he leaned his head back against the fence and closed his eyes.

Gaia came to a stop, staring at him, at his black beard and the distinct lines of his nose and eyebrows, disbelieving. *It can't be.*

"Hey, girly!" A jolly shout came from one of the crims.

Gaia hardly heard it. She took a step nearer. A mix of hope and horror was rising in her.

"Hey! Girl! Smile for us!"

Whistles and catcalls broke out around the yard, and the black-bearded crim beside Malachai turned his face, like the others, to scan up the hill. Even with the crim clothes and the deep tan and the beard, he was Leon Grey.

"Leon!" she called.

He came to his feet slowly, as if uncertain he was seeing correctly. "Gaia?"

The wondering joy in his voice was the sweetest thing she'd ever heard. She broke into an ecstatic smile and ran along the path, racing down toward the wooden gate. In the yard below, other crims took up her name. "Mlass Gaia! Give us a kiss, Mlass Gaia! Hey, girly!" Leon had Malachai by the arm, urging him forward, but the big man stayed against the fence, grinning and unmovable.

"That's enough!" came a loud voice. The guards pulled out their cudgels, fanning out from the barracks, but the crims only made more teasing noises, now directed at Leon, too. One of the guards was approaching Leon, his cudgel in hand.

"No!" Gaia called, but her voice was lost in the commotion.

As she ran, the declining path dropped below the sight-line over the fence, hiding the crims from her and her from the crims. She could see the gate now and two guards standing outside it. She clutched at her hat and skirt, still running full force.

"Let me in!" she said, gasping for breath. "I have to get in! My friend Leon is in there!"

The first guard appeared amused. "This is a prison, Mlass. You can't go in. Visits aren't until next Tuesday."

"This isn't a visit!" she said. She stepped back to project her voice over the top of the wooden doors. "Leon!"

She couldn't hear any specific reply, just the continued rumble of the disturbance inside.

"Let me in!" she repeated, grabbing at the heavy beam in the brackets that held the doors shut.

"Back up, Mlass," the second guard said, setting his hand on top of the beam. "You can't go in."

"But I have to! An innocent man's in there!"

The guard didn't budge. "You'll have to take that up with the Matrarc."

"Leon!" she yelled again. "Are you there? Can you hear me?"

Gaia listened for an answer, and then turned to run back up the path again. By the time she could see into the prison yard again, Leon and Malachai were gone, and the other crims were filing into orderly groups.

Gaia hurried back down to the prison gate.

"How long has Leon Grey been here? The new man from the Enclave?" she demanded.

The two guards looked at each other and she almost died of impatience.

"I guess they brought in a new man a couple days ago," the first guard said slowly.

Gaia balled her hands in fists. She wasn't going to get any information out of these idiots. She had to see the Matrarc.

"Give a message to Leon Grey," she said. "Tell him Gaia says she'll get him out. Okay?"

They nodded, but their ready agreement only made her suspicious that they wouldn't. They didn't care. Their job was to guard the door, and that's all they were doing.

She spun on her heel and ran up the road, but she had to stop far too soon. She hated not being strong. *Did Leon have the acclimation sickness yet?* she wondered. How would she help him through that?

Then another thought struck her: if he hadn't had the sickness yet, he could still leave.

Mlady Roxanne met her on the veranda of the lodge. "Where've you been? We've been looking for you. The Matrarc wants to talk to you."

"I want to talk to her, too," Gaia said. Murderous rage had overtaken her frustration. "Where is she?"

"She's in your room."

Good, Gaia thought, pulling open the screen door and charging in. She stormed past the mlasses who looked up from their books, down the hall past the kitchen where Norris worked, and into her little room.

The Matrarc stood before Gaia's barred window, facing outward, as if she could sense the light, and her red cane was angled rigidly to the floor.

"How long has Leon been here? Why didn't you tell me he'd come?" Gaia demanded.

The Matrarc turned. Her expression was furious. "Close the door," she said with ominous calm.

Rage and confusion warred in Gaia's heart, but the Matrarc's unyielding, steely eyes penetrated into her with uncanny precision, commanding. Gaia turned to close the door, even managing to do it without a slam.

"I need you to release him. Immediately," Gaia said.

"And I need you to explain that." The Matrarc pointed to Gaia's desk, where a dirty box was set. It was a wooden box, with neatly dovetailed corners and a lid, the sort of box made with care to last, and which might be used to deliver a gift or hold keepsakes. With no distinguishing marks, it could belong to any one of a thousand people.

"I've never seen it before," Gaia said.

"Look inside."

Gaia's heart beat strangely, and as she stared again at the dirt, the significance became clear to her: a box with dirt upon it had been dug up, which meant it first had been buried. The Matrarc was waiting, listening. Gaia stepped to the desk and lifted the lid. Inside was a neatly folded pile of rags, darkened with absorbed blood, now dried. On top lay a stem of blue cornflowers, dainty and just beginning to wilt. She gasped, stepping back.

"One of the boys, Sawyer, found it in the garden this morning. He thought it was odd to see fresh dirt under the apple tree," the Matrarc said.

Gaia felt the blood drain from her face.

"Explain," the Matrarc said.

"You've obviously reached the only conclusion," Gaia said. "Someone had a miscarriage and buried the remains."

"Who was it?"

"You can't think I'd tell you if I knew," Gaia said.

The Matrarc slammed her cane against the floor so hard that Gaia jumped.

"Don't fool with me. I asked you a question."

Gaia backed up, bumping against the rocker. "And I'm not answering."

"You mixed something in the kitchen last night," the Matrarc said. "The smell still lingered this morning, but Norris didn't think anything of it until I asked him to account for it. I can't make any sense of the pantry. That's all put away. But obviously you've started your medicines there, and it's more than likely you prepared something toxic last night."

"It's my job to prepare medicines," Gaia reminded her. "You asked me to take care of the pregnant women of Sylum. That's what I'm doing."

"Did you help someone have a miscarriage? Was it a girl in the lodge?"

"If someone wants to talk to me about a medical concern in private, it's a completely confidential matter," Gaia said.

The Matrarc clenched her jaw. "I will not have this."

"You told me to take care of the pregnant women. You must have known it would include this," Gaia said. "Why didn't you tell me Leon was here?"

"We're not done discussing this miscarriage."

"I'm done. I need to get back down to him. I have to find out if he's had the acclimation sickness yet."

"He hasn't."

"Have you talked to him?" Gaia asked.

"Of course I have. I talk to every newcomer who arrives here."

"Then why didn't you tell me? I don't get it. He looked like he didn't even realize I was here."

"He knows that you're here. He came on purpose to find you."

Gaia was more confused than ever. "You should have told me!"

"You were bedridden and half out of your mind. He was violent and dangerous. I expected him to leave."

"What?" Gaia said. "Are we talking about the same person, Leon Grey?"

"The newcomer said his name was Vlatir. He said he was raised in the Enclave but that he'd become friends with you. I found it impossible to trust anything he said. He tried to attack me."

Gaia couldn't believe it. "It must be a misunderstanding. He really is my friend. 'Vlatir' was his biological father's name, from outside the wall." He must have taken that name instead.

"Let me be clear about this," the Matrarc said. "I don't know why you left Wharfton with your baby sister because you've never given me a straight answer. But I was willing to give you a chance here because you seemed willing to try, and you have skills we need. Vlatir is another matter entirely. He's clearly some sort of escaped prisoner. He's a liability, or worse."

"You can't keep him in the prison," Gaia said. "He's done nothing wrong."

"Except threaten my life."

Gaia couldn't believe that. "He must have been seriously provoked."

The Matrarc frowned and slowly circled her cane in her fingers. "He matters to you, then?"

"Yes. Of course," Gaia said.

The Matrarc nodded and turned toward the window again. She reached out to touch a pane of glass, then glided her fingers downward, to the bottom of the sash, to hold her hand in the gap where the fresh air came in. Her silence made Gaia uneasy.

"You've inadvertently given me a very important tool," the Matrarc said softly.

Alarm flared up in Gaia. "You can't do anything to him," she said. "You've already taken Maya away from me."

The Matrarc turned her hand slowly in the open space. "I've been trying to think what to do with you. I've never known such a deceitful, lying girl."

"I am not," Gaia said, affronted.

"I know what you did in the morteur's barn," the Matrarc said.

Gaia was amazed. The only way the Matrarc could know was if Will had told her himself, but why would he?

"Chardo Will came to me," the Matrarc said. "He wanted to quit his job. He said he didn't want to deal with bodies or burials anymore. So, naturally, I asked him why. He's done an exceptional job for three years now. And you know what he told me?"

"I can't guess. I hardly know him."

"He wants to raise horses."

Gaia was so surprised she almost laughed. "I bet he'd be good at that."

The Matrarc turned to face in Gaia's direction. "He takes full responsibility for the autopsy. He wanted me to know about Jones Benny's uterus, but more than that, he wants you to have access to cadavers, with no secrecy, right out in the open, so if anyone wants to donate their body to your medical education or the study of the expools when they die, they can do it."

Gaia was amazed. "He said all that?"

The Matrarc folded her arms across her chest. "What did you do to him?"

"Me?" Gaia asked, taken aback.

"He's a good man. He'd never do this on his own. Do you know what would happen if this autopsy became commonly known? Everyone would wonder if Chardo Will has been doing secret autopsies on the people they love. It would break their hearts. What were you thinking?"

She seemed to think it was all Gaia's idea, despite what Will had said. "I wanted to help him," Gaia said. "That's all. And we discovered something important."

"It's useless. Unless you're planning to get the expools pregnant."

Gaia shook her head, part shocked, part disgusted. "Of course not."

"Did you even think where this might lead?"

"No," Gaia said, her voice low.

"You don't think much, do you?"

Gaia was stung. "I'll tell Will I'm sorry, all right? "

"You'll leave the poor man alone." The Matrarc's features settled into hard lines. "You've tied my hands in strange ways. I can't punish you for performing an autopsy or inducing a miscarriage without bringing these unsavory issues to light."

"So leave them in the dark."

"Sawyer won't be able to resist starting rumors," the Matrarc said. "That's why I need to act quickly. You need to tell me who you treated."

"Why? So you can make her a libby? An example to the other girls?"

"Yes."

"So what I did was illegal?" Gaia asked.

"What *she* chose was wrong, every part of it, from the fornication to the miscarriage, and she knows it. Her body would have betrayed her soon enough if you hadn't intervened."

"And then her pregnancy would have been her punishment? And giving up her child and her future? Who gave you the right to decide about that?"

"It's a community decision, not yours," the Matrarc said. "The price is high, but the girls know that. That's why they stay in line, and the flip side of it is that marriage is a sacred, respected tradition. Children are raised in intact families, with loving, devoted parents. When you get there yourself, you'll see what I mean."

"That is the most backward thing I've ever heard."

"Who is she?" the Matrarc demanded again. "Tell me."

"She can tell you herself if she wants you to know."

It seemed to Gaia that the Matrarc would explode with

fury, but instead she tapped her way toward the desk, then purposefully traced her fingers across the top, finding the box and closing the lid.

"If we didn't truly need you here," the Matrarc said soberly, "I'd send you to the wasteland now. Within the hour. Instead, I need a way to turn you into someone I can trust. Permanently."

"That's easy. Just trust me to do what I think is right," Gaia said.

The Matrarc shook her head, her hand resting pointedly on the lid of the box. "Obviously, your version of right is too far outside the bounds of what's acceptable here in Sylum."

"That box is a private matter," Gaia said.

"Not in a village where the people are going extinct."

"If numbers are all you care about, she's likely to have far more babies as a cuzine than she would as a libby," Gaia said.

"The numbers have never been all I care about," the Matrarc said. "It's much, much bigger than that, and you're a threat to it all."

"If I'm so dangerous, why don't you make me a libby?"

"You're not a libby. Even they have accepted the rules. You're something else entirely."

A stubborn, angry knot was tightening in Gaia's gut. She glared back at the blind woman. "You make me sound like some kind of moral freak."

The Matrarc's eyebrows lifted slightly. "Isn't that what you are?"

Everything inside Gaia revolted at the idea. She was not wrong. Or a freak.

"I want you to go down to the prison with me right now and let Leon out," Gaia said. "That's the first thing to do. He knows I'm no freak."

The Matrarc removed her hands from the box and straightened her shoulders.

"Do not delude yourself about who's in charge here. As of this moment, you are confined to the lodge until I directly give you permission to leave it," the Matrarc said. "You will not go to Mx. Dinah's, or Chardo's barn, or the prison, or anywhere. You will not see your sister. You will not even step out onto the veranda or out into the garden until I say you may."

Gaia didn't believe her. "What about the babies? How will I get my herbs?"

"Unless you're a reliable citizen of Sylum, completely trustworthy to me in every situation, you yourself are potentially more dangerous than any unattended childbirth."

"So I'm not even supposed to go to childbirths? For how long?"

"Until you're tame. A tame person would tell me about a miscarriage or an autopsy or anything else I asked. She would respect our customs."

Gaia felt the cold start in her fingertips. "What if I never tell?"

"You'll never get out. Vlatir will never be let out of prison."

"What does his imprisonment have to do with mine?" Gaia asked, her alarm increasing. "That's not fair at all."

"Call it leverage."

Gaia clenched her fingers in fists. It was the sort of thing Mabrother Iris would say, back in the Enclave. "You can't keep Leon in prison. He hasn't done anything wrong."

"Nobody cares about him, Mlass Gaia, except for you. He's just another man who wandered into a town that already has hundreds of surplus men."

"Don't tell me you keep every new man in the prison."

"If he threatens me, I do," the Matrarc said. "Are you going to tell me who you helped with the miscarriage and promise never to do it again?"

Gaia cared a million times more for Leon than she did for Peony. They couldn't compare. But deep in her heart, she knew she needed to care for pregnant women, in all their circumstances. It was what had driven her impulsively to follow the executed pregnant woman in the Enclave, and what had drawn her to Josephine, crying out in the night. It was who she was. Could she give that up for Leon?

"You're asking me to change completely," Gaia said. "To be someone I'm not."

"Yes. I suppose that is what I'm asking," the Matrarc said coolly.

Gaia found it hard to breathe, as if the oxygen had been sucked out of the air. "What if I won't?" she asked. "What if I just get up and walk outside?"

The Matrarc touched her hand to her monocle for a moment. "Then we'll lose the best midwife we're ever likely to have. Fortunately, we haven't gotten too used to having you with us." She started for the door.

"You're only teaching me to be sneaky," Gaia protested. "What will you do? Put bars on all the windows? Put a guard at every door around the clock?"

"You're your own guard," the Matrarc said. "It's very simple. If you step outside, even once, even a millimeter, you will prove you're untrustworthy, and that will be the end. Believe me, I'll know."

"You think you can keep me here? Without locks? What will it look like to everyone else? How will you explain it to them?"

"They won't mind. They'll trust that I've assigned you a period of reflection. I've done it to other women before."

"You have?" Gaia asked, then remembered Dinah had said something similar. "What happened then?"

"They gave in, of course. They all saw what was best, in time. You will, too."

"I won't. *You'll* have to change your mind," Gaia said, but the Matrarc's calm certainty brought a kind of horror unlike any Gaia had felt before. Doubt shook her. "Let me at least talk to Leon and Will, to explain."

The Matrarc seemed to consider, but then she shook her head. "I can relay a message for you. No letters. Outside contact would only confuse you. You may not speak to anyone outside the lodge or ask anyone else to relay messages after this. What would you like me to say?"

Gaia could barely believe this was happening to her, that there was no way around this intractable woman.

"Tell Will I'm sorry," Gaia said. "I never wanted him to be in trouble."

The Matrarc's eyebrows raised. "And Vlatir?"

"Tell Leon—" Her voice broke, and her toughness evaporated. She wanted to see him so badly. A raw truth struck her: this place would destroy him. She pictured him again, chained to Malachai. It had already started. "Please, Mlady Matrarc. Give Leon a horse and some supplies and let him go, soon, before the acclimation sickness hits him. Tell him I'm sorry. Tell him he won't ever get out of prison here if he stays. He deserves to know."

The Matrarc turned with her cane toward the door. "I'll give him the option of leaving," she said. "Now take that box to the kitchen and tell Norris to have Sawyer bury it again where he found it."

CHAPTER 8

a period of reflection

GAIA HEARD NOTHING of Leon, and thinking of him brought a kind of panicky buzz between her ears. She didn't even know if he had left Sylum, and she didn't see the Matrarc again to ask her. News of Will, Dinah, and Gaia's sister was minimal, and Gaia soon learned that the lack of information was another kind of wall, a silence to isolate her.

Otherwise, Gaia took small satisfaction in seeing that Peony was still circulating around the lodge in her normal way. Though a couple of times Gaia looked up to find Peony regarding her closely, they never spoke. Gaia started school in the atrium. The Matrarc's daughter, Taja, a tall blonde with an athletic figure and confident air, made a point of treating Gaia courteously, but the other mlasses avoided Gaia, and it was clear they understood she was in disgrace. *Reflection, nothing*, Gaia thought. *I'm grounded.*

After her studies, when the other mlasses left for archery practice and other activities, Gaia had nothing to do, and she considered it a mercy when Norris assigned her tasks to do in the kitchen. The teacher, Mlady Roxanne, set her to arrange

99

the books in the lodge's library, several shelves at the sunny end of the atrium. Mlady Maudie, the short-tempered blonde who ran the lodge, also put Gaia to work if ever she saw her sit for a moment, her hands unoccupied. Gaia focused on the work without complaint, whether it was shelling peas, spinning yarn, wiping down tables, or washing the clerestory windows, and while none of it was physically hard, there was a mind-numbing quality to the endless chores that gave her some relief from her worried preoccupation about Leon, at least sometimes. Gaia kept believing the Matrarc would realize she'd never give in.

She'd been in the lodge for several weeks when she woke early one morning to see, beyond the grid of her window bars, a diaphanous, ghostly fog misting the garden. She hadn't seen fog since she'd been in the Enclave, looking out at the obelisk in the Square of the Bastion, and it beckoned her with its shifting, cool shapes. She wondered if it was heavier down at the prison and if Leon was seeing it, too. Though she knew it would be better for him if he'd left, she couldn't help hoping he was still nearby.

When she stepped into the kitchen, the windows and door were closed up, and there was no sign yet of Norris. She touched a match to one oil lamp, then another. She pulled out the bread bowl and the yeast, but the room was so oppressively silent that even the smallest click of a spoon was magnified, so she opened one of the windows, swiveling it inward and up on its hinge to the hook above.

A gray, fog-enshrouded figure who had been stooping in the garden turned toward the sound. When the man straightened completely, she saw it was Chardo Will. She stepped back quickly against the farthest counter, and her heart began to thud in hard, slow beats.

She couldn't move. She was afraid to even acknowledge him in case he expected her to speak to him, but when he crouched down again, she stood on tiptoe, trying to see what he was doing. There was a soft, chinking noise of a blade in dirt, and then she realized he must be transplanting more herbs for her.

Unexpected gratitude filled her, just the way the quiet fog filled the garden. Until that moment, she hadn't realized how much it troubled her that they'd never spoken after the Matrarc confronted Gaia about the autopsy, but now she could interpret his presence in only one way: no matter how much he might have incurred the Matrarc's disapproval, he held nothing against Gaia. The morteur still counted her a friend.

When a noise came from beyond the fence, Gaia looked over to see Norris limping up the road. Will rose and dusted off his hands. She could hear the men's voices as a low murmur, and then Will moved away into the fog while Norris came up the garden path. She held the door wide for him as he stomped in.

He dropped a package on the counter. "What did you do to that boy?" Norris said, eyeing her suspiciously.

"Nothing. I didn't speak to him. You know I'm not sup- posed to. What did he say?"

He shook his head. "He wanted to know if you're well."

Gaia looked back out to the fog. Norris made a grunting noise and began moving around the kitchen, getting his apron, starting the fire, giving Una a nudge with his peg leg.

"Mark my words," he muttered in his gravelly voice. "The Matrarc's turned you into a mystery woman and a martyr all at once. What boy could resist you?"

"Will's hardly a boy."

"Don't give me that. He's a boy playing a game," Norris said. "The oldest game there is."

Gaia opened the second window and the third, swiveling

the heavy sashes up to hook them open. "Have you heard anything about my friend Leon in prison yet? Vlatir? Anything at all?"

"He didn't take the horse."

Gaia turned sharply. "What else have you heard? How is he?"

"He's causing the guards some grief. They had him in solitary last week. My cousin mentioned it last night."

She returned to the table. "Solitary. You mean, like in an isolated cell?"

Norris looked up from under his thick eyebrows. "Why do you want to know, Mlass Gaia? Will it make a difference? Are you going to give in to the Matrarc if you hear he's miserable? Did you think he wasn't?"

It was the first time Norris had spoken to her this way. She ran her hands slowly down the front of her apron and watched him, feeling her cheeks grow warm. It definitely made it worse to know for certain that Leon was in trouble. Suffering, even. She couldn't concentrate at all anymore.

Norris turned away with a disgruntled noise. "You might as well open these," he said, poking a finger into the package on the counter.

"Promise me you'll tell me if you hear any more about Leon," she said.

For answer, he merely pointed at the package again.

"What are they?" she asked.

"My cousin's a cobbler. He had some extras lying around. I figure you're going to be here awhile, and I'm getting tired of hearing your boots drag around all the time. I traced the bottom of one of your boots."

She unrolled the cloth wrapper to find two neat leather loafers inside, slender and soft, with thin, flexible soles. Wonder

102

rose inside her, tempering her anxiety. "For me?" She couldn't believe it. She shucked her heel out of her boot, slid off her sock, and tried the loafer. She tucked back her skirt and pivoted her ankle, trying to get a look. Her birthmarked tattoo showed clearly.

She looked up at him, puzzled. He was trying to make her feel better, obviously. "You didn't have to do this."

He shrugged. "Maybe I like that stubborn streak in you. Nobody's stood up to the Matrarc in a long time. No mlass, at least."

She studied him as he lit the stove and dropped the iron plate back in its groove. "I didn't do it on purpose," she said.

"No." He glanced up. "But you did it. You're still doing it, every day you're here."

Gaia hadn't thought that she was making the kind of statement that anyone else would notice, let alone respect. She wondered if Leon understood what she was doing. "You don't even know what I did to get in trouble," Gaia said.

"I know it had something to do with that box Sawyer found."

She remembered the box too well. "Do many other people know?"

"There's been some speculation. Most of the cuzines approve of what the Matrarc's doing with you, or she couldn't do it."

Most, she thought. *So not all.* "What about the men?"

"I can only speak for myself. I stay out of that woman's stuff."

It got worse after that. Every day, she hoped for more news from Norris, but he rarely had it and it was always the same: Leon was still in prison. No, Norris didn't know if he'd been back in solitary. No, he didn't know if Leon was well or not.

She began to wonder if he deliberately wasn't telling her things that would upset her.

The lodge itself began to feel tighter, smaller, its spaces dead, its walls claustrophobic, especially in comparison to what happened outside. The village had a big potluck dinner on the commons one evening, and Gaia brought dishes to pass out the door, but went no further. The dinner was followed by the thirty-two games, an athletic competition on an open field north of the village proper, and she could hear the cheering from the kitchen where she did dishes, left out completely. On another day, from an atrium window, she watched as three boys in their early teens were put in the stocks. They'd stolen the microscope that was used to determine who was an expool. On other days, men were put in the stocks for wife abuse, drunken fighting, and theft.

The public punishments never failed to remind Gaia what would happen to her if she ever stepped outside the lodge. The Matrarc would keep her word, and a merciless exile to the wasteland would mean death, like what had come to the man at the oasis. Yet if Gaia never submitted to the Matrarc, never told her about Peony's miscarriage, the lodge would become a living tomb for her, and Leon would be stuck forever with the crims.

She could see no way out unless she submitted, utterly.

The longer she stayed confined, the more she began to doubt herself. At night, restlessness drove her to the clerestory, where she paced around and around, trailing a hand along the smooth wooden balcony railing. By starlight, the sleeping village was an even hue of soft, deep purple, interrupted by bits of lamplight shining in the cabin windows, and Gaia could almost, but not quite, make out the prison down by the marsh.

Leon was still there, because of Gaia.

Pain sliced through her, and she cast her mind around for the millionth time, trying to find an answer.

She could tell about Peony. Peony would be cast out of the cuzines and join the libbies with no chance of raising her own children someday. Gaia would have to agree never to assist anyone else with a miscarriage, no matter what the circumstances. She feared what would happen then. Women desperate to end their pregnancies would still try to do so, in secrecy and shame. Gaia drew a hand back through her hair and squeezed.

Gaia didn't want to be taking a stand against the Matrarc for the rights of hypothetical women she didn't even know yet. It was such a small, small part of her job, so how had this become her issue?

She closed her eyes, leaning her forehead against one of the window jambs. She certainly didn't want to be taking this stand at Leon's expense. "What should I do?" she whispered. If she gave in on this, she could give in on anything. Once tamed, she would be at the Matrarc's service for the rest of her life.

But how was that different from Will, or Norris, or Mlady Roxanne? Certainly they'd made compromises, too, to exist in this society. Maybe the rules she'd learned in Wharfton at her mother's knee didn't apply here. Cooperating might just be what she had to do, as a survivor and a grown-up.

I'm not a grown-up. She didn't ever want to be one if it meant giving up who she was.

The cool night air drifted through the fabric screens, barely moving, and mosquitoes hummed on the other side, smelling her blood. The wild, insane birdcall rose from the marsh, and the echo of it made the hairs on her arms stand on end. She peered upward through the window, searching the heavens, and found the distinct row of three stars in Orion's belt. As she made out the rest of the constellation, she thought of her parents, missing them, and wondering what they'd advise her to do.

Another day. She would just get through another day, one at a time. She could do that. It couldn't go on forever. The Matrarc would have to let her out when she saw Gaia would never give in.

There was a tap on her door late one night, and Gaia woke instantly. "Come in."

The Matrarc entered quietly, keeping a hand on the knob.

"Norris's niece, Erianthe, is having a baby," the Matrarc said.

"I can be ready in a moment," Gaia said, swinging her legs to the floor.

"I need to know who you helped to miscarry."

Gaia gripped the edge of her mattress, looking up. The room was dark still, but Gaia realized the Matrarc wouldn't be affected by that. By the barest hint of moonlight, she could see her waiting, a gleam of gray along the length of her cane. Gaia licked her dry lips.

"I can't tell you," Gaia said.

The Matrarc waited a long moment, then took a step backward.

"Wait, please," Gaia said. "Let me come. Erianthe might need me."

"Only if you tell."

Indecision ripped at her. Someone now, in childbirth, needed her. How could she not go?

"Please," Gaia said. "There has to be a way. You have to let me come. Assisting with miscarriages will be such a small part of all I ever do, hardly a fraction. Why can't you just let this go?"

106

The Matrarc waited without speaking for another moment. Then she backed up one more step and quietly closed the door.

Gaia stood and hurled her pillow across the room, hearing something clatter on the desk and smash onto the floor. Stillness followed, charged in the dark air. With a moan, Gaia huddled onto her bed again, curling her head in her arms.

Erianthe had a boy. Norris told Gaia when she met him in the kitchen later that morning. He was in an unusually foul mood, and since she'd hardly slept, Gaia wasn't much better. *I'll never get out.* The refrain kept running through her mind. She would never get out, the Matrarc would never release her, and she'd be no good to any mothers ever again. Leon would live out the rest of his years in prison because of her.

She sank into the rocker near the hearth.

"I don't know what to do anymore," she said.

"Don't ask me." Norris smacked a ham on the table and reached for a cleaver.

"I'm not."

Mlady Roxanne peeked her head in the doorway, her arms full of books. "What happened last night? I thought the Matrarc came for you."

"I couldn't go with her unless I told her what she wants to know."

"Oh, Mlass Gaia," Mlady Roxanne said sadly. She came in farther and set her books on the counter, nudging a bowl of onions.

"What am I even doing here?" Gaia asked.

"This happens when people are confined for reflection," Mlady Roxanne said. "You'll need to sort it through."

"I'm not doing anybody any good stuck here in the lodge.

107

I don't even understand this place. Not the first thing about it," Gaia said.

Mlady Roxanne and Norris exchanged glances, and Mlady Roxanne leaned back against the counter.

"Can I help? Is there anything I can explain for you?" Mlady Roxanne asked.

Gaia tossed up a hand. What she needed was advice about what to do, but she couldn't ask for that without telling about Peony. Other information would have to suffice. "Everything. Why are the women in charge? What gives the Matrarc so much power?"

"There is something exceptional about Mlady Olivia," Mlady Roxanne said. She sent another glance to Norris and continued. "The cuzines have elected her, of course, but it's more than that by now. It isn't simply control or force. It's more like influ- ence, leadership. She really listens. I, for one, trust her implicitly."

"You can't help but respect her," Norris said.

Mlady Roxanne nodded. "She's the best of us, I'd say."

"But how did the women even take control?" Gaia asked. "How did Sylum get like this?"

"The women have always been in charge, ever since back in the cool age," Mlady Roxanne said, surprised. "You have to imagine how snow fell two meters high and lasted for months, so the people who lived hereabouts were used to hardship and a degree of isolation, even when they had oil technology." Her voice warmed with pride. "Our ancestors were uncomplain- ing, resourceful, no-nonsense types with a love of the land and nature."

"They drank a lot," Norris said.

Mlady Roxanne frowned at him. "Norris. That is com- pletely untrue. For work, there were some glasswork artisans living around Lake Nipigon, but most were poppy croppers and small-scale farmers. They ice-fished and raised hogs and married lumberjacks, frankly. A bus brought library books. Much of our collection is left over from one of those buses."

"There's the mine. That's from before. And there's the ruins near the mine," Norris said.

Mlady Roxanne nodded. "Right. We have a mine for iron oxide copper up on the bluff. The crims work there when we need them. The ruins aren't much: some archaic concrete foundations. Once, the government put a branch of the department of revenue here to try to provide some jobs, and there was a famous fish farm for generations, but even that didn't last."

Gaia looked over at Norris, who was cutting slices of the ham.

"It doesn't fit," Gaia said. "Why is the Enclave so much more advanced? What happened to your electricity and technology?"

"That all takes money," Norris said. "And planning."

"It's true," Mlady Roxanne said. "Nothing here was planned. As the lake receded over decades, the people followed it farther in." She gesticulated the tightening of a circle. "One night, a windstorm whipped through the area, killing many of the people and destroying their homes. The survivors banded together around a bonfire, seeking safety, and Sylum was born."

Gaia could see how that made sense. "Like 'asylum'? When did the number of women start to fall off?"

"A few generations ago it began to be noticeable."

"Why didn't the men just take over? Why don't they now?"

Norris jabbed his cleaver in his cutting board with a bang. He headed out the back door and let it slam closed after him.

"What did I say?" Gaia asked.

Mlady Roxanne shook her head. "Norris doesn't like to think about it. Now and then, the men grumble about changing things here, especially the expools like Norris, but they can't."

"I didn't know he was an expool."

Mlady Roxanne turned toward the window, and Gaia followed her gaze to where Norris was now heading out the gate. It changed something, knowing Norris had never even had a chance at being a father.

"He'll be back," Mlady Roxanne said. "He just has to cool down."

"He's upset that I didn't help Erianthe, isn't he?"

"No, that's not it. He doesn't blame you." Mlady Roxanne smiled sadly, the gap just showing in her teeth. "I don't want you to think the men aren't happy here. Most of them are. My husband and I have a beautiful family, and we have many unmarried friends from both the pool and the expool who are happy here, too. We're leading productive, meaningful lives. But Norris and some of the others, too—sometimes they wish things could change."

"Why can't they?"

Mlady Roxanne laughed and reached for her pile of books. "The cuzines like their power too much to give it up, for one thing. They, or I should say 'we,' also do a good job running things. People like order. Besides, the women are all trained archers, and we have a guard of two hundred loyal men, sons and husbands of the cuzines that we can call up any time. That's above and beyond the outriders and prison guards and such who keep order on a day-to-day basis. Those men in the guard want to protect what's theirs, believe me, and the best way to do that is to maintain the status quo."

"Have the other men never revolted, then?" Gaia asked.

"They did. Once." Mlady Roxanne idly turned around the top book in her pile. "There was a time just after Mlady Olivia became Matrarc when some of the unmarried men wanted to take over. They got the notion that the women should be shared. Can you imagine? The Matrarc brought every female together in the lodge, cuzines and libbies alike, and she positioned the loyal guard around us."

"What happened then?"

"We waited," Mlady Roxanne said. "It didn't take long for the men with wives and families to realize they had to put down the rebellion. They killed the men who started it. The rest gave in, and life went back to normal, but they never forgot."

Gaia looked back out the window, and Norris was coming back up the path of the garden, limping on his peg leg. There were so many things he'd never had a choice about.

"She won't ever let me out, will she?" Gaia asked.

Mlady Roxanne squeezed Gaia's shoulder gently on her way out of the room. "It isn't easy to give up what you believe in, Mlass Gaia. It just matters what you believe in more."

Weeks passed. A full moon came with another village potluck banquet and the traditional thirty-two games. When mothers were in labor, Gaia steeled herself for the Matrarc to come to her again, but she didn't.

Then one night, when Gaia was spinning wool by the fire in the kitchen, Peony came softly in from the garden door.

"I hoped I'd find you here," Peony said. Her face had gained a healthier color in the weeks since they'd spoken, but her eyes seemed even larger and her hair was back in a sober braid.

"How are you?" Gaia asked.

"I'm not supposed to talk to you. We don't have much time." Peony moved to the other doorway, where she could keep watch up the hall. "Have you talked to the Matrarc lately?"

Gaia peered across at her. "No. Your secret's still safe."

"My secret?" Peony frowned, turning to face Gaia. Her lips parted in an expression of surprise, then closed again firmly. "Mlass Gaia, I told her. Weeks ago."

"What?" Gaia couldn't believe it.

Peony wrapped her arms around herself. "I couldn't stand to see what she was doing to you. None of it was your fault. So I told her."

"I don't understand," Gaia said. "Why didn't you tell me?"

"I thought you already knew I told. I thought you were just being stubborn."

It boggled Gaia's mind. "She's known all this time? But you haven't been sent to the libbies."

"No. She worked out a deal with my mother," Peony said. "They settled it together privately that I'll marry Boughton Phineas two years from now, if I can behave myself until then. He's old, nearly thirty, from a good family. He knows, but he'll keep it quiet, and we're supposed to spend time together so it looks like love. It's possible no one will ever even suspect I buried the box."

Gaia couldn't wrap her head around it. "If she's known this, if you've worked this all out—" She could hardly breathe. "Then why has she left me here all these weeks?"

"She must want you to tell her yourself."

Gaia dropped her head back against the rocker.

"Just tell her already," Peony said. "She already knows. Give this up."

"I've been protecting you all this time. I can't believe you didn't tell me."

"I thought you were holding out for other girls like me in the future," Peony said. "Isn't that true?"

"Yes, but then why are you saying this?" Gaia asked. "Do

you wish you'd kept your baby? Do you think no one else should ever induce a miscarriage?"

Peony shook her head, her eyes gleaming. "I'm thankful for what you did for me. Believe me. But I think we need you out of the lodge. There's so much else you can do for us, and you need your own freedom. You're wasting away into nothing. When I asked for your help, I never guessed this would happen to you. I never dreamed you'd hold out so long."

Gaia's mind was whirling with the possibilities. "She sent you to say this, didn't she?"

"No. She told me not to talk to you. I came myself. And I brought you something else, too." Peony reached up her sleeve and extricated a folded bit of paper. She took another look out the doorway and then stepped near, holding it out.

Gaia felt a shiver before she even took it in her fingers. "Who's it from?"

"I think you know. I thought you'd want to hear from him."

"I'm not supposed to receive any messages," Gaia whispered. "If you ever tell, if the Matrarc ever knows, it will be as if I'd stepped outside the lodge." Sudden fear closed in around her. "Wait." She couldn't take it. She couldn't read it. As if it scorched her, Gaia dropped the folded paper onto the table. "I can't."

"Are you crazy? Do you know the risks I took to bring that to you?" Peony said. "I had to find Malachai's brother and get him to smuggle paper and ink in to Malachai, and then back out. Twice I had to try. It took forever."

Gaia shook her head. "It doesn't matter. I've stayed here weeks without going outside even one step just to prove to the Matrarc that she can't control me."

Peony looked utterly confused. "But she's controlled you this whole time," she argued.

"No. She hasn't." Gaia backed away from the table, her eyes still fixated on the little paper, knowing Leon had touched it, written on it. He had words just for her. She wrenched her gaze away. "You have to take it back."

Peony laughed in astonishment. "You are totally and completely mixed up. Do you know that? She's got you so confused that you don't even know what matters anymore." Peony marched forward, snatched up the note, and cast it in the fire where the paper hovered a moment and then burst into flames.

Gaia grabbed at the spinning wheel, watching the last, crinkling bit of Leon's message turn to black ash. "Do you even know what it said?" she asked.

"I have no idea. It was in some code. I'm going," Peony said quietly. "I thought you needed a friend."

"I do."

Peony's expression turned even more serious. "Then listen to me. Get yourself out of the lodge. Quit holding on to some ideal that won't ever fit here. Come back to life, Mlass Gaia."

Gaia spent a black night wrestling with herself, and when morning finally came, she asked Norris to send a message up to the Matrarc.

"Why? What are you doing?" Norris said.

"Just do it, please. I need to speak to her."

The Matrarc came a few hours later, just as the mlasses were finishing their lessons in the atrium. She came in the front door of the atrium, her belly noticeably larger than when Gaia had seen her last. Her red cane tapped softly along the floor, and Gaia left her books on the table to go join her.

"Mlady Matrarc," Gaia said softly. She felt sick inside, despising herself, and the whittled stump of her defiance tried once again to assert itself. But she forced it down. She'd made

114

her decision. She was a compromiser now. A survivor. A grown-up.

"Let's go to your room to speak in private," the Matrarc said.

Gaia could see the interested gazes of the other mlasses and Mlady Roxanne as she and the Matrarc passed through the atrium and down the hall. Gaia's bedroom was quiet, the window closed, her things in tidy order.

The Matrarc closed the door. "You have something to tell me?"

Gaia swallowed hard. "It was Mlass Peony. I gave her a concoction of herbs to induce her miscarriage."

The Matrarc's face relaxed in relief. Gaia waited for her to say something victorious, but she merely smiled. "This is a wise decision," the Matrarc said. "You won't regret it."

Gaia's chest hurt with each breath she inhaled. "I'm sure you're right."

"I need your assurance it won't happen again," the Matrarc continued. "You can refer anyone to me if they come to ask you for any such assistance again."

It took a moment for Gaia to grasp what she meant. "Instead of helping them, I'm supposed to turn them in."

The Matrarc nodded. "Yes. Although, once the word gets around that you're not safe to trust, my guess is no one will come to you."

"What will you do with them?"

"I'll be sure such a girl gets the support she needs until her baby can come to term. I'll have you in to examine her, as needed."

Gaia closed her lips tightly and looked down at the floor. That would be exquisitely difficult for Gaia to do. Another sliver of herself broke away. "All right."

"Now for Maya," the Matrarc continued. "Do you concede

that she belongs with her new family, and you won't try to take her back, ever?"

Gaia had seen this coming, too. "Yes. I give her up, permanently. But can I see her?"

"I'll arrange for you to have a short visit," the Matrarc said.

"Is she doing well?"

The Matrarc turned her cane in her hand. "Actually, she hasn't thrived the way I'd hoped."

Alarm shot through Gaia. "What do you mean?"

The Matrarc shook her head. "You'll see. I'll ask her mother when would be a good time for a visit and let you know. Don't be alarmed. She's not at death's door or anything, but we'll all be more comfortable when she takes on more weight."

Gaia pushed a hand back through her hair. *Let it go. You can't do anything*, she told herself. Before she could feel any more panic or despair, she forced herself to be calm.

"And Leon? You'll release Leon from the prison?" Gaia asked.

The Matrarc frowned briefly. "You're sure about that? Vlatir is a most troubled and difficult young man."

"You promised."

"I know," the Matrarc said. "I can always have him arrested again if he breaks the law." She took a deep breath, then exhaled. "I'll release him after the games tonight. There will be enough other commotion going on that no one will notice, and with extra guards on patrol, we can easily take him back again if we need to."

"Tonight, then?" Gaia asked.

"Yes. You can see him then."

She should have been happy, but stifling loneliness moved through her like a thin, gray shadow. She reached for her locket watch and slowly took it off over her neck. Opening the top drawer of her dresser, she carefully put it inside.

"What's that you're doing?" the Matrarc asked.

"I'm taking off my locket. I'll put it with my midwife supplies."

"Resume harvesting your herbs and building up your stock of medicines as soon as you can. I'll send the pregnant cuzines to you starting tomorrow, and you can go down to Mx. Dinah's to meet the pregnant libbies next."

"All right," Gaia said.

The Matrarc smiled. "It's lovely to have you on my side, Mlass Gaia, and to know I can count on you. It's most gratifying."

"I'm happy to serve," Gaia said.

And it was true. It had to be. It was only after she'd spoken that she realized why the words felt so familiar: she'd spoken them often in the Enclave.

"Tonight, I want you to sit with my daughter Taja and Mlass Peony at the games. Dress nicely. See if Norris will give you a haircut before then. I've heard you look quite shaggy. And for now, I'd like you to bring me a pitcher of cool tea out on the front porch," the Matrarc said. "I expect some of the other mladies to meet me there, and I'd like them to see you coming outside. That would be nice, I think."

The significance was not lost on Gaia. The Matrarc wanted the cuzines to see that she had won, and that Gaia was now permanently under her thumb of her own free will. Gaia felt exposed, humiliated.

"It will just take me a minute in the kitchen," Gaia said.

"With mint," the Matrarc added. "I like mint." She didn't wait for an answer, but turned for the door and let herself out.

CHAPTER 9

brothers

GAIA WALKED STIFFLY down the hall and into the kitchen, where Norris was rolling out piecrust on the big wooden table.

"It's done," she said. "The Matrarc has released me from the lodge."

Norris stilled his roller to regard her carefully. "And you're happy with that."

She didn't feel anything. Not a thing, except a residue of humiliation.

She looked out the windows to where the sunlight dropped brightly onto the greens and beiges of the autumn garden. "She wants a pitcher of cool tea for the mladies on the porch," she said. "With mint."

"The mint's not going to come walking in here by itself," Norris said. "I'll start the tea."

She stepped quietly to push the screen door open, watching her hand for the first moment the October sunlight fell on her skin. She held her other hand out, too, turning it in the light, and then she stepped down the two steps and pushed out into the garden where sun fell on her bare head and shoulders for the first time in weeks. She'd never noticed before that the warmth of it had an almost tactile, invisible weight. It burrowed into her white blouse, warming her through. She breathed deep, scenting the earthy tang of the garden, still waiting to feel happy.

A dog was barking in the distance. Walking to the garden gate, she set her hands along the top where the wood was bleached rough and warm in the sun. Beyond the fence, the world was waiting. She could go to visit Maya on the island. She could go to Will's anytime she pleased. She would see Leon tonight.

Nothing jumped inside her. It was as if her heart had moved underground, and the blood moved slowly, silently through her veins, all on its own.

The matina bell sounded from the tower, sending a rich, melodic bong reverberating through the air, followed by two more, and Gaia lowered her head and closed her eyes. Strangely, the one thing she could feel was gratitude. She was grateful to be alive on this gorgeous gift of a day. She lifted a finger and touched it calmly to her heart, to the empty place where her locket watch used to rest, and felt complete.

As Gaia arrived on the veranda with a tray, a posse of men on horseback was riding up the center of the commons, and the dog gave a last bark before it was scolded into silence. The Matrarc stood holding her red cane on the top step, with Mlady Maudie speaking in her ear. Gaia set the tray on the Matrarc's table and backed up beside Mlady Roxanne.

"What's going on?" Gaia asked.

"The outriders have brought in three newcomers," Mlady Roxanne said.

A bearded young man swung down from his horse. He beat dust from his shirt and pants with his hat, then put it back on, and as he tossed the reins toward a boy, Gaia recognized

Chardo Peter. It was the first time she'd seen him since he'd captured her by her fire in the wasteland, and saved her, and held her down in the dirt before the Matrarc.

He walked with a loose, easy gait toward the lodge.

"Chardo! Where did you find these newcomers?" said the Matrarc.

"To the west, Mlady," he said. "At the edge of the wasteland. There are three altogether, but I don't know if the last one will make it."

The Matrarc came down the steps and held out a hand. "Bring me," she said, and Peter guided her forward. In the middle of the posse, two of the riders had their hands tied behind their backs, and a third figure, slumped forward, had his hands tied to the pommel.

"Why are the men tied?" Gaia asked.

Mlady Roxanne moved forward and curled a hand around a porch stanchion. "They're nomads. They could be dangerous. We keep them bound until the Matrarc has a chance to interview them."

Gaia peered at the men. She'd never heard anything about her brother, Jack Bartlett, who had left the Enclave shortly before she had. She couldn't help hoping he'd found a way to survive in the wasteland, perhaps with nomads like these. The two sitting up looked rough and tired, covered in dust. They wore goggles, and their boots had dark buckles. Neither resembled Jack, but the unconscious one had his head wrapped in a concealing bandage. Gaia started down the steps.

As she stepped near to the prisoner's horse, she could see an edge of dark beard, but otherwise the man's face was pressed unnaturally against the horse's neck. Just as she reached for the man's bandage, Peter moved nearer to block her way.

"Mlass, wait. He could have a disease."

120

Gaia turned to the Matrarc. "Please, Mlady," she said. "I want to see this prisoner. He's hurt."

"Tell me what you see, Mlass Gaia," the Matrarc said.

Peter accommodated her then. "Allow me." He lifted the man's shoulder and turned his face. A fly flew away from the dead nomad's nostril, and a dribble of blackened blood oozed from his mouth. At least he wasn't Jack.

"He's dead, Mlady," Gaia said. "He has been for some time."

Peter released him. "I'll take him up to Will's."

"Do that. And after you've cleaned up, I want a full report," the Matrarc said. "Munsch, Leeds. Get these boys down to the prison. I'll follow. Dominic?"

The Matrarc's husband was already bringing the carriage to her.

"Would you like to go up the valley to deliver a body with me, Mlass Gaia?" Peter asked.

Puzzled, she glanced up at the dusty outrider. Half hidden in his beard was a tired, quizzical smile, and she was surprised. Wary.

"That's a different kind of invitation," she said.

"I could use a hand."

"I doubt that."

"I'm too stinky for you. That's what it is."

His relaxed voice caught her off guard and almost made her smile. His eyes, under the brim of his hat, were both welcoming and diffident, as if he expected her to refuse. She glanced back at the porch, where the other mladies were back to their knitting and cool tea. The other prisoners and the Matrarc were disappearing down the other end of the commons.

It struck her then that she was actually, truly free. She could go where she liked. She felt lost for a moment, directionless. Should she go down to look for Leon in the prison yard?

121

"Mlass?" Peter was waiting for a reply.

It had been so long since she had spoken to anyone outside the lodge. A walk to Will's barn would be a simple place to start, simpler than anything else, she reasoned. Or anybody else. Peter held out the reins of his horse toward her.

She reached to take them. "Come on, Spider," she said.

"You remembered his name."

"He's the first horse I ever met."

The big animal following her docilely, and she walked opposite Peter as he led the dead man's horse up the road.

"I wasn't sure you'd remember much at all from that day," he said.

She cast her mind back to that first brilliance of breathable light in the forest. The marsh had looked like a doubled sky below the horizon, and his arms had kept her and Maya safe: all of that belonged to Peter, as much as did the moment when he held her down in the dust. She reexamined her memories with new understanding and could no longer blame him for obeying the Matrarc so mercilessly.

"I remember a lot," she said. "Thank you for saving me and Maya. I'm grateful."

"I've worried about you," he said. "I heard you had a rough time adjusting."

"That," she said, "is the understatement of the year."

"Are things better now?"

She scuffed her loafers in the dust of the road. "As you see. I'm out of the lodge."

"When did your period of reflection end?"

"Today. Just now."

"Just now? Actually now?" he asked. "What perfect timing."

The trees arched over the road and intertwined their leafy branches above, like a great lace veil of changing color, and the air smelled, by turns, like honey and hay and the animal scent of the horses. The high buzz of the cicadas rolled invisibly through the branches, and Gaia soaked it all in. Even the dirt road felt different now under the thin soles of her loafers.

"Are you going to start being a midwife again?" he asked.

"Yes," she said. "I started working on the herbs before I was confined. Your brother brought quite a few from your garden."

"He did? I've brought a lot of our herbs back from when I was on trail."

"I hope he didn't deplete your own supplies."

Peter laughed, a warm mellow sound. "There were plenty. Are there any you're still looking for?"

"Motherwort," she said. "And shepherd's purse and lobelia. I hardly know what I'll do without them."

"We have some motherwort and shepherd's purse. I can get those for you. Describe the lobelia for me and I'll keep an eye out for it. You probably have the black rice flower and the lily-poppy already."

"What are those?"

"People smoke the black rice flower all the time," he said. "It mellows them out. The old doctor used to use the lily-poppy for pain. It's a small, white flower that grows all over the marsh. I can show you."

"It's a hybrid? An opiate?"

"Yes.

She would need to learn how to use it. "How do you know about herbs?"

"I guess I was always interested in them ever since I was a kid. I used to eat flowers. They looked so good, you know? Then I'd throw up."

"No surprise there. Most flowers are poisonous."

"I know that," he said, and smiled. "Now."

She laughed. She'd almost forgotten what laughing felt like, the way it lingered in her chest and behind her ears. It made her want more. She glanced over to see him picking a low-hanging leaf from a tree.

"Tell me what it's like where you're from," he said. "Is it wasteland all the way south, or is there another forest down there?"

"It's wasteland as far as I know," she said. "Wharfton is at the edge of Unlake Superior. You've heard of the Enclave there."

"Just the stories your grandmother told. Does it still have electricity? That's supposed to be a big deal, right?"

She tried to imagine how to explain electricity to someone who'd never seen a working light bulb, let alone a computer. "It runs all the important technology: the lights, the computers, the mycoprotein vats, the Tvaltar, everything. It's power."

"Like water here, running the grist mill?"

She smiled. "Multiplied by a thousand."

"Do you miss it, your life there?"

She missed the freedom she'd had outside the wall, and her old life before all the trouble with her parents and the code. Then again, she hadn't fully grasped the cruelty of the Enclave at that point. It made her edgy to remember Leon was just a kilometer away, in the prison. She would see him soon. Tonight.

"I miss parts of it," she said.

"Would you go back there if you could?" he asked.

"No. Not considering how I left it." She frowned. "Why? It isn't even possible."

"It's just a hypothetical question."

"Would you leave if you could?"

"I would."

He sounded so sure.

"Have you tried?" she asked.

When he didn't respond, a slow, expectant curiosity awoke inside her. She stopped walking. "Peter?"

He stopped, too, and turned to face her, unsmiling. In his dusty, worn clothes and his beat-up brown hat, he looked like part of the wasteland itself, dropped out of place on the shady road. His eyebrows were drawn together, squint lines edged his eyes, and he seemed to be contemplating something in the distance past her right ear.

"I have tried," he admitted. "I was trying when I found you."

Her eyebrows shot up in amazement. "How far have you gone?"

His voice dropped. "Pretty far. Different directions. I used to try to just go fast and far, but that got me sick fastest. Now I go slow. Once I went far enough to know I could have stayed out there, but there isn't anything out there. Not really. That's the problem. When I came back, I even had the acclimation sickness like newcomers get, though not quite as bad."

Gaia wanted to know more. "How did you do it, precisely?"

"I went slowly, only a little distance each day, and anytime I started feeling weird, I just stopped and stayed where I was a while, not going any farther and not going back. I just stayed mellow, watched the stars, and slept a lot, you know? I spent a full week at the oasis, and I was fine. Until I came back, that is."

She started walking again, curious. "You think going slowly was the trick?"

He fell into step beside her, keeping his voice low. "Part of it. I keep wondering if I ate something different then, or if the rainy weather made a difference. I don't really know why it worked."

"You should tell the Matrarc. Does your family know? Didn't they realize when you got the acclimation sickness?"

"They thought I ate something. I can't tell them I'm

essentially experimenting on myself. They'd only worry about me. Besides, I've only succeeded at it the one time so far. I'd like to do it again to be sure. Please don't tell."

"Nobody else knows?"

"My riding partner must suspect. Munsch. But only him."

Gaia frowned pensively at the road, and then glanced up at him. "I'm not a person to tell secrets to," she said. "If the Matrarc asks me, I won't withhold information from her. You should know that about me."

"I'll just have to hope she doesn't ask you." He smiled. "Don't worry so much. I'll tell her when I'm ready. When I figure it out for sure."

It was going to be strange for Gaia, not being able to keep secrets anymore. She felt like she was adjusting to a new version of herself. "I'm honored you told me," she admitted. "Especially considering you hardly know me."

His smile deepened, showing a hint of white teeth. "I've thought of you often enough. I guess I trust you. It seems like you ought to know there's hope."

She shook her head. "I'm going to try to forget it. Sylum is my home now. I can't go back. Are you the one who found my Enclave friend in the wasteland?"

"No. That was one of the other outriders."

"The Matrarc's letting him out tonight," she said. "I'm supposed to see him after the games."

"Nervous?"

She was. She was worried about what he'd think of how she'd changed and worse, she was afraid he blamed her for his own captivity. He must. She dropped one hand in the pocket of her blue skirt and watched the road before her feet.

"I'm sure if you're friends, it will work out," Peter said.

Surprised, she glanced up. "What an incredibly nice thing to say."

"I'm a nice person."

She laughed. "And modest, too."

"Glad you can tell."

She laughed again. They continued up the dirt road, passing yards where clothes were drying on lines in the bright sunlight. A wheat field was golden, and a chicken was pecking in the dirt. When she felt something graze her arm, she glanced down. Peter was lightly touching her sleeve where a pale, thin golden leaf had lodged. He pulled the tiny leaf away, twisting it between his thumb and forefinger, and a shiver ran along her skin.

"How old are you?" he asked.

She looked at him carefully, wondering why that felt like such a personal question. "Sixteen. And you?"

"Nineteen. What are you thinking?" he asked.

"Do you ever shave?"

He laughed, rubbing a hand along his bearded jaw. "Of course I do. When I'm here in the village. Why? You wonder what I look like under all this? I'm not always a dirtbag, you know."

"I'm just trying to see how much you look like Will."

He cringed. "Naturally you are. My brother got all the brains. And the looks and the modesty, come to think of it."

"You must have gotten something," she argued.

"I got the big feet."

She laughed again.

"You keep looking away from me," he said teasingly. "It's very annoying. Here, let me take Spider." He reached for the reins, but instead his fingers met hers, and instead of letting go, he held on.

Her feet came to a stop, and still he didn't let go. A tingling began in her fingers where her skin met his, completely unexpected, a live bit of current. Puzzled, she looked up at him.

"Aren't we not supposed to touch?" she said.

He jerked back, releasing her as if burned.

"I didn't even think," he said. His eyes blazed with dread.

"It's all right," she said.

"I've never done that to a mlass before," he went on. "Not ever. You won't accuse me?"

"Of course not," she said.

"I'm sorry," Peter said. "It won't happen again."

As she looked at her hand, it was as if her own flesh suddenly turned scaly and dangerous. "You can't touch me," she said. "But can I touch you?"

Peter's lips parted in surprise. "You wouldn't."

She let out a brief, self-conscious laugh, but the truth was, she couldn't help noticing how the dappled sunlight landed along his tanned skin. Perversely, now that she knew she shouldn't, she wanted to see if his forearm would feel as warm and smooth as it looked. Was that what it was like for him, knowing he couldn't touch a girl? It made the curiosity worse.

"Now you're just being mean," he said, half amazed.

She reached to twist her fingers in Spider's reins again. "I'm sorry."

"Not half as sorry as I am," he said. Though he'd backed up, he was still studying her and his expressive features ran quickly through pleasure, humor, and regret. "Your eyes," he said. "They're almost black in this shade. Or maybe it's that your eyelashes are so dark. Let me see."

She frowned, stepping a little closer to examine his eyes as well, and he took off his hat to let her inspect him better. His eyes had little rings of yellow around the pupils, but the outer

128

rims of his irises were a clear, translucent blue. They were nothing like the intense, consistent blue of Leon's eyes.

"Yes," Peter concluded quietly, still focused on her. "That's what it is. Dark lashes. And long. But your eyes aren't black at all. They're brown."

A statement of fact had never sounded so much like a compliment. She blinked away, and lifted her hand to cool her warm cheek.

"When you let me see them," he added softly.

She drew away from him and started forward again, returning to her far edge of the road with Spider behind her.

He put his hat on. "Are we done talking?" he asked.

She nodded. *Absolutely.* He laughed, and kept to his side of the road, leading his horse behind him. Yet even in silence it seemed to her like they were part of a dialogue, for their strides matched, and paced out a distinct harmony on the road.

As they came around the next bend, she saw a familiar fence, and then the Chardo place with the pasture behind. The new section of the barn was complete but still unpainted, and though Gaia listened for the sound of hammering, there was none.

"Glad to be home?" Gaia asked.

"I've never been so glad."

The front door of the cabin opened, and four men came out, calling greetings. Will outdistanced the others to pull Peter into a back-slapping hug.

"What are you doing here?" Will asked. "What have you brought?"

He took the reins of Peter's horse while the other two men enveloped Peter in a second series of hugs, and for the first time, Will glanced past the horse to Gaia.

129

"Mlass Gaia," he said, obviously surprised. "They've let you out of the lodge at last."

She nodded.

Will took Spider's reins from her. "Well, welcome! How long have you been out?"

"Just now," she said. "Just today."

"And you came here first thing?" Will asked.

A tiny jerk of hesitation caught her, but she nodded again. "Peter said he was bringing you a body."

Will laughed. "That's impossible to resist." Will's gaze flew to the body, then to Peter, then to her again, in an instant of assessment too quick for speech. "You can finally meet my father and my Uncle John," Will said. "And Uncle John's partner, my Uncle Fred."

The three older men were laughing at something Peter had said, but they turned now with welcoming smiles, and Gaia was introduced all around. Will's father, Sid, was a shorter, older version of Will, with a weathered complexion, short gray hair, and a wiry build. Uncle John, Sid's brother, was shorter still, with a round belly that bulged out the front of his overalls, a balding head, and a thick brown beard. Fred seemed a little younger, with a sweet, absent smile and dreamy dark eyes.

"Such a pleasure," Sid said. "Will's told us so much about you. I think he was more eager for you to get out of the lodge than you were yourself."

"Dad," Will said.

"You can't blame him," Uncle John said. "It's not every girl that's got him transplanting half the garden for her."

The older men laughed again.

Gaia glanced uneasily at Will. "Please tell me it wasn't half the garden."

130

"They're exaggerating," Will said, apparently more happy than embarrassed.

Peter looked from her to Will, then slowly back to her. "I didn't realize you knew each other," Peter said.

"We don't, really," she said.

"Not much at all yet," Will agreed, his smile genuine and warm.

Gaia could feel herself responding to his smile with real pleasure. *Maybe we actually do know each other,* she thought.

She glanced back to Peter to find his eyes narrowed faintly, studying her with an unspoken question. An awkward, triangular moment hovered. Will shoved a hand in his back pocket, waiting it out. What was she supposed to say?

Nothing, obviously. Like a dope.

"Why don't you come in?" Sid offered. "Have a glass of cool tea."

"You're very kind," she said. "But I really need to head back to help Norris get things ready for the banquet." She wished there were a way to talk to Will alone in the barn and make sure he was over the trouble about the autopsy, but it was impossible with his family standing around.

Gaia glanced once more at Peter, who still hadn't moved.

"Thanks again," she said. "For bringing me in from the wasteland."

He lost his stiffness a little and smiled again. "Think nothing of it. See you at the games?"

"Are you playing?" she asked. "I don't really know how they work."

The older men smiled.

"Of course I'm playing," Peter said, and glanced at Will.

"We both are," Will said.

She backed up another step. "Then I'll see you both."

CHAPTER 10

shirts and skins

THE MATRARC'S DAUGHTER, Taja, came by the lodge kitchen after the banquet to collect Gaia. Norris had given Gaia a haircut and a rose-colored, hand-me-down blouse from his niece.

"Ready?" Taja asked.

Gaia had spoken to her only half a dozen times since she'd come to Sylum, and Gaia wondered how Taja felt about essentially babysitting her on her first real outing. She was a tall girl, a year older than Gaia, with square shoulders and strong, lean arms. She was purportedly deadly with an arrow, and her poised manner made Gaia want to stand up a little straighter herself.

"Good luck tonight, Mlass Gaia," Norris said as she moved to the door.

"Good luck? Why?"

Norris gave her one of his rare, avuncular smiles. "Getting chosen, of course."

Gaia vaguely recalled Josephine and Dinah telling her about the thirty-two games, but it hadn't occurred to her she'd be eligible to be the prize.

"Aren't you coming?" Gaia asked Norris. "We can wait."

He waved them on. "I'll take my time with the old peg. Go ahead. Try to have some fun."

When Gaia and Taja reached the playing field, many of the villagers were already there. The east side of the field dropped off toward a dramatic view of the marsh, and she could see the evening sky reflect in coruscating patches wherever open water collected. Men gathered on the grassy slopes that enclosed the other three sides of the field, with a few women interspersed among them. Gaia spotted Dinah, Josephine, and other libbies near the top of one of the slopes, relaxing on blankets. Prominently figuring at the edge of the field on the half line, a wooden platform bedecked with colorful flags was slowly filling with important spectators: the Matrarc and her husband, Mlady Maudie, Mlady Roxanne, and a dozen other cuzines. Their families joined them. Over it all, the late October sun cast a golden, pearly light, and shadows were long on the green grass.

"Do you want to sit on the platform?" Taja asked. "We can."

"I'd rather not."

Taja turned and led Gaia to an area above and to the left of the platform where they'd have a good view of the field. Taja dropped her blanket on the grass and patted a spot on her left for Gaia.

"Here we go," Taja said. She tucked her blue skirt around her knees and sat straight.

"Do the mlasses ever play?" Gaia asked.

"We play a lot of soccer, but the thirty-two games are just for men in the pool," Taja said. "Do you play soccer?"

"No. I wish I did," Gaia said.

"Another thing for you to learn here," Taja said. Though her voice had none of her mother's musicality, her dry, regal tone had a distinctive quality.

"Here you are," Peony said, coming up the slope. Her yellow dress was sunny in the evening light, and she'd brought a sweater. She sat to Gaia's left as Gaia scooted over to give her more room on the blanket. "Glad to see you out," Peony said casually.

"Thanks." Gaia had to remember to act like she hadn't seen her just the night before and like she knew nothing special about her. "How've you been?"

Peony slapped her own arm. "Good. They'd better light the torches soon or the mosquitoes will eat us alive."

As Gaia looked around for the torches, she noticed guards around the perimeter of the field, their black sashes conspicuous. Sword scabbards and no-nonsense clubs hung from their belts. Others were strategically posted near the platform. Still others fanned out across the playing field to create a controlled pathway, and the reason became clear as a double row of crims came up the path from the village, passing between the guards. Even with the distance, she could hear their chains in the grass.

"I didn't know the crims would be here," Gaia said, instantly alert and looking for Leon.

"They always come," Taja said.

Seventy men or more, the crims kept crossing the field in their drab brown and gray garb. Most of their bearded faces were visible only in profile, and Gaia tried to narrow in on the ones with Leon's height and build.

"I wish the crims wouldn't come," Peony said. "They give me the creeps."

"Try motivating crims without any incentive and you won't be so quick to say they don't belong here," Taja said.

"There's Malachai," Peony said. "Remember him, Taja?"

Gaia's gaze shot to the tallest man, and walking beside him, linked by the chain on his ankle, was Leon. Her stomach dropped.

"I remember Malachai. He killed his wife a few years back," Taja said. "Sick guy. Poor Greta."

Peony spoke softly to Gaia. "I take it that's your friend with him."

Gaia nodded.

Leon's dark hair had grown, and he walked with slumped, heavy shoulders that looked nothing like what she remembered. The chain caused a hitch in his stride as he worked to keep in synch with Malachai. She was shocked by how old he seemed, and when he and Malachai turned to sit in a row with the other crims, she could see hardly any of his face between his dark bangs and his dense beard.

"Chardo's waving at you, Mlass Gaia," Peony said. "Look. In the red."

Gaia forced her gaze away from Leon and turned to the athletes occupying the center of the field, where a man was just lowering a hand. He lifted it again, and it took her an instant to recognize Peter without his beard. She was still too stunned from seeing Leon to be able to respond. Peter passed a ball to another man in a blue shirt, and Gaia realized he was Will.

Gaia looked back at Leon, and despite the distance, she saw he was slowly, methodically scanning the crowd of spectators. It was only a matter of time before he would see her. He'd been stuck in the prison, all this time, because of her. He'd sent her a note, and she hadn't even read it. Guilt swept through her and ignited an anxiety so intense, she feared she'd throw up.

"Are you okay?" Peony asked her.

She swallowed hard, nodding.

The sound of a horn's four-note melody carried through the air. The Matrarc stepped forward on the platform, and after a brief speech urging clean play all around, she opened the games.

"The first thing you need to know is there are two teams," Peony said. "The Shirts and the Skins, except the teams keep mixing up. And there are five rounds."

"They pick thirty-two players total to start with," Taja said, leaning forward slightly. "After the first round, the winning team of sixteen players advances to the next round, and they get split into two teams of eight. Each round, the teams get smaller by half, until finally there are only two men left, and they compete against each other to see who wins."

Peony looked annoyed. "I was getting to that."

Taja pushed her blond hair behind her shoulder. "I'm sure you were."

Closely guarded, the crims seemed as relaxed and curious as the other spectators. Malachai was saying something to Leon, pointing to the field. Leon nodded, then returned to his methodical inspection of the crowd. Gaia shrank lower between Peony and Taja, dreading the moment he would find her. For some inexplicable reason, she didn't want him to see her as she was, nicely dressed, with friends, ready for a game.

A referee in a black shirt and shorts moved to the center of the field, and in response, the athletes ranged into a rough line before him, facing the crowd. They were agile, strong, handsome young men, and it took Gaia only an instant to realize the significance of what Taja had said: before them was the pool of Sylum, the men who could marry. It wasn't enough that the athletes glowed with the confidence of youth and pulchritude, or that they'd come to play a game. They were answering an unspoken mandate to prove themselves, to compete visibly and physically before the scrutiny of their families and friends. No mlass could miss the significance, or the testosterone. It was clear in every move the men made, no matter how studied or nonchalant a gesture.

A spontaneous rumbling began in the crowd and then rose to a cheer, before the athletes did anything at all, just because they were there. The primal nature of it all stirred something within Gaia, and she looked again to Leon.

He had found her. He made no gesture, but across the distance, among the movement and commotion of the others, he alone sat completely still, a powerful, localized force focused exclusively on her. Time froze.

Then he looked away.

Gaia didn't know she was holding her breath until she had to gasp for another one. Instinctively, she reached for Peony's arm.

"Pull it together," Peony said quietly.

The ref was raising his hand, and a tall man with lengthy brown curls came forward to stand on a white O that was marked on the field to the ref's left.

"That's Larson Harry. He's the first captain of the Skins," Taja said. "The Larsons are carpenters. Good people."

With a flourish, Larson pulled off his shirt and tossed it to a boy who ran by for it.

"And the captain of the Shirts is, surprise surprise, Walker Xave," Taja said.

Gaia felt Peony stiffen beside her. A clean-shaven blond man strode forward to an X marked on the field to the ref's right.

"Is he the Xave who's the mother of Mx. Josephine's baby?" Gaia asked.

"Not according to him," Taja said dryly.

Xave shielded his eyes and turned toward the crowd, the picture of cocky arrogance, and there was a spattering of applause.

"Now they pick," Taja continued. "This is the important part. This is when we find out who gets to play."

People in the crowd started calling out the names of their favorite players. The captains were taking turns, picking one player at a time, and as the chosen players moved out to stand beside the captains, each team's line grew longer. The Skins players all tossed their shirts to a pair of waiting boys.

"Chardo Peter," called Xave for his fourth pick.

Peter ruffled the top of Will's head as he passed, and walked out to Xave's line, his red shirt bright among the blues, greens, and yellows. Peter stood with his weight back on one leg, his other knee bent in a relaxed, casual pose, but as he lifted both arms over his head and flexed them in a stretch, Gaia could almost see him buzzing with tension. This mattered to him.

One of the loudest voices in the crowd became more insistent, calling out the name of a favorite player, and others joined in.

A solid man with narrow shoulders and thick calves, the referee had a deadpan expression. He turned to face the rowdy crowd, saying nothing, and simply pointed to one section. A row of guards moved in.

"All right! We get it, Ref!" called Norris from the back. "Quiet down, you morons!" Laughter rippled out from around him, and as quickly as that, the mood shifted. The guards eased back and the referee returned his attention to the field.

Gaia turned, round-eyed to Peony. "Is it always like this?" Gaia asked.

Peony brought her face close so she could answer without yelling. "There was a riot once. That's why we have so many guards now."

Gaia looked out to the field again just as Will was picked for the Skins team. His movements were unhurried as he took off his shirt and passed it in. Will's shoulders were powerful, his torso lean as he rested a fist on his hip. She remembered him building the coffin, and his respectful handling of Benny's body, and the kind, silent way he'd planted herbs in the garden when she couldn't even speak to thank him. This was still another side of him she was seeing.

Was he playing in this game for her?

"I always forget about the morteur," Peony said idly. "He's really kind of handsome, isn't he?"

"If you want to see handsome," Taja said, "wait 'til his brother Peter takes his shirt off."

Gaia stared at her.

"What?" Taja said and laughed. "It's just part of the game. Try to have a little fun."

Gaia was not having fun. She had a bad feeling about the whole thing. Her skin kept prickling even though Leon wasn't looking at her whenever she checked.

Several more men were selected, and then it was time for Harry's last pick for the Skins team. "Where's Malachai?" he bellowed.

As one, the crims came to their feet. They cheered, rattling their chains, pumping their arms in the air. The remaining athletes started a harsh booing noise.

"Here we go," Peony muttered.

"What is it?" Gaia asked.

"Each captain can pick one crim," Taja said. "They don't always, but the crims love it when they do."

With the exception of the other athletes who aspired to be chosen, the rest of the crowd apparently liked the crim choice, too. Several guards gathered around the big, dark-haired man, and after a moment's delay while they released the shackle, Malachai strode onto the field. He came to stand beside

139

the last man on Larson's team and took off his shirt, revealing his massive arms and shoulders, hardened from physical labor.

"How about you?" Larson called to Xave. "Who's your last man?"

The Shirts captain was surveying the crims, and then he raised his finger and pointed. "I'll take Little Malachai," Xave said.

The noise of the crowd diminished as people tried to see whom he meant, but Gaia already knew. Her heart thudded heavily as Leon took one step toward the field and then stopped. His ankle was still caught in the chain.

A guard stooped down beside him to release his shackle, and Leon waited, unmoving. The crowd was laughing because, superficially, Leon did look like a smaller version of Malachai, with similar unkempt dark hair and beard. Once free, he didn't hurry but walked with long, slow strides to take his place on Xave's team. Gone was his hunched shuffle. Leon's shirt was threadbare and gray over his straight shoulders. Unlike the athletes, he wore work pants and rough shoes. He made no effort to stretch or warm up his muscles, as if he were too sore to move or too uncaring. He did not look again for Gaia in the crowd, but rather directed his unwavering attention toward the Matrarc's platform. The crowd's laughter died away.

Gaia couldn't take her eyes from him. Two things were clear from his proud stance: he agreed to play, and he despised them all.

the thirty-two games

SHE WAS ALREADY RISING.

"Where do you think you're going?" Taja said.

Gaia started down the slope, winding through the sitting spectators. She had to get closer. There had to be a way to talk to him. Several guards started forward, preparing to intercept her at the edge of the field.

"Come here," Taja said, following after her and tugging her arm. "You're blocking people's view. You're making a scene."

"I have to talk to him."

"Not now you don't." Taja pulled Gaia toward the platform and planted her along the side.

"Let go of me," Gaia said, pulling her sleeve free.

"After the game," Taja said. "You can see him then."

Peony caught up with them, carrying the blanket. "It's okay, Mlass Gaia," she said. "Just wait here with us."

"I need to see," Gaia said impatiently.

The ref was holding a soccer ball now, and a whistle dangled from his lips. Sixteen men on each team were ranged across the field: Skins on the left heading toward the south goal, and Xave's team of Shirts on the right, facing north. Xave directed Leon to a defensive position near the goal. Peter was positioned as one of the Shirts' center forwards. Will took a midfield position for the Skins. Like a great animal rolling in the sun, the crowd gave a slow, rippling shudder, and settled back to watch.

The ref blew his whistle and dropped the ball. The Shirts team, led by Xave, quickly gained control and pushed forward.

Leon began to walk, then jog in his zone of the field, keeping open in a position that echoed the movement of the ball. There was a lightness, a readiness that came to him as soon as the game commenced, and Gaia recalled he'd once told her he'd played soccer growing up. A Skins player gave a Shirts player a powerful shove, and the man pushed back, then twisted out of range in time to receive a pass and send it up to Xave. Up and down the field, the ball traveled in a zigzag of ricochets, while men shoved and flagrantly tripped each other.

"Why doesn't the ref call any of the fouls?" Gaia asked.

Taja looked surprised. "What fouls?"

I guess the rules are different, Gaia thought. It almost seemed there were none, other than that the players couldn't use their hands on the ball. The ref blew his whistle only when the ball went out of bounds. During all the action, Malachai crouched like a bear off the corner of the goal, hardly moving, but when Will ripped a long pass up the field toward Malachai, the big, bare-chested man trapped it with a clumsy foot and lunged with it toward the goal. Leon closed in from the outside, effortlessly stole the ball from between the giant's feet, and sent it back out, wide left, to an open shirts teammate.

"Nice save, Little Malachai!" yelled a voice.

Four seconds later, Xave drilled the ball into the net to score for the Shirts, and a burst of cheering filled the air.

"That's it?" Gaia asked.

"That's the end of round one," Peony said, nodding. "All those Skins players? They're eliminated."

Will stood panting, and then he turned with the other Skins players to leave the field. Four guards surrounded Malachai to escort him back to the crims' section, where the nearest crims pounded him on the back and roughed his head until he shook them off.

"Now what?" Gaia asked. "They pick again?"

"Yes. See the new Skins captain?" Taja said. "Xave picked him first last time, so since they won, he's the new opposing captain. There's some strategy involved."

Out on the field, Xave was returning to the X spot as the continuing Shirts captain, and on the corresponding O, the new captain for the Skins team took off his shirt.

The picking for the next round, two teams of eight, went rapidly, and Xave chose both Peter and Leon for his team. The intensity of the game changed significantly in round two as fewer players meant less of a scatter-shot mob style of attacking and more deliberate passing. Leon, again, played defense. It became clear, now, that Xave was a careful judge of where to position his players, and they passed around the Skins team with almost comic ease.

"Your crim friend can play," Peony said. "I think he's missing a finger or something on his left hand. What is that, Mlass Gaia?"

She didn't know. She couldn't bother to reply. She focused intently on Leon, trying to match what she was seeing with what she remembered of him, but it was like seeing a pebble that had always been dry and dusty suddenly thrown into a bowl of clear water. She'd never seen him run, never seen him with long dark hair flying, and fast as he was, he still seemed to be holding something back.

Peter scored off a hard instep drive from fifteen meters out, and the Shirts won again. Gaia kept expecting Leon to look over and find her again. He didn't.

"Now it should start getting interesting," Taja said, as the Skins players left the field and the others prepared for round three.

There were eight men total remaining on the field now, for two teams of four. The next new captain of the Skins moved to the O and took off his yellow shirt. The others stood in a rough semicircle. Peter wiped the sweat from his face with the hem of his red shirt. Leon stood quietly, flat-footed, his arms loose at his sides, while a man with black curls bounced lightly on his feet beside him, clearly eager to get on with it.

"That's Munsch, that man by Little Malachai. You used to have a thing for him," Taja said to Peony. "What happened to that?"

"Nothing," Peony said. "That was last year. He rides with Chardo Peter now, I think. Look. They're choosing."

Xave chose Peter first for his Shirts team, and then Munsch and one other. The Skins captain chose Leon last.

Leon walked slowly over to the Skins, pulling his gray shirt over his head, and for the first time, his chest was exposed to view.

Gaia stared. She remembered Leon most in a precise black uniform, his skin protected from the damaging sunlight, a hat brim always shading his features. Even his hands had always been lighter than her own. Now his torso was tanned, and the orange-hued sunlight that washed across the field cleanly defined the taut lines of his muscled chest and lean belly. Gaia's response was visceral and immediate.

Then Leon turned his back to the crowd.

It was clear, even from a distance, that scars mottled the

144

skin across the back of his shoulders in a vivid, savage pattern of white and brown.

Gaia felt sick. "No," she whispered. Hushed murmurs were spreading through the crowd as others noticed, too, and a gasp came from one of the mladies on the platform.

"That's not right," Peony said quietly.

"No one's been flogged like that here," Taja said. "Not in ages. He must have come like that."

"Who would do that to him? Why?" Peony asked. "He must have done something awful. Really awful." She turned expectantly to Gaia.

But Gaia was unable to answer. She pressed her knuckles against her lips, hating this. She couldn't bear to think of Leon being hurt. What if they'd done it to him back in the Enclave *because of her?*

She'd left him in the Sylum prison.

She hadn't even accepted his note.

"What have I done?" Gaia whispered. She turned to Peony, horrified. "What did you tell him about the note?"

"I never spoke to your friend directly. I told Malachai's brother the truth: that you refused to take it. Why?" Peony said. "Regrets?"

Gaia could barely breathe. *He must hate me.*

Round three began, four versus four, and this time Leon was playing defense for the Skins team, facing in Gaia's direction from the far north end of the field. Fierce concentration ruled his features. Xave's team tried to pass around the Skins like they had in the previous round, but Leon's team was quick to anticipate, and a teammate passed back to Leon, who feinted right, then dribbled left, and popped the ball up high and hard toward the goal, perfectly arced for a header.

Two players leapt into the air, straining toward the ball, and

145

a nasty cracking noise came as they collided and fell sprawling to the ground. The ref blew his whistle. Munsch lay still while the bare-chested player slowly sat up, blinking.

On the platform, the Matrarc stood. "Is there blood?" she called.

"Yes," called the ref. "Munsch is down, and Sundberg. They hit heads." He waved in a few of the other athletes to lend a hand.

"Bring them here. Where are Mlass Gaia and Mx. Dinah?" the Matrarc said.

"I'm here," Gaia called, moving forward.

Munsch was moving now, slowly rolling over on the grass, and he touched a palm tenderly to his forehead. Sundberg came to his feet and gave him a hand up, and with the others, the two walked slowly to the sideline before the platform. The crowd applauded out of respect.

"Resume play," called the Matrarc with a wave. "Mlass Gaia, take a look. See if there's anything you can do."

Gaia heard the ref's whistle and the action starting up again behind her. Sundberg was already looking better, but Munsch had a cut on his forehead, and a bruise was forming under his skin. His eyes seemed fine and he said he wasn't nauseous, but he looked a little dazed. One of the guards passed Gaia a basket of bandages and a bottle of water, and as she started dabbing at Munsch's cut, Dinah came up beside her.

"How are they?" Dinah said.

"I'm okay," Munsch said. "Just let me be for a minute. I want to watch."

"Hold still," Gaia said, and finished cleaning his wound.

"That crim's fast," Sundberg said.

Gaia glanced over her shoulder, then sat beside Munsch. The Skins captain had repositioned Leon to play forward. Only six men were left on the field, and it was now obvious to Gaia that though Leon's skills were decent, they weren't the best. What he had was speed.

On an inbound throw, Leon intercepted the ball and crossed it to his captain, who took a long, risky shot from way out. The deepest Shirts player ran it down, passed it up to Xave, and the Shirts began a punishing series of passes to move up the field again, dominating Leon's team. The crowd revved, voices massing into a wordless wall of sound as Xave closed in on scoring range

The Skins captain began to backpedal defensively toward his own goal.

"No! Forward!" Leon yelled, driving forward to cut off the angle.

Xave powered a shot high and wide over Leon's teammate's head into the goal.

The crowd jumped to their feet in a deafening roar of cheers. Gaia shifted her gaze from the ball in the net to Leon, who stood with his hands on his hips, his head down, his body working for breath. She felt the crush of vicarious defeat. A corps of guards was already moving onto the field to isolate him.

Leon lifted his head and looked over his shoulder toward the Matrarc. He wiped his forehead with his arm, and then, deliberately, he started walking toward the platform. It took the startled guards two seconds to respond, and then they circled tight around him. Leon made a grab for a guard's sword, but was instantly wrestled to the ground and pinned there.

Gaia couldn't see because the players were crowding in on the commotion. Peter was talking to the ref, pointing to Leon.

"What's going on?" Dinah asked.

"Peter's picking the crim, that's what," Munsch said with a laugh. "It's an insult to Xave and the other players."

147

"I don't understand," Gaia said.

The guards still held Leon to the ground.

"Xave won, so that makes Peter the other captain," Munsch explained. "Normally, they'd each pick one new teammate, but there's only one left since I'm out injured. Peter gets to pick a Skins loser instead, and he's picking the crim. It's diabolical. The other losers want to kill him. I don't blame them."

"We want the crim!" the crowd chanted.

Boys ran out with water bottles. Xave drank a long swallow and dumped the rest of the water on his upturned face while Peter, animated, continued to talk to the ref.

"Let's go," Xave said. He clapped a sure hand on the shoulder of his Shirts teammate. "Give Chardo the filthy crim, and let's get this over with."

The crowd laughed. The ref pointed his whistle at Leon. The guards lifted Leon to his feet, untied his hands, and marched off the field.

Leon walked to join Peter on the O. Peter pulled off his shirt, and his torso twisted in a supple economy of motion as he tossed it to a runner. Leon stood listening, rubbing his wrist, while Peter spoke in his ear. Gaia peered at the two shirtless men, trying to see what made them, nearly the same height and age, so different, and where Leon's stance was cautious, intense, coiled, Peter's personified an eager, magnanimous confidence.

"They are sweet, those two. No doubt about it," Dinah said, drawing out the syllables. "Where were they ten years ago is what I'd like to know."

"Mx. Dinah!" Munsch said.

"Mlass Gaia knows what I'm talking about," Dinah said.

She did indeed. She might be too polite to say anything, but she was far from blind.

The ref was lifting the ball.

As Xave and his teammate squared off against Peter and Leon, a cloud moved across the setting sun, dimming the light and shooting streaks of orange into the greeny blue of the sky. A slow wind came up from the marsh, audibly rippling the flags of the platform and lifting sparks from the torches that burned and smoked around the field.

Gaia forgot to breathe, and the ref dropped the ball.

Xave was fast. Leon was faster. He shot the ball wide to Peter, who pelted it down the field toward the goal. And it went in.

It was so sudden and unexpected that the spectators were silent a full two seconds. Then they went nuts.

Xave and his Shirts teammate stalked off the field to join the growing line of other eliminated players. Peter walked quickly to the O on the field, the last captain and sole remaining player of the Skins team. Leon strode to the X, where a boy ran out with a shirt. The gray material, ripped during an earlier round, clung in tatters to his sweaty back as he faced Peter, who was already crouching slightly, ready to spring.

It came down to this, one man against the other. Whoever won this point would win the entire game. Peter was the more skilled player by far, but Leon was faster, and Gaia sensed that Leon was hungry in a way that few had ever been before.

"Wait 'til I release the ball," the ref called. "Ready?"

The crowd went still and the flags stopped rippling as Leon and Peter faced off, primed for explosive attack. A spark from a torch floated silently across the field.

The ref lifted the ball high.

It dropped toward the green grass.

Grit and fury converged.

Peter lost.

CHAPTER 12

prize

THE SPECTATORS WENT BERSERK. Dozens of them rushed the field, where they mixed in pandemonium with the leaping, bounding athletes from the earlier rounds. The crims cheered even more wildly for one of their own. Men were throwing things in the air, kissing each other, hugging and slapping with unrestrained force, as if each one of them, personally, had scored the victory.

Gaia was too stunned to move. Peony charged beside her and jostled Gaia practically off her feet.

"Isn't it amazing?" Peony squealed. "Can you believe he beat *Chardo Peter*? I can't *believe* it!"

"Look at Peter," Dinah said dryly, joining them. "He can't believe it, either. And Xave. He's fit to be tied. I must say, that's a beautiful sight."

"Yes!" Peony said.

Half a dozen guards pushed onto the field, penetrating the congratulatory swarm around Leon and leveraging with their clubs to push the mob back.

Gaia lost sight of Peter, too, in the mass of reaching arms, and still the cheering went on, like a crashing brilliance of sound around her. The center of the swarm on the field gradually began to move, then took up more speed as the crowd delivered the winner and Peter to the area before the platform and a circle widened so they could be seen.

Leon gave his belt a slow hitch up his hip. His straggly hair was nearly black with sweat above his joyless expression, and he was physically spent. Peter, loose-limbed and gleaming with sweat, bore the air of a good sport fairly beaten.

The Matrarc lifted her hand. "My cousins!" she called out.

The rest of the noise simmered to a ripple of laughter and talk, and then subsided so that all could hear. The Matrarc kept her hand lifted until even the quietest hum desisted.

"My dear cousins," the Matrarc repeated in a clear, strong voice. "We've never had a game like this before. Vlatir," the Matrarc called out to him. "My husband tells me he's never seen anyone run so fast. What do you have to say for yourself?"

As Leon looked up, a furious, controlled burning emanated from him, a lethal tension that caused the guards to respond by pushing the rumbling crowd back, calling sharply to make more room.

Dominic leaned close to the Matrarc to speak in her ear.

"No, wait," the Matrarc said to the guards. "Speak, Vlatir. I want to hear your voice."

Leon's hand closed slowly in a fist at his side. "What would you have me say, Mlady Matrarc?"

His voice had the same cultured accents Gaia remembered from before, but now with obvious insolence. Obvious, at least, to her. She guessed that the Matrarc heard it, too, though many in the crowd took his words for a joke and laughed.

"We've never had a crim win our thirty-two games," the Matrarc said, providing him no further opening. "Before we can proceed, the cuzines have to make a decision. Come forward so

151

I can hear you, my cuzines. Step aside, please, the rest of you. I want the voters here."

She held out a graceful hand toward her left, like a great conductor, and the men cleared back to allow the mlasses and mladies to come forward. Gaia glanced around to see Dinah, who lifted an ironic eyebrow and shifted unobtrusively out of the way. The other libbies, likewise, were mixed in with Norris, Chardo Sid, and the other men.

Peony pulled Gaia's sleeve. "Come *on*," she urged.

Gaia followed with her, rising on tiptoe to keep an eye on Leon. She kept expecting him to acknowledge her, but he remained directed toward the Matrarc, as if no one else merited any attention. Nearly two hundred women now congregated on the field before the platform.

"Are they ready?" the Matrarc asked her husband.

"Yes."

"Then I want to hear them." The Matrarc raised her voice. "I need a baseline, my cuzines. Say 'Ay.'"

The voices of the women rang out in one, cohesive call, startling Gaia with the power of their unity. The call was followed by silence, and then a new, smaller wave of murmuring. Norris's scowl was as deep as Gaia had ever seen it. The men, excluded from the vote, were looking at each other, as if only now calculating their own numbers. She guessed that they'd never been assembled at a vote before, and it must strike them how many more of them there were, close to eighteen hundred men.

Does the Matrarc not notice? Gaia wondered.

Leon lifted his head, scanning the crowd beyond the platform.

"We have a new situation before us," the Matrarc said, in her clear, carrying voice. "The underlying assumption of letting a

152

crim compete has always been that a crim winner would be freed." She smiled. "We just never believed it could happen."

Laughter greeted her remark.

"Vlatir is a newcomer of two months' time, from the Enclave south of here," the Matrarc continued. "He's violent at the least provocation. He resists authority at every opportunity. He does not respond to any sort of discipline. But he is convicted of no crime, and you deserve to know this. You also saw him on the field today for what that shows of his character. So, this is your choice. We can accept this newcomer, Vlatir, into Sylum as any other man and confer upon him the rights of a winner, or we can deny him, keep him under watch with the crims, and grant the rights of the winner to the runner-up, Chardo Peter. What do you say?"

Excited debate broke out, both among the women on the field and among the men farther out. Gaia stood staring at Leon, watching how he put one fist on his hip and kept regarding the Matrarc. From his unyielding expression, Gaia could not begin to know what he was thinking. It surprised her that he didn't speak out on his own behalf, and then she wondered if she should.

She swallowed a knot of nervous fear. Across the crowd, she spotted Will, who was watching her closely. When he nodded infinitesimally at Leon, he seemed to be asking her a tacit question. Gaia was supposed to act. She knew that. But what was she supposed to do?

The Matrarc turned toward the women, expectant, and as the noise died away entirely, she lifted a hand.

"Have you made your decisions?" she asked.

"Ay," called the women.

"Wait!" Gaia called.

Those around her turned, startled. She pushed her way to the front.

153

"Wait," Gaia repeated. "Please, Mlady."

"This is not the time, Mlass Gaia," the Matrarc said.

"I just have to say one thing," Gaia declared. "Leon Vlatir's a good man. A brave one. He came a long way to be here and he deserved Sylum's hospitality, not its prison." She turned to project her voice farther. "The Matrarc promised me she would free him tonight. You can make that come true. Vote him the winner."

There was a murmur in the crowd, and then a smattering of indulgent laughter. They were amused by her? She shot her gaze to Leon, who stood stern and mute, still not looking at her.

"It seems he has a champion. And it's true, I did say I'd free him, at least until he needs arresting again. I suspect that will be any moment now if he lives up to his past," the Matrarc said, and more laughter followed. "For practical purposes, my cuzines, you are deciding between his status as a winner or a crim. Those in favor of denying Vlatir the rights of a winner, say 'Nay.'"

A chorus of "Nay" came from the women, and Gaia tried to guess how many had spoken. Was it more than half?

The Matrarc raised her hand again. "Those in favor of granting Vlatir the rights of a winner, say 'Ay.'"

Gaia lifted her voice to join the second chorus from the women. "Ay!" reverberated around the playing field and echoed away out over the marsh, and Gaia knew instantly it was louder. Laughter and cheering erupted from the men. The crims at their end of the field cheered triumphantly.

A small, strained smile turned Leon's lips, and he took a step forward.

Dominic spoke to the Matrarc, and she lifted her hand yet again, invoking silence. It took some time for the enthusiasm to be contained again.

"Well, Vlatir?" she said. "You have something to say now?"

"I do," Leon said. He made a slow, all-encompassing gesture to the men who ranged up the slopes and around the perimeter of the women. Like quick-silver, a current charged through the men from one to another, uniting them in a silent summons they'd never heard before, and the air crackled with anticipation. "All of you men," Leon called out. "If you're in favor of my freedom, say 'Ay!'"

A lusty bellow of "Ay!" rose up in the air, ten times louder than the calls of the women.

The following silence was deafening, ominous, and complete.

Next came the slick metallic sound of blades as the guards drew their swords.

"If you're inciting a riot, your return to the prison will be swift indeed," said the Matrarc.

Leon folded his arms across his chest, and though his lips smiled, his eyes glittered maliciously. There were no fewer than ten blades pointed at his throat. "Forgive me, Mlady," he said smoothly. "Living as I have with the crims, I haven't yet fully learned your customs. No offense intended." He lifted his voice to call to the men. "No riots tonight, my friends. Get that?"

The crowd laughed, its virile good humor tempering a darker undercurrent, and the Matrarc was quick to smile. "Lower your arms," she called to the guards. "Vlatir. Do you understand what happens next?"

"It's my prerogative to claim a female to live with me in the winner's cabin until the next games," Leon said, his voice carrying clearly. "Correct?"

Potor jerked forward half a step, as if he had only now realized the risk of keeping Leon in the game with him. Turning toward Gaia, he shook his head once and his lips parted in surprise, as if he couldn't believe what he was seeing. Gaia knew, then. She knew Leon was going to pick her. She searched for Will once more, and saw he was watching his brother with a pained expression. Will's gaze shifted to meet Gaia's, and the pain deepened.

"That's correct. Any mlass," the Matrarc said. "It is the tradition at this point for the winner to invite three young women to step forward."

"There's no need. I know who I want," Leon said.

Gaia reached for her locket watch, but it wasn't there, and she had nothing to hold while she dreaded the next moment, and longed for it horribly. He still wasn't looking at her, but she felt his attention as keenly as if he had an arrow notched in a bow, aiming for her chest.

"No," Peter said. He took a step toward Leon. "No, you can't." A guard blocked his path.

"Who do you choose?" the Matrarc asked.

Gaia stared at Leon, willing him to at least look at her before he called her name.

"I want Maya Stone," Leon said.

Shock froze Gaia's blood.

"You mean Gaia," the Matrarc said, her voice lifting in surprise. "Her name is Gaia Stone."

There was a shift around Gaia as people turned to get a look at her. Her heart lurched back into rhythm, nearly knocking her off her feet.

"No," Leon said. "I want her sister. Maya."

CHAPTER 13

loyalty

A SILENCE STILLED THE CROWD, and then Gaia moved forward to where the guards, as perplexed as everyone else, still maintained their circle around Leon.

"Leon," Gaia said. "I'm here."

He didn't respond. His blue eyes had turned to flint, and his unflinching gaze remained directed toward the Matrarc, who was conferring with her husband and several mladies on the platform. Gaia tried again. She had to speak between the shoulders of two of the guards.

"Leon, please. This makes no sense."

He turned then, finally, his scathing eyes burning into her with such intense hatred that she jerked back. His fingers closed again in a fist, and she saw up close the iron power contained in his grasp. She could not believe this was Leon, the same man who'd sacrificed himself for her at the great south gate of the Enclave. He looked like he'd happily rip her to shreds and throw her carcass in bits to wild dogs.

You can't be like this, she thought.

The Matrarc stepped to the edge of the platform again. "Let

me clarify," she said to Leon. "Are you aware that Gaia's sister Maya is an infant?"

"Yes," Leon said.

"What could you possibly want with a baby?" the Matrarc asked, openly mystified.

"I don't care to explain," Leon said.

"We would never let you harm a child," the Matrarc said.

"I wouldn't harm her. Far from it. I'll care for her most tenderly."

Gaia opposed the idea with every cell in her body. She didn't want her sister in Leon's control, not the way he was now. If Maya depended on him for care or affection, it would be torture for Gaia. Instinctively, horrifyingly, she knew that was his point.

"He wants what's mine," Gaia said.

The Matrarc shook her head. "But Maya isn't yours, Mlass Gaia. You know that. I've given your sister to Mlady Adele, out on the island. She stays with her."

"Mlady Adele may come to the winner's cabin, too, if she likes, or send a wet nurse. The details make no difference to me," Leon said, his tone frankly belligerent. "Are you going to follow your own laws, or not?"

Dominic strode forward. "Take the crim back to prison and beat some manners into him."

The guards instantly closed in again on Leon. "Matrarc!" Leon called out, his voice commanding. He struggled to try to break free, but they pinned his arms in a twist behind him. "You just gave me the rights of a winner. The rights I earned. All your voters here agreed. Or was that a farce?"

The Matrarc's voice grew hard. "The only farce here was the one you created. Every man of Sylum still has to follow our laws," she said.

"I am following them," Leon insisted. "You're the one who's reneging. I demand Maya Stone for one month in the winner's cabin. Send along anyone you want to care for her, but I claim her as my prize. It's my right. As far as I can tell, it's the *only* right I have. The only right *any* man has."

There was a grumbling of dissatisfaction among the men as Leon's logic sank in, and everyone heard it. The Matrarc could not disregard Leon's claim, not without risking a rebellion.

"It's not my fault your law has a loophole in it," Leon added mockingly. "Maybe you didn't think of everything."

One of the guards punched him in the gut and Leon clenched over with an *oof*.

"Release him," the Matrarc said.

Leon jerked free from their holds and spat in the grass.

"It's all right, Dominic," the Matrarc said to her husband, who was leaning near to her ear again. "He knows what he's saying. Hear this, Vlatir. You'll get the baby. That's your right. But if you do one thing to upset the child or Mlady Adele when she comes to care for her, you're going back to the wasteland."

"That's all I ask," Leon said dryly.

"Mlass Gaia, go with him first thing tomorrow to talk to Mlady Adele. I'll give you a note to take."

"Yes, Mlady."

The Matrarc lifted her hand to the waiting crowd again. "There's a change happening in Sylum, for all of us. You can feel it, can't you?" In a flash, her honest question penetrated the hearts of everyone there, and the very quality of the air hummed with surprise, then caution, then curiosity. Gaia was amazed at the sudden evidence of the Matrarc's power. It wasn't so much that she influenced people, but that she tapped into what was there, waiting for a lightning rod.

159

"We can be afraid, or we can embrace it," the Matrarc went on. "Watch out for each other. Care for each other gently. Come talk to me if you want to talk. We will find our way. We always have."

A palpable shift moved through the crowd, and then a young voice called out from the edge, "Matina!"

The Matrarc lifted her chin slightly, listening, and all around her, Gaia felt everyone pause to listen for the bell's reverberation, a sound that wasn't even there but was somehow all the louder for being collectively imagined, three resonating bongs. Then in the rich silence, the Matrarc touched her hand to her heart. The gesture passed outward in a great, silent ripple of unity. Gaia glanced over to Leon to find him watching her cynically. Slowly, she lifted her hand to her heart, too.

"Thank you," the Matrarc said simply, with heartfelt sincerity. "Let us go, now, my cousins. Let's remember to be grateful for all that we have."

The crowd of two thousand eased subtly, murmured, and then voices started up again. People laughed, turning to each other openly in a unified community, even as they began to disperse and leave the field. Gaia was impressed beyond words. The Matrarc had taken a potentially explosive situation and not only diffused it, but transformed it into something beautiful instead. Gaia had no idea how she'd done it.

Taja left with her family, and Peony walked slowly away beside Munsch. Will was moving against the crowd, toward her and Leon and Peter, but as Gaia spotted him, Dinah's bright red hair appeared near his shoulder and he turned to the libby. They became absorbed into the throng, and even the guards were drifting away as Gaia moved toward Leon and Peter.

"You got me back in the game. I won't forget it," Leon said to Peter.

160

"It was my mistake," Peter said. "I thought you'd be easier to beat than the others."

Closer now, she could see the filth that covered Leon, from his ripped shirt to the stains that darkened his work pants. His shoes were mere shreds of leather, and a line of blackish red was trickling down from Leon's elbow.

"You're hurt," she said.

He didn't reply. "Where's this winner's cabin?" Leon asked Peter. "Up on the bluff?"

"I'll take you," Peter said, looking at Gaia. "Mlass Gaia and I will."

"There had better be food there," Leon said.

She tried to examine his elbow more closely, and he deliberately turned away.

"There's no reason to ignore me," she said.

Leon turned back to her slightly then, and she felt the exact moment when his grim blue eyes met her own.

"You can send me a note if you have anything to say," he said.

She faltered back a half step. "I'm sorry."

Leon turned his back on her.

"She just stood up for you," Peter reminded him. "You should be grateful."

Leon let out a brief, incredulous laugh. "To her? Never again."

"Leon, please," Gaia began.

"Don't," he said. "Don't even start."

"I'm so sorry, about all of it," she said.

His teeth clicked together. "Two months I've spent in that hell-hole," Leon said. "For doing nothing worse than crossing a wasteland to find you. And what did you do? You told the Matrarc to offer me a *horse*."

161

"Okay, that's enough," Peter said, moving between them.

Leon pushed him with a flick of his fingers and backed away himself.

"The horse was so you'd have an option, so you wouldn't have to be trapped here," she said. "I knew she wouldn't let you out of the prison."

"Did you even try to persuade her?" Leon asked.

"I did. It only made her more determined to keep you there."

He shook his head, frowning. "I heard you were stuck in the lodge, confined there like a naughty kid," he said. "What did you do?"

"This isn't the place to tell you."

"No? When did you get out?"

"I was just released today," she said.

His eyes were sharp. "You know, you could have come down to the prison. I would have seen you over the fence. It's not like I haven't looked."

She swallowed hard, realizing now why it had been much, much easier to go with Peter when she was first released. "I was afraid to."

"You?" He laughed. "When has fear ever stopped you from doing anything?"

I was afraid you'd be angry. Like this. Shame burned through her.

"Let me get a good look at you," Leon said, his voice lower. He peered hard at her, until she could no longer meet his gaze. "I see what it is. They've ruined you." A strangled laugh came out of him as he tilted his face back toward the sky. "All this time," he muttered.

Doubt hit her hard. "What do you mean?"

"We should go," Peter said, intervening again.

But Leon didn't respond to him, and his blue eyes went cool

and curious as he regarded Gaia. "Aren't you going to ask if I'll let you visit your sister? My little prize?" he asked softly.

His question bit deep into her heart. It felt like a terrible, twisted game where she didn't know the rules, the sort of game his adoptive father the Protectorat might have invented.

"That's it," Peter said decisively. "I'll take you up to the winner's cabin. Mlass Gaia, why don't you head back to the lodge?"

She kept her focus on Leon. "I would like to see my sister. I'll beg if that's what you want. May I see her, please?"

Leon eyed her with dark satisfaction. "You do realize she won't remember you anymore, don't you?"

"Don't listen to him," Peter told her.

But she was already hurting, and mystified. She shook her head and lifted her gaze to Peter's. "He's not normally like this," she began.

Leon stepped so near to her that his face crowded her vision. His eyes glittered and his voice was rigidly controlled. "Don't you *ever* talk to him about me like that when *I'm right here.*"

She gasped in fear and then felt his focus drawn to her parted lips. A rapid ticking clicked on at the back of her mind as his gaze lingered, and then in the darkness of his beard, his own lips closed in a hard line. His eyes narrowed, and he pulled back a millimeter, watching her. Testing her. There was nothing kind or inviting about him at all, and yet she felt sucked into a compelling, black, uncertain shadow that belonged to him and her alone.

She finally found her voice again. "Don't boss me around," she said, in little more than a whisper.

Some lost, secret impulse flickered through his eyes for an instant, and then his loathing returned full force. "I'm going to the winner's cabin," Leon said. "I'm starving and I stink." He turned and started away across the field.

She covered her eyes a moment, just trying to freeze everything to make it all stop tilting.

"I should have beat him," Peter said.

She was too unhappy to laugh. "You let him win?" She opened her eyes again.

"No. Of course not," Peter said. "But if I'd known he'd treat you like that, I would have, somehow. I never would have picked him when I had the choice."

Leon hates me. It was still a total shock, as if the sun had turned black or the force of gravity had doubled. Foreshortened by distance, Leon's dark, isolated figure was receding at the far edge of the field, past a smoking torch, and then he turned out of sight.

"I wish I could do something for you," Peter said.

"Would you take care of him, please?" she asked. "He has nobody here, and he doesn't want me near him."

Peter considered her, then took a deep, visible breath. She lifted her gaze to meet his direct regard. Handsome didn't begin to describe him. He still hadn't put on a shirt, and she realized now she'd hardly looked at him, even though he stood there, barely a meter away, arms akimbo. She glanced once more at the sheen of cooling sweat on his skin, and then away, ashamed and confused.

"Of course, Mlass," Peter said.

It was the perfectly polite thing to say, yet even that seemed completely mixed up and wrong to her.

The men always cut loose after the thirty-two games, but this night was by far wilder and louder than the other times

164

she'd seen. She was certain Leon's gesture of inviting the men to vote had something to do with it, as if he'd awoken a slumbering, destructive force, and the Matrarc's moment of the soundless matina didn't carry over to the urges of the night. From the clerestory, she could see a glow reflecting up into the trees from bonfires down by the marsh, and she saw torches heading toward the glade site in the woods where she'd once spoken to Peony, too.

For hours, it wasn't safe to go out, but as the night finally crept toward dawn and Sylum grew quiet, Gaia couldn't wait anymore to see Leon. Taking her blue cloak from its peg, she pulled on her old white boots. The early air was surprisingly cold as she let herself out the kitchen door and headed up the road.

The sound of breaking bottles had been replaced by crickets, and as the full moon set behind the bluff, a peculiar, ashy light hovered over the road. Gaia strode rapidly, feeling her breath condense in the air before her face. She turned a familiar corner, and the Chardo place spread before her on her right. The house was dark, but a lamp hanging high in the barn filled the open doorway and cast an inviting yellow parallelogram onto the driveway, almost as if one of the brothers was beckoning to her. Gaia didn't stop.

The road narrowed as it began to rise along the face of the bluff, and soon she hit several switchbacks. To the east, morning light was creeping over the black, sullen rim of the earth, and the surface of the marsh began to glow with ribbons of lit water.

At the top of the bluff, Gaia paused, uncertain of her way. She remembered overhearing once that the winner's cabin stood by a meadow. A stump stood beside the road with an abandoned axe propped in its top, like a mute sentry marking the entrance to another world, and she headed to the right. A line of half a dozen cabins gradually emerged, lightless.

When a distant door slammed, a hollow, sharp bang in the stillness, she turned toward the noise and found a narrow track that wound even farther along the ridge. The pines were older here, with thick, massive trunks. Many of the lower branches had broken off over time, leaving sharp spikes pointing horizontally out of the trunks, like blind arms into the mist.

At last the trees parted, and Gaia stood at the edge of a small meadow where the fog hovered knee-high. Across the meadow, perched at the brink of the bluff, stood a sturdy, low-slung cabin with a deep wraparound porch and stone steps. Smoke rose straight and thin from a stovepipe on the left side of the roof. Weathered to the same color as the early morning grayness, the stone and log cabin seemed to grow naturally out of the rock. An enormous oak stood beside it, the tips of its upper branches stretching over the roof, each individual leaf silhouetted against the pink in the sky.

Bright geraniums were planted in two pots beside the cabin's steps, red velvet in the growing light, and a water urn hanging from the porch reminded her of home. *Home.* As she reached for the railing and set her feet upon the stone steps to the porch, an ache stirred in her. She stared through the screen door to the empty, dim entryway beyond, and her intuition told her she'd come to the right place.

She tapped softly on the wooden frame, and her eye caught on the iron scrollwork of the open interior door. A creak of movement came from farther inside, and a moment later, a dark, solid figure stepped into view. Leon Vlatir stood on the other side of the screen, his expression obscured by the mesh, and yet she knew there was no welcome in him. *How can it be worse to see him than to not see him?*

Gaia reached for the door that separated them. "Hey."

"I'm not ready to see you," he said.

She faltered and her hand stopped in mid-air. "Are you all right?" she asked.

He gave an infinitesimal shake of his head.

"I'm sorry," she began.

"No," he said. "I don't want your voice. I don't want anything about you here."

Gaia was startled. Unbelieving. He couldn't be sending her away. Not after they'd both come so far. "I'm supposed to go with you to get Maya."

"Come back later. Or better yet, meet me on the beach."

"I just have to see you," she said. "Just for a little. I want—" Her voice closed in on itself. "Let me talk to you. Please."

The spring squeaked as she pulled open the screen door. Leon turned his back and walked farther into the cabin. She watched him descend a couple of steps, pass through the main room, and head out the opposite door to a back deck that overlooked the valley. She followed him as far as the door, but there was something so off-putting, so private in the way he stood and leaned his hands upon the top railing, that she couldn't go farther. Yet neither could she leave.

The back of his head was a mess of damp, nearly black hair, grown full and shaggy, entirely unlike the crisp military cut that she'd known before. His sleeves were carelessly rolled, and the tail end of his brown shirt hung loose over the seat of his homespun trousers. He'd grown slightly taller, and his shoulders were dense where they tested the seams of his shirt. Streamlined as ever, he was clearly stronger than he'd been in the Enclave. Much. She'd never seen him without boots before, except once when he'd inspected the freckles on his ankle, and now his bare heels on the wood of the deck seemed to be the only vulnerable thing about him.

A stillness immobilized him, as if he had schooled his body to remain motionless despite a starved, inner disquiet.

She pushed through the door and stepped softly to the railing beside him, where she could finally see his profile. His beard was gone. Instead of surveying the valley below, he had his eyes closed, and his fingers were clasped tight around the wooden railing. A row of colorful little pebbles was lined up along the top of the rail, as if the last occupants had left them there for a greeting, and they were incongruously playful in the early light.

"Leon," she began softly. "I can see you're angry with me. I hardly know where to begin, but I'm so sorry."

"Don't," he said. "I don't want your apologies."

She gulped back the rest of her words. *But I am sorry*, she thought. "Did you really cross the wasteland to find me?" she asked.

Cleanly dressed and shaved, he should have looked more like the old Leon, but when he finally turned, dark bangs hung to half conceal his blue eyes, and his expression was openly hostile.

"Believe me," he said. "I regret it."

Her pulse jumped, and she swallowed thickly. "I never wanted you trapped here."

"That isn't why."

"Isn't there a chance you could be happy here, despite how you started?"

He let out a broken laugh and ran a hand back through his hair in an old gesture she recognized.

"This is what I don't need yet," he said. "You, talking to me. Asking your questions. I don't want to say any of this."

"But I don't want you to be so unhappy."

He shook his head. "Just don't. You're not the same person you were," he said. "It's not like I'm talking to the old Gaia. I can't forget that."

What would you say to the old Gaia? "How do you know I'm so different?"

His expression grew cooler still. "You burned my note, for one thing. That was hard to miss."

"Peony burned it."

"You let her. Same difference."

She didn't know how to explain it, but her only pride, her last defiance had come from not breaking the rules of her confinement. "I couldn't accept it," she said. "As long as I didn't step outside the lodge, I was still resisting the Matrarc. Your note was part of that."

"That's ridiculous," he said bluntly.

It must seem like that, especially since she'd capitulated shortly after that. How could she explain how lonely and awful it had become in the lodge, how her last strength had vanished as she watched that scrap of paper burn? "It was your note that made me finally realize I had to give in."

"I don't get it."

Gaia turned toward the marsh. "The Matrarc made me give up something. She wouldn't let you out until I did." She didn't want to feel this hurt and confused again. She'd made her decision.

"I'm entitled to know what she asked you for," he said.

She stared bleakly toward the horizon. "I helped someone miscarry her baby, and the Matrarc wanted to know who. She made me promise not to do it again."

169

"It was Peony, wasn't it? That's why she helped with the paper." His eyes narrowed in amazement. "Why didn't you just agree, Gaia? You could have agreed on day one, and then done whatever you wanted to secretly."

"Lied, you mean?"

"Wasn't letting me out of prison worth one lie? Why does the Matrarc even deserve your honesty?"

He was confusing her more. Honesty came from within. It wasn't what someone deserved. "You know how bad I am at lying, even if I wanted to," she said. "Which I don't. Even when I tried to be discreet about Peony's miscarriage, the Matrarc knew about it in less than a day. I could never lie to her over years. Besides, I wanted her to see I wouldn't give in. I wanted *her* to change her mind," she said.

"But then *you* did."

"I had to go on with living. I had to get you out."

The stillness came over him again, alarming her. He wasn't satisfied with her answer. It wasn't good enough, what she'd done, and he certainly wasn't grateful. In the end, he hadn't even needed her to get him out of prison. He'd done that himself by winning the thirty-two games.

He peered over at her again. "Look at you. You used to be Gaia Stone from outside the wall. You had nothing to lose and nothing could stop you. Now you're one of them."

"I've had to adjust, that's all. I'm not especially proud of it."

"Why not be? You're a girl now," he said.

"What are you implying?"

"Just what I said. You're a girl in a place where the girls rule."

She frowned. "You think I just want to be part of the ruling class."

"I'm sure you'll find it very convenient."

She instinctively recoiled. Their positions were reversed, she realized, as neatly and completely as a flip of a card. In the Enclave, he'd been a person of privilege and power, while she'd been a poor midwife from outside the wall, entering it only to become a prisoner of Q cell, and finally a fugitive.

"Now you know what it was like for me back at home," she said.

"I have just spent two months in prison, shackled to Malachai, for no reason at all," he said. "I think I've got you beat."

"Really?" she demanded. "You think two months of prison beats years, no, generations of neglect and abuse?"

"What do you think the men here have been putting up with?" Leon asked. "What do you think my future's going to be like? No man here is free. Even if they're not in jail, they're still slaves."

"They are not," she disagreed. "I've seen plenty of happy men here."

"Those are just the ones who've succeeded in pleasing some girl. The rest of them are all warped and stunted from trying to."

Now he was exaggerating. "That is totally untrue," she said.

He laughed strangely. "You don't even see it anymore. That's how myopic you've become."

"But you see everything clearly," she said, getting her own edge of sarcasm. "At least there's food and shelter for everybody here, not like in Wharfton, where you Enclave people doled out your meager drips of water for the rest of us, and spied on us, and killed the people who resisted you."

"Now we're getting to it," he said.

"Just don't try to tell me it was better there."

"I'll concede it's better here, for you," he said.

"It's not just better for me! You're like any other man of

171

Sylum now. You can do anything you want: work, build a safe home, eat your fill. You can even marry and have children some day, if you can get someone to love you."

His eyes flashed darkly. "Yes. The Matrarc's husband informed me I get to join the pool if my sperm are viable," he said. "Naturally, I'll have to be tested. He wants it done soon."

Embarrassed, she looked over the rail toward the distant marsh. "I'm sorry," she muttered.

"He's sure it will just be a technicality," he added. "And then, as you say, there's the problem of getting anyone to love me. Even if the male-female odds weren't ridiculously bad, there's the fact of how utterly unlovable I am. Thanks for reminding me."

She looked down at the deck, wishing she could take it back. It was just that he could get her so mad. "I didn't mean to say that," she said.

"But you did, didn't you?"

"I'm sorry."

"You apologize more than anyone I've ever known and it doesn't fix a thing."

She poised a fist on her hip. "Then what do you expect me to say? You obviously hate everything here, but it's our new home. I, for one, am trying to find a way to survive in it, and excuse me if I hope to find some measure of happiness."

"Didn't you learn anything in the Enclave?" he asked. "A system that exploits any of its people is inherently unfair. Did you hear the men last night, when I asked them to vote?"

"That was your fault."

"My *fault*? Gaia, wake up," he said. "The men are not happy here. They might act like they are, they might even think that they are most of the time, but this whole place is a tinderbox. The right spark, and it would go up in flames."

"Are you going to be the one to destroy it?" she asked.

"Why not? At the moment, I can't think of anything I'd rather do."

She didn't believe he could destroy Sylum, but she didn't like that he wanted to. "Is this what you were like when you first arrived?" she asked. "Is that why the Matrarc didn't release you immediately? She normally holds newcomers in the prison only until she knows they aren't dangerous."

He lifted one eyebrow ironically. "All it took was for them to see my back, and they started asking idiotic questions. I fought back when they tried to tie me, so they shackled me to Malachai. I refused to follow orders when some stupid guard tried to humiliate me, so then I was a discipline reject, which meant they could hit me all they wanted and stuff me in solitary. You never knew?"

She found it difficult to meet his gaze. "Norris told me a little."

"A little," he said quietly. For a long moment he searched her eyes, seeking deeply. "And still you left me there."

"I didn't know what else to do," she said. "I'm sorry."

He raked a hand back over his ear. "All that time, I was worried about you. I just wanted to see you and know you were okay." His lips twisted. "When I heard you didn't even read my note, I thought *that* was unbearable. But *this*—"

For an instant, an ache of promise yawned before her, a glimpse of what had driven him to leave the Enclave and follow her into the wasteland.

Suddenly he slammed his fist against the railing. She jumped in her skin. The pebbles trembled.

"They took the guts out of you," he said. "That's the worst of it. I didn't think anything ever could. Enough of this. I can't talk to you anymore."

She backed up. "I was only trying to be honest with you," she said. "But the more I try, the more you despise me."

He wouldn't look at her. "I won't lie."

An insidious pain knifed through her. She didn't need this. She wished she could hurt him somehow, too. He seemed to know exactly what to say to make her feel awful about herself. A small, mean flame burned inside her.

"Why is your back ripped up?" she asked, watching to see if the memory was painful to him.

He lifted his left hand, splaying the fingers, and for the first time, she saw that the top of his ring finger from the knuckle up was gone.

"They wanted to know where the ledgers were. The one we stole," he said.

"He tortured you? Your own father?"

Leon's eyes went flat and lifeless. "Until he saw that it hurt Genevieve worse than me." He lowered his hand and resettled his grip on the railing. "Don't misunderstand. He would never sully his hands with such work himself, but he routinely checked back in on me." He ducked his head, turning his neck as if to relieve soreness there. "Resisting only delayed them, anyway. They checked on all your friends and figured out who had hidden you. They advanced Emily's baby. You probably didn't know that."

She shook her head, horrified.

"He was a little old, but they took him anyway," Leon continued. "Emily even gave back the birth records, but they still kept her son. They think she had a copy made."

Gaia didn't want to believe him. "What can we do?"

He let out a laugh. "That's brilliant, really. You can't do anything. You're a wasteland away, in your precious new home."

She felt dirty, sick at heart. Trying to hurt him had backfired.

She turned and paced to the far corner of the deck. He'd been hurt defying his father for her sake, and Gaia's dearest friend had lost her child because of Gaia. The guilt was unendurable, and she couldn't begin to imagine how Emily must be agonizing. She pressed a hand to her forehead and squeezed.

"I'm pleased to see you still have some natural feelings of loyalty left in you," Leon said finally. "Not that they've done me any good."

Raw, isolating loneliness swept into her. "Why are you doing this to me?"

"You know perfectly well," Leon said. "I risked my life for you back in the Enclave. I crossed a wasteland to find you, and you offered a horse to send me back. You left me in prison for months when one little lie would have set me free. Or don't think back so far. Not twenty minutes ago, I told you point blank I wasn't ready to see you. I didn't want to say any of this, but you couldn't leave me alone."

She was struck by his words. It was true. All of it. She turned slowly and gazed down to where his bare toes peeked from under the edge of his trousers.

"If you feel that way about me, why did you choose Maya?" she asked.

He looked as if he wouldn't answer, and then he laughed in self-derision. "Suffice it to say, I thought it would help me get over you. I didn't know it would work so fast."

She hugged her arms tight around herself, hurting. "For that purpose, you could have just chosen me," she pointed out.

"True. Funny thing. I couldn't abide the idea of you being trapped as a prize in the winner's house. With anyone." He scooped up the row of pebbles and pelted one hard over the railing. "You seem to enjoy being trapped, though. I didn't think of that."

She turned away again and blinked back a sting. "There's nothing left between us at all, is there?" she asked.

For a long moment he said nothing, and the pebbles made a clicking noise in his fingers.

Then, as if it gave him no pleasure at all, he replied. "Whose fault is that?"

CHAPTER 14

riding double

GAIA FALTERED BACK a step, registering his undisguised bitterness, and then she turned and strode back into the house. She didn't stop until she'd gone out the front door and down the stone steps. Her inner compass had turned upside down. She'd thought she was a compassionate person trying always to do what was right, but one conversation with Leon had exposed her for what she was: ungrateful, disloyal, weak, and mean.

She let out a laugh of disbelief and pressed a fist to her heart, where a crushing sensation made it hard to breathe. She felt a fierce, sudden longing for her mother, who would be nice to her and understand her and let her hide. How she longed to hide.

"Mlass Gaia?"

She glanced up. Chardo Peter was dismounting from Spider with a second horse trailing on a lead rope. The last shadows of dawn were dissolving with the mist, and sunlight touched the russet oak treetops behind him.

"Are you all right?" Peter asked. "What are you doing here?"

She didn't see how she could talk to him.

There was a noise behind her, and Leon stood at the top of the porch steps, carrying a pair of boots.

"What did you do to her?" Peter asked him.

"Wouldn't you like to know?" Leon began shoving his feet in the boots.

"Nothing," she said quickly to Peter. "He didn't do anything."

"If he touched you—" Peter began.

"No. I said. He didn't do anything," she insisted.

"Then why are you upset?" Peter asked.

Gaia sent a look back toward Leon, who lifted his eyebrows slowly, mocking her. He stomped his heel in the boot, twisting his foot.

Peter looked back and forth between the two of them. "I don't understand," he said.

Gaia felt her cheeks turning a deep, guilty red.

Leon came down the steps and reached for the second horse. "What's its name?" Leon asked.

"Hades," Peter said.

"Nice." Leon swung into the saddle and pulled at the reins with natural command.

"You won't get lost?" Peter asked.

"Don't get your hopes up," Leon said. "I'll meet you at the shore in an hour, Gaia. That should give you enough time to chat with your boyfriend. Hey!" he said, urging his horse forward with a sharp movement. They took off across the meadow.

Gaia watched his brown shirt catch sunlight once, and then he disappeared in the trees. She slowly turned back to the porch and sat on the steps, sweeping her cloak beneath her to avoid the geraniums. Wearily, she dropped her face into her hands and pressed her cool fingertips against her warm eyelids.

"What's going on?" Peter asked quietly.

"He just reminded me of some things. Some true things."

She sensed him standing just below the steps, watching her, yet she couldn't bring herself to look at him.

"Does the Matrarc know he was your lover?" Peter asked.

That brought her head up. "He wasn't my lover."

"You can tell me."

"No. He was never even my boyfriend," she said. "We just went through a lot together," she said. "You can't think— Peter, I've never slept with anyone."

Peter sat slowly beside her on the top step.

She frowned. "Have you?"

"No," he said. "I shouldn't have asked. I just had my doubts after I saw you two together. You must have had quite a past with him."

"Well, we did. We do. We did."

"Which is it?"

Gaia smoothed her skirt over her knees, wishing she knew the answer to that herself. It wasn't what it used to be, but it didn't feel over, either.

"I don't know," she admitted.

She should have felt strange having such a personal conversation with Peter, but none of the normal rules seemed to apply anymore. She glanced sideways at his fresh white shirt, at his clean hair in the morning light, and it hit her that she was sitting on the steps of the winner's cabin, with Peter. This could have been them, for real, if he'd won.

Peter would have had no compunction about claiming her for a prize. Of that she was certain. She didn't know if that made him less or more noble than Leon.

Spider nudged his big head down into the long grass beside the porch and switched his long tail.

"This may seem a little strange," Peter began. "But it's a new life here for you. You can choose how you want it to be."

"I can't choose who I am."

"Maybe you could," he said. "You can at least choose who you spend your time with."

She shook her head, not certain of anything. "What if I don't like who I'm becoming here?" she asked.

"There's nothing wrong with who you're becoming. Nothing at all. Is that what he made you think?"

She turned enough to really look at him, at the regular lines of his jaw and the even angles of his nose and cheekbones. Now that his beard was gone, she saw a pale scar, slightly longer than an eyelash, which marred the complexion of his right cheek like a permanent smile line. With wide-set, perceptive eyes, he watched her patiently, waiting. The truth was that Peter was an innately genuine, trustworthy person, and as she felt the strength of that, something inside her eased slightly, then lightened, like a tight band letting go.

"You don't care why the Matrarc kept me in the lodge or why she let me out, do you?" she asked.

"Of course I care," Peter said. "When you're ready, I hope you'll tell me. Until then, I know you did what you thought was right."

His answer made her feel a little better. Leon was wrong about her enjoying being trapped. She wasn't trapped just because she'd joined the system. "Tell me something," she asked. "Do you think I have a warped view of Sylum? Do I misuse what power I have because I'm a girl?"

"Not at all," he said. "I find you're one of the most respectful mlasses I've ever known."

She felt a slip of disappointment. "You're just comparing me to other girls here."

"What else can I do?"

She twisted off one of the geranium petals. "I think it was a mistake, coming up here this morning."

"You shouldn't be alone with him. The Matrarc doesn't trust him."

"He'd never hurt me."

"It looks to me like he can hurt you just fine without lifting a finger," he said. "How well are you sure you know him?"

Of course she knew him. "He saved my life, Peter."

"So did I."

Startled, Gaia had to pause. It was true. She glanced out to the meadow, to where cornflowers made a dotted array of blue where the fog used to be. "Of course," she said. "I owe you my thanks."

"I don't mean it like that," Peter said. "I just don't want you to think he's the only one." He stood and walked over to Spider, who had wandered down the length of the porch, pulling grass in big mouthfuls. As he ran a hand along his horse's neck, she absently watched the strong, silky motion.

He was certainly easier to talk to than Leon. She dropped her crushed petal.

"You need to start down to meet him soon," Peter reminded her.

"You don't like him much, do you?"

Peter did a subtle thing with one eyebrow that turned his expression both ironic and amused. "What do you think?" he asked. "Come on. Let's go. Your sister's waiting." He brought Spider around and held out a hand to help her into the saddle. She hesitated, thinking of the taboo against touching, but his fingers beckoned toward her left boot. "It's fine," he said. "No one will see. I'm just handing you up."

181

She reached for the pommel, then gave him her left foot. On three, he bounced her lightly up into the saddle.

"Good?" he asked.

She shifted her skirt under her seat, aware that the fabric rode high up her legs, and the stirrups were too low for her boots unless she stretched on tiptoe. "Thanks."

As he took the reins to lead Spider, she frowned.

"Aren't you riding, too?" she asked.

He looked up at her, clearly hesitating. "I guess I could as long as we're in the forest."

"Wouldn't it be faster?"

Peter led the horse next to the steps and pulled himself up behind the saddle. She kept her back straight, expecting to feel the pressure of his chest behind her, or his legs behind her own, but he held himself in a way so that they didn't touch.

"All good?" he asked, the quiet voice behind her ear again. "You have no idea how many times I've thought of this."

She felt a shiver along her neck and took the reins herself. "Which way do we go?"

The saddle moved with the rhythm of the horse beneath her, and she shifted along with it, quickly learning how to direct the horse. They descended down a different path, through the forest, and the silence of the morning was broken only by the sound of the horse's footfalls on the packed earth and the bird notes from high above.

When the path opened at the edge of the valley in view of the first cabin, Peter wordlessly slid off the back of the horse to walk beside her. She pulled on the reins to stop Spider.

"What are you doing?" Peter asked.

As she dismounted, her boots landed hard in the dust. "I can't ride when you're walking," she said. "I feel like some sort of royalty."

"Dismounting is a political statement, then?"

"Politics. Personal. It's all the same here," she said.

"Exactly what I was thinking." He smiled. "Or not."

She laughed.

"There. Finally. A smile," he said.

She closed her lips again. *He makes me happy*, she thought, surprised by the discovery. It seemed like an important thing to know. She pulled off her cloak and folded it over her arm.

"Thanks," she said.

"Feeling better now?"

She nodded. "You're good for me." The words came spontaneously, and when his eyes lit up, she was glad she'd spoken.

"Do you want me to go out to the island with you and Vlatir?" he offered. "I could."

"Really?" She liked the idea. "That would be nice."

They'd nearly reached the Chardo ranch, approaching the pasture from the back where the path narrowed through a shady area beside a fence. Gaia could see the back of the barn and the new addition.

"Is Will home?" she asked.

"Probably," he said.

Still holding Spider's reins with one hand, he unlatched the gate and held it open for her. As she passed through before him, she inadvertently snagged her cloak on the post and paused to free it. She glanced up, ready to laugh, and found him close. Her mirth caught silently in her throat.

The overarching branches of an autumn maple cast golden shadows and dollops of sunlight around them, and the light pooled in his blue eyes. He didn't move, while the horse waited patiently behind him. "I don't know how to say this," Peter began. "But I feel something between us. Maybe the best thing I've ever felt."

She crumpled her cloak in her hands and told herself to keep moving through the gate, but she couldn't. Some truth in what he was saying felt right to her. He released the horse's reins, and then he let go of the gate, which creaked once on its hinge and stayed open. Deliberately, always watching her, he tugged at her cloak.

"What are you doing?" she whispered, but she let him take it and fold it over the top of the gate.

With one finger, he reached out to touch where her fingers were knotted together, and a spark shot into her, a tiny charge that changed how she breathed. She knew he wasn't supposed to touch her, but he was making a deliberate choice to do so, and she was letting him. *What are we doing?* she thought, staring at the exact place where his finger met hers.

Then he wrapped his index finger around hers, just one link, no more. She had to be nearer to him. She could trust Peter. She liked him. He never jerked her around emotionally or accused her of twisted, dark failings. She didn't dare look up into his eyes, but all it took was for her to tug his finger, the tiniest bit, and he slid his strong arms around her.

"I have wanted to hold you my whole life," he said.

She closed her eyes against his shoulder, breathing in the smell of sunlight in his shirt. "That first ride when I was asleep most of the time doesn't count," she reasoned. "You've only known me since yesterday."

"That's my whole life."

The strangest, most amazing thing was, she kind of knew what he meant. He certainly spoke as if he believed it, and she'd had very little of such sweetness. Instinctively, she knew what could happen if she tilted her face up, but she couldn't guess yet how it would feel, how it would be different from with Leon. She wanted to find out. It would help. She lifted her gaze to see his sturdy chin first, and then his little scar again, and then his eyes, expectant and beaming. Peter audibly caught a breath between his lips, so she could almost see it hovering there in the gap.

Spider whinnied.

Peter's arms reflexively tightened. Gaia glanced over, across the meadow, to where Chardo Will was standing at the back of the barn, a beam of lumber over his shoulder, his attention fixed in their direction.

CHAPTER 15

chicken

PETER RELEASED HER. Embarrassed confusion erased her happiness, and then, when she realized the trouble Peter could face, fear set in.

Will rested one end of the wooden beam on the ground, still looking at them. She kept hoping he'd leave, just go back into the barn, but he didn't.

"Will he tell?" Gaia asked.

"I don't think so. I don't know."

"I'd never accuse you."

"It wouldn't matter." Peter tossed her cloak to her and drew Spider through the gate. "A witness is just as damning as a mlass's accusation. I should have been more careful. I'll talk to him."

"Wait, I'm coming, too," she said, starting forward.

"It would be better for you to go down to the marsh. I'll join you as soon as I can."

"No. I'm not leaving you."

"Mlass, please."

She shook her head stubbornly and began marching across

the pasture toward Will. If Will wanted a confrontation, he was going to get it.

"It wasn't your fault," Gaia said. "Besides, nothing happened."

"Nothing did?" Peter said, striding beside her.

"I mean. You know what I mean."

"I'm not sure I do," he said.

Will leaned the beam of wood against the barn wall as they reached him.

"Hello, Mlass Gaia," Will said cordially. "Why don't you put Spider in the barn, Peter?"

"Nothing happened, Will," Peter said. "I have it on the best authority."

She met Peter's shooting gaze, and could only conclude he was hurt.

What? What did I do? We didn't even kiss.

"If you don't mind, I'd like a word with Mlass Gaia," Will said.

"I'm still going with you out to the island," Peter said to her.

"Give us a minute, then," she said.

Peter took Spider around the corner of the barn at a rapid clip, but even after they were alone, Will said nothing. He merely looked at her, skeptical. Disappointed.

A sort of frantic desperation rose inside her. "What?" she protested. "I couldn't help it."

"You'd better," Will said. "It's no joke here. I don't want to see him hurt. Or you." He put a hand in his back pocket, lounging his weight on one leg. "It's a lot for you. I get that. Especially with your old boyfriend in the game now, too."

"Why does no one believe he wasn't my boyfriend?" she insisted.

187

Will's lips turned in a sardonic half-smile. "If you have to touch someone, just make sure you don't do it in public. The rules are very clear. It can only lead to disaster."

He made it sound like she had to touch all sorts of people. "Duly noted," she said, annoyed. "Will that be all?"

Will glanced over his shoulder, then dropped his voice. "I've done three more autopsies."

It was the last thing she'd expected. "I thought the Matrarc told you not to."

"She wouldn't let me quit being morteur," Will said, "but I can't not be curious now that I've started. Two more expools had uteruses, so Benny wasn't just a freak anomaly. There could be a lot of others who do, too."

Gaia peered at him closely. "It's systemic. Why? What could be causing it?"

"That's what I've wanted to ask you. Could it be genetic?"

She wished she knew. Leon might. "It could be. It could also be some response to something in the environment."

"Something left over from the fish farm?" he asked. "I can't think of anything else that used chemicals on a large scale here. But that water is long gone by now."

"Without a lab here, there's no way to really find out," she said.

"I'd take any reasonable theory. It's been driving me crazy."

Gaia frowned at the new planks of wood in the barn wall behind him. "I could ask Leon what he thinks. He knows more than I do about genes and epigenetics and such."

He shook his head. "Please don't. I can't have word get out."

She was about to say Leon was trustworthy, but then she realized she didn't know that anymore. "Aren't you going to tell the Matrarc?"

"No."

Gaia turned and glanced uneasily across the meadow. "I know people trust you and we can't undermine that, but we can tell *her*."

"She told me point blank not to do any more," Will said. "I'm flagrantly disobeying her. The punishment for treason is exile."

"Then stop," she said. Will was doing exactly what Leon had said Gaia should have done to get him out of prison: lie, and then secretly disobey. "Why did you tell me?"

"Because you're the only one I *can* tell," he said. "We need answers."

"I don't have any!"

"Without a solution, we'll die here. It might take a couple more generations, but that's it."

"I think that's the point," she said. "I think that's the Matrarc's plan. Acceptance."

Will stared at her. "What did she do to you?"

She lashed out a hand. "Not you, too. I'm fine, all right? I'm just following the Matrarc's orders, like everybody else. And right now, I'm going out to the island for my sister. Let me just be grateful for that."

"I'm beginning to think gratitude is the opposite of curiosity," Will said.

His disapproval was obvious, and she didn't like it.

"That's supposed to be an insult, isn't it?" she said.

His frown softened somewhat. He reached a hand around the back of his neck, and her gaze went to the small mole at the base of his throat. "I didn't mean it to be," he said. "I apologize."

"All right then." She started away.

"Wait," he said. His brown eyes were troubled, and tension

189

was obvious in every line of his body. "Don't leave mad at me. The truth is, I've wanted to tell you something else, too, but I never see you alone."

She wrapped her arms around herself and waited grudgingly.

Will cleared his throat. "I'm here for you, Mlass Gaia. That's all," he said. "Anything you need. Anytime."

When he said no more, the silence stretched, filling with bigger implications.

"Will," she said uncertainly.

"I just thought you should know. You're it for me."

It was not a small thing he was telling her. And his timing was horrible. Then his mouth curved in a slow, honest smile, and his warm eyes told her all that his words couldn't.

Leon made her so miserable she wanted to die. In Peter's arms, she nearly liquefied. Will just had to smile, without even touching her, and she was purely confused. He certainly didn't seem too old for her anymore, if she'd ever consciously thought he was. She took a big, gawky step backward. She'd heard of love triangles before, but a love square?

"I can't believe I told you," he said.

She let out a laugh. "Well, you did, and I really have to go."

"I know. Go. Run."

She hurried toward the road and broke into a sprint. *Will!* she thought. *Peter.* And even worse: *Leon.* She let out a little squeak and then banished them all to think only of her sister.

Sunlight splashed around her in bright buckets of light as she ran in and out of the shade of the big trees, gripping her cloak around her arm. The familiar road curved past the lodge, then the willow and the pump, then past the smaller cabins. Soon the shore spread out before her, with morning light bright on the marsh, and the dark bulk of the prison in its yard on the right.

As the breeze turned, she caught a whiff of sour ash, and

saw the charred black remains of a bonfire with part of a burned stump still faintly smoking. A dozen men and women were grouped loosely beside a row of canoes that lay with their bottoms up, like giant, sleeping fish. Leon was among them, and a gust of wind blew to ripple his brown shirt and hair.

"Ready to go?" he asked.

"Aren't we expecting a note from the Matrarc?" she asked.

"I gave it to Vlatir already," Dinah said. "We think someone went out last night to tell Mlady Adele's family to be ready," she said. "But officially, they haven't heard yet."

"What if Mlady Adele doesn't want to come?" Gaia asked.

"She'll still have to give up the baby," Dinah said. "That's why we were discussing more canoes. The Matrarc said she would rather keep the security here in the village if you don't really need them." She nodded to another group of men farther along the beach, and Gaia realized they were guards.

If it came to taking Maya forcibly, Gaia didn't want to be part of it. She had memories of taking babies to give to the authorities in the Enclave, and didn't ever want to do anything like that again, not even to get her sister.

"I don't think I can do this," Gaia said.

"You're coming," Leon said flatly. "You do what the Matrarc tells you, remember?"

It was true. She looked back up the road for Peter and was relieved to see him coming down the slope. "Peter offered to go with us," she said.

"At least one person in the canoe will know how to paddle, then," Dinah said, amused.

Gaia hadn't thought of that.

"I can see I'll have to get involved," Dinah added. "Vlatir, I'll go with you. Mlass Gaia and Peter can take a second canoe. I may be able to help with Mlady Adele and the baby anyway."

"Fine," Leon said. Without another look at Gaia, he took an end of the nearest canoe to carry it into the water, and Dinah reached for the other.

"Need a hand?" Peter called as he neared.

"You're bringing Mlass Gaia," Dinah said. "We'll meet you out there."

Dinah knotted her red shawl across her chest so it couldn't slip free. With one quick, deft step into the water, she pushed off the canoe and settled in the stern. The wind caught the locks of her loose hair as she reached for her paddle, and with Leon in the bow, they pulled away from shore.

It took only a few minutes for Gaia and Peter to get arranged in another canoe, with Gaia in the bow, and she held tight while he pushed off.

"What do I do if we tip?" she asked.

"Hold on to the canoe and we'll swim it to one of the hillocks."

"I don't swim," she said.

"What?"

"I grew up by an unlake," she said. "In a wasteland. Nobody swims there." Gaia wedged her knees against the gunwales of the canoe to keep steady, and tentatively picked up her paddle.

"I won't let you tip." His smile was audible in his voice. "Most places it's so shallow you can stand anyway. Here. Watch what you're doing."

Her paddle banged against the side of the canoe. "What am I doing wrong?" she asked, pivoting on her seat to see him behind her. His light brown hair was almost blond in the sunlight. "Shouldn't you be wearing a hat in this sun?" she asked.

"Where's yours?"

"I forgot it. I had my cloak when I left the lodge this morning."

192

"I forgot mine, too." He jerked his chin up. "The clouds will help a little. You want to go, don't you?"

She did.

"Then put your right hand down here, by the blade," he explained, demonstrating with his own paddle. "And you keep your upper arm pretty much straight. Kind of roll with it. Use the power in your back and try to keep your strokes long and smooth."

"Like this?" she asked, trying. It felt different. Awkward.

"Not so stiff. And if you keep the blade flat, parallel to the water to feather it forward again, it cuts through the wind."

"There isn't that much wind."

"You like to argue, don't you?"

"I'm just saying," she said, trying another stroke. The water felt like black syrup.

"Air resistance instead of wind, then," Peter said. "When we go faster, it matters more."

On her next stroke, the water seemed thinner, and she was surprised by how easily her paddle moved until she realized Peter was propelling the canoe from the stern. She had to pull harder to feel like she was making any contribution to their momentum, and soon the canoe was winding through the labyrinthine water trails of the marsh. Peter could steer them within centimeters of a muddy hillock of reeds and bushes without grazing it, and then turn the other way a few meters later.

Gradually, they began to go faster. She liked the power of paddling, the rhythm of her strokes timed with Peter's, and the smooth, graceful swiftness of the water below her blade. It felt so, so sweet to be moving and using her muscles for something besides cleaning or peeling potatoes.

"Pace yourself, Mlass Gaia," Peter said. "It's going to take a while to get there."

193

She glanced ahead and couldn't see the island at all.

"It's there," he said, and she paused from paddling, looked back, and saw him pointing to his right. "The water path circles around this way," he said, "and then back. Like an S with a few extra loops."

"Why does Mlady Adele's family live out here?"

"Mlady Adele's mother and her mother before her always owned the island. Mlady Adele does now. Luke's a bit of a loner, too, so I guess it suits them."

She untied her cloak and dropped it into the canoe behind her. The water made a hollow noise against the belly of the canoe, and she could smell the sun-warmed mud in the marsh.

"What's that?" she asked, pointing to a box fixed to a pole, coming out of a hillock.

"That's one of Luke's station boxes," Peter said. "He tracks water temperature and other things in the marsh. It was your grandmother who got him started. That was even before he married Adele and moved out here. I think he's kept it up."

"What was he looking for?" Gaia asked, curious.

"I don't know, actually. You should drink," he added.

She pivoted to look back and saw him scooping with his hand.

"Right out of the marsh?" she asked.

"It won't kill you," he said, smiling. "Just don't scoop up anything big."

She didn't think he was joking. "But what about germs? Or fish poop? Don't you need to boil it at least?"

Peter laughed. "We do at home. But I never knew anyone to get sick from a little marsh water. Aren't you thirsty?"

She was, but she shook her head. "I'll wait."

"You can't swim, you like to argue, and now you're afraid of a little fish poop?" He laughed again. "Remind me why I came along with you."

She looked doubtfully down into the water, peering through her own dim reflection, while the sound of him drinking made her even thirstier. She tentatively dipped her hand and tasted the cool water, surprised at its freshness. "It changes everything, having all this water," she said. "You have no idea."

"How did you get water back in Wharfton?" he asked.

"The Enclave drew up water at the geothermic plant, then purified it for us," she said. "We got it from spigots in the wall."

"So you were completely dependent on them, weren't you? Was there enough water for you?"

She looked around at the marsh, and the seemingly endless supply of water right beneath the canoe. "Yes. Barely. I hauled it all the time."

"Did you ever think of digging your own wells?"

"Actually, my dad had ideas about that. He thought we should go to the bottom of the unlake and start drilling there." She remembered all the ingenious ways her dad had improved their home and garden. "But he never had time. Or a drill."

It was the first time she'd thought of him without a crushing sense of loss, she realized.

"You miss him?" he asked.

She nodded. "And my mother. But it's a little better." She looked around her again. "They would like it here."

He smiled gently. "I'm glad."

In the stillness, she heard the even notes of voices over water. She glanced back to see Peter wipe his wet fingers on his pants and reach for his paddle.

"They're not much farther ahead," he said. "Want to catch them?"

She did. The skin inside her thumb was raw, so she shifted her grip on her paddle as she pulled again. Most of the waterway was intricately twisted and narrow, but soon they came around another bend to find Dinah and Leon floating, their paddles across their knees, and the waterway beyond them opened up to a wider expanse five hundred meters long, like a proper lake.

Dinah was laughing. Leon was peering dubiously into his cupped palm full of water, and then he drank. He looked more relaxed than Gaia had seen him yet.

"Five-legged frogs," Leon said. "Mx. Dinah thinks that's normal."

"The wasteland boy thinks he knows more about the marsh than I do," Dinah replied.

Leon silently lifted his eyebrows, looking at Gaia for confirmation.

"Five-legged frogs are definitely not normal," Gaia said, smiling.

Peter, Leon, and Dinah began to debate the issue. Gaia glanced across to where a black and white bird, finer than a duck, was silhouetted against the water.

"Is that a loon?" she asked.

"Yes," Peter said. "And that's the lily-poppy just behind it. That white flower."

Just then the loon dove, vanishing.

"The weather's turning," Dinah said. "There'll be lightning. We shouldn't linger."

The sky overhead was still clear, but to the west behind them, a bank of clouds was gathering in a line that hardly appeared to move. This would be the second storm since she'd arrived, and she liked rain.

"We don't get much rain back home," Gaia said. "It mostly comes in the winter."

"Rain is rare for us, too," Peter said. "Those clouds could take all day to get here and then never rain."

Gaia glanced over to see that the canoes were even and she was head-to-head with Leon.

"Beat you to the end," she said impulsively, nodding down the clear, straight stretch of water.

"Want to make it interesting?" Leon asked.

"A bet?" she asked. She didn't have any money. "What for?"

"Winner gets a wish," Leon said.

"Who ever heard of a bet like that?" Dinah asked, laughing.

"What kind of wish?" Gaia asked. It was such a whimsical idea coming from him.

"Something small," Leon said.

Gaia glanced back at Peter, who shrugged.

"I'm in," Dinah said. "On your mark, get set, go!"

They shot down the straightaway. Gaia pulled her paddle with all her might and plunged it in again, over and over. Skimming the dark water, the canoes barely seemed to touch the surface. Foam gurgled under the front of Gaia's canoe. Her muscles burned, and she could see Leon's canoe gaining a lead on her right. She pulled even harder. Bow to bow, they flew toward the end where the waterway turned abruptly. Unless one canoe pulled ahead to win, both would converge in a crash.

Gaia didn't care. She was laughing inside, fully alive and paddling for all she was worth.

A wrenching drag caught back her canoe. Leon's canoe shot past. Dinah's laughter floated over the water and an instant later, the winning canoe was out of sight.

Gaia lifted her paddle out of the water, and leaned forward over her knees, her heart pounding. Peter, she realized now, had obviously dragged his paddle to slow them at the last possible moment to avoid a collision.

Now we know who the party-pooper is, she thought, and laughed, still gasping for breath. Peter began to paddle again, but Gaia didn't. Her arm muscles burned too much.

"That was fun," she said, and turned.

Peter's cheeks were ruddy from exertion, and his blue eyes were brighter than ever, the color of the sky in front of the thunderheads.

"Have you ever played chicken with Mx. Dinah before?" she added.

"No. But I knew she wouldn't stop. She has nothing to lose."

"That's deep," Gaia said, trying to look serious.

He smiled at her. "I should have let us tip so you could drown. Are you going sit there like royalty?"

"I'm thinking yes."

He made a motion to splash her and she laughed, gripping her paddle again.

As they came around another bend, the island rose in a gentle slope to meet a limestone cliff, and then shot up. Wind-twisted trees abounded. Dinah and Leon were already on the rocks, pulling up the other canoe. As Peter maneuvered their own canoe close to the shore and her vantage point shifted, she looked up the cliff again, finally discerning the edge of a roof at the top. A more windblown, isolated spot would be hard to find.

Gaia was about to step into the shallow water when Leon held out a hand.

"Allow me," he said.

Surprised, she reached for his hand, but then he shifted. In a strong, fluid movement, Leon braced one arm behind her back, the other behind her knees, and swept her up into his arms to carry her to shore. Caught off guard, Gaia was even more startled by the sensation of hard contact where her clothing met his. When he set her on her feet, his hands secured her with a light touch around her waist to be sure she had her balance. Her lips parted, her locked breath started again, and she lifted questioning eyes to his. His blue irises gleamed steadily through his dark bangs.

"You didn't need—" she began.

"Shh," he said softly, letting her go. "Wish granted."

He strode back into the water to lift the bow of the canoe and pull it up on shore.

That was your wish? To carry me ashore?

She was in trouble.

CHAPTER 16

bachsdatters' island

"YOU ARE AWARE she could put you in the stocks for that," Dinah said to Leon.

"Is that so?" he said dryly, like he couldn't care less, and handed Gaia her blue cloak.

Gaia felt her cheeks warm with color. She looked rapidly from Dinah to Peter, silently begging them to keep the uncondoned contact secret. The hug she'd had with Peter only that morning leapt to mind, and she could see the memory of it in his eyes, too. Why had Leon's maneuver felt even more intimate?

"Don't worry, girl," Dinah said. "We don't carry tales. I don't suppose anybody cares about my wish."

Peter gave a forced laugh. "Of course we do. What is it?" The second canoe made a hollow noise as he inverted it on the stones.

"I'd like a fire lit for me when I get home," Dinah said, smoothing her hair back from her face so her wide gray eyes showed clearly. "I bet it will be raining by then, and if, for once, somebody else set a fire in the grate and got it going, that would be my wish."

Gaia glanced over at Dinah, who always struck her as so competent and independent, and yet here she had this quaint

little request. She wondered if Dinah realized the lonely vul-
nerability she was revealing. Gaia glanced to Leon, who was
regarding Dinah thoughtfully.

"I'm on it," Peter said.

"Hello," came a voice from behind them. "Mx. Dinah! Chardo!
How are you?" A man strode forward, and Dinah made introduc-
tions.

To Gaia, Bachsdatter Luke looked like an extension of the
island itself. His worn, tidy clothes had been mended and washed
so many times that they were the same weathered color as the
stones on the beach. His beard was a soft brown, and his hair
was tousled and stiff from the wind. Deep set and dark, his
eyes gazed out from beneath straight black eyebrows.

"And at last I meet Mlass Gaia," he said. "Our daughter's
sister. Welcome."

"How is she?" Gaia asked.

"Considering how fragile she was when she came to us, she's
all right. These haven't been easy weeks." Bachsdatter glanced
toward Leon. "I know why you've come, but I can't credit that
you'll really take our daughter from us. You look like a decent
young man."

Leon didn't smile. "I'm not."

Bachsdatter scratched slowly at his chin and then made a
gesture to the sky. "Whatever we do should be decided before
this storm. Come along."

They began to climb a steep path that was, in places, chis-
eled out of the rock, and Gaia looked back over the distance to
see that Sylum was in shadow now. Around her the yellow
birch leaves rippled with a rushing noise in the wind.

At the top of the path, Gaia was surprised to find a little
settlement of half a dozen stone structures. They seemed older
than everything back in Sylum. An orchard and a garden lined

the far eastern edge of the hilltop, and chickens and goats wandered freely. A fenced area enclosed one long, low stone house and a profusion of bright flowers.

A woman was taking laundry off a line. Full-figured and strong, she nevertheless had a fragile, youthful profile. Her loose brown hair fluffed around her head as if made of spun silk and static electricity, and when she paused to face the visitors, Gaia saw her fine, narrow features were scattered with freckles.

"Adele," Bachsdatter called, opening the gate and leading them in. "Boles was right. We have visitors. Chardo and Mx. Dinah have brought out Vlatir and Mlass Gaia."

Adele took one long look at Gaia, lifted her basket and turned for the house.

"Adele, wait," Bachsdatter said. "We have to at least listen to them."

"They're not taking Maya," Adele said. "Make them go. I don't want them here."

Bachsdatter moved beside his wife and gently took the laundry basket from her. "We knew this could happen," he said softly.

"But she promised. Mlady Olivia promised!" Adele said.

"You don't have to be separated from your daughter," Dinah said. "It's only for a month. He wants Maya in the winner's cabin, but you can go, too."

"And leave our home? Why? Because he has some fetish?" Adele asked.

"I have no fetish. She'll be well cared for." Leon nodded toward Gaia. "I'll do everything I can for her, and her sister will be there, too."

"Her *sister*," Adele said, "nearly got her *killed*."

Gaia narrowed her eyes, looking more closely at Adele, taking in the sallowness of her complexion and the puffiness of her fingers. Shadows under Adele's eyes told a tale of deep fatigue.

"You're nursing Maya, aren't you?" Gaia asked.

Adele looked affronted. "Of course."

Bachsdatter stepped forward. "Don't you dare accuse her of neglecting Maya. If you could see what we've been through."

Gaia couldn't be entirely sure without examining Adele more closely, but the wary, angry expression in Adele's eyes confirmed what she suspected. Adele knew, even if Luke didn't yet, that she was pregnant. For her own health, and for the child she was carrying, she should not be nursing.

"Where is she?" Gaia asked.

"She's sleeping. You can't disturb her," Adele said.

"We have a letter from the Matrarc," Dinah said quietly. "Vlatir. Show them."

Leon uncrossed his arms and pulled a paper out of his trousers pocket. Dinah passed it over.

"I won't read it," Adele said, as if it were poisoned.

"Do you want me to, then?" Dinah offered, still holding it. "Don't you care what Mlady Olivia has to say?"

"Let the Chardo brother read it," Adele said. "Come here, Chardo," she added imperiously.

Surprised, Gaia turned to see Peter had remained back by the fence. All his normal casual grace was absent as he came forward in response to the summons.

"Avoid me for three years, and then you show up here," Adele said. "I believe you've grown a little taller even. Won't you say hello?"

"Hello, Mlady Adele," Peter said. A muscle tensed in his jaw. "Have you been well?"

"I have, as you see," Adele replied. "Now, was that so hard?"

"Don't do this, Adele," Bachsdatter said quietly.

Gaia watched the unfolding exchange with amazement.

Adele put her hands on her hips in a belligerent pose. "How's your big brother?" she continued.

"Will's fine, thank you," Peter said.

"He never did marry, did he? I suppose there's still hope for you, isn't there?"

Peter looked away, his ears red.

Adele pointed at the letter. "Read it," she commanded Peter abruptly. "I want you to be the one who tells me what the Matrarc says."

Peter slid a hand in his pocket. "I can't read."

Adele laughed harshly. "That's right, I forgot! Will's the smart one in your family, isn't he?"

"You don't need to harass him," Gaia said, snatching the letter from Dinah. "I'll read it." She wasn't the smoothest reader herself, but she spoke up for everyone to hear.

My dearest Adele and Luke,

I know you will greet this news with heavy hearts, but I plead with you to accept patiently what I must say. The bearer of this note, Leon Vlatir, has won the thirty-two games, and for his prize he claims a month with a female in the winner's cabin, as is his right. He claims your daughter, Maya.

The peace of our community now depends upon you. Vlatir, a newcomer, has been voted by the cuzines into full citizenship as a free man in Sylum, and I'm sure you can appreciate how delicate the situation is for all of us cuzines if we deny him the one privilege a man can legally claim. He has fairly won his prize. Indeed, he has overcome extraordinary obstacles to do so.

Please bring your daughter to the winner's cabin for one month. Your family will find no shortage of hospitality

in Sylum. Alternatively, you can give Maya into Vlatir's
care for the requisite time. I promise you no harm will come
to your daughter, and that I will be forever in your debt.
You may choose any compensation that is within my power
to give you to ease this sacrifice on your part.
In peace,
Olivia
Matrarc

Gaia glanced up as she finished and saw Adele sit down slowly on the stoop of her house. The change in her was sudden and complete, as if her essence had been erased.

"No," Adele said.

"It's all right," Bachsdatter said. "We can close up here for a few weeks. I'll come back to tend the animals. Or maybe I can get someone to come out. Barrett maybe." He peered around the yard in a lost sort of way.

"No," Adele said again, more loudly. She lifted empty eyes to her husband. "I think I always knew we'd have to give her up. I've tried to shield my heart from her. I've tried." She stopped, unable to go on.

A small, soft wail came from inside the house.

"Maya," Gaia whispered.

The cry came again, more plaintively. Gaia watched one moment longer to see if Adele would stir, if she would go inside to tend the crying baby like a loving mother would, but when Adele only leaned her head down into her arms, Gaia lurched past her and flung open the door.

The darkness of the stone house's foyer blinded her for a moment, but the cry came again from her left, and she squinted toward a small, low-ceilinged living room. The house was perched on the crest of the cliff, with a breathtaking view out a span of windows, but Gaia hardly noticed in her hurry toward the crib.

A tiny baby lay in the blankets, her hands waving in distress, her little mouth wide in a silent cry that, when she sucked in another breath, burst from her again. By then, Gaia held Maya in her arms, and she caressed the little head and body soothingly, hushing her. Ineffable joy spiraled through Gaia, even as her heart ached for the tiny girl. After a last cry, the baby tucked her head into Gaia's neck and made a soft, smacking noise.

When Gaia turned, Leon was standing behind her, his hand on the doorjamb. Emotion welled up inside her, gratitude and sorrow and alarm.

"She's so light and small," Gaia said.

She stepped to the window with the baby to see her better. With growing anxiety, she wiggled her fingers into the blanket to extricate the spindly legs of the baby. Maya should be bigger by now, with more fat on her bones.

Gaia peered at the baby's ankle. Faint, smudged, and only partly visible were the marks she'd tried to tattoo in her sister's skin the night she believed she was dying, only an hour before Peter had found them.

•

•

•

•

"It's really her," Gaia said, rubbing her thumb over the little marks. When Maya's gaze drifted toward Gaia's face, Gaia saw her father looking out from the solemn, infant eyes. It was uncanny.

"I don't know much about babies," Leon said, "but she doesn't look any bigger than she did back in the Enclave."

"She's not well at all," Gaia said. "She should be stronger by now. Look, she's almost three months old but she can hardly keep her head steady. Something's wrong with her."

"What would cause that?" he asked.

"Maybe Adele didn't nurse her enough. Or maybe Adele's milk doesn't agree with her." Gaia cast about for ideas, becoming increasingly irate. "Maybe she's allergic to something here. I don't really know, but she needs a change."

Leon came nearer, keeping his voice low. "You can't accuse Mlady Adele of not nursing her enough. The woman's distraught as it is."

"Leon, look at Maya!" Gaia said. She had to be mad at somebody, and who else but Adele?

The little baby's forehead was furrowing with distress, and she began to cry.

"You're upsetting her," Leon said.

Gaia spun away with the baby, cradling her near, and shushing her sweetly again. Her little, fuzz-covered head was so warm in Gaia's fingers, and tenderness that Gaia hadn't felt in weeks eased out of her sore, stymied heart, half breaking her open. She'd missed her sister more than she'd ever dreamed. What would her mother think if she knew she'd let Maya go out of her life?

She turned toward the door. She was coldly furious at everything in sight.

"What are you doing?" Leon said.

207

"I want some answers."

He stepped in front of her to block her way.

"It's enough that we're taking their baby," Leon said. "Do not go out there like this. I mean it."

She blinked hard at his solid frame, wondering if he'd really make her push him out of her way, and then, with a crumpling sensation, she turned back.

"I haven't done anything right," she said. "Not one, single thing since I got here. All those weeks wasted in the lodge! What was I thinking? I should have given in right from the start and bugged the Matrarc nonstop until she let me come out here to be with my sister. I should have found her a better wet nurse or weaned her onto something, like goat's milk or rice milk or something."

She glanced over at Leon, half hoping he'd contradict her, but she could see he agreed.

Looking at her sister again and the limp little way her fingers curled made Gaia want to cry. And she never cried. She hugged the baby tenderly against her chest, and fought back tears. She wished, for one awful minute, that Leon would hold her. She wished she could simply lean into him and have his arms around her, just this one time. He'd gotten his wish, after all, to carry her to shore. Shouldn't she get one? When she needed him?

Instead, he took a step backward, away from her. The distant, lonely sound of a goat bell tinked in the yard, and she looked past him toward the bright doorway.

"Promise me you won't be mean to Mlady Adele," he said.

"Now I'm the one being mean?" she asked. "You're the one who came out here to take her baby."

"Should I change my mind? Do you want to leave Maya here?" he asked.

208

She shook her head. There was no possible way she was leaving her sister on this island. "Did you know she'd be like this?"

"No," Leon said. He set a hand on a little yellow blanket that was resting over the back of a rocker. "I just knew that the Gaia I remembered needed her sister."

She lowered her face over the baby, holding her near, letting her hair hide her face from him.

"Thank you," she said softly.

He gave the rocker a little push to set it in motion and then stepped to the door. "Think nothing of it," he said, and let himself out.

bow and stern

ADELE NURSED MAYA once more in private while Gaia, Leon, Peter, and Dinah waited in the yard, watching the storm line progress slowly forward to cover half of the marsh in a dark, foreboding shadow. Wind came in fits, causing Gaia's eyes to water. Bachsdatter came out finally, carrying the baby.

"Adele and I are staying here," he said. "She's pregnant. There will always be a home for Maya with us here, but I can't disrupt my wife any more." He handed the baby in her yellow blanket gently to Leon, and then a bundle of clothes. "Some of her things," Bachsdatter added, then stopped to clear his throat.

"Come anytime to the winner's cabin," Leon said.

Bachsdatter nodded. "There's one more thing," he said, passing a small book to Gaia.

"What's this?" she asked, turning the volume in her hand.

"It's the records of the marsh I kept for your grandmother. I kept them up for a while after she died, but not as frequently. I think you should have them. Some of the notes are hers, and I expect you don't have much to remember her by."

She thumbed open the pages, seeing temperatures and other

measurements, records of weather and storms. "What do they mean?"

"She was always looking for evaporation patterns," Bachs-datter said. "The only one that ever made sense to me was that the water was getting lower year over year, but anyone could see that." He nodded at the clouds. "The storm made me think of it. That's the sort of thing she wanted me to write down." He looked once more at Maya, his deep-set eyes growing sad. "Go now. Quickly, please."

He said no more, but lifted a hand briefly in farewell and went back into the house. Gaia heard the muffled cry of Adele's voice from inside, and turned rapidly toward the path that led back down to the water.

"This is terrible," Dinah said, following after her. "Vlatir was so nice on the way out here. I was sure he would change his mind about the baby."

"It's simple. He has no heart," Peter said.

"Don't say that," Gaia snapped.

"Leave it, Gaia," Leon said.

"And it's not 'Gaia' here," Peter added. "It's 'Mlass Gaia.'"

Leon looked at Peter with obvious disdain. "If she tells me to call her 'Mlass,' naturally I'll oblige her. Heads up." He tossed Peter the bundle of baby things.

Leon led the way down the steep path. On the shore, they hurried to flip the canoes and ready them in the water.

"Can I have Maya?" Gaia asked Leon.

He nodded, bringing the baby near. "Hold her tight," he said.

Without further preliminary, Leon lifted Gaia again into his arms. Gaia held her sister in one arm and curled the other around his neck as he stepped into the water. He aimed her into the bow so that her feet landed in the triangular space before the wooden seat. Then he released her, touching his hand along Maya's blanket as he let them go.

He spoke next to her ear. "All set?" he asked softly.

She nodded, and since he was clearly waiting for her to look up, she did. He was very near. His expression was uncertain, curious, and then a satisfied light changed the opacity of his eyes.

Dinah coughed conspicuously. "Don't let us hurry you. All the time in the world."

Gaia looked down at little Maya and felt Leon straighten away. The canoe rocked slightly as Peter got in the stern, and then it jerked to life as he began to paddle. She kept her eyes on Maya, strangely aware that her pulse was still racing and that she was resisting an urge to look back for Leon. She adjusted her cloak around Maya, too, and watched as the baby was lulled by the rhythm and the watery noises until her little eyelids grew heavier. Gaia took a deep, even breath of her own.

"Is she asleep?" Peter asked eventually.

"Not quite. Soon, though."

Gaia caught her windblown hair out of her eyes and turned carefully on her seat so she could look back at Peter. He was concentrating on the water, sterning expertly through a narrow section, and she noted they'd already left the other canoe behind.

She remembered what Adele had said. "Is it true you can't read? Not at all?" Gaia asked.

"Why does it matter?"

She didn't like to think he'd never had a chance to lose himself in a book. "It just does," she said. "It says something about Sylum. So can you?"

212

He kept paddling. "I never learned."

"Can you write?"

"What's your point, Mlass Gaia? You want me to feel stupid, like Mlady Adele? Because it's working."

It wasn't like that at all. "I'm sorry," she said, startled.

"Apology accepted."

She needed to be more careful with him, she realized. Just because he was strong and considerate all the time didn't mean he couldn't be hurt. "Will you tell me about your history with Mlady Adele?" she asked.

"It's over, is what it is."

That clinched it then. She should turn around and let him paddle in peace, she thought, or in anger as the case may be, but when she started to turn, she heard him muttering.

"What?" she asked.

"I'm curious about your past, too."

Gaia braced a hand on the gunwale and shifted her knee to a more secure place. "What do you want to know?"

He shot his gaze briefly to hers, and then he paddled with strong, relentless strokes. "How did you ever get mixed up with someone like Vlatir? I don't get it. He's rude. He's cruel. He jerks you around. Is that what you like?"

"No. He's not always like that. He never was before. Or, actually—" That wasn't completely truthful, either. Leon had seemed cruel to her, back in the Enclave. Heartless, in fact. But then he'd changed, at least toward her. Now, with Adele, he'd used his cruelty on Gaia's behalf. Was it wrong to be selfishly grateful for that?

"This is strange for me," she admitted. "Where I'm from, I was never considered special. No boys ever paid attention to me. I figured I'd always be alone, with my work as a midwife. That was enough for me."

213

"Until you met Vlatir?"

She frowned, wondering how much to say. "There was nothing between us at first," she said. "I didn't even like him. But then, he began to change. He did things for me, like when I was in prison, sort of protecting me. Then he helped me unravel a code and get to my mother, who was also imprisoned." There were many memories there, more than she could ever summarize for someone who wasn't there. "He helped me, like now," she said slowly, tracing Maya's little hand. "Getting my sister back."

"You said he saved your life."

She nodded. "He did, when we were escaping the Enclave," she said. "There was a moment, this unbelievable moment, when he was able to push me through a closing door. It saved me, while he was trapped. I didn't know he planned to do it. But he did. I think—" She paused, struggling for the right words. Then her memory leapt back to earlier that same evening, and she could see the old Leon again, the one who had stood with her in an open doorway while the rain poured down just beyond, when there had been no reason to believe either of them would survive the night. "Is that all you do? Respect me?" he'd said.

She looked past Peter, back into the marsh, knowing the same person was back there now, no matter how different he seemed. "He must have cared for me more than I knew," she said at last.

Peter paddled another stroke and then paused. "Did you love him back?"

The question made her go very quiet inside, listening. "I don't know."

Peter's laugh brought her back to the moment.

"What's so funny?" she asked.

"It's not so much funny. But no matter how powerful your

gratitude and admiration are, they aren't a promise," he said. "He knows that."

We weren't talking about promises, she thought. "You know, you can be pretty annoying."

He laughed again, sounding even more relieved. "So can you."

"Tell me about Mlady Adele."

"Like there. That's annoying."

"I told you about me and Leon," she argued.

"You didn't really," he said.

"I certainly did!"

He smiled. "Not *everything.*"

She closed her mouth primly. He would just have to use his imagination for the rest, such as it was.

"Okay," he said. "But Will won't like it that I'm telling you. He hates this story."

If Will was involved, too, she had to know. "Tell me everything."

He squinted one eye against a gust of wind. "Mlady Adele used to be very different, nothing like she was today," he began. "I mean, she was always intense, but she was happier. Very sweet and creative. She was always coming by the barn, and Will fell for her hard. This was a good three years ago, I'd say. In any case, I used to tease him about how she was going to ask him to marry her." He shot her a quick grimace.

"I take it that didn't happen," she said.

"Worse. She asked me instead."

"But you—" She tried to calculate.

"I know. I was sixteen. She's only a couple years older than me, so the age difference wasn't so strange, but I knew how Will felt about her."

"So you said no?" she guessed.

Peter nodded, still paddling. "Adele's pride was hurt more than anything else. Men like me don't turn down women like her. But then she turned around and said she might as well take Will."

"Ouch," she said. That had to sting. It didn't take much to imagine Will a little younger, and idealistic, and disappointed.

Peter made a humming noise in the back of his throat. "Yes."

"Just how old is your brother?" Gaia asked.

"Now? He's twenty-two."

"So what happened then?"

"Well," he said, drawing out the word. "Will said no, too. A week later, the Matrarc assigned me to the outriders and told Will he'd make a good morteur."

"He didn't choose his job?" *But he's so good at it.*

Peter shook his head. "I know. He's good at it. But it wasn't raising horses like he wanted, and let's face it: being a morteur ruined any chance any other woman would want him. He's never had another offer. Never even come close."

Adele's revenge seemed unfair to her. Gaia glanced down toward the inner ribs of the boat as she pondered Will's predicament. She cared for Will. A lot. Just how much, she wasn't sure, but she valued what he'd told her behind the barn. It meant even more now that she knew he'd been burned before.

"Mlass Gaia?" Peter said slowly.

She needed to concentrate. She was missing something about Will, something that didn't quite make sense, and her cheeks were growing warm.

"And you?" Gaia asked.

He was still looking at her strangely. He'd stopped paddling.

"I mean, you must be—" she stumbled over her own tongue. "The mlasses obviously like you," she finished.

But he was still gazing at her with a faint crease between his eyebrows.

"You like my brother, don't you?" he asked. He calculated further. "Does he know? Of course he does."

She huddled into her cloak. "You make it sound like I can't like more than one person."

He let out a laugh. "He won't talk about you. My dad's always teasing him about you, and he won't talk about you at all."

"Peter," she began, but then realized she had no idea what to say. "I just got here a couple of months ago, and most of that time I spent in the lodge." She laughed helplessly, trying to explain. "I still hardly know anybody here, except maybe Norris."

"And you've got Norris wrapped around your finger, too."

He began canoeing again in earnest, and when she turned forward again, she could see Sylum growing larger on the shore. He didn't speak for a long time, and the reeds and lily-poppies passed in a steady blur of green and white. Then a hollow, knocking noise reverberated from the marsh behind them, followed by a ripple of Dinah's laughter.

"I said 'J-stroke,'" came the libby's voice, carrying clearly over the water. "It's about finesse, not muscle. You're not murdering the water."

Peter let the canoe glide silently forward. "They've switched positions," he said. "She's teaching him how to stern."

"Are you sure?"

There was another bang, and then more of Dinah's laughter. Apparently, she and Leon were getting along better again. Gaia listened intently, wondering if Leon was laughing, too. She'd never heard him laugh much. A frog croaked nearby.

217

"The Matrarc's asked me to stay in the village," Peter said. "She wants extra guards around for security since Vlatir's vote last night. She's called in a dozen of the outriders."

Gaia turned to see him again. "She has?" Her mind sifted the possibilities. "It's an opportunity for you, isn't it? Even at a ratio of nine to one, there have to be more mlasses in the village than there are out on your patrol."

"I met one out there," Peter said. "She turned out to be not so bad. I can't quite get a read on her, though, especially now that I know she likes my brother and she's reminding me I can meet other girls."

She was starting to blush again. "I'm sorry. I don't know what else to say."

"I've just never felt like I have so little control."

"You have to trust that things will work out all right," she said, shifting on her hard seat. "Sometimes it's not about control."

"Do you really believe that?" he asked.

She thought a moment, hesitating. Maya's eyelids were closed, and her tiny lashes splayed over her pale cheeks. Gaia stroked the soft skin wonderingly, noticing its contrast with her darker finger. A raindrop fell on the back of Gaia's hand and magnified the pores. "Yes," she said finally.

"Mlass Gaia," he said quietly, so that she looked cautiously up at him again. "I can see things are complicated for you. I'm not going to pressure you. But will you just promise me one thing? Will you please promise not to choose Vlatir while you're up in the winner's cabin?"

Her eyes opened wide in amazement. "You can't possibly mean what I think you're saying."

"I see how he looks at you."

Nervous energy swarmed in her gut, and she shook her

218

head decisively. "Half the time he despises me," she said. "There's no danger of me choosing him. None." She tilted her face, peering at him, and nearly laughed.

He shrugged. "Fine, then. Don't promise."

He sent the canoe skimming around another corner.

"Would it really make a difference to you?" she asked.

"Let's just say it's not going to be fun for me, knowing you're up there with him. My imagination is bad that way."

Looking up, Gaia saw the shore was not far ahead. A flicker of lightning lit the horizon, followed by a low growl of thunder. Soft plinks of isolated drops pattered the water around them in a gentle chorus.

"All right," she said. "This is the strangest promise I've ever made, but here goes: I won't make any commitment to Leon while I'm up in the winner's cabin. He won't ask, either."

"That part's not up to you."

"It still won't happen," she said. "I know him."

"Exactly. That's what concerns me."

Gaia tucked her sister more securely into her cloak and hovered over her to shelter her from the raindrops. She wondered if Peter would tell his brother about the promise, and considered it best not to ask. Peter drove his paddle deeply into the water, and the canoe shot forward around the last curve, skimming over the open water before Sylum just as the rain began to fall in earnest.

The other canoe caught up with them shortly after they reached shore, and with a final nod to Gaia, Peter went off with Dinah to take care of her wish about a fire. Gaia wanted to find Josephine as soon as possible, and Leon accompanied her to a part of Sylum Gaia had never seen before, where the cabins became smaller, as if beaten down by the rain. Men lingered under porch awnings, smoking, and watched wordlessly as they passed.

Down one muddy lane, the cabins became smaller still, until they were little more than shacks. The last one, hardly bigger than Gaia's chicken coop back home in Wharfton, had a wispy trail of wood smoke coming out of a pipe in the roof. A dark cliff rose up behind the cabin, and rain fell loudly on an over-turned washtub by the door.

"You think this is it?" Gaia asked, and Leon nodded.

"It's what Dinah described."

She settled Maya in her left arm and stepped forward to rap on the wooden door. No response came. Gaia looked at Leon, listening, and then she rapped again, harder, to be heard over the noise of the rain. There was a bumping noise from within, then a softer shuffling before the door opened. A shirtless man held the door wide and scowled.

"Yeah? What do you want?" He scanned his eyes up and down Gaia, then eyed Leon. "You're that crim, aren't you?"

"Is it for me?" asked a voice behind him.

"I'd say so," the man said, scratching his hairy chest. "Sure enough isn't company for Jezebel." The man hocked and spat out the door, narrowly missing Leon's boot. He moved out of the way as Josephine stepped into view, neatly if poorly dressed in a pale, loose shirt and gray trousers. She smiled in surprise.

"Mlass Gaia! What are you doing here? Don't mind Bill. He's my roommate's boyfriend, and a more piggish person would be hard to find."

"I heard that," came from the interior. "Where's my chaw? I just had it."

"How many of you live here?" Gaia asked, unable to mask her astonishment.

"Three and a half. The half's Bill."

"I heard that," came from the interior.

Josephine rolled her eyes. "What can I do for you?"

It turned out it wasn't hard to persuade Josephine to relocate to the winner's cabin and help nurse Maya. Josephine scooped up a few essentials, wrapped her daughter in a blanket, and headed out with Gaia and Leon.

the winner's cabin

LIFE IN THE WINNER'S CABIN gradually fell into a routine for Gaia, Josephine, Leon, and the babies. At first, Josephine was openly happy to take on the extra nursing of little Maya, rising to the demand with generosity and endearing modesty. But after three days and nights with little sleep between the feeding demands of the two infants, Josephine settled into weary determination. She drank and ate copiously and napped as often as she could, leaving diaper-changing, burping, and soothing of both babies to Gaia and Leon.

"Just call me a cow," Josephine said in her matter-of-fact way. "I don't mean to complain. You know I'd do this for you for free. I'll never forget what you did for me when I was having my baby."

"Don't be silly," Gaia said. There was a standard compensation for wet nurses in Sylum, and once the Matrarc learned that the Bachsdatters were staying on the island, she arranged for Josephine to be paid fairly.

One late afternoon, Gaia sat by lamplight in the old rocker, holding Josephine's daughter Junie while on the opposite side of the fireplace, Josephine nursed Maya. Outside, it had been overcast for eight days, ever since the storm, as if the sky were too stubborn to finish raining or fully clear. Wind rattled in the chimney and stirred the ashes, even with the flue closed.

"It's like having twins, I guess," Josephine said for possibly the hundredth time. "Bring me a cup of tea, won't you?" she added, lifting her voice enough so they all knew the request was aimed at Leon.

Near the glass of the window, where the darkness of the late afternoon cast a blue coolness over his skin, Leon aimed his gaze toward the deck and the valley beyond. At Josephine's words, he obligingly turned and walked into the kitchen. His boots made a hollow sound on the wooden floor.

"This beats having Bill around, let me tell you," Josephine said. She'd said that before, too.

"I'm sure," Gaia murmured.

"I just wish Xave could see me now. Do you think he'll ever come visit?"

"No."

Gaia glanced across the room, over the half-wall partition that divided the living room from the kitchen, to where Leon was dipping water from the bucket by the sink. He'd rolled his sleeves up his forearms, and the brown cotton delineated his muscles as he moved. She looked away. She lived in dread that he would realize how often she liked to study him, because the truth was, to her dismay, she had discovered just how easy it was to watch him perform even the most mundane task. There was a kind of efficient grace to everything he did, something in his smallest manipulation of a diaper pin or ladle that fascinated her. *This is beyond stupid*, she told herself.

As it happened, he performed a lot of mundane tasks.

Josephine seemed to take perverse pleasure in asking him to do the least thing for her, from handing her a napkin or bringing her a shawl, to adjusting a candle on the mantel so it wouldn't be in her eye. Leon never failed to assist her politely, as if he completely accepted that Josephine had every right to command him.

Gaia, on the other hand, couldn't bear to ask him to do the simplest thing for her. She felt indebted to him for having Maya back in her life and she was relieved that he was never again openly hostile, but never could she find a sign from him, like the day when he'd lifted her in and out of the canoe, that he cared for her at all. At worst, she had the feeling she was disappointing him. At best, he ignored her as much as possible, given that they were living in the same cabin.

It was driving her mad.

That madness, in turn, made her lonely for the comfort of Will's barn, and thoughts of Will made her edgy about Peter, too. It was new territory for her, all of it, and she didn't like being perpetually unsettled.

Leon brought Josephine the requested cup of tea and set it on a stool near her hand. His finger with the missing knuckle passed over the rim.

"Thank you," Josephine said, then yawned, covering her mouth. "You didn't bring Mlass Gaia any."

He looked gravely at Gaia. "Tea for you, Gaia?"

"Of course she wants some," Josephine said, laughing. "I don't understand how you can call her 'Gaia' and still be so formal." She yawned again, luxuriously. "I'm sorry. I'm so sleepy. It's this darkness. Start a fire for us, please, Vlatir."

Gaia felt him still looking at her. "I don't need any tea," she said softly. "Thank you."

"If you'll excuse me, then," Leon said, gesturing toward the hearth.

Gaia shifted her legs to be out of his way while he laid the tinder and the wood. He opened the flue, struck a match, and leaned forward. The flare of light outlined his profile as he held the match to a bit of bark, waiting until a tendril of smoke wisped toward the chimney and the first crackle sounded. He'd had someone cut his hair, and her eye was drawn to the bare spot of soft skin behind his ear. She half missed his wilder locks, but at least he'd kept some a little longer in front.

He turned, lifting his gaze to hers. Caught staring, she tried to look away, and couldn't. A sizzle came from the new fire.

"Excuse me," he said quietly, and gestured to her socks.

It took her far too long to realize she was blocking his way again.

"I'm sorry," she mumbled, tucking her feet farther back so that he could rise.

He reached to the mantel. "What is this?"

She glanced up. "My grandmother's sketchbook," Gaia said. The Matrarc had sent the package over to her the day before, and she'd put it with the notebook from Bachsdatter, but she hadn't had a chance to examine either of them.

"She was the former Matrarc, right? Mind if I take a look?" he asked.

"Not at all. I want to, too."

Josephine's eyes were closing with the soporific effect of the warm fire, and she surrendered Maya out of her lax fingers. With her black curls and a delicate pink in the dusky hue of her cheeks, Josephine looked very young, Gaia thought, especially falling asleep. She wondered if Leon ever noticed how pretty Josephine was.

He was busy settling the sleeping babies together like two cocoons in the bassinet. She moved quietly with him toward the other end of the room, where a table and hutch of dishes made up the eating area.

"How long do you suppose they'll all sleep?" Leon asked.

"Five minutes?"

He smiled slightly. If she didn't count unconscious people, Gaia was alone with Leon. She wished it didn't make her feel wary, but as she came nearer to the table, the room felt a little smaller, as if the panes of cloudy, late light that faced over the deck had moved inward several centimeters. She pushed back her hair from her face and stretched her arms overhead to loosen her stiff shoulders.

Several maps lay open across the table. "What's all this?" she asked.

He spread his hands on the wooden surface, leaning over it, and glanced up. "I borrowed them from Dominic the other day when he called me in to see him." He gave his head a little jerk to get his bangs out of his eyes. "I'm in the pool, by the way. For what that's worth."

"Congratulations?" she said, feeling awkward.

He met her gaze only briefly before looking away. "Thanks."

She turned back toward Josephine. "Maybe I should—"

"No. Stay," he said, and pushed one of the maps toward her. "This map's the most current, even though it's several years old. I'm trying to get a sense for how big the forest is, and why nobody can leave. Malachai said it wasn't worth trying."

"He's your friend?" Gaia asked, interested.

"Yes."

"He killed his wife, I heard."

"Yes. Strangled her. She'd abused him for years, and then he found her hurting their nine-year-old son. He couldn't let that start."

Gaia had never thought of a wife abusing her husband, and it was a stretch to think of big Malachai as a victim. "Is he sorry for what he did?"

"For killing his wife? Yes. For saving himself and his sons? No. I can't say I blame him." He drew one of the older maps toward him. "He's in for life." He spoke with finality, and Gaia sensed the subject was closed.

She swiveled the map in her direction. It was a well-worn paper, tattered around the edges from much handling. Faded lines extended out from the center of the village, like the spokes of a wheel, and an outer ring designated the perimeter of the forest, roughly oval, except where it bumped up against the marsh. Little X's and Y's and numbers had been carefully marked in clusters around different points, a palimpsest of records.

She hitched up her sock and took a chair, sitting on one of her ankles, while Leon occupied a chair kitty-corner to hers. "What's this?" she asked, pointing to a dotted line.

"That's the border the outriders travel, more or less." He tapped a point to the west. "This is where they picked me up, Dominic said. Here's where they picked up the nomads that came in the day of the thirty-two games." He glanced up at her. "You heard, right, that your brother Jack traveled with them?"

"What?"

"We got talking down at the prison. Those nomads were from a tribe that picked Jack up out of the wasteland."

"That means he's alive," she said, amazed. "Are you sure?"

"As sure as I can be. They heard I was from the Enclave and wondered if I knew him."

"Did they know anything about Old Meg?"

"I asked. They'd never heard of her," Leon said.

It was hard for her to believe the old woman had perished, even though that was most likely. *Old Meg was a tough old bird,* she thought. Conversely, she was happy to know her brother was alive, even if she never had a chance to be with him. "Did

227

you ever know a boy named Martin Chiaro back in the En-clave?"

"He was in the grade ahead of me at school," he said. "Kind of a skinny loner. His family makes the fireworks. He got in trouble once for starting a fire in the school playground, but that's all I really know. Why?"

"He's my other brother, Arthur."

"Really?" He pondered a moment, looking at her closely. Then he shook his head. "I'm sorry I don't remember any more. We were never friends."

What she really wanted to know was if Arthur had grown up happy, if his family had been good to him, but she'd proba-bly never know. "It's still something," she said. Gaia turned the map again and wondered where Peter had captured her. "The trail south doesn't go farther than the oasis," she said. "Did you go there?"

"No," he said. "It's odd that people here have never explored south, considering your grandmother obviously told them about the Enclave."

"They haven't been able to leave because of the gateway sickness," Gaia reminded him. "A hundred kilometers of waste-land is no small barrier, either. It's like we know there's a moon, but we don't try to go there." She reached for the book Bachs-datter had given her. "I don't even really know why my grand-mother left Wharfton in the first place. Why would she abandon her family?"

"Maybe she wanted to find somewhere better. When did she leave?"

"When I was one or two. I remembered her monocle, actu-ally, the one the Matrarc wears, but I don't remember her at all."

"After you were scarred, then, right?" he asked.

She glanced up at him. People rarely mentioned her scar

here, almost like they didn't even see it. In Wharfton, it had defined her so completely as an ugly outcast that she'd hardly ever been able to forget it. Now, it struck her that Leon saw her clearly, flaws and all, but in balance.

"Yes," she said.

"Why don't you wear your locket watch anymore?" he asked. She instinctively touched the bare place on her chest. "It doesn't feel right to. I can't describe it better than that."

"When did you take it off?" he asked.

"When I told the Matrarc about Peony."

"When you capitulated."

She shifted in her chair, resting her elbow on the armrest, and let herself look up at him directly. "Sometimes I feel like you understand me so clearly."

He tilted his face slightly, his dark eyebrows lifting. "I was just thinking what a complex mess you are."

"How so?"

He shook his head. "I don't want to get drawn into this with you. Not again. We're getting along fine for once. Let's leave it at that."

She stared down at the book in her fingers, feeling color warm her cheeks. "You started it, asking about my necklace."

"I just wanted to be sure you hadn't lost it."

"I didn't. It's with my midwifery things in my satchel."

"Fine, then."

She hunched back in her chair, taking the little book Bachsdatter had given her. She forced herself to focus on the pages before her, finding lists of dates, temperatures, and weather records for the swamp. They went on for four years predating her grandmother's death, daily, with obsessive precision. Then, ten years ago, Bachsdatter's handwriting continued less frequently, and finally tapered off altogether two years ago.

She peered closely, flipping the pages slowly, wondering why little brackets had been marked in the margins around some of the dates, with more in the winter months. Then she remembered Bachsdatter commenting on the storm, and checked the weather comments again.

"It looks like she was keeping track of the overcast days," she said.

"Let me see," Leon said, and she shifted so he could look over her arm.

"Why would she do that?" she asked.

He flipped a few of the pages. "There are dots here, too, by the evaporation numbers. It would make sense that there's less evaporation from the marsh on overcast days."

"But why go to all this trouble to confirm that? Was she trying to connect the evaporation to something else? To health problems?"

"Possibly."

"What's in the sketchbook?" she asked.

Leon passed it over, and as she opened it, a sheaf of folded papers fell out from under the cover, tied with a red string. The outer sheet was clearly addressed in black ink.

To Bonnie and Jasper Stone

"It's to my parents," Gaia said, astounded. "How can this be here?"

"Your grandmother must have written to them, hoping they'd find this here," he said.

She unfolded the letter, and a white card slipped out onto the table. The letter had no normal writing, but several pages of symbols.

It made absolutely no sense to her.

"Not again," she said. "What is with the people in my family? Why can't they ever write anything normal?"

Leon reached for the card and flipped it over. "This is normal," he said. "Better than normal."

She leaned nearer to see. There, painstakingly rendered, was a pencil drawing of a sleeping child, hardly more than a baby, her eyes closed, her little hand bunched under her chin. Each finger was carefully, perfectly drawn, down to the tiny fingernails. The artist had gazed closely at the child for a long time, and with unflinching skill, had also rendered the raw, burned skin that marred the baby's left cheek.

Gaia touched the card wonderingly. "It's me," she murmured.

"It hurts to look at it," Leon said quietly. "It must have killed her to draw it."

Gaia had never seen such a lifelike drawing, and it fascinated her. She wished the baby would open her eyes and look back at her.

"Are there any more?" she asked. "Are there pictures of my parents?"

She shook the leaves of the book, hoping for others to fall out, and a small black feather drifted to the table. The two white, squarish dots in the black made her think it was from a loon like the one she'd seen in the marsh. Gaia lifted it, turning it in the light to see its sheen, then held it over the drawing to hide the scar. How different, how untroubled the baby seemed then, with the evidence of her agony concealed. She shifted the feather away again to see the face complete with its scar.

Leon's chair creaked slightly, and she glanced up to see he was watching her closely, his eyes pensive. "You had people who loved you," he said.

She nodded slowly. It was an amazing, profound heritage to have, she realized. Her grandmother wasn't just some record keeper or political figure; she wasn't some elusive old woman with no personality or motivations. Gaia felt like she was tapping into something much deeper, something that was alive in her, just as it had been alive in her parents, too. For a moment, holding something as ephemeral as a feather, she felt like she and her mother and grandmother were the same person, sharing the same pain and love, just repeating in different generations.

"I don't know what this letter says yet," Gaia said, "or why she wrote it in code, but I bet it has to do with survival. She came to Sylum for a reason, and she believed my parents would follow, but I also can't think she'd go to all that trouble to lead them to a dead end. She must have been trying to find a solution, some way to reverse the girl shortage or leave again if she had to."

"How did she die?"

Gaia shook her head. "I don't even know that." But she would find out.

She set the feather aside to lift up the letter, turning it different ways. She examined the negative space between the symbols, but that didn't work. She shifted her foot out from under her, curling her knee up before her on the chair. "Why do you suppose Old Meg and my mother both told me to go to the Dead Forest? Mabrother Iris told me this place was a fairy tale."

He reached for the little black feather and stroked it idly over the table. "In the Enclave, we knew other communities must exist. How could they not? But I never heard of Sylum, specifically, until I came here. The Dead Forest figured as a magical, evil place in many of our children's fairy tales, full of witches and spells and fire, like a Land of the Dead. The Unknown. Mabrother Iris probably thought you were talking about that."

His voice trailed away, and she studied his profile, surprised to see that his focus had shifted to her hands. She held them still while a faint shiver crossed her skin.

"We had the same fairy stories outside the wall," she said. "But my mother was so certain, sending me to look for my grandmother. Like she'd heard of Sylum. I can't help thinking some nomads gave my mother a message or something, or just told her my grandmother was here. Will said the nomads call this place the Dead Forest."

"It makes sense that your mother knew something Mabrother Iris didn't," Leon said.

"You didn't believe in the Dead Forest, either," she reminded him.

"But you did. That was enough for me."

She looked across at him, watching him with the feather. There had been something in his voice that was different, almost tender. A faint ruddiness rose in his cheeks, though he wasn't looking at her.

She sat back, smoothing the fabric of her skirt close around her knee. "What's going on?" she asked quietly.

A shifting noise came from a log in the fire, and Gaia knew without looking that Josephine was starting to stir. She kept her gaze on Leon, who set down the feather and started to rise. A flash of lightning lit up the valley.

"Good luck with this," he said.

"You're giving up? I thought you were going to help me." She spread her fingers over the code. *You said we were getting along.*

"Maybe later."

"Aren't you curious?"

"I am. But this isn't a good idea, working with you."

"Why not?"

The delayed roll of distant thunder came up the bluff and rattled one of the window panes.

"Because of this." Very deliberately, he leaned forward to where her hand rested on the code, and brushed his knuckles across the back of her fingers, just once. Invisible electric particles hovered over her skin where he'd touched her, and she didn't dare move. Wide-eyed, she lifted her gaze to his face, and still he wouldn't meet her eyes.

He tightened his fingers in a fist and examined his hand, as if questioning the sensitivity of his own skin. "You see, that's a little problem," he said calmly. "At least for me."

She couldn't even move. *For me, too.*

He turned, strode up the steps, and headed out the door. Moments later, she heard the unmistakable thwok of wood being split, and the noise kept up with tireless regularity for the next hour.

CHAPTER 19

lightning bugs

O VER THE NEXT FEW DAYS, Gaia was careful not to be alone with Leon again, and where before she'd been watching him, she now had the sense that he was watching her, and not with any particular pleasure, either. He unsettled her in a way that touched everything. If he was in the same room, she was aware of him. If he wasn't, she kept expecting him to return. Worst of all was when he went down into the valley for supplies and more water, because he could be gone for half an hour or half a day. The only thing that gave her relief was when she was inside and could see him out on the deck, where he sometimes took Maya or Junie and paced slowly, looking out over the valley. Then she knew where he was and what he was doing, and that he wasn't looking at her.

"You're so fidgety," Josephine said one night. "I'd say to smoke some rice flower, but you don't do that, do you?"

"No."

Josephine sighed. "It's the darkness getting to you. Everyone always smokes more as the days get shorter. It would make you feel better."

Gaia was alarmed. "You're not smoking while you nurse, are you?"

"No," Josephine said. "But honestly? I'd be tempted to if I weren't. Jezebel smokes all the time, whenever her headache starts, and she's much more mellow when she does." She laughed, waving a hand to indicate the living room. "This sure beats having Bill around. Are you still working on that code?"

"Yes," Gaia said.

Josephine was changing Junie's diaper, but when she finished, she came to look over Gaia's shoulder. Gaia leaned back to let her see. In the new sling Gaia had made, Maya was awake, looking around placidly, but her little eyes focused on Gaia, and after a concentrated look, Maya gave her baby smile, all gums and pure joy. Gaia couldn't help grinning back.

"It could just be nonsense, you know," Josephine said. "Your grandmother was crazy."

"I beg your pardon?" Gaia said.

Josephine sat in one of the armchairs by the table. "Nobody wants to tell you, but she was crazy by the end. She started wading in the marsh at night. Did you know that?"

"What are you talking about?"

Josephine nodded. "Ask Mx. Dinah or Norris. Or the Matrarc. They'll tell you."

"Why don't you tell me? What else do you know?"

"I was just a kid, but I'm pretty sure that's why the cuzines voted her out."

"What?" Gaia had thought her grandmother died as the Matrarc.

Josephine raised a hand to her mouth. "I'm sorry. I thought you knew. She was a great Matrarc until near the end. Then she got crazy ideas. She tried to make the expools leave Sylum.

236

I don't know what all else because that's about when the cuz-ines voted her out."

"Then what happened?"

"Mlady Olivia moved in with her and took care of her, up here in her place on the bluff, and then she ran away that time and Norris found her. You know, dying."

Gaia didn't want to believe her. Josephine did not strike her as the most accurate source for information, but at least a little of what she said must be true.

"I didn't know," Gaia said. She rested a hand around Maya and looked again at the sketchbook.

"I just don't want you to pull your brains out," Josephine said. "That's all I meant. It might not make any sense." She switched Junie to her other shoulder. "What else is in her sketchbook?"

"Tons of drawings, of water towers and pipes, mostly."

There was a thumping noise out on the porch, and both of them started.

"That must be Vlatir," Josephine said, and went to get the door.

Gaia scrutinized the code again. If her grandmother had in-deed been mad, she'd had a very precise, tidy madness. Gaia didn't buy it. She remembered putting pencils between the lines of the last code she solved, and reached for a wooden spoon, trying it this way and that. With the spoon in a vertical position, she paused.

She peered more closely, fiddling the spoon along the edges of the letters. They didn't quite line up, but then she thought she saw something.

Josephine's laughter came from outside.

Gaia peered again at the symbols, wishing she had a pencil and some clean paper. She rose and went to the bookshelf where some supplies were stored and dug around until she found a quill, a bottle of ink, and some scraps of paper.

Josephine was laughing again, and Gaia looked up as she and Leon came in. He had his hands carefully clasped together before him. As he looked at Gaia, his eyes were warm, and a smile hovered at the edge of his mouth. He looked happy for once.

"I've brought something for Maya," he said.

Gaia's heart turned over. She pulled her sister out of her sling, propping her upward in the nook of her elbow so she could see, and Leon came nearer.

"Ready?" he gently asked the baby.

He slowly opened his hands. On his calloused palm was a long black bug, completely unremarkable until it glowed green for a steady instant. Gaia gasped, delighted, and then it went black again. The baby, unimpressed with the bug, was staring at Leon's face with her intent concentration, and then she smiled again.

Leon laughed. "The meadow's full of them." He closed his hands again before the lightning bug could fly away. "Come see."

"What are they doing out in November?" Gaia asked. She'd never seen lightning bugs this late.

"It makes no sense at all," he said, "but you have to see them."

Gaia left her things on the table, slipped the sling off over her head, and carried Maya out to the porch. Leon held the door for Josephine to follow, but Josephine, smiling, shook her head.

"I saw," Josephine said. "They're beautiful. Junie's asleep, though. I'm going to sleep while I can, too. Maya ought to be able to go for a few hours, but call me if she needs to nurse."

Gaia paused on the porch beside Leon and stared in wonder. It seemed all the stars that had been missing from the sky for the last two weeks had come down to delicately gleam in the meadow. Tiny moving lines of light blinked on and off, overlapping and skimming with no noise of their own, while crickets kept up a persistent chirping that filled the night air with vibrating sound. She'd never seen anything so lovely. She walked barefoot down the stone steps, drawn to the ineffable beauty. Even the night air smelled soft. Dry grass prickled between her toes as she stepped gingerly into the meadow, where soon the tiny lights were all around her.

"It's amazing," Gaia said.

"I thought you'd like it."

She looked back, just able to make him out by the faint light from the cabin. He leaned a shoulder into one of the pillar beams of the porch and slid his hands in his pockets, lounging and relaxed. She wished she could see his eyes. She held up her hand in the darkness, wondering if one of the lightning bugs would land on her, but they came no nearer to her dark fingers. The whole thing made her laugh with pleasure.

"They're like music," she said.

"I know. Or flying."

She zoomed Maya smoothly through the air in three big, slow swooshes, careful to support her little head. "Come out with us," Gaia said.

"I'm good here," he said.

"Why not?" she asked.

"You know why."

She looked over. "I don't," she said. "Is it that you like me and don't want to, or that you don't like me?"

"None of the above."

The light from behind him faintly outlined his shirt, revealing only that he wasn't moving. She felt something strange and magnetic between them, something that defied labeling, yet it was tinged with sadness, too, or longing.

"You're deliberately being enigmatic," she said.

He laughed. "Not at all."

"Then come out with us."

"That sounds suspiciously like a girl command," he said lightly. "You're learning from Mx. Josephine."

"No, I just want—" She broke herself off.

"Yes?"

You near, she thought. She couldn't say it. A twisting feeling happened inside her, making her hug Maya tight again.

"You enjoy the bugs, then," he said. "I'm heading in."

He straightened away from the post and let himself in the screen door, closing it softly. Gaia turned slowly in a complete circle to see all the lightning bugs glowing around her. They were still beautiful, still incredible, but without him to share them with, they'd lost their transcendent enchantment. She held Maya near to her neck and scanned the dark sky, not finding Orion or any stars through the cloud cover, while inside she just felt confused. Just plain uncertain and anxious and hungry. It was an awful combination. Shivering, she stepped carefully toward the cabin again.

She slipped in the screen door, blinking toward the lamplight in the living room, and as she stepped forward, he came into sight on the far side of the dining table. He was inspecting her grandmother's code, fiddling with the spoon.

"There's something here," he said. "With the symbols. But they don't line up."

His manner was direct and openly curious. She hesitated, considering. Perhaps, as long as they restricted their exchanges to a practical level, they could last all the way through a normal conversation. At least there could be a chance of a friendship with him this way.

"I know," she said, coming down the stairs with Maya over

her shoulder. She would try, at least. "Look, here." She pointed. "Right next to the spoon, it looks like half a letter's missing, and then the next one below it, too. I think she sliced letters apart, and then squished the halves together."

"Down the page?" he asked.

She nodded. "It must be, because going across doesn't work at all. I was going to redraw them."

"Why don't you try? I'll hold Maya."

She passed over the baby, then opened the ink and dipped the quill. Carefully, she copied each character from the first column directly beside the next, only running left-to-right across the fresh sheet instead of from the top down.

kaavethenniasmaadddictsandgo

She straightened slightly to see the message. She puzzled over the long string of letters until she could separate them into distinct words:

leave the miasma addicts and go

"Is *miasma* even a word?" Gaia said.

"It's an atmosphere, a fog," Leon said.

Gaia stared at him, her mind scrambling, and saw he was thinking fast, too.

"It's not the water of the marsh that's toxic," she said. "It's the fog. The evaporation. It's in the air around us all the time."

He nodded. "I'm not ruling out that the water might be toxic, too, but the miasma makes some sense. An odorless gas local to the marsh could certainly be addicting."

"Especially if it's based in the lily-poppies," she added. She was already reaching for the quill again. "Like they're essentially cooking in the sunlight. We're always breathing. That means we're constantly getting a low-grade fix. Could we all be addicted to the miasma without even knowing?"

"Think about us when we first came," he said. "We had to adapt to the air, but once we did, we didn't have any symptoms anymore. Everyone else has been used to the air here since they were born."

"And think of Maya," she said. "She had a terrible time out on the island. She was a baby on drugs."

"The miasma could be even stronger out there," he said.

"I think my grandmother was studying everything she could about the marsh because she was looking for a cure for the miasma addiction."

"That's likely. But the miasma addiction doesn't explain the shortage of girls," he argued. "All those X's and Y's on the map are probably births of girls and boys, by location. She was trying to find a pattern there, too."

"They could be two unrelated things," Gaia said. "Suppose the miasma addiction keeps people here. Something else could turn the girls into boys." She reached again for the letter to her parents.

"What did you say?" he asked slowly. "About the girls?"

"I just mean the girl shortage could have a separate cause."

She fingered the pen to copy out more of the letters, but Leon reached for the bottle of ink and moved it out of her reach.

"What else do you know?" he asked. "What do you know about the girls?"

Gaia glanced up. He regarded her intently.

Too late, she realized what she'd said. "I have a theory about the girls," she admitted.

"Let's have it."

"I think girls are being turned into boys," she said. "Maybe there's some hormone left over in the marsh from when it had a fish farm, something that's getting more concentrated the more the water evaporates, or something that seeped into the soil of the marsh and keeps bleeding into the water. Is that possible?"

243

"There was a fish farm here?"

She nodded. "For years."

Leon regarded her pensively. "Some fish farms used hormones to raise only male fish. They were more uniform in size that way, which made processing them easier. We thought about it for hens back in the Enclave, in reverse, but it wasn't practical." He tilted the ink bottle idly, not quite spilling it. "Could the hormone mimic originally intended for fish now affect humans? It's a stretch. I suppose, hypothetically, the expools could be XX males who were exposed. It would have to be early, while they're in utero," he said. "They would be born as boys, but their chromosomes would be female. That would make them infertile."

"They'd still look like men, though, right?" she asked. "But with female parts inside?"

He studied her before he answered. "They could. This is an unsubstantiated theory, I'm assuming. Right?"

She couldn't reveal what she knew from doing the autopsy with Will. "Whatever I know is in confidence."

His chair creaked as he leaned back, still holding Maya, who had dropped off to sleep in his arms. "A secret," he said. "You have a secret that could make a difference, and you won't tell me. You'll tell the Matrarc about Peony, but you won't tell me some random thing about the expools."

She shifted uncomfortably against the table. "I can't. And it doesn't make a difference. It's a dead end. There's no way to reverse the hormone mimic, is there?"

"No. You can't cure a man of that kind of sterility, and if it's in the water, it's in everything. You can't purify it out of the environment to prevent future XX males. What if I promise to keep it a secret, too?"

She hesitated, then shook her head, steadfast. "I still can't. I made a promise."

"A secret and now a promise," he echoed. "You do realize a promise is a level of loyalty. Are there any secrets of mine that you keep from anyone else?"

"Of course."

"Such as?"

She hesitated, reluctant to exhume the twisted, haunting loss of his sister.

He waited.

"I'd never tell about Fiona," she said quietly.

For a long moment he stared at her, expressionless, and then he shrugged. "People here can't speculate about rumors they've never heard, so they'd never ask you. Maybe there is one good thing about this place," he said dryly. "Tell me just this: Is it Peter's secret you're keeping?"

She had one of Peter's secrets, too. "Don't ask me, Leon," she pleaded. "It doesn't make a difference. We've identified the miasma addiction and that's all that really matters. I'll just decode the rest of these pages, and we'll go from there to find a cure, all right?"

He stood slowly. His lips closed in a taut line. "You know, I told myself I wouldn't do this, but here I am again, anyway. Trusting you."

"You *can* trust me."

"No," he said quietly. "I can't. Not when you pick through my brain and won't let me into yours. Take her, please." He passed the sleeping baby carefully into Gaia's arms.

"What about the lightning bugs?" Gaia reminded him.

His gaze flicked to hers and then away. "They were too pretty. They conspired against me. I'll know better next time."

He went to his bedroom and closed the door.

Gaia sank back in her chair, miserable and confused. It was easier, by far, when he kept his distance, but he could reach into her faster and more tenderly than anyone she'd ever known. *Lightning bugs.*

She groaned.

She frowned down at her sister, jealous of the baby's peaceful sleep, but too restless to go to bed herself. A few minutes later, when she heard the sound of water out on the porch, she lifted her head, listening. He had to be washing up.

She curled her leg up beneath her, keeping Maya in one arm, and reached for the quill. Carefully, she copied over her grandmother's code, separating the symbols into logical words as she went, and starting a new line for each group of symbols.

> *leave the miasma addicts and go*
> *i have no proof none believe me*
> *labor wasted on fools if*
> *you read this my bonnie*
> *obtuse not be smoke i*
> *regret i ever left you or urged*
> *relocating to a better*
> *ideal place none exists go back to*
> *cruel unlake for gaias sake*
> *else we all die*

Gaia read the message over, and each time her heart sank more. Regret, urgency, and scorn. Were these her grandmother's legacy to her, after all? Why had she bothered putting this bitter, spiteful message in a code to keep it secret? So none but her parents could read it, she thought.

She set the pen down and cuddled Maya closely. "But how do we leave?" she whispered. "If Sylum is a death trap, how do we escape?"

She left the poem and her notes on the table in a tidy pile for Leon to see when he awoke. If he cared to.

The next day, Gaia headed down to the lodge with Maya in her sling to pick up more of her midwifery herbs and found Norris in the kitchen, peeling potatoes. Sawyer, who had found Peony's box under the tree, was helping him, but when Norris saw Gaia, he urged her to stay for a visit and sent the boy out. He stopped peeling to inspect Maya, and his stern features softened.

"She's cute," Norris said. "How's the winner's cabin? I could come up and chaperone you, if you want. I talked it over with the Matrarc."

She set her basket on the counter. "Mx. Josephine's enough," she said. "I appreciate the offer, though." The truth was, she'd come down to the lodge in part to avoid the awkwardness of seeing Leon again that morning. She could feel Norris's gaze upon her and knew she was starting to blush.

He made a humming noise. "You watch yourself," he said "The idea is, a man's supposed to give you a chance to get to know him. He's not supposed to pressure you in any way."

"Leon doesn't. We hardly speak most of the time. Besides, I'm not technically his prize."

Norris chucked a potato in a pot with a bang. "He doesn't seem like the sort to let a technicality get in his way."

"You're worried about me, aren't you?" she asked, smiling.

"Course not."

Gaia laughed, pleased. "Did you know you look like a pirate, Norris?"

"Okay. Enough. Get out."

She laughed again, taking a stool and picking up a potato.

Norris passed her a paring knife. Maya slept peacefully in the sling, her warmth snug against Gaia's side while Gaia peeled. "Mx. Josephine told me my grandmother was crazy. Can you tell me anything about her?"

"Mlady Danni? Sure. She was full of new ideas when she came," Norris said. "Like the water towers, and it was her plan to irrigate farther up to where the cornfield is now, too. People had been worrying about the girl shortage privately, but your grandmother took it on directly. She made having children a top priority, a civic duty. Very forthright she was, and people listened to her. I think they were relieved. That's why the cuzines chose her for our leader."

"She wrote my parents a letter warning them to leave if they ever came here," Gaia said.

"That fits," Norris said. "Ironically, people become more complacent with all the improvements she started, but your grandmother got more and more worried." He paused in his peeling to point his knife for emphasis. "She predicted the girl shortage was going to get much worse, and fast. It drove her frantic that people weren't listening to her. She wanted us all to leave Sylum, but of course, we can't. By the end, she was obsessed with trying to go herself. That's what killed her."

"Mx. Josephine told me you found her," Gaia said. "But I don't know any of the details."

"Your grandmother was headed south, toward Wharfton. She made it past the oasis down that way. It was an ugly death, Mlass. She had seizures and shakes." Norris propped the point of his knife on the table. "If you really want to know, she was trying to claw her own eyes out when I found her. I'll never forget it."

"What did you do?" Gaia asked, appalled.

"What could I do? I packed her up on my horse and raced

back with her as fast as I could, but she was too far gone. By the time I pulled into the commons, she was dead."

Gaia couldn't get over the idea of her grandmother clawing out her eyes, as if she had been seeing things. Hallucinating.

"There's something else," Norris said. "I never told this to anybody. Your grandmother was opposed to smoking anything. She liked to say that smoking made us all shiftless and boring, actually, but when I found her, she had a pipe full of the lily-poppy. Mlass Gaia, nobody smokes the lily-poppy. It isn't mellow like the rice flower. I think she was experimenting on herself and it went wrong."

She tried to remember something Peter had said about the time he had left. "Did you smoke anything yourself?" she asked. "On that trip?"

He nodded. "I smoked a little rice flower. I did regularly back then."

"I've never seen you," she said. "Did you quit?"

"I quit the day I lost my leg." He rubbed at his knee. Una came around and jumped in his lap, and he let go of his knife to pet her with his broad hands.

"You never told me about that," she said.

"You never asked," Norris replied. "I wanted to leave Sylum, too. I figured if your grandmother could try it, so could a big strong expool like me. But no. My horse rolled into a ravine and broke its neck. I lay trapped under him for half a day before Chardo Sid found me and brought me back. The doc sawed off half way down my shin, cauterized the end, and there you have it."

She felt her eyes going wide as she imagined the mechanics of sawing through a man's bone. "What did you have for the pain?" she asked.

"I had me a nice-sized pouch of black rice flower, so I packed up my pipe and I smoked all of it while I was under that horse," he said. "Or do you mean for the surgery? I passed out from the shock. Didn't think I'd ever wake up." Una made a loud purring noise and closed her eyes as he rubbed between her ears. "I promised to be grateful for what I have and give up smoking, if only I survived somehow. I won't say I don't miss it from time to time. The Matrarc, she helped me. She gave me the job here in the lodge and told me I couldn't predict what I'd been kept alive for. I've thought about that lately, with you here."

Gaia glanced at Maya, lingering on the beautiful little face. "I'm afraid I'll let you down, Norris."

Keeping his hold on Una, he reached up, took down a small jar of honey from a shelf, and tucked it in her basket.

"What's that for?" she asked.

"I know you like it in your tea," he said. "You can share with Mx. Josephine and Vlatir, but only if you want to."

Gaia picked up her basket and pointed to the honey. "That, right there, is why you were kept alive," she said.

He laughed, jogging his big eyebrows. "And you won't let me down, Mlass Gaia. Never worry about that."

Gaia considered telling Leon about Norris's ideas, but she never had the chance. He developed an uncanny ability to appear only when Josephine was also already present and evinced no interest in resuming their conversation.

In time, Maya began to grow. First her fingers filled out from bony stubs to slender, curving, flexing fingers. She seemed to change by the hour as her cheeks filled out and her head wasn't as wobbly. Junie was sleeping through the night, and Maya's length between night feedings began to stretch from four hours to five. The first night Gaia was able to sleep six hours in a row with no babies waking her, she rose astonished at how well-rested she felt. The timing was especially sweet since she'd been at a childbirth earlier in the night and had badly need the rest.

Josephine smiled from the other bed in the room they shared. She was already nursing Junie, and Maya, miraculously, still slept, her cheeks rosy and serene as she lay in the little bassinet. Beyond her, through the window, it was as gray and overcast as ever, but inside it felt sunny to Gaia.

"I have a good feeling about today," Josephine said.

Gaia curved her cheek into her pillow again, smiling. "I agree."

"You'll never guess who dropped by while you were gone last night. Mlass Taja," Josephine said. "I hadn't talked to her in ages, not since before the trial for Xave, but she was very nice. She says there's rumors about you."

"Not bad ones, I hope."

"Are you trying to help the men get to vote?" Josephine asked.

"I think they should vote," Gaia said, startled. "That doesn't mean I've done anything about it. Who's saying that?"

"Mlass Taja wanted to know if you'd said anything. I told her no." Josephine fluffed her dark hair. "I'm sure it's nothing but her normal paranoia. She's ultra protective of her mother. Want to know a secret?" She smiled mischievously.

"What?"

"Vlatir washes out his shirt each night in the tub on the porch. I've seen him. I think he hangs it in his room to dry overnight. Isn't that sweet?"

That had to be what he'd been doing the night of the lightning bugs when she'd heard water outside. Gaia guessed that he valued clean things more than ever since his time in prison. She'd felt the same way. "He should hang it near the fire to dry faster," she said, "and he needs more clothes."

Josephine laughed. "That's just what I was thinking. Should we make him another shirt?"

Considering all her father had taught her about sewing, making a shirt was well within Gaia's sartorial abilities, but there was no way she would do anything so personal for Leon. Just the thought of handling fabric that would cover his skin made her feel strange.

"Count me out," Gaia said.

"Why not? What's with you two, anyway?" Josephine asked. "I mean, he's so incredibly handsome and smart. And intense. Those eyes." Josephine exaggerated a brooding squint.

"All right. I get it," Gaia said, sitting up and pushing her pillow away.

"No, really, Mlass Gaia," her friend insisted. "Why don't you try being nicer to him?"

"Me be nicer? He's the one who's so distant," Gaia said. "He may be courteous on the surface because he can't help it, but deep down, he doesn't trust me. He's told me so. I thought we were doing a little better, but now he hardly even speaks to me anymore."

She'd never guessed that strained, ongoing awkwardness could be its own art form of torture, but it felt like it. The winner's cabin had probably never resulted in less interaction for the winner.

"What are you talking about? You're the one who hardly talks to him," Josephine said. "He's always baking stuff for you, and putting flowers on the table for you, and washing diapers."

"He's doing that for both of us, and for the babies," Gaia explained.

Josephine let out another laugh. "Okay, if you say so. But

then why is he all itchy and moody whenever you're gone? Why is he watching you all the time? Again, with the eyes."

"Please don't. It isn't funny."

"I'm just saying. He's a lot cuter than both of the Chardos combined, and that's saying something. Peter alone about kills me."

Gaia felt her cheeks burning. "You're being ridiculous."

Josephine smiled brightly. She poked a finger at Gaia. "You should see your face. Mlass Taja told me the Chardos have been asking about you, too."

"Leon didn't happen to be in on this conversation, did he?"

Josephine tilted her face to consider. "I don't recall. He was coming and going, like he does." She sighed. "I'm going to miss living up here."

Gaia reached for her skirt and her blouse. The pointless eternity in the winner's cabin couldn't end soon enough to suit her.

innocence

L ATER THAT MORNING, the Matrarc sent up for Gaia to attend another childbirth, so she headed down to the mother's cabin on the commons, and arrived just as Mlady Beebe's labor seemed to stall. She rolled up her white sleeves, washed her hands, and planned to stay through the rest of the day. Most of helping Mlady Beebe involved keeping her comfortable and calm, and trying a slow walk around the backyard. It was Mlady Beebe's eighth child, and she was weary but not anxious. "My labors are always slow like this," she said. "I'm sorry the Matrarc even called you so soon."

"It's really fine," Gaia said. "I'm glad to help."

In a lull, when Mlady Beebe's husband Roger stepped out of the room and they were alone, she set a hand on Gaia's arm. "I have a friend who's pregnant again for the fifth time," Mlady Beebe said, lowering her voice. "Her last child is only a couple months old, and she says she can't handle another baby so soon. She wants to know if you could help her with a miscarriage."

Gaia looked down at her hands and shook her head. "Tell her no. If she asks me directly, I'll report her to the Matrarc."

"Are you sure?" Mlady Beebe asked.

It was there inside her, a mutiny of frustration, but Gaia strangled it off. "I'm only able to help you now because I promised the Matrarc not to induce miscarriages, in any situation."

Mlady Beebe smiled tiredly. "I didn't know it was true. All right. Forget I asked."

Gaia didn't know if she'd been tested or if Mlady Beebe truly had a friend in trouble. It disturbed her to think of it at all, especially since now she was worried about Mlady Beebe's pregnant friend.

"I'm sorry," Mlady Beebe said. "You aren't mad at me?"

"Of course not," Gaia said, and turned to check the supplies in her satchel again. She would try to forget. That was all she could do.

Mlady Beebe's children came frequently to give her hugs, and neighbors dropped by to check on the mother's progress. By late afternoon, several uncles came to take the kids to their house for dinner. Nightfall came early with the overcast sky, and Mlady Beebe's labor started in again, gradually progressing until the baby was finally born: a healthy boy. Gaia, exhausted from assisting births two days in a row, sighed in relief as she passed the tiny boy to his mother, who welcomed him with trembling, grateful fingers. Roger tenderly kissed Mlady Beebe on the forehead.

"What should we name him?" Mlady Beebe asked.

The man's hand looked enormous as he gently caressed the infant's little head. "I want him to be free some day," Roger said. "I want to name him 'Liberty.'"

"For a boy?" Mlady Beebe said.

"We'll call him 'Bert,' if you want."

Mlady Beebe shook her head. "I don't know, Roger."

Roger smiled down at his son and glanced over to Gaia. "Will it happen, Mlass Gaia?" he asked. "Will men ever vote here?"

"Why do you ask me?"

Mlady Beebe and Roger exchanged a glance. "We were hoping," Roger began. "Well, some of us men have been hoping you'd take the issue to the Matrarc for us, seeing as how you've stood up to her before."

"Why don't you?" Gaia asked Mlady Beebe.

"I just don't think it's right," she said. "There's already more trouble with the men lately. I just want things to go back to how they were. We've got kids to think of. You shouldn't have mentioned it, Roger. I asked you not to."

Gaia looked at Roger, who averted his gaze to his newborn son and said no more.

Mlady Beebe gave a heavy sigh and then reached a hand for Gaia. "You've been so good to us," she said. "I'm sorry politics had to come up. We're so grateful."

Gaia started cleaning up and putting her supplies back in her satchel. She looked again at Roger, who hadn't moved, and that's when Gaia had an odd feeling, like she was having a glimpse into a marriage with hidden layers.

There was a knock on the front door, and Roger left to answer it.

"Please, Mlass Gaia," Mlady Beebe said. "Don't mind what he says. I don't want him in trouble if something gets started."

"What do you mean?"

"I mean it for your own sake, too," Mlady Beebe said. "We don't need a rebellion here. Not now. The backlash would be bad for us all."

"You don't think the Matrarc would permit the men to vote?"

Mlady Beebe's eyes were tired and worried. "No. It would mean too much upheaval. It's better to keep things as they are, especially as we go into the decline."

Gaia could hardly contain her surprise. "There's a plan for the decline?"

"Not really a plan. But it's obviously coming, isn't it?" As Roger returned, Mlady Beebe put her hand on Gaia's. "Don't bring us into any trouble. Please."

Gaia gave her hand an uncertain squeeze.

"Chardo's here to escort you back up to the winner's cabin," Roger said. "He's out with the horses."

"Which brother?" Gaia asked, and to her surprise, she discovered she didn't know which one she hoped for more.

"The younger one." he said.

Peter, she realized, would do very nicely. It felt like forever since their canoe ride in the marsh. She tried to hide a smile.

Mlady Beebe laughed. "It's about time. I'd like to see something good happen to the Chardos. You're just what they need."

Gaia blushed, picking up her satchel. "You're all set, then?"

"We're good. Go on. And thank you, for everything," Mlady Beebe said. "Can you let yourself out?"

"Of course."

Mlady Beebe reached out a hand for her husband, who sat obediently beside her and looked up once more to thank Gaia.

As she stepped into the other room and put on her cloak, Gaia couldn't help wondering if Mlady Beebe had kept Roger beside her deliberately so that he couldn't speak to Gaia alone. She opened the heavy door and stepped out, closing it behind her. With a hand on the latch, she peered into the darkness and hitched her sachel up on her shoulder. She heard a horse snuffle a murky breath somewhere to her left.

"Peter?"

"I'm here."

His quiet voice was part of the cool evening darkness, silky and inviting. As her eyes adjusted, she saw him waiting at the edge of the yard. In the distance, beyond the big, shadowy trees that ringed the commons, the lodge's windows glowed faintly, indicating others were awake there still.

"How late is it?" she asked, walking carefully forward, trying not to trip in the dark grass.

"After ten. Not too late," he said.

She headed toward his voice. "Did you bring Spider?"

She came up against Peter in the darkness. She let out a soft "Oh!" expecting him to step back, but instead she felt his hands close around her arms to steady her, and he didn't let go.

"I've wanted to see you so badly," he said.

Her heartbeat leapt. "Peter," she began, glancing around. "It's not safe here."

"It's dark. No one will see."

He backed up a step, drawing her along with him, and then another. She could just make out the shape of his face and the line of his jaw. She tentatively touched her fingertips to the front of his shirt. Heat lay beneath the fabric.

"Are you okay?" he asked. "Is he treating you all right?"

"Of course," she said, smiling.

"You sound tired."

"I just delivered a baby."

"How's your sister?" he asked.

"She's good. She's gaining weight, and she actually slept six hours straight last night."

"That's wonderful. You must be happy."

"I am. You can't imagine." She felt his hands slide around her back, and then he was pulling her gently nearer.

"What do you do up there all day?" he asked. He was so near his voice was hardly more than a whisper.

A tingle started in her gut and spread outward. "I help

with the babies," she said. "There are always diapers to wash. And I cook some."

"That's all? You don't play cards or anything?"

"No, why?"

Her satchel slipped down her shoulder and he caught it for her, lifting it away to hook it over the saddle.

"You don't walk in the meadow?" he asked. His arms slid around her again.

She laughed. "We're far too busy for that," she said. *Though one night we watched lightning bugs.*

"I'm trying to picture it," he said. "What's the most interesting thing you've done?"

Inside her cloak, one of his hands moved lightly up her back, and it was getting hard for her to think.

"The most interesting thing?" she said. "We found a letter to my parents in my grandmother's sketchbook."

"You and Mx. Josephine?"

"Me and Leon."

"You and him." He sounded as if she was finally telling him what he wanted to know. "What did it say?"

"It was in a code. She told my parents to leave Sylum if they ever came here." She peered up at him, wishing she could see him more clearly. "It made me want to ask you about that time you left and beat the gateway sickness. Did you have any withdrawal symptoms, like shakes or hallucinations or anything?"

His hands stilled where they were. "I already told you," he said. "I was starting to feel strange, like headachy and nauseous. I wouldn't say they were hallucinations, but I lit up and that took care of it."

"You smoked rice flower?"

"Yes. Why? Do you think that mattered?"

Gaia thought of Norris smoking, too.

"I don't believe it," she said. She impulsively tugged on his shirt. "Peter, that's the solution. The rice flower was why you were able to avoid the gateway sickness." Her mind was flying. "Why didn't I see it? Norris smoked, too, when he went to rescue my grandmother. Since he went just as far as she did, he should have died, too, but he lived to bring her back *because he was smoking the rice flower*. Do you hear what I'm saying?"

"We could leave," he said quietly.

"I know!" she said. She'd never been so excited. She couldn't wait to tell Leon. And the Matrarc. "This changes everything," she said. "The people of Sylum don't have to stay here and die off. I want you with me when I tell the Matrarc. She'll be thrilled."

"You want to go now?"

"Sure. Why not?"

He laughed, low in his throat. "You sound so happy."

"Of course I am," she said, grinning. "This is huge!"

"You're so pretty when you're happy," he said, and his arms tightened around her.

His absurdity amused her beyond anything. "I can't be pretty in the dark," she said, laughing.

"It isn't dark for me."

Gaia's breath caught. Her joy was transformed by sweet pleasure, and then he drew her nearer until her shirt met his. Tentatively, she moved her arms around him, while something anxious inside her wondered why he felt so good to her. She felt a feather-light touch along her right cheek, and the softest kiss followed. She couldn't inhale anymore. Her heart forgot how to work.

When she tipped her face up, his mouth was already there, barely any distance away. All she had to do would be to tilt up a little farther, and her lips would meet his. She didn't know how she could tell that he was still smiling, but she could, and then his lips touched briefly against hers. It was just enough so that she knew precisely where he was. He tasted like the night air, pure and clear. And then he just tasted of happiness. She closed her eyes, leaning completely into him, and let herself get lost.

She became dimly aware that a banging had started on a door. "Mom!" yelled a child's bright voice. "Mom! Open up! Show us the baby! Is it a girl?"

A moment later, the area was filled with the rush of footsteps as Mlady Beebe's children returned home, and when the door was thrown open, light illuminated every corner of the yard.

Gaia broke away from Peter, but it was already too late. Other people were in the yard, too, and they were turning in curiosity.

"Come on in, children. Hurry now," Roger said. The little ones scampered in.

"Can you open the door any more there, Roger?" came a man's deep voice. "We need the light. You all right there, Mlass?"

"I'm fine," she said quickly.

"Mlass Gaia?" came Mlady Maudie's voice. "Is that you?"

"You'd best stand aside, there," came the man's voice again, warningly. He started toward them, his striped shirt catching the light. "Chardo Peter?"

"Hello, Doerring," Peter said calmly. "Mlady Maudie."

Mlady Maudie took a step into the light. "You should know better, Chardo," she said. "How long have you been out here? Roger, what do you think?"

"Not long. He came maybe fifteen minutes ago," Roger said.

"Long enough," Mlady Maudie said. "Doerring, take him."

261

The men began to circle around Peter.

"Wait a minute," Gaia objected. "He didn't do anything. There's nothing wrong with me."

"That was an uncondoned embrace," Mlady Maudie said. "We all saw it, clear as day. I just hope the children didn't."

"Mlass Gaia, it's all right," Peter said.

She stepped before him into the light cast from the doorway. "No. I'm *telling* you," she insisted. "Look at me. I'm perfectly fine. There's nothing wrong."

"Please, Mlass. It's the law. Attempted rape is a matter for the tribunal," said one of the older men.

"Attempted rape? Are you serious?" she said. "It was just a kiss. Nothing more."

"He actually kissed you?" Mlady Maudie asked.

"Mlass Gaia, no," Peter said and groaned.

"That's it," Doerring said. "You going to come easy, Chardo?" The big man crowded nearer.

It was going too fast.

"Get away from him," Gaia said, backing near to Peter again to shield him from the other men. "For the last time, he didn't do anything."

To her amazement, Peter stepped around her into the light and didn't resist at all as two of the men grabbed his arms.

"Roger, stop them!" Gaia called. "Mlady Maudie!"

"I'm sorry, Mlass," Roger said. "He went too far. I've got a daughter of my own."

"Just don't say anything more," Peter said to Gaia.

One of the men hit him across the face. "Don't mess with her. You've done enough."

"Peter!" she called. "Are you all right? Leave him *alone!*" She grabbed at Doerring's arm.

262

"What on earth is going on here?" came a new voice from the road.

"Norris!" Gaia called, spinning toward the voice. "They're arresting Chardo Peter for attempted rape. Make them let him go!"

"The girl's completely out of control," Mlady Maudie said.

"I'm not the problem!" Gaia protested.

Norris came in the yard and crossed quickly to Gaia. "Take it easy there, Mlass," he said softly.

"Chardo kissed her and who knows what else," Mlady Maudie said, stepping nearer.

"Get away from me!" Gaia said. "You never liked me!"

"See what I mean?" Mlady Maudie said. "You try to handle her."

Norris laughed. "Take the boy, now. I've got Mlass Gaia. She's not going to cause any fuss, not this late in the evening when the kids are all trying to settle down."

Something in his tone made her listen. A warning. She looked back at Peter. Already a drip of blood was coming from his mouth. His hair was messed over his eyes, and his lips moved silently in the light from the doorway: *Please.*

"What are you going to do with him?" Gaia asked.

"We'll hold him down at the prison until the tribunal," Doerring said.

"Tribunal!" she said. *This can't be happening.* "Can't you all just forget about this?" she pleaded. "Believe me. Nothing happened." She turned toward Mlady Maudie. "Truly. Look at me, I'm fine."

Mlady Maudie let out a brief laugh. "Fine you are not."

"Mlass Gaia," Peter said, his voice low and deliberate. "You must stop." His quietness alarmed her most of all. In a moment

263

of charged silence, she stared around her, grasping finally that these people would not yield to reason.

"I'll find the Matrarc now," she said to Peter. "I'll make her let you go." She turned toward the horses.

"Norris, go with her," Mlady Maudie said. "Talk sense to her."

Frustrated beyond belief, Gaia heaved herself up, threw her satchel over her shoulder, and pulled at the reins. She took a last look at Peter being hustled away by the men, and with a sense of near panic, she took off with Norris.

"Unbelievably moronic," Norris said as they rode out of earshot. "Kissing, right where you could be seen. You had the whole ride back up to the bluff. Couldn't you wait five minutes?"

She caught a glimpse of his irate expression as they passed the lodge. "I didn't know he was going to kiss me. It's not like I planned anything."

"He could have, if he had a brain in his head."

"I told them I was fine," she said, still infuriated. "This is all a stupid fuss for nothing."

"If you'll calm down for a minute, I'll try to explain."

"I know already," she said. "Touching isn't condoned. It's the most idiotic thing I've ever heard of."

Norris kept riding, aiming up the road that led toward the bluff, and she could tell from his silence that he wasn't going to answer her until she calmed down.

She took a deep breath. "All right. I'll listen," she said. "But just don't tell me something ridiculous or I'll lose it again."

"Intimate physical relations are the absolute basis of our entire society here," Norris said. "You have to remember, there are nine men for every woman. Nine. They're competing all the time, and the rules are very precise to keep it fair. If one man crosses the line, it's unfair to everyone else."

"I get all that. But Peter didn't cross a line," Gaia said.

"It doesn't matter if you personally welcomed what he did. Once he can touch you or kiss you or whatever, you're naturally going to care more for him. He's playing on your sympathy, on your desire."

"Don't I have a choice about my own desire?" she demanded.

"He's using your own body to influence your reason, not the other way around."

"But what if I want that?"

He grunted in the darkness. "I am not getting through to you."

"No. You're not. Because you're wrong."

"Let me put it this way. Are you ready to choose Chardo Peter over any other man, permanently, for the rest of your life?" Norris asked.

She frowned, thinking of Will and Leon. "Of course not."

"So then, you were just playing with him."

"Norris! I'm not like that."

"You're either incredibly dense or just plain mean. He took an enormous risk for you. Think, Mlass Gaia. He was unbelievably stupid, but whatever you two just did in the dark meant a lot more to him than it did to you. It *mattered*." Norris kicked his horse. "I'm no good at this," he said.

It began to come clear. The rule against touching didn't just raise the stakes legally, it raised them emotionally, too. Peter must deeply care for her, and by accepting his kiss, it must seem to him that she cared that much, too. She'd raised his expectations exponentially.

265

"I never should have kissed him," she said, horrified.

"Now you're getting there." Norris pulled to the right, and Gaia saw they'd arrived at the Chardos' ranch.

"What are you doing?" she asked.

"What do you think? Rotting peg leg's no good in a stirrup," he added under his breath.

"I can't talk to the Chardos," Gaia said.

"Don't be a coward," Norris said. "Come on."

She watched him head up the driveway, toward the cabin where light gleamed in several windows. "I'll just keep going up to the Matrarc's," Gaia called.

"It's a bad idea getting her up when she's with her family. She won't do anything tonight, anyway. Wait, and talk to her calmly in the morning."

"But Peter will spend the night in prison," Gaia said.

"It'll give him a chance to wise up," Norris said. "Take my advice on this one."

She itched to do something productive, but it was possible Norris was right. She rode up the driveway to where he was already dismounting. The door opened on his knock, and Will stood framed in the doorway with lamp light behind him.

"What's going on?" he asked. "Is there a death?"

"It's Mlass Gaia. She needs an escort back up to the winner's cabin," Norris said.

"I thought Peter was taking her."

"There's been a problem," Norris said. "I'll let her explain. Let me talk to Sid." He stomped up the step and passed Will.

"Mlass Gaia? Are you all right?" Will asked.

She wanted to rip up the night and tear it to shreds. She pulled her horse around, realizing only then that, unlike the last time she rode, her feet met the stirrups comfortably. Peter,

266

so considerately, had adjusted them for her height when he'd saddled her horse.

"I think I'm going to scream," she said.

"Wait," Will said, already reaching for Spider. "I'm coming."

She headed impatiently back down the driveway.

"What happened?" Will asked as he caught up. "Are you hurt?"

The clouds had thinned to let through the light of a gibbous moon, and though the horse picked its way smoothly over the road, she could see only outlines and she was glad. She didn't want Will to see her face.

"I kissed your brother. Or he kissed me," she said. "It doesn't matter. Some people saw us and now he's been arrested for attempted rape."

The horses' footfalls beat stolidly on the dark dirt road, underscoring Will's wordless silence.

"And now you hate me," she added.

Will's voice was careful. "I'm just surprised. Are you sure you're all right? He didn't hurt you in any way, did he?"

"How can you even ask that? Of course he didn't. And please don't say you warned me. I feel bad enough as it is."

"I'm sure it wasn't your fault."

"It *was* my fault, as much as his," she said. "I'll talk to the Matrarc first thing tomorrow. There has to be a way to explain."

"You have to be careful about what you say," he said. "You don't want to make it worse."

"What do you mean?"

"If you're too passionate in your defense of him, they'll wonder why you're not impartial."

"Of course I'm not impartial," she said.

"Listen to me," Will said, his voice warming. "If witnesses saw you and they can prove he kissed you, then the law is very clear. He's going to the stocks and then to prison. Can they really prove it? Where did this happen?"

It was getting worse and worse. "I admitted it myself," she said, her voice tight. "We were in the yard of Mlady Beebe's house, and Mlady Maudie and several others saw us. I was trying to persuade them it was just a kiss."

He lifted a hand to the bridge of his nose. "That's it, then," he said.

"Will, no. We can explain. They'll have to listen to us."

"Peter won't be there."

"What?" she demanded.

"He won't be at the tribunal. You say you had witnesses. You admitted yourself, in front of them, that he kissed you. That's attempted rape."

"But I kissed him, too! And nothing more happened! What about presumed innocence?" she demanded.

"That's it exactly," Will said. "You're presumed innocent. That makes him the guilty one."

She could not believe this. "There was no crime."

"Whether you agree with it or not, it's the law here that a man can't touch you until you've made a choice to marry him." Will audibly flicked his reins. "That's just how it is. If he breaks the law, he goes to the stocks and then to jail. Peter knew that."

"You're talking about your own brother like you don't even care!"

"Of course I care," he said sharply. "It's taking everything I've got not to go down there and wring his neck. And then yours."

Gaia caught her breath. He wasn't kidding.

"You want to know what's really funny?" Will said. "We

drew straws tonight to see who would pick you up from Mlady Beebe's."

She could hardly accept what he was saying, barely imagine that scene between the two brothers. Her mind twisted around the possibilities. This might never have happened if Will had met her at Mlady Beebe's instead of Peter, but something else might have.

"I never would have tried anything with you, if that's what you're thinking," he added. "And not because I have any fear of the stocks."

"No. You might be jealous, but you'd never think of kissing me," she said, not really caring whether she made sense or not. She was getting angry all over again, as if he were implying that what she and Peter had done was truly unnatural and criminal.

"Give me credit for some subtlety," Will said. "I'm saying I would never put you in the position he's put you in."

"You're too decent, you mean," she said.

"Don't hold it against me." He kicked Spider into a faster pace.

She gripped her reins and dug in her heels to catch up with him, riding in stubborn silence while she tried to sort out her emotions. She didn't like having tension with Will on top of everything else. The path rose through the trees, and eventually reached the more open ridge at the top of the bluff.

"There's an obvious thing to do," she said. "We need to change the law."

"I know."

"And I guess it's up to me to do it," she said.

"You can try."

A corpse would have sounded more optimistic. As they came around the next corner, she saw a faint glow from the windows of the winner's cabin at the far edge of the meadow. The lightning bugs of the other night were gone, and the crickets had subdued to occasional chirps. She slowed her horse, then drew up by the stairs.

"Will you tell your family I'm sorry about Peter?" she asked. "I never meant to get him in trouble. I hardly know how I'll ever face your father again." She slid off her horse and made sure she had her satchel.

"Peter knew what he was risking, even if you didn't," he said.

"That's what Norris told me, too," she said, but it didn't reassure her any. "I wish I had realized what it meant."

A long moment passed, and she looked up to where he sat in the saddle, faintly silhouetted against the night sky. A thicker cloud passed over the moon and glowed white and gray above him. "I'll take your reins," he said, reaching toward her.

As she passed him the reins, she noticed he was careful not to overlap with her fingers, and the lack of touch was suddenly charged with meaning. She understood. It wasn't that he cared any less than his brother. He just had a different way of showing it, a way that played within the law and managed to transcend it, too. He gave any choice completely to her.

There's nobody in the world like Chardo Will, she thought.

"If I can do anything for you, let me know," he said.

"You aren't going to wring my neck, then?" she asked.

"Much as I'd like to, no."

There was nothing left to say except good night, and then he was gone.

cinnamon

SHE CAME QUIETLY through the door, dragging her satchel by the handle, and dropped it just inside. A rich, heavenly smell of sweet pumpkin, cloves, and honey pervaded the air, and she breathed deeply. Against the globe of the kitchen lamp, a moth pinged, then fluttered away toward another oil lamp in the living room farther below. She listened for the sounds of babies, or of Josephine stirring in the bedroom to her right, but even the sound of the wind had died down, leaving the cabin quiet.

"Leon?" she said.

She closed the door softly behind her and stepped farther inside. He was asleep with his head on the table, the maps and her grandmother's sketchbook spread out before him under the soft yellow glow of the lamp. One hand was pressed under his cheek, and his dark hair fell across his eyes. A gray blanket had slipped off his bare shoulder, revealing that he wore no shirt beneath.

She hung her cloak on a hook, silently shucked off her boots, and tiptoed sock-foot into the kitchen where the warm, homey redolence was even stronger. It helped her calm down slightly.

He had tidied up, leaving a bowl overturned to air-dry by the sink. Gripping the oven door, she swung it open for a quick peek and found two loaves of pumpkin bread, risen and golden brown. She grabbed a towel for a hot pad, jimmied the pans out, and set them on the wooden counter to cool.

By the time she looked out to the table again, Leon was awake, blinking heavily in her direction.

"You're back," he said.

She came down the two steps. "Your bread was done."

He rubbed his nose inelegantly and nodded. "There isn't any cinnamon here. Have you noticed that? It won't taste right, but I had a craving—" His voice trailed off and his gaze turned attentive. "What's wrong?"

"I've done something terrible."

"Is the baby okay?"

She moved nearer into the lamplight. "The baby and mother are fine. It's Peter."

Leon lifted his eyebrows, then he hitched his blanket over his shoulder and leaned back, crossing his arms. He was fully awake now. "This would be Chardo Peter. Boyfriend Number Two. Am I right?" His voice turned lazy. "Or is he Boyfriend Number One now?"

"Don't tease me." She spread her fingers on the table and slumped into a chair kitty-corner to his. "This is really bad. I have to go down again in the morning. There's going to be a trial."

"What did he do?"

Until that moment, she had not guessed how impossible it was going to be to tell Leon what had happened. Telling Will, by comparison, had been nothing. She loosened her hair from behind her left ear to let it slide forward and ducked her face down.

272

"You always do that. That thing with your hair, when you're upset," he said quietly, and leaned forward. She felt his touch skim her hair, and then he gently tucked the loose lock back behind her ear again. Her scar tingled. She held still, frozen, while his hand slid down her white sleeve to her hand. It made it even worse that he was being nice.

She curled her fingers into a ball and drew back from him.

"Don't, Gaia. Just tell me what's wrong," he said. "It can't be that bad, unless you did something stupid, like kiss him in public."

She thunked her face into her hands.

"You didn't," he said.

"I didn't mean to."

Leon stood, pushing his chair back. "I'm going to get a shirt on," he said. "Don't you move."

"They're going to put him in the stocks, Leon! And then prison! I don't know for how long."

"And *this* is what bothers you? That he's going to prison?" he demanded.

"It's the whole *thing!*" she exploded. "All I did was kiss him. One kiss! It just *happened*. And now he's accused of attempted rape. I can't take this place anymore. It's just not right. Any of it."

"*Now* you see."

She glared up at him. "Don't give me that," she said. "I saw it before, too, but I didn't see any way to make it change. Now we don't have a choice."

" 'We,' " he echoed. His expression was a mix of mockery, confusion, and anguish. "How could you do it, Gaia?"

She faltered back in her chair. "I don't know what you mean."

"What did he do, that it just 'happened'?"

273

She gripped the armrests, hard. To her alarm, he hitched his chair nearer and sat again so that his face was level with hers. He set his warm hands over hers, lightly pinning hers to the armrests, and the motion left his blanket to slide loose from his shoulders again. Warmth like she'd never felt before traveled up her arms.

"Was it like this?" he asked, leaning nearer.

She licked her lips, shaking her head. "Leon," she said. She leaned back in the chair, but somehow that only brought him nearer, so that she could almost feel the smooth warmth in his chest. She tried to draw away her hands, but instead her fingers intertwined with his and ended up on her lap, where the fabric of her skirt rumpled slowly up her legs.

"What I wouldn't give to know what you're thinking," he said.

Just whatever you do, don't kiss me right now, she thought.

But he leaned forward until no more than a millimeter of lamplight separated them. For a long moment, she resisted the appeal of his intent gaze, wondering how he could feel for her what she saw there, and fearing what he did to her. If anybody could use her own instincts against herself, it was Leon.

"I lied, all those weeks ago. About my wish," he said. His eyes gleamed with a quiet, private light. "This is what I was really thinking."

His lips touched hers and she closed her eyes, letting her head sink back against the chair. With unhurried restraint, he kissed her softly, and long, and slow, until she was a tangle of melting pleasure and frustration.

"That," she murmured, stopping to swallow and catch her breath. "Is not fair."

"Good," he said.

He kissed her again, only not so softly anymore.

She didn't know quite how it happened, but she was fully on his lap, with his bare arms around her, and everything about him felt warm and strong under her fingertips, even the scar lines she found across the back of his shoulders. She shifted her weight, and he broke away suddenly, holding her quite still.

"I think we're going to have a little problem," he said. "Hold still."

She looked into his face, surprised. Her eyes felt hazy, as if she were coming back from another land. She touched a finger to his jaw, liking his faint, tactile shadow of beard. "What's the matter?"

His laugh was low and rumbly. "Nothing. It's just funny that Peter's the one going to the stocks for what he did."

She'd forgotten about Peter. She'd forgotten about everything. Now she tried to disentangle her arms from around him.

"No, you don't," he said. "Stay there."

"What is wrong with me?" she asked. "It's like I have no self-restraint at all."

He laughed again. "I see. Please tell me you didn't get this far with him."

"I can't be on your lap," she said.

"Well, excuse me. You are. I would know."

She brushed her hair back around her ears and tried to straighten her blouse, but it was hard with his arms still around her, and even worse when he tried to help a little. She gave him a shy, embarrassed smile.

"I'm really sorry," she said. She badly wanted to kiss him again.

"Don't say that."

Slowly she got up, steadying one hand against the table. He dropped the blanket across his lap, and as she guessed the significance of that particular gesture, her embarrassment quadrupled.

Her gaze flew up to his face, and he shrugged, relaxing his arm casually around the back of the chair.

She wanted to die.

"It's okay, Gaia," he said.

She threw out a hand. "I'm just so bad at this."

"As if I'm any good at it?" He laughed, his smile sweet. "Don't be embarrassed. I'm fine. In fact, I have a good idea."

"What?" she asked, still mortified.

"Why don't you marry me?"

paradise

"MARRY YOU? Are you out of your mind?" she asked.

"Not at all. Think about it. It would solve all kinds of problems."

"Like what?"

"Like Peter won't kiss you again and get sent to the stocks. I'd kill him first."

"Leon! This is not helpful."

"It makes perfect sense to me. Have you thought about what will happen next month, when I'm not here?"

"What do you mean?"

He ran a hand around his jaw. "I doubt the next thirty-two captains will pick me to be on either team. If I can't play, I can't win again, either."

She was still missing something.

"You really don't see it, do you?" he asked. He braced his hands on his knees. "So modest. Forgive me if I point out the obvious. You'll get chosen by the next winner. Someone else will have the same opportunities with you that I've just had."

Her mind went blank white. Then it slammed back on and

horror shot through her. "I can't," she whispered. "I can't be the prize."

"You don't think so?" he asked. "Not even for Peter if he's out of prison by then? Or how about that other one who was captain last time. The big blond. Xave."

The idea repulsed her. She hadn't been thinking forward at all. Now it all hit her: the cycle of the thirty-two games drove things not only for the men who had a chance to compete, but for all of the mlasses, too.

"The only way to not be eligible," she said slowly, "is for me to pick someone. To get engaged. Or become a libby." That's what Dinah had done, and Gaia began to see what it had been like for her, getting picked as the prize month after month. Gaia couldn't let that happen to her, especially not now. "What am I going to do?"

"At last you see the brilliance of my proposal."

She studied his watchful blue eyes, and now she saw he really meant it.

A tiny voice in the back of her head reminded her that Peter had warned her of such a moment, the same Peter who was now in prison because of her. She'd messed up everything.

"I can't," she said. "You must know I can't. We've hardly been talking to each other."

His expression became grave. "It isn't always easy between us. I admit that. But it's right between us, always."

She held very still.

"Every tiny, happy thing makes me want to share it with you," he went on, leaning forward. "I thought I would get over this, but I can't, and I'm done trying. I understand you like no one else here ever can. Even now, you're just afraid. You're worried you'll hurt Peter's feelings if you rush into something. Right?"

"It isn't fear," she said. "It isn't that simple."

"Then what is it?" he asked. "You can't really like him. Not more than me. Do you?"

"No." *Not more. Differently.*

His eyes flicked in the light. "You can't believe what this is like for me, living up here with you, getting pushed away every other minute. You belong with me. When will you see that?"

She didn't understand how he could be so sure. It was actually freaking her out a little. She leaned back against the table, frowning. "You aren't even that nice to me all the time," she said.

He choked out a laugh. "Like when? When you lie to me?"

"I don't lie to you. I just can't tell you everything. And why should I? You scare me sometimes."

"Me?"

"What about after the thirty-two games?" she reminded him.

"Do I really even need to apologize for that?" He stood, pacing away from her toward the window. She watched him lean his head against the glass for a long moment. In the kitchen, the oven made a ticking noise as it cooled, and inside her, a knot twisted itself even tighter. He turned finally, his eyes troubled. "All right," he said in a low voice. "I'm sorry. And I'm sorry for the next morning, too. Of course I am. And for everything I ever said when my heart—" he stopped. He ran a hand back through his hair, glanced to the side, and then back to her. "Don't make me do this. Leave me some pride."

She gripped the edge of the table, stunned by the enormity of what he'd admitted. He'd loved her all that time, when she hadn't even known, when loving her had brought him suffering and prison and heartache.

"I'm sorry, too. About a lot of things," she said. Her cheeks grew warm with shame. "Including what happened with Peter tonight." She did regret that. Already her moment of happiness with Peter seemed ages past, permanently obscured by what had happened since. "I'm sorry about what's going to happen tomorrow, too."

He folded his arms across his chest. "You're going to his trial to try to free him, aren't you?"

"I have to."

He considered a long moment, then spoke quietly. "I can't help noticing that it's him in trouble that makes you want to change things."

Gaia felt her heart half break. She should have done it for Leon. She knew that now, but it had taken Leon coming back into her life, waking her out of her blindness, for her to see it. It was all twisted around. "I'm sorry," she said. "But you do see, don't you?"

"I suppose you can't help it. You have to be noble." He closed his eyes briefly, and then regarded her again without smiling. "What will you do for him?"

She let her gaze travel over the maps on the table, and ended up peering at the globe of the lamp and the glowing flame within.

"I'll try to reason with the cuzines," she said. "And if that doesn't work, I'll try to change the law."

"And if that still doesn't work, what then?"

Anxiety coursed through her. "I don't know exactly. Something."

"You won't give up, will you?"

She shook her head. "I can't have someone else punished unfairly because of me. Not again."

He stepped nearer to her, beside the table, and reached for the loon feather peeking out of her grandmother's sketchbook.

"Aren't you concerned that the Matrarc will exile you if you fight her?"

Her gaze froze on the feather. "Being exiled wouldn't be a death sentence anymore," she said. "We've found an antidote to the miasma, Peter and I."

"What are you talking about?"

"I was so happy when I realized it," she said. "That's why I didn't think when I was, when he, when we were—"

"I get the point. What did you discover?"

She ignored the heat in her cheeks and reached impulsively for the sketchbook. She pulled out the poem she'd deciphered and held it flat under the light. "It's the black rice flower. Smoking it eases the withdrawal symptoms from the miasma addiction."

"That's not bad," he said, impressed. "If the miasma is opiate-based as we thought, a lesser drug can take the edge off the worst withdrawal symptoms."

"My grandmother came so close! Why didn't she see it?" Her gaze caught on the most puzzling line again: "Obtuse not be smoke i," and a new idea came to her. Perhaps it was a directive: "Obtuse not be. Smoke." The i might go with the next line.

leave the miasma addicts and go
i have no proof none believe me
labor wasted on fools if
you read this my bonnie
obtuse not be smoke i
regret i ever left you or urged
relocating to a better
ideal place none exists go back to
cruel unlake for gaias sake
else we all die

281

She leaned over the table, peering more closely at the poem. And then she saw the other clue, the hidden one, right in plain sight.

It was coming down the poem acrostically, the first letters of each line: *lily or rice.* Gaia was stupefied. A shiver ran through her, lifting the hairs on the back of her arms, and her eyes rounded. "Unbelievable."

"What do you see?" he asked.

She ran her finger slowly down the poem. "It's here," she said. "Lily or rice. She actually knew. She'd narrowed it down to two possible cures. She wrote them here so my parents would know. Only my parents." She told him briefly about Norris's account of her grandmother's death. Then the truth came clear to her. "She chose the wrong one. She smoked the lily-poppy instead, thinking it would save her, and it killed her."

He set the feather gently beside her fingers. "Are you sure?"

"It's all I can think. But now we can leave. We just have to tinker with the right dosage."

"Do you realize what you're saying?" he said, turning to face her. "Would you seriously leave Sylum and go back to the wasteland? Or the Enclave?"

A chill passed through her, and she looked up to meet his gaze. "We might all have to go," she said.

Dawn, with its gray light, was working through the window when Gaia woke to find Josephine nudging her shoulder. "The Matrarc's here for you," she said softly.

Gaia blinked heavily and rolled up. Aside from staying up late with Leon, she'd been awake with Maya crying in the night, and when she had returned to bed, she'd found it nearly impossible to sleep, anxious as she was about Peter.

Josephine gave her a quick hug when she was ready. "Good luck."

Gaia wanted to see Leon before she left, but his bedroom door was closed.

She tiptoed nearer and tested the latch, listening. The door opened noiselessly. On a narrow table, a shaving brush and a dish with a nugget of soap lay beside a straight razor that gleamed in the gray light. His pants were folded over the back of a chair, and his shirt was on a hanger propped on the edge of the open window. She peeked around farther to his bed, where he lay on his stomach in deep slumber, his mouth agape, his dark wool blankets in a tangle. One pale-arched foot hung off the mattress.

She instinctively looked for the birthmarked tattoo on his ankle, but the angle was wrong. Even without finding it, she realized she was looking for Orion. An elusive sadness and comfort, both, sifted through her as she remembered her parents. Leon would always be a bind to them, to home.

She could hear his quiet breathing, and with protective tenderness, she couldn't wake him just to say goodbye. She backed up and softly closed the door.

She checked her satchel to bring her supplies with her as she habitually did, and paused to wind her locket watch, twisting the tiny peg back and forth. The ticking was loud in the silence. A tingle of nervousness ran through her as she thought of what lay ahead, and on instinct, she looped the necklace over her head again. Then she grabbed her cloak and stepped outside.

A carriage waited at the door, its shape sharp and black in the cool gray light. The Matrarc's belly was so large that her cloak couldn't cover it, and she'd tucked a dark blanket around herself. Her husband spun down from beside her as Gaia descended the step.

"Good morning, Mlass." Dominic handed her up. "Can you drive?" he asked.

"You're not coming with us?" Gaia asked.

"I'm staying with the children. It's Jerry's birthday, so hopefully the tribunal won't last too long. Here, take these," he said, passing her the reins. "The horse knows the way. Come back to us soon, Olivia."

"I will," the Matrarc said.

Gaia gripped the little metal armrest while she wedged her feet against the dash, and then she lifted the cool leather of the reins in her two hands. She looked doubtfully ahead at the horse's ears.

"Ha!" Dominic said, giving the horse a slap on the rear to get them going.

Gaia lurched back, and then forward again.

"Loosen up a little," the Matrarc said. "Even I can tell you've got him too tight."

Gaia complied, and the horse headed into the morning mist. Down below, the marsh was lost in a soft layer of fog that drifted up into the valley, and far out, the Bachsdatters' island lifted out like a distant ruin. Gaia shivered. Now that she knew the miasma was addictive, it was like watching an insidious poison blanket the village.

"How's Peter?" Gaia asked.

"He's fine. How are you is the question."

"I'm perfectly fine, of course," Gaia said. "This whole thing is really unnecessary. Can't you just let him go?"

The Matrarc put her hand on the dashboard as they rattled over a rough spot in the road and started down the bluff.

"You'll have to trust the cuzines to come to a fair decision," the Matrarc said. "It's not within my power to release him

284

without a tribunal, thankfully. I wouldn't care to have that responsibility on my hands."

"But they'll listen to you, won't they?"

"You have it backward. I listen to them. They decide."

Gaia steered the horse around the bend, and the road flattened out again.

"Mx. Josephine said the cuzines voted my grandmother out because she was crazy," Gaia said. "She said my grandmother waded in the marsh at night and tried to kick the expools out of Sylum. Is any of that true?"

The Matrarc laughed. "Your grandmother liked the bioluminescence, but she was far from crazy. And she resigned. Were you able to decipher her letter?"

"You knew about that?"

The Matrarc nodded. "Dominic reminded me of it. I used to wonder if it was a suicide note."

"It was a bitter, angry note saying she'd wasted her efforts on fools," Gaia said. "She urged my parents to go back to the Enclave."

"That fits," the Matrarc said. "It's strange to think now that the girl shortage she predicted came true even faster than she expected."

"Then isn't it time to do something about it?"

"Like what? I know what Chardo Will found, and there's no cure for that," the Matrarc said. "Your grandmother urged the expools to experiment with leaving, and many of them died. No. Hope is a kind of curse, Mlass Gaia, just as destructive as despair."

"So Sylum is better off without hope? You've actively discouraged curiosity."

"I didn't have to discourage it," the Matrarc said. "It's much easier for people to be grateful. Think about it, my dear. In many ways, it's a paradise here, a simple, beautiful life of abundance. Once people accept that and focus on their own lives and their own families, they're happy."

As they passed the Chardos' place, she glanced over her left shoulder and saw the cabin windows were dark. The Matrarc sat back again and smoothed the blanket over her lap.

"Your own children could be the last generation here if no more girls are born," Gaia said. "Mx. Josephine's baby Junie could be the very last girl. Doesn't that terrify you?"

"Terrify? No. I'll grant that we've reached a critical time. It's my hope that we'll stay civilized for as long as possible, right up to the end."

It sounded awful to Gaia. A death sentence for the entire community. "Is that really better than trying to leave?"

The Matrarc laughed. "Where to? That nihilistic, abusive place you come from? Even if we could, why should we give up our peaceful ways to go there and be destroyed? No. There's no disgrace in dying here, and that's what we want to do, without being frustrated by false hope."

"Are you sure?" Gaia asked.

"I beg your pardon?"

"Are you sure your civilized death in paradise is what the majority wants?"

The Matrarc's eyebrows drew together as she turned toward Gaia. "Tell me something," the Matrarc said in her melodious alto. "Are you aware of a way we can leave Sylum? Be truthful with me now."

Gaia let the horse pull the carriage a dozen more paces while she tried to decide how to reply. The Matrarc would see through any lie, but the more she thought of it, the more reluctant she was to hand over her discovery about the rice flower.

286

"I was going to tell you, but now Peter's on trial," Gaia said.

"At least you aren't lying to me outright yet. That you've found a way to leave is quite amazing, actually," the Matrarc said. "You could cull out all the healthy, strong, young people and leave the rest of us here to die off more quickly. The young families will be thrilled."

"That's not the idea," Gaia said, appalled.

The Matrarc's sightless gaze turned distant. "No?" she said. "How did I lose you again so quickly?"

"You haven't lost me," Gaia said, growing confused. "I've obeyed you as I promised. I've been good." She gave the reins an extra flick, urging the horse along.

"I fear for you, Mlass Gaia," the Matrarc said. "You should be trusting me, not trying to undermine me."

Gaia didn't know how the Matrarc was making her doubt her own mind again, but she was. She could see the lodge ahead now, and the sunlight dawning into the commons. The four stocks were still in shadow, but she already imagined and feared what could happen there. She pushed back her uncertainties and focused on one thing she knew.

"I won't let you put Peter in the stocks if I can help it," Gaia said. "He's no more guilty of a crime than I am."

The Matrarc didn't reply. She smoothed a hand over her belly, and then straightened her back conspicuously. Gaia knew she was due in another week or so and wondered if she would say something about beginning labor, but the Matrarc only sighed.

"Tired?" Gaia asked.

"Always."

Gaia guided the horse toward the lodge, and it came to a stop at an angle before the front porch. "We're here," Gaia said.

"Set the brake. Get Norris or someone to help me down."

Several men were rising from the benches in the commons. Chardo Will was there with his father and his uncles. In a gesture that struck Gaia as poignantly ironic, it was Peter's father, Sid, who came forward to help the Matrarc down from the carriage and lead her into the lodge.

CHAPTER 23

the tribunal

THE MATRARC TAPPED with her red cane, and her cloak remained parted over the full swell of her belly as she headed into the lodge. Judging her silhouette, Gaia saw that the baby had dropped, and she had the sense that the Matrarc could go into labor at any time. Gaia bet that the Matrarc knew it, too.

Chardo Sid passed Gaia on his way out and nodded politely. She glanced behind her to see Will standing with a hand on his hip, watching her wordlessly. Clearly they intended to wait there, just outside, until Peter's verdict was determined.

Inside the atrium, two tables had been pushed together, and eight women were assembled around them, Mlady Maudie and Mlady Roxanne among them. Gaia had expected something more formal, but they were chatting, and two of them had their knitting out. Gaia recognized Peony's mother and several others, like Mlady Eva, who were regularly at the lodge with the Matrarc. One was nursing her baby, and when she glanced up, Gaia was surprised to see it was Mlady Beebe. She looked tired, but her hair was clean and tidily back in a bun, and her face was scrubbed. She gave Gaia a faint smile.

"You should be resting," Gaia said.

"I'm all right," Mlady Beebe said. "It's only for a few minutes, and then I'm going back to bed."

Mlady Maudie pulled out a chair for the Matrarc and brought a stool so she could prop up her feet. "Thanks, Mlady Maudie. You're always so thoughtful. Sit here, Mlass Gaia. By me. So I can hold your hand."

"I'd rather not."

"You will do so nevertheless," said the Matrarc.

Startled, Gaia looked around at the other women, who regarded her soberly. The chatting had stopped. Gaia took her place on the straight-backed chair and shifted it closer to the table. She set her satchel on the floor. The Matrarc's left hand was open, palm up on the table, and as Gaia lightly set her hand in hers, the Matrarc's warm fingers closed around her own. There was no possible way Gaia could pretend to be calm.

"There. We're ready," the Matrarc said. "Thank you all for coming on such short notice. I really hope to have this resolved quickly so you can get out and about soon."

"It's no trouble," Mlady Roxanne said, adjusting her glasses. "We're glad to help."

"Mlady Beebe, why don't you begin," the Matrarc said.

"First, I want to say how grateful I am to Mlass Gaia for all her help yesterday. She's a first-rate midwife. We're so lucky to have her with us."

"Duly noted," the Matrarc said. "Tell us what happened when she was leaving."

"The last I saw her, she took her satchel of supplies and left the bedroom," Mlady Beebe said. "After that, I heard her go out, but I didn't actually see anything more myself. Mlady Maudie has a better idea than I do after that. She's the one who saw them in the yard."

"When did Mlady Maudie arrive?" the Matrarc asked.

Mlady Beebe lifted her baby over her shoulder and patted his back in a slow, firm rhythm. "I'd say fifteen minutes after Mlass Gaia left. Twenty tops. But I wasn't really paying attention."

"Thank you. Mlady Maudie, what happened when you arrived?" the Matrarc said.

"Excuse me," Gaia said. "I was there. You could ask me."

The Matrarc squeezed her hand lightly. "You'll have a chance soon, child," she said. "We need to establish what the witnesses saw first."

Mlady Maudie rested her arms on the table and dovetailed her fingers together. Her blond hair was cut in a clean line that curved at the base of her neck, and she sat straight, speaking succinctly as if she'd prepared what to say. "I was coming back with Mlady Beebe's kids and their uncles when we came into the yard and saw horses there. I looked over, naturally, and there were two people closely embracing in the shadows. When Roger opened the door, the two people took a moment to move apart, and then we all saw they were Mlass Gaia and Chardo Peter."

The calm precision of Mlady Maudie's testimony made Gaia anxious. The other cuzines were certain to believe anything she said.

"Chardo has no prior misconduct, has he?" the Matrarc said.

The women didn't speak, but there were several quick glances around the table.

"We don't count what happened with Mlady Adele," the Matrarc said. "Was there ever anything else?"

"No," Mlady Roxanne said.

"Then what happened next?" the Matrarc said.

291

"I asked Roger's oldest brother Doerring to apprehend Chardo, who did not resist," Mlady Maudie continued. "Mlass Gaia, on the other hand, became extremely upset. She tried to interfere with Doerring."

"The whole thing was totally unnecessary," Gaia broke in. "I was completely fine." She itched to take her hand away from the Matrarc's.

"Be calm," the Matrarc said to her quietly. "Were they both fully clothed when they were discovered?"

Gaia flinched. It was insulting. An awful idea struck her: if this interrogation were about her and Leon, how different the answers would be. She could feel heat beginning in her cheeks.

"Yes," Mlady Maudie said. "She was a little mussed, but nothing more."

"Was there any other evidence of contact between them? Anything else that was directly observed?" the Matrarc asked. "It must have been quite dark."

"His hands were under her cloak when the light first fell on them," Mlady Maudie said.

Gaia blushed more deeply, humiliated, but could not argue.

"Anything else?" the Matrarc asked.

"She admitted, herself, and I quote, 'It was only a kiss,'" Mladie Maudie added coldly.

"Only to persuade you that nothing more happened," Gaia said.

The women began to whisper.

Mlady Maudie sat back with a sad, satisfied smile. "You see? Such disgraceful conduct I'd never seen. I hardly knew how to deal with her. Thankfully, Norris Emmett came by then and he was able to reason with her."

The Matrarc spoke quietly to Gaia. "You admit it?"

292

Gaia took a deep breath, scrambling to regain her temper and barely succeeding. "What I did with him is nobody else's business. That's what I should have said."

The Matrarc shifted in her chair and repositioned her elbow, as if holding hands were uncomfortable for her, too.

"Please," Gaia said, flexing her fingers and trying to draw away.

The Matrarc's clasp closed more firmly. "You'll stay where you are."

On the other side of the table, Mlady Roxanne tapped a finger against the wooden surface, then tucked her dark hair behind her ear. "If you please, Mlady Olivia," she said. "She's young. She's new to us. There is no doubt she didn't know the severity of what she was doing."

"That, I'm afraid, is the point," the Matrarc said. "Chardo knew. How old is he?"

The women looked around the table at each other. Gaia waited, but no one seemed to have the answer.

"Nineteen," Gaia said. "Peter's nineteen."

"And how old are you?" Mlady Roxanne asked.

"Sixteen."

There were more looks around the table.

"Three years' difference," Mlady Roxanne said quietly.

Mlady Maudie began flipping through a small book of papers.

"The law is clear in such a case," the Matrarc said. "Attempted rape. First offense. Three years' difference with the girl at sixteen. That means twelve hours in the stocks. A week in prison. Do I have that right, Mlady Maudie?"

Gaia could not believe what she was hearing. Her fingers twisted briefly in the Matrarc's hand before the Matrarc's fingers tightened again to still her.

Mlady Maudie nodded at a page in her book. "Yes. You always do."

"If he did something," Gaia protested, "if he really tried to rape me, such a sentence might make some sense, but for a kiss? You can't call a kiss attempted rape. You can't even put it in the same category as a violent crime. It's an insult to any woman who's ever really been raped."

"It's the law," Mlady Maudie said.

"Then it's time to change it," Gaia objected. "Aren't we in charge?"

"We don't change our laws on a whim," Mlady Roxanne said. "This is only a small tribunal called in an emergency to hear Chardo's case. The kind of change you're talking about requires all the cuzines here, and we'd have a lengthy debate."

"Then call everyone," Gaia said.

"We're scheduled to meet again in three days," Mlady Maudie said. "We can put it on the agenda for then."

"Then postpone Peter's sentencing until then," Gaia said.

The Matrarc was shaking her head. "It's better to get it over with," she said. "Over and done. If it weren't Chardo, we wouldn't even be hesitating. We can't appear to play favorites."

"Your instinct to play favorites is leading you toward fairness," Gaia argued. "You know the law is wrong."

"I don't," the Matrarc said. "It protects our mlasses. It gives them the chance to consider the men freely and comfortably without ever being pressured, and the men learn respect."

"Compulsory respect," Gaia said.

"What's the difference?" Mlady Maudie said.

"Accept it," the Matrarc said. "Every society has its customs and laws. You just chose to ignore one that matters here. Or more accurately, Chardo did. Would you care to tell us which of you reached for the other first?"

294

Startled, Gaia thought back, remembering how she'd bumped into him unknowingly in the darkness and how easily he'd drawn her back with him, putting his arms around her.

The Matrarc's fingers clasped hers firmly again for a moment, as if she'd felt Gaia's answer in her hand.

"I thought not," the Matrarc said. "I'll grant you one concession. I don't think it would be right to keep Chardo in limbo for three days, but if it is truly likely that we would change the law, I would allow it." She gestured around the table. "We're a fair sample of the cuzines right here. From us, we can guess how a vote among all of the cuzines would go. How many of you are in favor of revising the law regarding attempted rape? Say 'Ay.'"

Gaia said "Ay," and she heard an echo from across the table as Mlady Roxanne agreed with her. They were the only two voices.

Then, very softly, Peony's mother spoke. "Ay," she said.

The other women at the table looked at her. She said nothing more.

"Those opposed, say 'Nay,'" the Matrarc said.

Six voices rose in a negative, and the sound fell away to nothing.

Gaia jerked her hand out of the Matrarc's. "You're just cruel, all of you," Gaia said.

"Watch yourself, Mlass Gaia," Mlady Beebe said. "We're keeping our girls safe. You just have to be more careful next time."

"Not to get caught?" Gaia demanded.

"No. Not to let yourself get in such a situation at all," Mlady Beebe said.

"You'll learn to respect our ways in time," Mlady Eva added more gently. "They're good ways."

"When an innocent person gets punished, that's not good," Gaia said. "I know that much. The men would never support such a law."

"So now you're suggesting that the men should be allowed to make the laws? Do you think they should vote?" Mlady Maudie demanded. "Is that what this is really about?"

"If that's what it takes to have justice," Gaia said.

There was an outburst around the able, and laughter as well. The Matrarc frowned and rapped her knuckles on the table.

"My cuzines, please," the Matrarc said. "We will stick to the matter at hand, and that is Chardo Peter's crime. You need to understand this, Mlass Gaia. Even though you consider him innocent, he still committed a crime against the law as it stands now." She made another gesture around the table. "The sentence holds? Say 'Ay.'"

The council agreed, unanimously even Mlady Roxanne and Peony's mother. Gaia was in such shock she couldn't speak.

The Matrarc touched a hand to her monocle. "Then tell his father, Mlady Maudie, and have him fetched up from the prison immediately. The time starts as soon as he can be put in the stocks. The days are shorter now, and I don't want him out in the dark any longer than he has to be. Remember, no food or water. Mlass Gaia, will you drive me back up to the bluff? It's my son's birthday," the Matrarc said to the others. "Little Jerry. He's four."

The women smiled, relaxing into casual chat, and began to rise from the table. Mlady Maudie went out the front door. That abruptly, the meeting was over, and Gaia was stunned. The arrogance, the confidence of the women was staggering, as if they hadn't taken one word she'd said seriously. Mlady Beebe was showing her new son to the woman beside her, who set aside her knitting to coo. Disgusted, Gaia reached down for her satchel.

"Mlass Gaia," Mlady Roxanne began. "I hope you'll understand."

Gaia glared at her teacher, backing away. "I don't want to have anything to do with you."

Noises came from above, and she looked up to see several of the mlasses coming out of their rooms. Sunlight was pouring in through the clerestory above. The day was beginning. People were going about their business. Norris must be back in the kitchen, starting breakfast.

She pivoted on her heel and strode rapidly out the front door to the veranda, where she gripped the railing and looked out to the commons. Peter's brother and father and uncles stood in stoic silence near the stocks, clearly having just received word of the verdict, and Will lifted a hand to his father's shoulder. Gaia couldn't bear it. In the commons, other people were gathering to hear the news. She expected them to look somber, concerned, but strangely, perhaps because it was the first time in weeks that the sun had appeared and the day promised to be spectacularly clear and beautiful, there was an undercurrent of joy in the way people smiled, greeting each other. Already a child was playing with a toy truck in the dirt at his father's feet.

From the other end of the commons, several men came riding in on horseback. More people were following on foot behind, and as Gaia squinted to see more clearly, she identified Peter in the middle of the riders. Someone was leading his horse, and as he came nearer, she realized his hands were tied behind him. She had an awful recollection of the last occasion when she'd seen him ride in, only that time, he'd been an outrider leading in prisoners and one of them had been dead.

Now Peter was the prisoner.

The people in the commons gathered nearer, leaving a path between them for the procession. The Matrarc came out to the porch, tapping softly with her cane, and stood to Gaia's right. Good, Gaia thought. *She should at least be here to witness this.*

From the right came the sound of wheels, and Gaia looked over to see Dinah driving a wagon. Josephine sat beside her on the bench, holding her baby, and as the wagon turned before the lodge, Gaia saw Leon was in the back, holding Maya. She hadn't realized how badly she wanted them there until she saw them.

"Is that Mx. Dinah's wagon I hear?" the Matrarc asked.

"Yes," Gaia said. "She's brought Leon and Mx. Josephine and the babies."

"She would."

The entourage from the prison arrived before the lodge, and the guards dismounted into the dust. Peter's profile was aimed toward his father, who silently lifted a hand. One of the guards spoke to Peter and reached up to him, and then, with his hands still tied behind him, Peter swung off the horse. Several buttons of his pale blue shirt had come undone, and his lip, from where he'd been hit the night before, was discolored.

"He looks bad," came a soft voice from Gaia's left, and she realized Peony and the other mlasses had come out to the porch beside her. "I'm sorry, Mlass Gaia."

I can't stand this, Gaia thought. She shrugged away from the others and started down the steps. The guards were moving Peter forward. Four sets of stocks were positioned to the right of the lodge. Each device of heavy, weathered framework had three holes cut between two hinged beams of wood. Peter would have his head in the middle hole, his wrists in the outer holes, and he could stand, leaning over, or kneel against a board

298

at the base of the stocks. She could already imagine that the discomfort would be only partly caused by the stocks themselves, but the time, pinned there, would cause his own body to strain against itself, and there'd be no relief, not even for a moment. Thirst and hunger would torment him under the noonday sun. Mosquitoes, at nightfall, would be another kind of torture. She only hoped he'd be numb to it all by then.

They stood him before the nearest stocks, facing the commons, and untied his hands. As if he'd been tied so long that his muscles were stiff, Peter curled his arms forward and hunched up his shoulders for a moment. He stared bleakly at the stocks. The voices in the crowd fell silent. He carefully did up the buttons that had come undone on his shirt. Finally, with slow fingers, he straightened his collar.

The small gesture of dignity sliced through her like nothing had before, and that was when she made her decision.

She turned to the wagon where Dinah and Josephine sat watching with sober expressions. Near them, Leon stood holding Maya against his shoulder. Gaia quietly set her satchel and cloak in the back of the wagon and briefly touched her locket watch to be sure it was around her neck.

"Leon," she said. "I need you."

His blue eyes met hers squarely and for a long moment he studied her. Then he nodded, ready to do whatever she needed. He passed Maya to Dinah so his hands were free and pushed up his sleeves.

They were lifting the top bar of Peter's stocks as she strode forward. She wasn't going to say anything to Peter at all. She couldn't. She was already trembling with fear. The hinge squeaked as they brought the bar down on top of his neck and wrists, and she heard the click as a peg was dropped in the slot to keep it closed. There was no need for a lock. No one would dare undo the stocks until the full term of the punishment was meted out.

Gaia kept walking, with Leon following, until she came to the second stocks, but she was too shaky to be able to open up the top part herself. She turned to Leon.

"Help me in," she said.

"You can't," he said quietly.

"I must."

She couldn't look to her left, where Peter was. She couldn't look beyond him to Will or the cuzines on the porch. But she could lift her pleading eyes to Leon, and she knew that she could count on him.

He lifted the top bar of the stocks.

"Look after Maya for me," she said.

"I will."

"What's going on?" came a voice from the crowd.

Gaia tucked her hair behind her ears. She set her neck over the center dip in the wood. She felt along the top of the beam until she came to the places for her wrists, and set them there, and then she closed her eyes as Leon set the top beam, carefully, back in place, and audibly dropped in the peg to keep her there.

CHAPTER 24

the stocks

SHE COULDN'T LOOK UP to see them, but she could hear their voices.

"But she didn't do anything wrong."

"Did the Matrarc sentence her, too?"

"He's in for twelve hours. Is she, too?"

"Isn't she supposed to be up at the winner's cabin?"

"Look at the Matrarc. I've never seen her so furious."

And then a nearer voice, a man's voice. "This is just wrong. You there. Let her out."

"She doesn't want out," Leon said.

"But she's innocent," the man said. "I was there last night. I know." She recognized the voice of Doerring, the big man in the striped shirt.

"She believes that Chardo is innocent also," Leon said.

"I can't stand to see her in there. It's obscene."

Gaia heard the sound of metal clearing from a sheath and hoped Doerring wasn't armed. It wouldn't do her any good if Leon was arrested now, too.

"Stand back, Doerring." It was Will's voice. His boots came

within her line of sight, black and solid in the brown dirt before her. "She stays as long as she wants to."

"You're crazy, the whole lot of you," said Doerring.

She heard more shuffling and saw more booted feet surrounding her.

Then she heard Doerring's voice, moving farther away. The sound of metal came again, more quietly. "Who ever heard of protesting a law by getting in the stocks?"

"She'll grow tired of it," came another voice. "I left my laundry soaking. Come get me if anything happens."

Gaia was already growing tired of it. Five minutes in, she started feeling a strain in her ankles, of all places. She tried kneeling, and that was better for a minute, but then her knees began to hurt. It was warmer than she'd realized, too, with the morning sun weighing heavy in her full skirt. Was that a spider, very tiny, dropping down a spindle of web to her right?

"How many are we?" came Leon's voice.

"I count eleven. I can go for some weapons, some pitch forks and shovels if you think we'll need them," said Will.

"I don't think so," Leon said.

"No weapons," Gaia said.

"She says no weapons," Leon repeated.

She tried to turn her head, but couldn't twist far enough to see Peter's stocks. She felt the slight tug at her neck as her locket watch bumped against the wood. "Peter?" she said. "Can you hear me?"

His voice sounded distant. "Yes. You've made your point and I appreciate it. Now tell Will to let you out."

"It isn't just about you anymore," Gaia said.

He answered something she couldn't hear.

"What? What did he say?" she asked.

"He says kissing you was worth it," Leon said. "Would you care to reply?"

"No."

She squirmed to think of Leon as the go-between for such a conversation. She quit trying to look to the side and instead focused downward, seeing the frame of the stocks and the dirt directly below her head. It was going to be awkward sorting out things with Peter eventually. *Far worse than awkward, actually.* She tried shifting her shoulder a little. Her arms felt a little achy, like the blood wasn't getting to them right, but if she relaxed to let them sag, it hurt her wrists.

"I'm taking Mx. Josephine and the babies to my place," Dinah said. "She's really upset. But I'll be back after I get her settled. You plan on staying?"

"As long as it takes," Leon said. "I'd get in the stocks myself if I thought that would help."

Dinah laughed. "Somehow I don't think you'd garner quite as much sympathy."

"Tell Mx. Josephine not to worry," Gaia said. "It's really not so bad."

"It looks like a regular picnic," Dinah said. Then her voice softened. "I'll tell her."

Gaia tried straightening her legs again, and her knees felt strange from the kneeling. The little spider went down farther. Her hair had come loose from her ears to hang toward the ground, further limiting her vision. She closed her eyes and concentrated on breathing deep. Over the first hour, it was her arms that went numb first, and then her wrists. When she tried to move them, it made it worse, so she focused on keeping her head turned slightly, tucking her chin partly into the wood. That way she could rest her neck and still breathe. She was better standing than kneeling, too. By the second hour, standing and kneeling were equally bad, so she stayed down.

"Any word from the Matrarc?" she asked.

"She decided to stay down here and keep an eye on things," Leon said. "She's in the lodge. She could look out the window and see you if she weren't blind."

"She's going to have her baby soon," Gaia said. "From the way she held herself sometimes, I think she was having contractions already."

"Does her husband know?"

Gaia licked her lips and swallowed thickly. "It's his son's birthday. He stayed up on the bluff with the kids."

"Will you get out of the stocks if she needs you?" Leon asked.

"Not unless she lets Peter out first."

There was quiet for a moment, and then voices, farther out.

"How many of us are there?" she asked.

"It's about twenty-five, now," Leon said. "They're sitting around you and Peter, here in the sun. Not just men. Three libbies came a few minutes ago. They were telling jokes when they first came, and then they decided to stay."

"Hey, Mlass Gaia," called out a woman's voice to Gaia's right. "We're with you, girl. Down with the cuzines."

Gaia smiled slightly, but she'd been thinking, too. "Leon, I think we need to send a message to the Matrarc to make things very clear. Tell her we object to the cuzines making laws without everyone's input. If she'll concede she's wrong about punishing Peter, and if she lets him out to show she's willing to let everyone vote, then I'll get out, too, and come take care of her when she's in labor."

"Did you get all that, Will?" Leon asked.

"Yes," Will said. "And what if she says no?"

304

"Then I'll stay here," Gaia said. "As long as Peter does. I can't make any promises for after that."

There were voices to her left, and then Will crouched down where Gaia could see him if she turned her face slightly. His brown eyes were clouded with concern.

"Peter says he wants you to drink something," Will said. "He says it's not a restriction for you."

The mention of drinking made her thirst worse. "The sentence is the same for both of us," she said.

He watched her another moment, then nodded. "All right," he said. "I'll bring the Matrarc your message." He straightened again and was gone.

A fly buzzed by, and Gaia thought she could hear her locket watch ticking. A rough place in the wood just below her chin was rubbing a raw place in her skin, and she was careful whenever she moved not to make it worse.

"Leon?" she asked.

"I'm here." His voice was near, to her left. She saw the homespun fabric of his trousers bend over his knee as he sat in the dust beside her. He leaned a little nearer, so she could see his face.

"You okay?" he asked.

She wasn't really. She wanted him to talk to her. "Do you think about the Enclave much?"

He slouched lower on his elbow, settling into an angle where she could see him easily. "That's what you want to know?"

She smiled a little. "Just tell me something."

His seemed to consider a moment. "I worry a little about Genevieve."

"Your mother? Why?"

"She's the one who helped me out of V cell," Leon said. "I worry that life isn't very easy for her."

"You never told me how you got out," Gaia said.

Leon's gaze turned inward and his voice became subdued. "I don't know how many interrogation sessions I went through before she came. Genevieve brought Myrna Silk to cauterize my finger and do what she could for my back." He winced briefly, then shrugged. "When I told Genevieve I wanted to leave, she put together some supplies and took me to the North Gate."

"Did your father know what she was doing?" Gaia asked.

"He knew. The Protectorat knew." Leon raked his hair back from his forehead. "Genevieve said he wasn't pleased with her, but then, Genevieve wasn't pleased with him, either." He smiled oddly. "She said he never knew how to handle me."

She doubted anyone really knew how to handle Leon, least of all his father. His *adoptive* father, she corrected mentally. She shifted slightly and her knees felt better for a moment. "Why doesn't that surprise me?" she said. "Do you always call your mother by her first name?"

"No. Not when I'm with her," Leon said. As he spoke, he doodled lines in the dirt with a little stick. "Just when I think about her. I guess I always have." His smile warmed into something genuine. "My sister would have liked you."

"Really?"

He laughed. "Why is that so strange?"

Gaia was diverted by the idea of meeting Evelyn again some day under different circumstances. "I doubt Evelyn would be impressed if she could see me right now."

"Evelyn would like you, too," he said. "But I was actually thinking of Fiona."

She felt oddly honored that he'd meant his favorite sister Fiona, the fragile, wild one. His family would always be complicated, she realized, even in memory. Moving away hadn't changed that.

"There's something I've wanted to know," she said, glancing at his doodles lines. "I didn't know how to ask."

"I'm listening now."

She blinked as a fly passed close to her cheek. "What did you say in that note you sent me? Back when you were in prison? Peony said you wrote it in code. Was it my father's code?"

"A simpler version. It doesn't matter now."

"I'd still like to know," she said.

He frowned slightly, not quite meeting her gaze. "It said 'Orange.' "

No single word could ever have been a stronger plea to her, or, considering that she'd refused to read it, a stronger reproach. "I hope some day you'll forgive me," she said.

His blue eyes met hers directly then. "There's nothing to forgive. I understand now what you were up against." He turned in the direction of the lodge. "Will's coming. I won't be gone long." He shifted out of her line of sight as he stood.

She heard voices again, and then Will crouched nearer.

"Mlass Gaia?" he asked. "Are you all right?"

"What did she say?"

"She said nothing. I delivered your message, and Mlady Maudie told me the Matrarc had no reply. She's gone into labor."

Gaia felt a new heaviness in her chest as her hope dwindled.

"Thanks, Will," she said.

"You know you don't have to do this," Will said. "We can find other ways to negotiate with the cuzines." He dropped his voice. "I can tell them what we found in the barn, if that would help."

"Please don't," Gaia said. She didn't want Will in trouble with the Matrarc, too. "Everyone trusts you. I don't want that to end. What we found is a separate issue."

Will looked away, towards her left. "Have you told Vlatir?"

"No." She swallowed with an effort. "He'd keep your se-cret, though, if you told him. How's Peter?"

"He's holding up. And you?"

It was getting harder to lie. "I'm fine."

As the sun rose higher, a dizziness came to her, and she no longer bothered trying to listen to the voices around her. Her lips grew parched. She wet herself, with a sense of relief, and then her urine dried down her legs. She knelt now, slumping backward, so that her jaw and the back of her head were wedged in the wood, and she could breathe through her nose. She couldn't feel much anymore except the sun on her face where her hair didn't cover it, and an exquisite burning sensation in the skin along her nose and cheeks. Her scar pulsed slowly with pain, and she thought of her mother, burning her on purpose to keep her safe.

"Mlass Gaia?" It sounded like Dinah's voice, but distant.

"I think she's sleeping," Leon said.

Gaia tried to move her tongue around her mouth. She cracked open her eyes and saw Leon's legs again where he was sitting beside her in the dust.

"Should her hands be that color?" Dinah asked.

"Probably not," Leon said. "Does the Matrarc want to nego-tiate?"

"She says she won't be coerced. She wants me to try to convince Gaia to give in."

Gaia moved her lips slowly to form the word. "No."

"She won't," Leon said.

"The Matrarc wanted to know if I'd help her with her labor," Dinah said. "Me. Can you imagine?"

"Who is helping her?"

"Mlass Taja and Dominic, and a couple of the cuzines."

"Not Norris?"

"No. He's here with us," Dinah said. "I'm guessing that's the end of his job cooking for the lodge."

"Everyone's risking their jobs and more if this ends badly," Leon said.

Gaia shifted forward slightly, and an ache shot down her legs. "Peter?" she asked.

"Peter's not talking much," Leon said. "He hasn't moved in a while, either. His father's sitting by him. Will's been talking to people in the crowd."

Dinah's narrow boots angled into Gaia's view, and then she crouched down so that Gaia could see her face. "Are you doing all right?" Dinah asked.

"Numb," Gaia said.

"That's good, I suppose." Dinah grimaced. "I had no idea you could be so stubborn. Remind me never to get in a fight with you."

Gaia smiled inside, even if her face didn't move.

"I can't believe all these people," Dinah said.

"Who?" Gaia said.

Dinah shifted to sit down in the dirt to Gaia's right. "There's about two hundred, I'd say. Men mostly, and a dozen of the libbies. My boy Mikey and my brother's family are here. I don't know when Mlass Peony and her mother came, but they're here. They're the only cuzines. Boughton Phineas just came by to sit with them, too. Have you met him?"

"No."

Gaia was glad that Peony was there. Then her mind slipped a little, and she tried to remember if the Matrarc was in labor. Had someone said that? She couldn't remember where her satchel was. She closed her eyes again.

"Tell her more," Leon said. "She's listening."

"Let's see. Some of the men have a pack of cards, and they're betting for rice flower," Dinah said. "You'll be smelling it soon, I expect. One of the Havandish boys, he's maybe thirteen, he's sitting with his grandfather, back to back. There are a lot of other people in the commons, watching us. I don't know if they're just curious or if they're going to join us. What do you think, Vlatir?"

"They'll join us."

"There are armed guards around the lodge," Dinah continued, "and a few cuzines are in the bell tower with their bows, but they're just watching."

Gaia was half listening, but it was easier to let her mind wander to the back porch of her parents' home and remember how cool it had been in the mornings when she woke up under the mosquito netting. *We should be raising more chickens*, she thought. A little chick pecked its way out of a shell, but then it began pecking at her eyelid. That wasn't right. She couldn't have chicks in her eyeballs.

"Don't cry, Mx. Dinah," Leon said. "Here. I thought you libbies were supposed to be tough."

"It's just she looks so awful," Dinah said in a tight voice. "And there's still hours and hours to go."

"The Matrarc will change her mind. You'll see," Leon said. "Dominic came to the window a minute ago. He must be talking to her. Go tell them Gaia says she won't give in."

Dominic. Dominoes. Gaia used to play with dominoes, white ones with black dots. The dots floated upward, always small no matter how close they came. The baby chicks grew afraid. Gaia tried to shoo the dots away, but that brought a twisted burning to her wrist.

Stay still, Gaia's mother said. *No more moving.*

Listen to your mother, squirt, her father said.

310

"Okay," she whispered. She listened to her mother. She did not move. And in time, she was able to forget the chickens and the dots burning in her face, and sleep.

It was much later that the pain woke her. It was in her wrists first, spreading like fire along her arms, and then it was in her neck and her face. There were hands on her, savage, terrible arms, tipping her. She opened her eyes partly to see nightmare trees rolling overhead, and her limp, burning hands were lowered at an impossible angle onto her own chest. She couldn't move anything herself, not the smallest muscle, except her eyelids, and they burned, too.

"Be gentle. You're hurting her."

"On three."

No, she thought. *Don't shake me.*

There was counting, and then they shook her all over. It was the most complete pain she'd ever experienced, a shattering explosion in every molecule of her body, and in three seconds she was gone again.

CHAPTER 25

the matrarc's choice

Her ears came alive first, hearing the quiet sound of water moving in a bowl.

"They waited too long," came a voice in the darkness. "It's their own fault."

She was afraid to open her eyes, afraid she would start to hurt again, and then something cool and soft touched her face. It was a merciful, beautiful sensation, and her cheeks welcomed the sweetness of it.

"I think she's coming around. Gaia, can you hear me?" Leon asked.

"Peter?" she asked. *Did they free him?*

The coolness vanished.

Then a woman's voice came, and the coolness was light and dabbing again. "Peter's here, too," Dinah said. "They released him first, just as you wanted."

Gaia tried to move her head, but sharp pains ran down her neck. She gasped and held still.

"The Matrarc's husband wants to know if she can come," said a man's voice.

"Tell him there's no possible way," Leon said.

312

"It's urgent."

"See for yourself," Leon said.

As cool air moved around her, she opened her heavy eyelids for the first time. She was in a quiet room, a small living room, and when she saw the shelves of books and the rose-colored lamp, she remembered Dinah's place.

"We got trouble breaking loose all around the village," the man said. "I'm just saying. If you could get her up there to the lodge, it might help."

"Get out," Leon said. "Now."

She tried moving her finger and found she could.

Did the Matrarc have her baby? she asked, but no words came out.

"Here, Mlass Gaia. Try this," Dinah said.

Gaia moved her lips against the rim of a cup, and a pure sip of water wet her tongue. She tried to lift her hand for the cup.

"It's all right, I've got you," Dinah said.

She was helping her up enough to drink, and more of the liquid was smoothing along the dryness of Gaia's throat. Gaia let out a moan of pleasure and greed. "More," she said hoarsely. She wanted to see Leon, but she couldn't find him without turning her head. There was a person-shaped lump on the cot opposite hers, and when she saw his light brown hair, she realized he must be Peter, only his face was burned bright red, and he was all crumpled looking, like he'd been dropped by a giant and squashed by the giant's foot.

"Giant," she mumbled. That was kind of funny, actually.

"Can you understand me?" Dinah asked. She was dabbing Gaia's face with a damp cloth again.

Gaia shifted her gaze to the libby's face, and slowly licked her lips. "Yes," she whispered, concentrating.

313

"They left you in the stocks for ten hours," Dinah said. "Nearly the whole time of Peter's sentence. Do you remember?"

She did. Much of it. She remembered the spider, and Leon's voice always near. She remembered pain unbelievable when they took her out.

"Where's Leon?" she asked.

"He's here," Dinah said.

She had to wait until he moved into her line of sight, and finally he did. He'd never looked so serious, with his dark eyebrows lowered and his intense blue eyes regarding her carefully. Dinah gave her seat to him. Gaia felt the tightness in her throat easing again.

"We won?" Gaia asked.

He tenderly lifted her hand, bending near to press his cheek against her knuckles. "We did," he said. "You did. There were over eight hundred people with us by the end, and more were coming. The Matrarc had to let you go. If she'd waited another two hours, we would have had a majority, and she knew that."

"Eight hundred?"

How could she not have known that? How long had she been unconscious? A banging noise came from outside, and then a cheer and laughter.

"They're outside, most of them," Leon said. "They followed us here, and they're waiting to see if you're all right."

"I'm good," she said.

He smiled, but he was wincing, too. "You're not good," he said. "Your poor little hands."

He turned over the one he held, and she saw a raw, bruised discoloration ran around it in a ring just where her hand widened beyond her wrist. The weight of her arms and sagging body had hung from there and from her neck, too. That must be why it was so painful to turn her head, even though she hadn't broken anything.

"We have to finalize it," she said. "I need to talk to the Matrarc. We need to assemble everyone for a first vote."

"In time, but first you need to rest," he said. "You're nearly dead."

"How's Maya?"

"She's fine. Josephine's in the bedroom with her and little Junie, too."

Gaia looked more carefully at Peter and found he was still out cold. "Did the Matrarc have her baby?" she asked.

"Not yet."

That concerned her. Gaia tried to move again, but her muscles were too weak, and all she managed to do was smooth her fingers over his. "Do you have a stretcher or something?" she asked. "To take me up to the lodge?"

"I said you're not going," Leon said.

"Just this one last thing," Gaia said. "You helped me before."

He touched the hair on her forehead, smoothing it back, and his eyes turned unbelievably sad. "I should be shot for having any part of it."

"You don't mean that."

He ducked his face away right when she most wanted to see him. She reached slowly to thread her stiff fingers through his dark hair. "Leon, what's this?"

"I had to sit beside you and do nothing, all that time," he said.

She hadn't guessed what that would be like for him. She tried to pull his hair, and when he looked up again, the traces of agony were written plainly in his features.

"But now we can get rid of the stupid laws," she said. She knew how he hated injustice. "It'll be completely different here, fair for all the libbies and men, too."

315

"That's what kills me," he said. "You did it in part for me."

"Of course I did," she said, surprised. "I just wish I'd realized what I needed to do before I kissed Peter. I'm so sorry about that."

"Please don't. I can't stand to have you apologizing to me." He gently smoothed back her hair again, as if he couldn't resist touching her.

"That's right," she said, smiling. "I apologize all the time and it never fixes a thing."

"Gaia, don't be mean. You know I never meant that."

She kept hoping to evoke an answering smile in his eyes, and finally it came, warm and sad and just for her. He truly was endearingly, killingly handsome when he smiled.

"I need you to do something for me," she said.

His smile vanished. "No."

She laughed, and it didn't hurt so much. "How did you guess? Take me up to the Matrarc. I really need to go. Maybe you could ask eight hundred people to carry my cot."

"How do you think we got you here?" he said.

A dozen lamps glowed in the atrium, and the mladies and mlasses cleared to make room for Gaia's cot and the men who carried her in. Gaia had never seen men in the atrium, and they seemed inordinately large now, filling the space with their tall, strong bodies.

She sat up carefully. The clean blouse and trousers she'd borrowed from Dinah felt loose on her. She'd drunk some willow bark tea and eaten a little, enough so that her mind was clear even if she was still incredibly weak and sore.

Above, at the second-floor railing, Taja appeared and looked down at her. "You're here at last," she said. "Come up quickly."

Gaia took a look at the staircase and put out a hand to Leon. "Carry me?"

Leon slung her satchel over his shoulder and lifted her securely into his arms. She held tightly to his shirt, and as he carried her up the steps, she concentrated on trying to hold still, because even the little bumps of his footfalls traveled through her sore body, bringing new vibrations of pain. She was sweating by the time he passed into the Matrarc's room.

One look at the Matrarc told her she was in very bad shape. Dominic, Taja, and Chardo Will all looked up expectantly.

Leon set Gaia gently on a chair beside the bed, and she leaned forward slowly to brace her elbow on the mattress and prop her chin on her hand, supporting her neck.

"Olivia, darling," Dominic said gently to his wife. "Mlass Gaia's here."

The Matrarc's voice was slow and sonorous, and she spoke distinctly despite her obvious exhaustion. "I didn't think you'd come."

"You should have let her out of the stocks hours ago," Leon said.

"Leon, don't," Gaia said instantly.

"It's Vlatir?" the Matrarc asked.

"Yes," Dominic said. "I'll make him go."

"It doesn't matter," the Matrarc said. "He can stay."

Gaia glared at Leon. He shrugged, leaning back against the wall. "Gaia's nearly dead," Leon said. "You'd know if you could see her."

"That makes two of us," the Matrarc said.

Dominic turned to his wife, and the others went still for a moment.

Gaia beckoned to Leon to bring her a basin and water, and she straightened to wash her hands. The Matrarc lay on her right side, her blind eyes staring toward the black window, her huge belly extended before her. Dominic held her right hand in both of his. Taja was backed into a corner near the door. Will sat at the foot of the bed, his sleeves rolled back and a roll of bloodied towels in a basin beside him.

"When did you come?" Gaia asked him.

"As soon as she let you and Peter out. I've been useless, though, I'm afraid."

Drying her hands, Gaia gave the Matrarc a long, searching look. "You agreed to let all the men and libbies vote when you let us out of the stocks. You realize that, don't you?"

"Of course I do. It's the end of Sylum."

"Olivia, you need to think of yourself now, and the baby," Dominic said. "Let it go."

The Matrarc clenched her face as a contraction came, and with growing concern, Gaia saw it lacked the intensity and duration to be productive.

"How long has she been in labor?" Gaia asked.

"Ten hours," Dominic said. "She delivered her last four babies in half this much time."

"Have any of you examined her?" she asked, turning to Will.

"I tried," Will said. "It didn't feel right, but I had no idea what to do. There's been a trickle of blood on and off."

Everything about this looked wrong to Gaia.

"Do you feel movement from the baby?" she asked the Matrarc.

"Sometimes. Not as much as before."

"She didn't tell us that," Dominic said, looking anxious.

"I think it would be best if I sat on the side of the bed. I need to be able to examine her and I can't stand well," Gaia said.

Will shifted out of the way, and Leon helped her.

"Lift her gown for me," she said.

Dominic reached to pull the Matrarc's gown up, and Gaia saw an alarming pattern of black veins already spreading across the mother's belly.

"Mlady Olivia," Gaia said. She rested her wrist lightly on the Matrarc's arm. "Tell me whatever you can. What do you feel?"

"I feel like I'm plugged. Like I'm pushing all I can, but the baby's just plugged in."

Gaia spread her hands on the woman's stomach, palpitating slowly, and then she put her ear to the warm skin and listened carefully for the faint, fast heartbeat of the baby within. It always made her think of butterfly wings, and it was there, urging her to hurry. She straightened to feel around more carefully, until she could feel knees and the back, and knew the baby was lined up normally, which was at least something.

"I'm going to examine you internally now," Gaia said.

Gaia ignored the creaking pain in her own arms and gently reached inside, feeling carefully for the cervix, which was fully effaced but only about four centimeters dilated. Where the hard lump of a baby's head normally should be, she found a tight, stretchy substance instead, and as her fingers continued to prod, in her mind's eye she constructed an image of what she was feeling. The mother was, indeed, plugged. The baby's placenta had grown across the opening of the uterus, like a living mass of purple dough over the funneled opening of a soft chute, and even though it had torn partially, there was no way for the baby to come through. If it tore much more, the baby would die quickly.

Gaia pulled out and sagged back. She reached for the basin again, and Leon held it while she dipped her hands in the water, where the blood swirled.

"You see?" the Matrarc said.

319

"Yes," Gaia answered. Her heart grew heavy. There was a choice to be made soon. It might already be too late.

"Taja?" the Matrarc said.

"I'm here, Mom."

"Get the others. I want to say goodbye to my children."

Taja glanced at Gaia, her expression stunned, and then she slipped out the door. As it clicked closed, Dominic seemed to wake up.

"What are you talking about?" Dominic said to his wife. He turned to Gaia. "What's wrong?"

"I'm sorry," Gaia said as gently as she could. "The baby's placenta is blocking the cervix."

"What does that mean?" he demanded.

"The organ inside the womb that feeds the umbilical cord, the placenta, has grown across the opening of the womb," Gaia said. "It means the baby can't get out. It's plugged in."

"Then cut the thing away," Dominic said. "Pull it out."

"Go in with a blade? The baby would die in the process, even if I could do it quickly," Gaia said. She could imagine all the blood.

Dominic laughed helplessly. "We can't just leave the baby in there forever." He searched Gaia's face, then looked back at his wife, distressed. "Let the baby die, then," he said. "Save my wife."

Gaia didn't know what to tell him. She couldn't take the placenta and the baby out without massive hemorrhaging, and she knew what happened then. That was how her own mother had died. Fear backed up inside her, cold and hard.

"I can't," Gaia said.

"Are you telling me you won't?" Dominic demanded. "We have seven other children who all need their mother."

"Dominic," the Matrarc began.

320

"No. I don't care," Dominic insisted. "I'm not going on without you, Olivia. We're losing this one. I know how you feel about it, but we'll have others. It'll be okay."

Gaia looked up at Leon to see if he understood what she'd been trying to say. Then she reached for her satchel and stiffly pulled out the smaller bag of tinctures and herbs.

"It's not that Gaia won't," Leon said. "It's that it's not possible. She can't save your wife by sacrificing the baby."

Dominic frowned at Gaia, obviously trying to process the information. "Are you telling me you can't save either of them?"

"It's not that. There's a chance I could save the baby," Gaia said.

She watched Dominic's horrified expression as the implications became clear to him.

"No," he said flatly. "Olivia, did you hear that? I'm telling you no."

"Dom," the Matrarc said softly.

"No!" he said, standing. "Get out of here! I don't want you here," he said to Gaia.

Gaia felt Leon's hands on her shoulders.

"No, Dom. I want her. Wait, please," the Matrarc said.

Her face contorted during another contraction, and she reached for her husband's hand. Dominic sat again beside her, his face grim, his eyes furious.

"Don't make it harder for me," the Matrarc said softly to her husband.

The following silence was terrible, and then a soft knock came on the door.

"Cover me up so the children don't have to see any blood," the Matrarc said. "Be sure about it. Give us a minute as a family, but then, Gaia, you have to come back. Promise me."

"I will. Take this, now. Open your mouth." She leaned near

321

with a tincture of witch hazel and shepherd's purse, and carefully placed the drops under the Matrarc's tongue.

"What's that for?" Dominic said.

"For the bleeding," Gaia said.

The door was opening and Taja, her eyes enormous, was
peeking in. "Mom? We're all here."

"One minute," the Matrarc said.

Gaia packed a clean towel between the Matrarc's legs again
while Will collected the bloody ones in a basin. Dominic sat
motionless, stricken, as Leon spread a clean white blanket over
the bed.

"Okay. We're going now," Gaia said. "Leon?" She reached
for his arm, but he simply lifted her off her feet again, and they
went out to make room for the Matrarc's children. Jerry, the
birthday boy, sucked his thumb. The youngest, a toddler, was
carrying his bear. Will closed the door behind them.

They moved down the balcony toward a bench, and Leon
set her gently on her feet. Across the atrium space on the opposite balcony, a couple of mladies waited to be of any assistance, but Gaia waved them off.

"You holding up okay, Mlass Gaia?" Will asked.

She felt his concerned gaze, and nodded. "I'm going to need
your help soon," she said.

"There's no way you can save the Matrarc, too?" Will said.

"I'll try, of course, but I've never sewn anyone up after a
blade delivery, and she'll lose a lot of blood no matter what I
do. Once we start, we'll have to do it fast." She considered,
feeling rather sick. Even if she succeeded in extricating the
baby and sewing the Matrarc closed, there would be nothing
to prevent infection. She hadn't had time to learn more about
the lily-poppy Peter had said the old doctor used for pain. "I
think we'll have to tie her down. I only have motherwort for

the pain. It won't be nearly enough." She touched a hand to her forehead.

"Can you get Gaia some tea?" Leon asked.

Will gazed at her a moment, then nodded and turned for the stairs. As he left, Leon sat, pulling Gaia tenderly beside him. She couldn't relax, but she leaned her cheek against his shoulder.

"It's hard for me to believe you're not furious at the Matrarc," he said quietly.

"Why?"

"She left you in the stocks for hours. That's something I don't think I'll ever forgive, and you're helping her as if it never happened."

Gaia turned over her hand, seeing the raw, bruised circlet in her flesh, but she was already thinking ahead about the surgery. "She's a pregnant mother and she needs me," she said. "This is what I do."

"Remember how she punished you for inducing a miscarriage?" Leon asked. "I can't help noticing her husband would have no qualms about sacrificing his own full-term child now that it's the Matrarc's pregnancy your dealing with."

Gaia hadn't thought of that irony. "He's desperate. It's awful. All of it."

"She's stubborn like I've never seen before," Leon said.

Dominic's suggestion was bothering her. Gaia remembered a conversation she'd had with a doctor back in Q cell, when Myrna had proposed that a hooked forceps could be used vaginally to pull out a placenta like this one, sacrifice a baby, and save a mother. Gaia had no such tool and no such skill, but part of her wondered. If she'd been released from the stocks earlier, when the Matrarc was still strong, before she'd had much blood loss, could Gaia have cleared the placenta and the baby by hand so that the Matrarc would have lived? There were many *ifs*, but it almost made the Matrarc's decision to keep Gaia in the stocks a suicide choice.

"She wasn't just stubborn," Gaia said. "She valued Sylum the way it was. Enough to die for it."

Leon watched her closely. "What are you saying?"

She shook her head. It was pointless to speculate anyway. The Matrarc was now so weak that her body was shutting down and killing the baby along with her. "It feels wrong to play with life and death."

"You're not," he said. "Just do the best you can."

"If I do nothing, they'll both die."

"Then do what the Matrarc wants you to do," Leon said. "It's her choice."

When the Matrarc's six sons and Taja came out, they looked bewildered. Jerry took the bear from his little brother and tossed it over the balcony, which made the toddler cry. Taja scooped him up into her arms, and the mladies hurried forward to meet them.

"Mlass Gaia," Dominic called.

Gaia stood stiffly and leaned on Leon's arm to go back in, dreading what lay before her in that room. Will joined them, bringing a fragrant pot of tea on a tray to set on the table. He had brought more clean towels, too. He closed the door.

"I want you to take the baby out now, Gaia, while it's still moving," the Matrarc said.

Gaia sank onto the edge of the bed.

Dominic shook his head, burying his face into the pillow beside his wife. "Please, no."

Gaia lifted her bruised hands, thinking of the strength and skill she would need. She had a flashing memory of her mother's death and knew it was coming again. She glanced at her satchel, then at Will, and then back to the Matrarc. "Are you sure?"

"Absolutely," the Matrarc said.

"You'll die," Gaia said. "I'll do what I can, but it's beyond my skill. You need to know that."

"I want my baby to live," the Matrarc said. "That's all that matters to me now." She clenched her jaw while her body worked in another contraction. They were becoming weaker and more infrequent, and soon, Gaia knew, her body would give up entirely.

"Dominic, you have to let me go," the Matrarc said.

"I won't," he protested, speaking quietly and urgently to his wife. "Please, Olivia. I can't manage without you."

"Kiss me," the Matrarc said.

Gaia looked away, hiding her face against Leon's shirt while he held her closely. She could hear Leon breathing and feel his strength, and when, moments later, it was time to deliver the baby, she did.

CHAPTER 26

power

Soon after, the Matrarc was dead. Her youngest child, a son, slept in his father's arms.

Gaia never wanted to see another dead person for the rest of her life. It would take her forever to forget the sight of cutting into the Matrarc to rescue her baby, let alone everything that had come after, and the fruitless effort to save her life. The motherwort had done nothing for the pain, and though the Matrarc had bit on a tightly rolled cloth, her screams still echoed through Gaia's mind. While she'd been doing it, she'd focused with a cold, efficient part of her brain, but now she trembled everywhere and felt sick with a kind of loathing.

She washed her hands a last time while Will covered up the body. He would have one mess of a job with the cadaver.

"Take her monocle," Dominic said.

Gaia couldn't look him in the eye. "I don't want it."

"You don't have a choice," Dominic said.

I always have a choice, she thought.

"Leon," she said. "Take me out of here."

He put an arm around her as she walked slowly out of the room and along the balcony. Taja, without a word, passed around her to go in with her father. At the top of the steps, Gaia wavered, and Leon lifted her against him once more. All she wanted to do was sleep, deeply, for ages, preferably without having to move out of his arms.

He carried her down the stairs, careful not to bump her toes against the walls during the turns, and set her gently on her feet at the bottom. She straightened the waist of her trousers, gazing wearily at the gathered men and women in the atrium.

Gaia moved forward and braced herself on the back of a chair. "The Matrarc's dead," she said. "But her son's alive."

In the silence, some of the people began weeping, and others turned to hug each other. Gaia couldn't bear to look at the Matrarc's younger children, who were gathered up by several of the mladies and brought up the stairs.

Mlady Roxanne rose from a seat near the fireplace where a half dozen of the cuzines were gathered. She looked like she had been crying already. "What do we do now?"

"The first thing is to plan the funeral," Mlady Maudie said soberly.

At her words, Gaia was jolted out of her fatigue. She half expected to see a list of notes already in Mlady Maudie's hand. If no one stopped them, the cuzines would arrange the funeral, and then it would be natural for them to plan the next thing, and the next.

"No," Gaia said. "You don't plan anything. Dominic can plan the funeral with Will."

"Don't be so worried," Mlady Maudie said. "We'll just make it easier for him."

Gaia took a step back, alarmed. "Leon, how many people are outside?"

"Hundreds still. I've been watching," Leon said.

"We're going out." Gaia lifted her voice to carry clearly

327

through the atrium, even over the sorrowing noises of those who hadn't noticed her exchange with Mlady Maudie. "Come out to the commons," Gaia commanded. "If you want any part of the decisions for Sylum, come outside. Now. All of you."

Painfully, she walked through the screen door and stopped on the top step of the veranda. It was the same place Gaia had seen the Matrarc occupy, ages ago, when she had first come to Sylum. Like golden, winking eyes, torches filled the commons and burned their black smoke into the air. By their light, the men of Sylum, who had been sitting and resting while they waited for word, rose to their feet, and there was a visible ripple as they moved forward, gathering.

"The Matrarc's dead," Gaia said in a loud, steady voice. "She died a few minutes ago. Her baby's alive. A son."

Mumbling began, and Gaia began to make out individual faces: Will and Peter's uncles, then Roger, and Xave. Leon stood just behind her, and the people who had been waiting in the lodge were streaming out the door. Norris came along the porch rail to her left, bringing his rolling pin, which seemed odd to her until she looked more closely at the crowd and saw a scattering of pitchforks and hammers.

This is not good, she thought.

"Look there!" came a man's voice.

There were startled cries and arms pointing upward. "They're armed, in the bell tower! The women are going to shoot!"

"Nobody's shooting anybody," Gaia said loudly. "We're here for a vote. A civilized vote. That's what the Matrarc agreed to when she let me and Chardo Peter out of the stocks. Equal rights for all."

"If we're so equal, why are they armed?" yelled another man.

"Put your bows down!" Gaia called, turning back toward

the doorway. "Tell them to put their bows down. Mlady Rox-anne, are you there?"

"Put them down, or we'll burn the lodge to the ground!" called another man.

Angry voices erupted from the crowd.

"Mlady Roxanne?" Gaia called again.

"She went in to talk to them," Will said in his quiet voice, coming out the door.

She glanced from him to Leon, making a quick decision about who would have more inflence.

"Talk to the men," she said to Will. "Quickly."

Will glanced briefly toward Leon, then stepped forward to the front of the porch and lifted a hand. Torchlight flickered over his straight frame. "You heard her," Will said, his voice carrying with calm authority. "Go tell everybody who's still home. We're having an election right here. In fifteen minutes' time."

The buzz lifted into the night air, and the men swarmed. Torches scattered in every direction.

Gaia spotted Peony hovering farther down the porch.

"Go ring the bell, Mlass Peony," Gaia said. "That will wake people up."

Mlady Maudie turned from a group of cuzines. "But Mlass Gaia, that's just for the matina," Mlady Maudie said.

"Ring the bell," Gaia repeated to Peony. "And keep ringing it. They'll know it's no matina. Tell the archers to come down. We're not having any of that. Will? Can you make sure?"

He and Peony went back inside and Gaia glanced again at Mlady Maudie, who folded her arms across her chest, frowning.

"You're making a mistake," Mlady Maudie said. "I'll keep the archers near." She headed into the lodge. Gaia went slowly down the stairs and turned to look up at the bell tower, where the archers had withdrawn out of sight.

Peals broke into the night air, sonorous and strange, far more than had ever been rung in a string together. They filled the dark air with their insistent rhythm. She looked for the moon to the east over the marsh, knowing it must be nearly full, and caught a glimpse of it low on the horizon, still hidden in the trees. Residual horror hovered at the edge of her mind, and she veered away from the nightmare she'd just gone through with the Matrarc. Then, as the bell peals reverberated away into silence, far out in the marsh, the loon answered with its elusive, haunting call. Gaia listened, waiting for more, and shivered when it didn't come.

"Here, let me give you a hand," Leon said, coming to help Gaia back up the stairs.

"I never thought I'd see this day," Norris said, putting forward a chair for her.

"It isn't over yet," she said.

"She needs something to eat, Norris," Leon said. "She's hardly had anything."

"What I really want is more willow bark tea. Can you make it strong?"

"Will do," Norris said, and went inside.

Gaia sank gratefully onto the cushioned chair. Her wrists and neck had started to pulse with soreness, and it felt best when she held still. Torches were moving in the commons, illuminating glimpses of beards and hats and pitchforks as men returned.

"Is this going to work?" she asked Leon.

"It might. If nobody burns the lodge down first."

That's what she was afraid of, too.

"We should have Peter here," she said, and realized his uncles must have gone for him.

The torches were returning, more than ever. The crowd swelled to the edges of the commons. Children, grandfathers and uncles amassed until they were jammed in doorways and windows, until they had climbed the trees and the stocks, and still more people came, nearly two thousand strong.

Josephine and Dinah came, bringing the babies. Little Maya's eyes were bright, but when Gaia reached for her, Dinah kept her against her shoulder. "I've got her. You take care of business."

A snatch of laughter drifted over the crowd, and a clinking noise.

"Are they drinking?" Gaia asked.

"Some are," Leon said.

A man on horseback was progressing through the commons, and as he came nearer, Gaia recognized Peter in the torchlight. His father and uncles helped him down when he reached the lodge. He'd had a chance to wash and change his clothes, she saw, and though his face was haggard, his pace labored, he met her gaze and smiled warmly. He came up the steps just as Will returned.

"Have a seat," Will said, setting another chair beside Gaia's.

The discoloration of Peter's lip was nearly gone, and she felt a flutter of nervousness as he slowly sat beside her.

"You really delivered the Matrarc's baby?" Peter asked Gaia.

"It was awful," she said.

"Are you okay?"

"I will be, if we can settle this vote once and for all."

He reached out to put his fingers over hers, clasping her warmly, and she saw he had the same circle of bruise around

331

his hand. Her heart beat in irregular thuds as she carefully pulled her hand away from his. His frank gaze lifted to hers in a question.

"I think we've earned the right to hold hands," Peter said gently.

Gaia glanced up at Will and then Leon. She licked her lips, then turned to Peter again. His eyes were as blue and direct as ever, and the tiny smile scar beside his mouth still beckoned. She didn't know how to begin.

"What is it?" Peter said.

It was bad enough having no privacy, but she couldn't talk at all with Leon and Will looking on. "Leon," she said. "I think I need a few minutes with Peter alone. Will, do you mind?"

Will backed up. "Not at all." He started down the steps, taking his father and uncles with him, and only once looked back over his shoulder before they mingled into the crowd.

Leon was studying her closely, but then he nodded.

"I'll see if Norris needs a hand," Leon said.

"Thank you," she said.

"What's going on?" Peter asked, his voice low. He did not sound happy.

There was no nice way to say it. She tried to still the clamoring in her veins. "I think I'm falling for Leon," she said.

He stared, visibly registering her words. "Do not say that. You can't possibly say that."

"I'm sorry."

"We were just in the *stocks* together for *ten hours*," he said. "You're just confused."

She shook her head infinitesimally.

"No," he protested, his tortured gaze burning into hers. "What has he done? I don't believe it. Mlass Gaia, we have something. You can't just say it isn't there."

332

"I know," she whispered. "But it isn't enough. It doesn't compare."

He jerked back up out of his chair. She could feel eyes turning in their direction. Peter looked like he was going to burst out of his own skin.

"I'm sorry," she said, her voice aching.

"When did this happen? How could this happen?" he demanded.

"At the winner's house."

"After you and I—" He stopped, lowering his voice again. "After I was arrested?"

She nodded.

He sat down again, facing her, and this time he took both of her hands in his with infinite care, gently turning them over and tracing the lines of her bruise. A shiver ran over her palm, disturbing her further. Maybe she wasn't as certain as she thought.

"Look," he said, quietly decisive. "We did this together. We have the same marks."

"I know," she said. It was just getting worse. "You think this is easy for me to say?"

"Then don't say it," Peter said. "You can't be in love with him. I don't believe it. You'll change your mind."

"Peter," she began, but her heart twisted inside her, and she couldn't speak. She closed her eyes, lowering her head.

Peter bumped his knees into hers, shifting close. "Why him? He isn't even nice to you. You deserve so much better."

"He *is* nice to me," she said.

"Don't you hear yourself? You're just persuading yourself."

"No, I'm not. He understands who I really am."

"*I* can understand you," Peter protested. "We just need a chance together."

"It wouldn't be fair," she said.

"I don't care what he thinks."

"It wouldn't be fair to you," she clarified. "Don't you see? That's why I'm telling you now. I don't want to lead you on."

"You wouldn't be leading me on," he said, tugging her hands. "Let me hold you. Let me just hold you again."

She wavered, then shook her head, fighting back tears.

"You were so happy with me. I know you were," he said.

"I was," she admitted.

"Then what happened? I don't believe this," he said again, his voice low. "Why did you get in the stocks with me?"

"I did it for justice," she said.

"For justice," he repeated, as if the concept eluded him. His hands stilled on hers then, and after an unbearable moment, he let her go. "You really mean it." He let out a brief laugh. "You could see how I might think you had a different reason."

"I didn't mean to hurt you."

When he didn't reply, she had to look up at him, but his searching, lonely expression was too terrible to bear.

"Well, you did," he said. "How bizarre. I thought having you in the stocks with me was the worst thing ever, but that was bliss compared to this."

"Don't say that," Gaia said. "Please, Peter."

"Not your sweet voice. Not after what you've just done." He rose to his feet.

"Where are you going?"

"I don't know. Anywhere but here."

"You can't go," she said. "We need you."

He let out an astonished laugh. "Do you think I care?"

"We're going to have an election," she added. "You have to be part of it. It's what we fought for."

"It's what *you* fought for," he corrected her. He turned toward the stairs.

"Peter, please," she urged him. "Please stay."

He spoke over his shoulder. "I would never have done this to you, Mlass. Do me a favor. Don't use me politically ever again."

He walked stiffly down the stairs. Gaia felt an urge to cry out after him. Everything was going wrong. She clutched her arms around her middle, holding herself tight as if that were the only way to keep herself together. Peter was joined by his family as he met the crowd, and after a moment, Will came up the stairs again.

"What did you say to him?" Will asked.

She shook her head.

"You told him about Vlatir, didn't you?" Will said calmly, sitting down beside her.

"I feel so stupid," she said. "This is all so messed up."

She looked back out and saw that Peter's father was helping him up on the horse. Soon he was moving, and the crowd rippled around him to let him pass.

She glanced back to Will. "You'll leave me next, won't you?" she asked.

He laughed. "No," he said, drawing out the word.

He only confused her more. "Why not?" she said. "I'm a disaster for anyone but Leon."

"I don't much mind a disaster, I guess," Will said. "Let's get this election squared away."

Leon returned then. "Hey," he said quietly. When he lowered a warm mug into Gaia's hands, he wrapped his own fingers around hers to help steady the drink and lift it to her lips. She couldn't meet his gaze. Instead, she forced herself to take a swallow, and then drank more, willing the warm tea to ease down her tight throat.

"Where's Peter?" Leon asked.

Gaia peered mutely into her cup.

"I believe he's defected," Will said.

Leon glanced across at him. "But you're here."

Will merely waited on Gaia's other side, his hands resting on his knees, saying nothing more. She felt Leon's gaze return to her, speculative. There was nothing to say about Will. Nothing at all. And even less to say about Peter. If she even tried, she knew she'd become an incoherent mess.

Leon leaned closer to Gaia. "I know that can't have been easy," he said, and gently tucked her hair behind her ear for her. "You okay?"

She nodded unhappily. "I'll be fine."

Leon smiled slightly. "You're having a very bad day, aren't you?"

"That's what it is," she said, with a choked laugh. How he could make her feel a little better, even then, she didn't know.

"We need to do this soon," Mlady Roxanne said, coming out the door. "Are you ready, Mlass Gaia?"

The crowd by then was enormous, and an air of excitement buzzed through it, even stronger than the implicit threat of the crude weapons. A bat swooped down into the torchlight, banked away, and was gone. Gaia set aside her mug.

"We're ready," Gaia said. "Are all the cuzines here, too? Where's Mlady Maudie?"

"She's on the porch, there, and we brought all the archers down, too," Mlady Roxanne said, pointing to an overflow of women near one end of the lodge. "They're on edge, but they'll wait to see what happens."

"Okay," Gaia said. "We need more light." She came stiffly to her feet as Will and Leon and several others brought torches nearer.

The glow around the lodge steps grew as bright as daylight, but orange in hue and sharply scented with smoke.

Gaia stepped forward into the light. Her body was nearly broken from her hours in the stocks, and she was aware that traces of dried blood from the childbirth smudged her blouse and trousers. She felt old, and sad, and afraid of all that lay before them, but as she looked out at the crowd, she also felt that this moment was right, that it belonged to her. A calm came over the crowd, rippling slowly outward from the focal point of Gaia, and some new, solemn power came into her.

There was a soft click behind her, and she turned to see Dominic standing beside the door, watching. A shiver ran along her arms, lifting each tiny hair, and she turned to face the crowd again. She waited, knowing soon the right words would come to her.

"I think, first of all, I'd like to call for a moment of silence," she said, touching a hand to her heart. "Please put down your weapons and take a minute to remember Mlady Olivia, our Matrarc. There's no one who ever cared more for the people of Sylum."

A shift and soft clatter followed, and then a stillness spread outward, uniting them. Gaia felt the steady count of her heartbeat beneath her fingers, and then, silently, Mlady Roxanne slid her hand into Gaia's. Gaia took a half step back and reached for Leon's hand as well, and looking out in the commons, she saw others joining hands until a quiet, powerful current physically connected them all.

She heard a sniff behind her. "Thank you," Dominic said quietly.

Gaia released Mlady Roxanne and Leon to step forward

again. "It's our time to choose a new leader," Gaia said, lifting her voice so it would carry. "The Matrarc spoke for the cuzines before she died, and she conceded that the vote belongs to all of us now. Anyone who can understand me and raise his or her voice can vote, and should." She waited to see if anyone would question this, but the silence waited, expectant. "We'll start with nominations," Gaia said.

"I nominate the teacher, Mlady Roxanne," called out a woman from Gaia's right, and there was a spattering of applause from the cuzines. A hopefulness was growing.

Mlady Roxanne moved forward and stood beside Gaia. Her gap-toothed smile showed as she lifted her hand in a little wave. "Thanks."

"Okay, who next?" Gaia called.

"Chardo Will, the morteur," called out a man's voice. "He'd be good."

Gaia was surprised, but it made sense. Will glanced questioningly at Gaia, and then moved around her to stand beside Mlady Roxanne.

"Anyone else?" Gaia asked. "Do the libbies want to nominate anyone?" She looked for Dinah.

"You," Dinah called. "I nominate Gaia Stone, the midwife."

The responding cheer startled Gaia. She turned to Leon, who nodded at her, and then to Will, who smiled. Mlady Roxanne shifted, making room so the three candidates could stand evenly along the edge of the porch, equally visible.

Gaia rested a hand on the pillar beside her.

"I'm honored," Gaia said. "Of course I am. But I have to tell you something. It matters if you're going to consider me for your leader." She took a deep breath. "I believe the shortage of girls means the end of us here, and not in the distant future, but soon. Mx. Josephine's daughter might be the last girl ever born here." She gestured toward where Josephine and Dinah stood holding little Junie and Maya.

Voices mumbled in the crowd.

"What's your point? We know this," Mlady Maudie called from the cuzines.

"We don't have to stay anymore," Gaia said. "It's a miasma from the swamp that's keeping us addicted here, and there's an antidote. We can smoke black rice flower and get away."

Astonished gasps and laughter rose from some in the crowd, followed by another ripple of voices.

"Is that for certain?" Will asked her.

"Yes," she said. Now was when she really needed Peter to explain what he'd done to escape.

Norris came forward. "Let me through here," he said gruffly. "Listen up!" he called. "The girl's right. I was smoking rice flower when I fetched back our last Matrarc, Mlady Danni. You remember. And I survived when I should have been dead like she was. I didn't put that together until just now. We should have been experimenting and trying to leave all this time."

Voices called out, and Norris raised a hand to settle them again. "Just listen to Mlass Gaia. Hear what she has to say," Norris said. "The girl's got some sense, even if she is one of the cuzines."

As the men laughed again, Gaia could feel the tension easing and genuine curiosity focused in her direction. Her gaze settled on Dinah, and the way Maya was sucking on her little fingers.

"It's just this," Gaia said. "I think we need to move away now, with this generation, while we're still strong. All of us. I don't mean tomorrow, but as soon as we can reasonably put together a plan. If you elect me, you have to know that's what I'll try to do."

339

"If you ask me, the girl's right," Norris said, and went down the stairs. A knot of men converged around him, and everyone was talking out in the commons and along the porch. Voices were excited now, lifting into the air with charged energy.

Leon lifted his eyebrows, smiling at her. "Cause trouble much?"

"I had to be honest," she said. "I'm not going to be someone I'm not, especially if they might elect me."

He laughed. "No kidding."

"It's more than they can handle, though," Mlady Roxanne said, drawing near to Gaia. "With all respect, Mlass Gaia, you shouldn't have told them like that."

Will and Dominic stepped nearer, too.

"You're underestimating the men," Will said to Mlady Roxanne. "We deserve to know. It matters to us maybe even more than to the women."

"You think they want to leave?" Mlady Roxanne asked, gesturing to the men in the commons. Conversation there was rising to a cacophony.

Will glanced at Gaia. "If there are more women out there, the men will want to leave. It'll take them only two seconds to realize that."

"You see?" Gaia said to Mlady Roxanne.

"Did you tell my wife about this?" Dominic asked. "Did she know?"

Gaia hesitated, then nodded. "I told her this morning. She was afraid the information would divide the community. I'm hoping it will unite us."

"Mlady Olivia knew what was at stake," Mlady Roxanne said. "I can't believe the very first vote is about destroying Sylum. No wonder she left Mlass Gaia so long in the stocks."

"This vote isn't destroying Sylum," Will said. "It's about making Sylum survive."

Without another word, Dominic stepped aside and moved further down the porch, touching the wall on his way, as if his sense of balance had been thrown off by his loss. Taja came from the other direction and gently drew her arm through her father's.

Mlady Roxanne adjusted her glasses with delicate fingers. "I, for one, am in no hurry to leave Sylum, even with the men involved in the governance now. I suspect the other cuzines will agree with me." She stepped forward and raised her hand. "All right, my cousins!" she called. "I need your attention."

The crowd settled again.

"Thank you. We're going to keep this simple," Mlady Roxanne said. "We'll first hear the votes for Chardo Will, and then for me, and then for Gaia Stone. Ready?" She pointed to Will. "All those for Chardo Will, say 'Ay.'"

"Ay!" came a loud surge of male voices, and then a spontaneous burst of applause and laughter. It was the first time the men and libbies had ever voted for real, and their joy was contagious.

Will put out a hand, gesturing to Mlady Roxanne. "And now," he said. "Those for Mlady Roxanne, say 'Ay.'"

Another loud "Ay!" echoed through the commons, with a stronger mix of female voices. Of the two votes, Gaia guessed Will's had been a little larger, but she couldn't be sure.

Mlady Roxanne turned to Gaia and put a hand on her shoulder. Gaia looked briefly to Leon, who watched her steadily, a slight smile curving his lips, and then she turned to face the crowd.

"And finally," Mlady Roxanne said, "those in favor of Gaia Stone, say 'Ay!'"

The sound that followed was deafening, a roar of approval from every corner of the commons, and then the cheering began.

further

WHEN SHE FIRST sank into a hot bath, the heat seeped deeply into her sore muscles. Like some limp, boneless thing, Gaia didn't even try to move. Her chin hovered at the surface of the water, and she closed her eyes, imagining she could hear the minute bubbles layering over her skin. She didn't let herself think of the Matrarc dying under her blade, or the people of Sylum, or the future, or Leon or Peter or Will or Maya; she simply existed, and when at last the water began to cool, she worked soap into a lather to wash her hair, dunked, and hauled herself out, half blind, only to fall asleep the instant she hit her bed.

She made it to the funeral the next day, but otherwise she rested in the lodge, listening to anyone who had concerns about Sylum and how it was going to be run. She ate slowly, finding even a soup spoon heavy. She asked Mlady Roxanne, Will, Dinah, Dominic, Mlady Maudie, and half a dozen others to serve as advisors, and though Dominic declined, the others began to draw up a framework of basic laws that would be fair to all. Dominic, Taja, and the rest of the Matrarc's family stayed up on the bluff, and Gaia knew they mourned deeply. Dominic offered to vacate the Matrarc's house up on the bluff for her, but Gaia declined. She moved back to the lodge, to the little first-floor bedroom she'd slept in when she'd first arrived, but with the bars removed from the window.

"You could live with me," Dinah offered. "We'd have fun."

"The lodge has a nicer bathtub," Gaia confessed. "And it's just easier to run things from here."

It would be days before Gaia could move again without aching, weeks before the last pain in her neck and wrists was gone. Josephine took a bedroom in the lodge, and the mlasses shared the work and pleasure of raising little Junie and Maya. Leon and Norris agreed to oversee conditions at the prison and determine which cases warranted review, so Leon spent his days divided between the prison and the lodge, where he was often near Gaia. At night, Leon slept in an extra hammock in the cabin Norris shared with his cousin's family, where he wasn't too far from the lodge. Mlady Roxanne took charge of expanding the school to include the boys and men who were most interested. On a practical level, many things went on as before, but everything felt different, full of promise and trepidation, both.

Whenever anyone asked Gaia how soon they'd leave Sylum, she said it was too soon to know. Conversations about who might go and who might stay were rife, and Gaia decided it best not to push anyone too hard, for now. She trusted, in time, the majority would persuade the others in their families.

Peter went back out to the perimeter, where he and a dozen of the other outriders began a series of expeditions south, experimenting with doses of the black rice flower and scouting sites for the future exodus.

"Will he ever want to see me again?" she asked Will after a meeting once in the atrium.

343

"Honestly? We don't talk about you," Will said. "He hardly talks at all, frankly. But if I had to guess, I'd say no, he won't want to see you. I think the nicest thing you could do for him would be to leave him alone."

The thing was, she missed Peter. She hated feeling like she would never be able to put things right with him, or laugh with him again, or see his eyes all warm and joyful. Even worse, she couldn't escape the feeling his unhappiness was her fault, and guilt plagued her. Though Leon offered to listen, talking to him about Peter was impossible for her, so she did the only thing she could: she locked the black swirl in a box in the back of her mind and tried not to remember it was there.

As the days progressed toward the full moon, it became clear that most of the men wanted the tradition of the thirty-two games to continue. Gaia realized the competition would be an important emotional outlet and serve as a celebration to give credibility to the new regime. So she proposed a change that was immediately popular: only women who were present at the games and at least fifteen years old could be chosen as prizes. Mlasses who didn't want to be chosen simply had to stay away.

"Are you going to the games?" Leon asked her once in passing.

She smiled. "What do you think?"

He smiled back. "Just checking."

The night of the games, Peony stopped in the lodge kitchen to see if Gaia wanted to walk with her down to the shore for the bonfires that would follow.

"An excellent idea," Norris said to Gaia. "People need to see you, especially since you won't be at the games. They have to get used to you as the new Matrarc."

Gaia still wasn't used to having the title refer to her. "I thought I'd go to bed early with a book," she said.

"No hiding. You need to get used to yourself as Matrarc, too," he added. "When Mlady Olivia first took over after your grandmother, she was always around talking to everybody."

"You told me. I've been doing that. You've seen me," she argued.

"But tonight's important. I can watch Maya for you, or Mx. Josephine can, but you need to get out there."

"I see," she said, smiling. She stroked Una's soft fur and glanced up from the rocker. "You just want to take over with Maya. Grandpa."

"Can I help it if she adores me?" Norris said. "And it's Uncle. Uncle Emmett."

Gaia walked down to the shore with Peony and helped throw extra logs on the five bonfire piles that were ranged down the beach. They could hear the cheers from the field, distant and unified. Even the laughter came in waves.

The sky streaked orange and purple over the marsh as the sun dropped below the bluff, and after the games ended, more and more people began milling between the bonfire piles. Partiers were supplying cider, and she caught whiffs of rice flower smoke. Guards, too, were present in pairs at the fringes. She'd assigned the same number that the Matrarc had designated the month before and hoped, with the new climate, it would be enough.

Peony unfolded a couple of blankets, and they sat down by the wood pile nearest the main road.

"Is this visible enough?" Gaia asked.

Peony nodded. "Norris would approve. I'm glad it hasn't gotten too cold yet. That red's a good color on you. Where's Leon?"

Gaia glanced down at her new sweater. "He's at the games. I asked him to keep an eye on things there for me."

345

Peony flicked some sand off her blanket. "I didn't know he takes orders from you. That's so, I don't know, ordinary. Like a regular guy from Sylum."

"He doesn't," Gaia said. "One of Norris's nephews was bugging him about it, saying how the last winner ought to at least show up even if he doesn't play. Besides, I thought he'd have fun going."

"So you sent him?"

"No, he was going anyway, so I asked him— Why am I explaining this?" Gaia asked.

Peony laughed. "I think it's nice. You took a totally wild crim and tamed him."

Gaia curled her knees up in front of herself and hugged them. "That's not true."

"It's what my mother said. I think so, too. Everybody does."

Gaia rested her cheek on her knee and gazed absently at the big logs, puzzling it over. She wasn't the only one who'd changed, she realized. Only a few weeks ago, Leon had openly fought the guards on the thirty-two field and practically jumped down Gaia's throat. Now there was something happy and generous in the way he treated everyone, and not just Gaia. It was in the courteous way he addressed Mlady Maudie, who still ran the lodge, and the way he hefted things for Norris in the kitchen between their discussions of the crims. When she went looking for Maya, she often found the baby over his shoulder, even when she could have been sleeping in her crib.

But none of that made him tamed. "It's really not like that," Gaia said. "He's just being who he always was inside."

Peony tossed a pebble toward the pile of wood. "It's sweet to see, in any case. Say, I never thanked you for what you said to my mother."

While she was making rounds of the village in the days

after the election, Gaia had gone to find Peony's mother and assure her that Peony's miscarriage would remain confidential, even if she didn't go ahead with the arranged marriage. Peony's mother had thanked her and said the family would consider that.

"It wasn't much," Gaia said.

"It turns out I'm sort of liking Phineas." Peony dropped her voice. "Will you induce any more miscarriages if someone asks you?"

"I've been thinking about that. I know the Matrarc wouldn't want me to, but I still think it's a private decision. Do you regret what we did?"

"No. It's different now, too," Peony said. "If I got pregnant now, and got kicked out of the cuzines, I'd still have the same rights as any other woman. They can't take babies from libbies anymore, can they?"

"Never again." It gave Gaia tremendous joy to know Josephine would never be separated from Junie.

The beach thronged with people now, some throwing yet more wood on the bonfire piles and others passing cider. Young boys hunched over on the dock, peering down into the dark water. The light of the sky was retreating behind the bluff, and someone lit the farthest bonfire.

Gaia looked toward the road, but instead of Leon, she saw Will walking across the sand with more men from the games. He peeled off to join them, and Dinah arrived at the same time.

"Hey, Will," Gaia said. "Who won the games?"

"Walker Xave. He picked one of the young mlasses, a fifteen-year-old named Leila."

Gaia would have to check that the girl had an astute chaperone at the winner's cabin. She glanced at Peony, who was blushing faintly and didn't meet her gaze. Dinah spread out her blanket, and her son Mikey, running by, stopped to give her a hug.

"Did Peter come to the games?" Peony asked.

"No," Will said.

Gaia shifted uncomfortably. "Did you see Taja there?" she asked Will.

"No. I heard she stayed up on the bluff with her dad," Will said. "They've got their hands full, but I guess it's working out to have Mlady Beebe's family next door. Was that your idea to send them up?"

"I'm sure it would have occurred to her if I hadn't suggested it. She saw immediately that it was the thing to do," Gaia said. "She's good to nurse both babies."

As Dinah sat, Mikey curled up beside her, and she passed him a handful of sunflower seeds to shell and nibble.

"Are you joining us?" Dinah asked Will. "Or just standing around? We have room."

He glanced at Gaia, then took a place on Dinah's blanket and lay back on an elbow, crossing his ankles. Dinah's son passed him a seed. So far, none of the libbies had asked to have their biological children restored to them, but Gaia wondered if any would. That would take some delicate handling.

"I've been thinking," Dinah said. "A lot of our men are excited to leave Sylum, but the Enclave might not be pleased about two thousand refugees showing up on their doorstep."

"That's a complication," Gaia said. "We'll have to prepare. We can't arrive all needy, and we have to be able to defend ourselves."

"You could teach all the men to shoot, too," Will asked.

Gaia picked up a flat, circular stone to twiddle. "We could. The problem is, no matter how much we train, our arrows and swords won't stand a chance against the Enclave's rifles. We're

348

better off going prepared to negotiate. We have something they want."

"What's that?" Dinah asked.

"We're a new gene pool."

The Protectorat, Gaia was certain, would immediately see the potential of her new people. *He might be interested in having his son back, too,* she thought uneasily.

"That sounds scary," Peony said. "Like they'd experiment on us."

"No," Gaia said, laughing. "Their medicine isn't that advanced. I just think our unmarried men from the pool will be especially welcome inside the wall to help diversify the gene pool there. It's a win-win situation."

"You're sure?" Dinah said.

"Nothing's sure," Gaia said. "Would you rather we head west? Or become nomads? I don't know how they even survive."

The others exchanged glances. "At least we have some idea what we're going to with the Enclave," Will said. "They have resources there."

"Not to mention we know it exists. That's a plus," Peony added, and the others laughed.

Gaia looked toward the road again for Leon, but he still wasn't coming. It began to feel vaguely lonely to her. Stars were coming out one by one, and the eastern horizon glowed where the moon would soon rise over the marsh. Some men farther down the beach began to sing. She wondered where Peter was, and what he was doing, and if he were alone. She curled her knees up again, snuggling into her sweater.

One of the guards arrived with a torch. "Hello, Mlass Matrarc," he said, and reached in to touch the flame to the dry kindling at the heart of the wood pile. Then he lit two more places. Gaia loved the first scent of smoke.

"Thank you," Gaia said. "How's everyone doing?"

"Good so far. You enjoy yourself now."

Gaia turned her face from the growing heat to look once more toward the road, deepened now with the shadows of last dusk. Finally, she saw Leon. Finally, he was coming, and she inhaled deeply as everything inside her felt whole again. He looked different in a white shirt that caught some of the firelight. He'd brought Maya. He paused near the upper edge of the shore, scanning the crowd, with the trees behind him and the last of the daylight tainting the sky a rich indigo above him.

She waved, and when he didn't see her, she rose stiffly to her feet and waved again. When he still didn't see her, she turned her back on the fire and began crossing the dark sand toward him, moving slowly as she had ever since her day in the stocks. He was gazing farther down the beach, standing with his profile to her, his expression as focused as always. She liked the way he absently patted the baby in her yellow blanket and the curving, casual line of his back. When he finally turned to see her, he broke into an easy stride, and then he was smiling, too.

"Hey," she said when they met. "What took you so long?"

"Maya was nursing, so I had to wait to bring her down," Leon said. "I thought she'd like to see the bonfires."

Gaia cupped her fingers loosely around the baby's little head, and saw that her eyes were closed in contented sleep. She thought Leon was incredibly sweet. "She doesn't see much when she's asleep, you know. New shirt?"

"One of Norris's cousins offered me an extra. They're nice people," Leon said. "You know, Josephine told me she tried to get you to make me a shirt and you said no."

"I'm going to kill her."

Laughing, he shifted the baby into the nook of his arm.

"Dominic sent something down for you," he said. He slid something into her palm, and she knew by the cool solid weight that it was the Matrarc's monocle.

Gaia's mirth seeped away. "I told him I didn't want it."

"I know. He wants you to have it anyway, evidently. I think you should accept it."

Gaia closed her fingers around it, feeling the metal and glass warming in her hand while her thoughts churned.

"She's complicated for you, isn't she?" Leon said.

She nodded. She didn't know if she'd ever understand it. Her relationship with the Matrarc had been a labyrinth of submission and rebellion, coercion and pleading, but her death had been the worst of all. It wasn't at all the same as what had happened with Gaia's mother.

"She made me a killer for real this time," Gaia said. "I know she was only thinking of her baby, but if feels like she did it to me on purpose." It sickened her, what she'd done.

Leon put an arm around her shoulder. She felt awkward, stiff, but she let him rock her nearer.

She lifted the monocle to see firelight catch in the lens, and then thought back to the morning in the atrium when the Matrarc had gently touched her face, learning who she was. It still made her uneasy to think of the strange, charismatic power the Matrarc had had over her, as if she'd been able to see deep inside her. The Matrarc's strength and influence hadn't vanished just because she was dead. If anything, she had proven how strong she was when she chose death to let her baby live. Logically, by daylight, Gaia knew that.

But the nightmares. She couldn't hide from self-loathing there. Her nightmares were awash with death and blood.

Leon gave her shoulder a squeeze, and she deliberately made herself let go of some stiffness.

"You're so hard on yourself," he said. "You know what I think?"

"What?"

"You were the only one who could help her. The only one, Gaia."

She nodded slowly. "I'll think about that."

"And her baby's alive because of you. Think about that, too."

As Gaia pulled the chain of her locket watch from around her neck, Leon let her go. She undid the clasp, looped the monocle on, and reattached it. When the necklace fell on her chest again, it was a little heavier and bulkier than before, but after all, it did belong to her.

"I'll have to thank Dominic," she said.

"You okay?"

She nodded.

"Really?"

She smiled. "Yes. I really am." She glanced ahead to the bonfire where her friends sat. "You know what Peony said? This is strange. She thinks I tamed you."

Leon laughed. "You don't like that?"

"It's just not right," she said.

"No, not exactly," he said. He shifted to face her more directly. "I wonder if you'd clear something up for me."

"What?"

The flickers of the bonfire cast gleams over his complexion and turned his hair a satiny black. He paused to tuck Maya's little hand into her blanket, and then he still didn't speak.

She started to smile. "You going to tell me, or am I supposed to guess?"

He peered down at her, oddly frowning and hopeful. "It's just, when you turned me down that time, up at the winner's cabin, I couldn't tell if you were just saying you couldn't decide

352

then, or if you were turning me down permanently. Like with a hatchet: done."

A tingle started behind her heart and became a small, painful twist.

"I couldn't decide then," she said. "That's all I was saying."

"I see. So not the hatchet."

"No," she said. Is that what it had felt like to him?

He patted Maya's little back. "So, where does that leave us now?"

She dug the toe of her loafer into the heavy sand while she tried to figure out what to say.

"Gaia," he said gently. "I kind of need to know."

The heat of a blush rose in her cheeks. She'd been falling in love with him. She knew that, so why was she holding back? "A lot's happened lately," she said. *With Peter and everything.* She touched a finger to one of the buttons on his shirt, peering at it hard while she smoothed the fabric around it.

He didn't say anything, which made it worse.

"I don't think I can give you an answer tonight," she said.

"Such wild enthusiasm. I think you just did."

She cringed. "Leon, no. Really. Please, I just need a little time."

"I'm not going to do well with being kept hanging." He covered her hand with his to keep it still. "Because, from my side of it, I don't have any doubts. Maybe I didn't make that clear."

"I know," she said.

"So what is it, then?"

"I don't know exactly. What if I say yes now and then change my mind or something?"

"You won't change your mind."

"But I could hurt you again," she said. "I don't ever want to do that."

353

"You won't."

"I can't make a commitment until I'm completely sure," she said. "That's what you want, isn't it? For me to be completely sure?"

"And you're not."

She'd been tricked by her own feelings before, and the hesitation that held her back now was real. How was she supposed to know if what she felt for him would last, that it wasn't some mistake that would take them both to disaster? She had to be honest with herself and fair to him, too. "It's such a big decision. All I need is a little more time," she said. "Just to be sure. Is that too much to ask?"

"It's a lot to ask, actually," he said. He ran his thumb over her fingers, slowly. "I guess I should be happy you're being honest with me. Would it be different if you weren't running Sylum?"

She hesitated. "But I am running Sylum now."

"That's what I thought." He was quiet for a moment. "If I give you more time to decide, I want you to give me something, too."

"What?"

"Promise me you won't go sneaking off to be alone with Peter. Or anybody else. Take the time you need to think things over, but just about us, you and me, with nobody else dropping in to say 'Hey, Mlass Gaia, let's take a little ride through the woods.' You know what I mean? You're the Matrarc now."

Peter wanted nothing to do with her. There was no danger of any little ride. At least, not another one. She glanced over to the bonfire and could just make out Will through the flames, sitting beside Dinah, splitting seeds for her son. She wondered if Leon ever knew about Will.

"What's that mean, 'I'm the Matrarc now.' Don't you trust me?" she asked.

"I trust you. But plenty of these men would love to get close to you, and they'll be trying all the time, especially now that the rules are changing." His gaze narrowed briefly. "It would kill me to have you peeling off with them. I have to know you won't do that to me."

"I wouldn't."

"I mean it," Leon said quietly. "Tell me now. We don't have to go any further."

Further. That was where she wanted to go with Leon.

Maybe they could go further while they weren't getting chased around the Enclave or overthrowing the cuzines of Sylum. Maybe they could have some normal life together while they prepared to lead an exodus of two thousand people across a hundred kilometers of wasteland to a walled city that might very well be hostile when they arrived there. Then again, maybe normal would never be possible.

She slid her arm shyly around his waist and felt his arm go around her, too, drawing her close even as he cradled the sleeping baby in his other arm.

"I can be loyal, Leon. I know what that is."

He laughed. "Finally, the girl gives me a crumb."

She focused on the collar of his shirt and the warm gap next to his neck. The truth was, even if she wasn't brave enough to make a commitment forever, she did love him. She was who she was because of him. Certainly he must know that. She thought of how she'd felt the day he got her sister back for her, and the way he'd kissed her, up in the winner's cabin, and the way he'd helped her into the stocks and been there when she woke up afterward to turn her bruised hand in his. She knew what it felt like to be with him, right then, with an aching happiness just teetering inside her, ready to spill.

"What is this?" he said. "I know you love me back, Gaia. I can see it in you."

She nodded. "What I feel for you, it's like this, right here between us. It's everything we've gone through, and Maya, somehow."

He tilted his forehead against hers and held her tight. "Don't be afraid of it, then," he said. "It could be what's ahead for us, too."

"Soon, okay?" she said.

He had to give her a little more time. Had to. She searched his eyes, anxious, until finally his smile eased, turning lazy and warm.

"All right," he said. "Come here."

She was already there, but she managed to get closer still. The loon called far out across the marsh, and all along the shore, humans tried to mimic the wild cry, hooting and whistling back from around the bonfires, and then laughing at each other, but Gaia hardly heard them. She was perfectly busy kissing Leon.

When at last she looked down the beach again, scatters of sparks were cascading upward into the deep sky. The moon, a glittering, full orb, was rising over the marsh to illuminate a shimmering path along the water. Dovetailing her fingers with Leon's, she drew him toward the sweet, shifting smoke of the bonfire.

And for once, she was happy. Very.

acknowledgments

Prized evolved into this story only because my editor, Nancy Mercado, encouraged me to grapple with what matters, so I offer her my warmest gratitude. Thanks, also, to my agent, Kirby Kim, for having faith in my work. I'm grateful to Amy Sundberg O'Brien, Francine McNiel O'Brien, and Nancy O'Brien Wagner for trusty input on dodgy drafts. I'd like to thank my children, William, Emily, and Michael LoTurco, both for sending me off to Gaia's world and for asking if, on any given day, I made it off the couch. As always, I thank my husband, Joseph LoTurco, for everything.

Caragh M. O'Brien
November, 2011